PUB WALKS IN UNDERHILL COUNTRY

Nat Segnit lives in London. His journalism and stories have appeared in several national newspapers, and his play, *Dolphin Therapy*, and two co-written comedy series, *Strangers on Trains* and *Beautiful Dreamers*, were broadcast on BBC Radio 4. This is his first novel.

Pub Walks in Underhill Country

NAT SEGNIT

FIG TREE
an imprint of
PENGUIN BOOKS

FIG TREE

Published by the Penguin Group
Penguin Books Ltd, 80 Strand, London WC2R 0RL, England
Penguin Group (USA) Inc., 375 Hudson Street, New York, New York 10014, USA
Penguin Group (Canada), 90 Eglinton Avenue East, Suite 700, Toronto, Ontario, Canada M4P 2Y3
(a division of Pearson Penguin Canada Inc.)
Penguin Ireland, 25 St Stephen's Green, Dublin 2, Ireland (a division of Penguin Books Ltd)
Penguin Group (Australia), 250 Camberwell Road, Camberwell, Victoria 3124, Australia
(a division of Pearson Australia Group Pty Ltd)
Penguin Books India Pvt Ltd, 11 Community Centre, Panchsheel Park, New Delhi – 110 017, India
Penguin Group (NZ), 67 Apollo Drive, Rosedale, North Shore 0632, New Zealand
(a division of Pearson New Zealand Ltd)
Penguin Books (South Africa) (Pty) Ltd, 24 Sturdee Avenue, Rosebank, Johannesburg 2196, South Africa

Penguin Books Ltd, Registered Offices: 80 Strand, London WC2R 0RL, England

www.penguin.com

First published 2011
1

Set in Dante MT Std 12/14.75 pt
Typeset by Palimpsest Book Production Limited, Falkirk, Stirlingshire
Printed in Great Britain by Clays Ltd, St Ives plc

A CIP catalogue record for this book is available from the British Library

ISBN: 978-1-905-49057-8

www.greenpenguin.co.uk

Contents

Foreword

I first came across the work of Graham Underhill during a long, hot summer in which I was trying and failing to write a novel. For some years I had been spending July and August in a charming little writer's retreat in the Malvern Hills. Goodness knows why, as distanced from the social and intellectual stimulation of the city the last thing I felt inspired to do was write. Whole afternoons – whole *weeks* – would pass in which I did little else but sun myself in the garden, or slap about the house in flip-flops, looking for anything that might distract me from the yawning emptiness of my day. And it was during one of these aimless afternoons that I unearthed a yellowing pamphlet in a drawer full of out-of-date bus timetables and flyers for local attractions. *More Pub Walks in the Malverns and Beyond* was, on the face of it, an even less promising read than the 'haunting sagas' and 'evocative travelogues' left on the shelves by my bookish predecessors. Nonetheless, something compelled me to take it into the garden, where, by the second page, I was seized with the almost chilling certainty that I had, unlikely as it sounds, made a once-in-a-lifetime discovery.

To look at the pamphlet was indistinguishable from one of those self-published, poorly photocopied local-walks books you might find in a rural newsagent or tourist-information bureau. Indeed, this is exactly what it was, judging by the price – £2.99, discounted in biro to 25p. Start to read, however, and within a couple of paragraphs, rich in Underhill's unique mix of natural history, philosophy and endearingly innocent personal reflection, you'd discover what so quickened my pulse that August afternoon sipping wine in the garden. Graham Underhill could not only write. He might, without too much exaggeration, be considered one of the most instinctive writers of prose in the country.

More Pub Walks in the Malverns was, according to the back cover, the last in a series of six: *Pub Walks in the Cotswolds*, *More Pub Walks in the Cotswolds*, *Pub Walks in the Brecon Beacons*, *Pub Walks in Shropshire and the West Midlands*, and the two volumes covering 'the Malverns and Beyond'. Leaving my novel to moulder in a shoebox, I set off to comb the region's newsagents and bookshops for copies. I drew a blank. No one had even *heard* of him. Then, a week before I was due to leave Malvern and head back to civilisation, a chance encounter in the pub yielded pristine copies of all six existing *Pub Walks* titles, the original manuscript of a seventh – *Pub Walks in Underhill Country*, compiled over a period of two years but as yet unseen – and the information not only that I knew his wife but that Graham Underhill had gone missing four months previously and not been heard of since.

The exact circumstances of Underhill's disappearance are a matter of public record.[1] The exact *reasons* for it will perhaps always remain uncertain, and are in any case for the reader to tease out in the pages that follow. Unhappy as his private life may have been, however, I feel Underhill himself would have preferred we focus on the vitality of his prose. No work of non-fiction is complete these days without a personal journey of some sort – and *Pub Walks in Underhill Country* is at times personal to the point of indiscretion. But it's as a 'psycho-geographer', a cartographer of human consciousness in the exalted tradition of Roger Deakin, Richard Mabey and Robert Macfarlane – the three Rs, as Graham liked to call them – that Underhill most deserves to be plucked from obscurity. Always searching, uncon-strained by the conventions of more 'sophisticated' nature writing, Underhill guides us towards a conclusion that Kant, and Coleridge, and Wainwright had drawn in their turn: that walking lies at the heart of human experience. When our earliest ancestors first stood and walked, their hands became free, demanding of the budding human brain an expansion commensurate to the body's new capacity for manipulating its surroundings. Four million years on, men have

1. See, for example, Keith Frampton, 'Rambler "vanishes" following disappearance of wife', *Ledbury Evening Star*, 15 April 2008: 3.

walked on the moon, dreaming with each weightless step of further journeys, wilder achievements on the long path of human ingenuity that includes, in its small way, the work of Graham Underhill – of which *Pub Walks in Underhill Country* is both the summation and crowning achievement.

My role in that process has been minimal. I take no credit for bringing these pages to a larger audience than their author, a local council official, could ever have hoped to reach. Anyone in their right mind would have leapt at the chance. Clearly, any walking guide worthy of the name relies on the precise, objective descriptions of the routes it contains, and where typographical errors and the odd instance of tangled syntax might have prevented readers from following the walks properly, I've sought in the most light-handed way to correct them. Tragically, in the case of *Pub Walks in Underhill Country*, the author never got the chance to redraft what at times amounts to an uncomfortably intimate portrait of a marriage, and if some of the lengthier and more incoherent asides in the final few walks have been omitted, readers need not regret their requisition by the relevant authorities.

I would like to thank Jasmine Reed, who, for the price of a sympathetic ear, and five glasses of Chardonnay, entrusted me with a literary legacy of whose value she seemed scarcely aware. I can only wish her, and her new husband, all the best for his eventual release from prison. To the other friends and colleagues of Graham Underhill named in the text I owe a special debt of thanks, and the assurance that, whatever the sensitivity of the material, its unique merit gave me, as a writer, no choice but to take it to a publisher. But by far the greatest debt I owe to Graham Underhill himself. We never met. I don't even know what he *looked* like. Unusually in this image-saturated age, no photograph of him exists in the public domain, and although there is footage on YouTube of a rambler Jasmine insists is Graham, it's raining heavily, and the figure's face is obscured by the hood of his kagoule.

But in a sense all this is immaterial. Graham is fully visible – vividly present – in his prose. So please. Read on. Better still, don some sturdy boots, slip this book into a waterproof jacket cover, and do the walks in the pages that follow. You will at the very least be assured of a great day out in largely attractive countryside. Or you may feel, as I have, in moments as fleeting as the racing edge of cloud-shadows on a windswept mountainside, the oddly comforting sensation that Graham Underhill, wherever he is, is walking beside you.

N.S.

West London, February 2009

To S

A Note to the Rambler

The author has taken considerable pains to alert the reader to any hazards they may face undertaking the walks in this book. Due caution should be observed, however, as *under no circumstances can I accept any liability whatsoever for any injury or loss of life sustained on the routes that follow.* Walking is by and large a safe, healthy and enjoyable activity, but the potential for disaster remains, and some of the more challenging walks in this guide can pose considerable dangers to the inexperienced rambler. Remember – if in any doubt as to your safety, it's better to head back to the pub at the beginning than become yet another of the statistics that yearly blot the rambler's landscape.

G.U.

Ledbury, April 2008

Walk 1: Malvern to Ledbury

Nothing so lifts a foul mood as the perspective a stroll on high ground can give on the lower slopes of life; the diarist John Evelyn called the view from the Herefordshire Beacon 'one of the goodliest in England'. This walk, beginning in the mostly charming spa town of Malvern, is a personal favourite of my wife's and mine, not least because, as a prelude to its third and final section, when the spirit is beginning to flag, a refreshing 'wild swim' is on offer against the dramatic backdrop of an abandoned quarry face. Mildly strenuous, the route should not be attempted in misty weather, and can be treacherously muddy in its latter stages, but provided simple safety procedures are observed this should prove a ramble to remember.

Start by turning right out of the main entrance of Malvern Link railway station. Properly equipped walkers should note that there are often teenagers smoking in the car park here. While their presence can be intimidating, Malvern is by and large a respectable town,

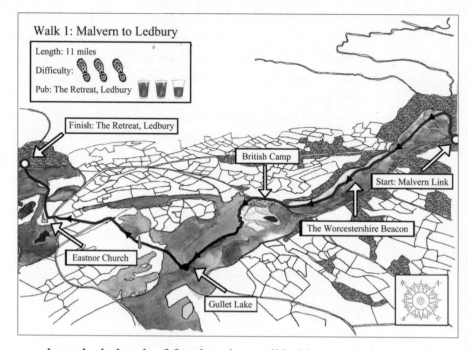

Walk 1: Malvern to Ledbury

Length: 11 miles

Difficulty:

Pub: The Retreat, Ledbury

Finish: The Retreat, Ledbury

British Camp

Start: Malvern Link

The Worcestershire Beacon

Eastnor Church

Gullet Lake

where the bulwark of family values still holds against the national tide; keep your eyes on the route ahead and you should escape with nothing so much as a snide remark about the gaiters, insulated jacket, or carbon-composite walking pole without which no attempt on high ground is advisable.

Turn right and walk up the busy main road for half a mile, passing a newsagent, where you might like to stock up on water or something from proprietor Iqbal's mouth-watering range of self-packaged sweets. There's nothing like a well-timed Fruit Pastille to propel you up that mid-ramble incline! Turn right on Hornyold Road and shortly afterwards, at a pair of field maples under which it may interest readers to know I first asked Sunita to marry me, take a left uphill along Trinity Road. At a fork, bear left along North Malvern Road, in a short while passing on your right a photographer's studio, Photography by David, whose services it was my pleasure to retain when, almost exactly a year after that first 'stab' under the winter-naked maples on Hornyold Road, Sunita finally agreed to become the second Mrs Underhill, in spirit if not technically in name.

Walk 1: Malvern to Ledbury

Walk 1: Malvern to Ledbury

We had met by the loans desk at Malvern Library. Sunita had been refusing to pay a fine of £25.20 on the grounds that two pages were missing from one of the six books she had been three weeks late in returning. The librarian, a large woman in traditional African dress, was threatening to rescind Sunita's tri-county library membership, and to avoid any further unpleasantness I took the liberty of stepping in and settling the fine, securing the librarian's eternal contempt and Sunita's agreement to join me at the Nags Head on Bank Street for a glass of whatever she fancied. Incidentally, it was an irony we were both later to enjoy that the book I had been queuing to take out was entitled *Coping with Grief: A Recent Widower's Guide*. Up to that point in my life, women as beautiful as Sunita had been like illuminated manuscripts in reference libraries: to be examined under the hushed invigilation of one's own sense of disentitlement. But here I was, taking one out, and in my flush-faced astonishment at the turn events had taken I left the grief book unstamped on the loans table.

At a gap in the wall on your left, climb steps into dense tree cover. Ramblers at all familiar with the pressures under which writers, paint- ers and other electively underfunded freelancers operate will understand Sunita's reluctance to make too firm a commitment after those first few dates over ale, white wine and ready-salted crisps. Then again, walkers at all familiar with the beauty of Bengali women will understand my eagerness to get her to the altar as quickly as possible! Joking aside, at the time of my first proposal, Sunita had only been in the Malvern area six months, and having moved here from west London precisely to find the peace and quiet in which she might write her long-gestated memoir of growing up *Motherless in Calcutta*, quite understandably felt she lacked the 'mental and emotional space' to undertake such a serious step as marriage. My loss, literature's gain! Even if she has yet to find a publisher.

Emerging into a municipal car park, turn sharply left onto a broad, stony track by an information board, detailing the local bye-laws it would behove a certain very small minority to study with closer attention than has, I regret to say, recently been the case. Walkers venturing onto the ridge before sunrise should be aware that certain 'activities' have been

3

known to take place in this car park under cover of night; the police have been informed, but in the unlikely event that you do come across potentially multiple figures with their backs to you, intent on a vehicle that although parked may be rocking, rest assured that passing ramblers will be the last thing on their minds, and – a good rule of thumb, this, while we're at it – keep your eyes fixed on the path ahead.

Follow this attractive route, giving views over Great Malvern, and the remarkably level Severn Valley beyond, for half a mile before turning sharp right at a stone indicator marked 'North Hill'. Ascending steep paths like this, I often get the contrary sensation, tested lungs notwithstanding, of descent; survey a map of the area and the great ridge erupting from the flatlands appears as a wound, a gash whose deepest point is, according to a more objective reality, a summit, as if by pressing on and up you were getting steadily closer to the bottom of things. Completing this first climb, you might like to strip off a layer or two. In conditions liable at once to be cold and productive of considerable amounts of internal warmth, I find a storm-proof tri-climate jacket with removable inner fleece gives a good level of flexibility, especially when worn over a good-quality technical T-shirt, heavily peached for comfort and treated with anti-bacterials to reduce odour. Mind you, that motionless afternoon last June we did the walk as newlyweds, Sunita sported nothing but a summer dress, and while I had to frown at the flimsy silver ballet shoes she insisted on wearing in lieu of walking boots, she looked lovely as summer itself, free and unencumbered and light on her feet as our shadows stretched like Giacometti figures across the col.

You might like to pause here to 'drink in the view'. Though negligible compared to the vertiginous glories of the Lakeland Fells, or the Munros of Scotland, the Malvern Hills rise so abruptly from the surrounding landscape that they afford the sort of yawning vantage associated with ranges of far greater height. Westward over the hushed undulations of Herefordshire lie the Brecon Beacons; to the south, the blue-green rumour of the Forest of Dean; to the east, like a female form on its side, recline the haunch and tender midriff of the Cotswolds, lazy through the haze above the sprawling Severn Vale. This truly is the

'Heart of England' – or, I always like to think, its lower abdomen, if Cornwall is its right leg, and Kent its left, submerged up to the knee off the white cliffs of Dover. As he lay dying, Elgar, who loved these hills, reportedly told a friend not to be alarmed if, out walking among them, he ever heard anyone whistling the famous refrain from his cello concerto. 'It's only me,' croaked the grand old celebrant of Albion, and indeed, spanning the saddle as the realm yearns before you for the skyline, you can almost hear Jacqueline du Pré mount the assault on the north face of that majestic cadenza, at least if you shut out the incessant roar of the M5, whose junction with the M50 sits in a regrettably amphitheatrical depression a little under four miles to the east.

Continue towards the Worcestershire Beacon, easily identifiable by the 'nipple'-like triangulation pillar at its summit. The hills here are as fretted with paths as the cracked surface of an old oil painting, but keep the nipple in your cross hairs and, like Wordsworth, guided by a wandering cloud, you cannot miss your way. Whichever path you choose, you might like to step up the pace, particularly if, like me, your companion comes down strongly on the 'get on with it' side of the great 'get on with it'/'view-drinking' debate, and, unless you plan to spend the rest of the walk lonely *as* a cloud, you have a yard or two of ground to make up! Anthropologists like C. Owen Lovejoy, of Kent State University in Ohio, claim that bipedalism – walking on two legs – evolved when our pre-human ancestors, fed up with scrapping with other four-footers for food, stood up and walked off in search of less competitively harvested areas. Or when the males did, anyway. In females bipedalism evolved much later, in part because the raised hind-quarters of quadrupedal posture were just the sort of welcome home a chap needed after a long day's ramble through the thickets, in part to limit the female's ability to wander off, allowing the males to hunt for nourishment free of the anxiety that their lady friends were off consorting with the dissolute but irresistibly charming *Australopithecus* in the valley next along. Scientists I suspect motivated as much by gender politics as the value-neutral search for truth have since cast doubt on this convincing case for monogamy as man's (and woman's) natural state. Petty wrangling aside, however, the idea that women came to walking later than men – that, in evolutionary terms, the male rambler is far, far older than his female counterpart – might in some part explain Sunita's occasional reluctance to *live* in the walk, as it were, *experience* it, as opposed to look forward every step of the way to the fabled 'Underhill Footrub' at the end.

Marbled White butterfly

That glorious afternoon in June we ascended the Worcestershire Beacon just as a raincloud rolled under the sun. At 1,395 feet (425m), this is the highest point of the Malverns. Note the circular toposcope indicating the distribution of notable landmarks visible to the naked eye. Butterflies including Peacocks and Marbled Whites feed here on sprays of ox-eye daisies, although in lesser numbers when the summit is crowded. You should be aware that this *is* a popular spot with tourists. If I take particular satisfaction in the enduring popularity, in the face of more immediate gratifications, of hill-walking as a national – and truly democratic – pastime, I am only taking my place in a tradition that dates back, as readers will no doubt know, to the Romantic ideal of Nature as a category free of the distortions of privilege and inequality. It was on common land that William Wordsworth 'daily read / With most delight the passions of mankind', saw most clearly

> . . . into the depths of human souls,
> Souls that appear to have no depth at all
> To careless eyes.

But there *are* limits. Would Wordsworth, one wonders, have considered it 'careless' to impute depthlessness to a 'soul' that insists not only on *sitting* on the toposcope, but on singing 'Angels' by Robbie Williams at the top of his voice? Oblivious both to his *fortissimo* and nearly avant-garde tunelessness by virtue of the earphones piping the original into his inconsiderate head? Seekers after the 'calm / That Nature breathes among the hills and groves' may prefer to strike on southwards, following the course of the ancient Shire Ditch, or Red Earl's Dyke, so named after a boundary dispute between the 'carrot-topped' Earl of Gloucester, Gilbert de Clare, and Thomas de Cantilupe, Bishop of Hereford, who among other things introduced the melon to England. Without which Andrew Marvell would have had nothing to stumble on some four centuries later in his poem – favourite of 'solitary wanderers' everywhere – 1681's 'The Garden':

> Stumbling on Melons, as I pass,
> Insnar'd with Flow'rs, I fall on Grass.

Famously, of course, the speaker of the poem harks back to a happier time for 'that . . . Garden-state, / While Man there walk'd without a Mate'! Personally speaking, I'm far happier in company, and it's my great pride to report that it was at this very spot, on a wintry walk the November before last, that I finally and definitively wore Sunita's resistance down! Before picking her up at the station I'd stopped in at our old haunt, the Nags Head – despite its lack of an apostrophe a gem of a pub offering a range of well-kept local ales – but when push came to shove she accepted my proposal almost before I had summoned the courage (Dutch or otherwise) to make it. Yes, she breathed, and softly shut her eyes. In the silence that followed I recall a swathe of grass rippling in an unheard gust of wind, as if taken aback at the unlikeliness of the match. At forty-six I was nearly fifteen years Sunita's senior, and in all honesty some distance shorter of the male physical ideal than she was of the female.[1] But I had persistence in my favour, and as a senior council officer, well-regarded local watercolourist and author of six successful self-published walking guides, I hope it doesn't sound too conceited of me to say I represented a degree of stability and social standing to which, by her own admission, Sunita had long aspired. With her book on indefinite hold she felt

---

1. I have, however, been told by men and women alike that I have exceptionally nice legs.

'able to devote herself' to a new and arguably rather more arduous project – me – and for my part I was in a position to provide her with the material support she so sorely needed after several years surviving on odds and ends of freelance copywriting work. As my good friend the local poet[2] Alan Oakeshott puts it, 'We walk on lonely paths until they meet.'

A little less than a mile after the gentler crest of Summer Hill, the route bends right and descends through maturing turkey oaks to enter the appealing hamlet of Upper Wyche. Turn left along Beacon Road, passing the pleasantly proportioned yellow cottage that Sunita rented before moving in with me. 'Malvern View' is, I'm told, advertised in the back pages of the *London Review of Books* as 'ideal for writers seeking tranquillity and inspiration in a semi-rural setting', although last time I passed by I saw Sunita's successor sitting shirtless in the garden at a laptop computer, by a fractional wrongness in the position of his head clearly pretending to write as he people-watched the traffic on the footpaths. Turn left at the car park at the junction with West Malvern Road, if needs must taking advantage of the well-presented public toilets, and cross the busy B4218 to climb concrete steps by a metal rail. Hereafter the path climbs steadily upwards, and you may feel – as my wife certainly did – Perseverance Hill well named as you labour towards its 1,066-foot (325m) peak. Perhaps this would be the time for that emboldening Fruit Pastille! Descend a steepish slope, bearing in mind that however taxing the upward slogs and knee-fatiguing declivities on this section of the walk, any trembling you may feel in the legs will just as likely be down to the London Midland service that burrows underneath on its journey to Birmingham New Street.

Climb again to reach Jubilee, and shortly afterwards Pinnacle Hill (1,174 ft / 358m), to receive ample compensation for your efforts. The views from here are, if anything, more stirring than the prospect from the Worcestershire Beacon. That afternoon last summer the looming nimbostratus had threatened to dampen our fun, but as

2. And member of the Ledbury town-centre management committee.

Sunita and I drew level with the Worcestershire Golf Club, doing our best to ignore the insensitively sited industrial estate to its east, a vista opened up over Evendine and Herring's Coppice to the concentrically ridged earthworks of the Herefordshire Beacon. This Iron Age hill fort, otherwise known as British Camp, was at first sunk in a deceiving gloom that flattened its ridges to an unremarkable smoothness. But then the sun broke through the clouds in four splayed shafts, not only throwing each ridge into gilded green relief, but framing the entire Beacon in celestial quotation marks. The cliché 'picture-postcard scene'. Sunita had at this point opened up a lead of twenty paces, and by the time I caught up with her a wet-blanket raincloud had effaced the evidence for God's 'ironic sense of humour' to the extent that the observation fell understandably flat. But I was pleased to have observed it, and had reached that stage of the walk where the circulation of blood seemed to have sluiced the alluvia of stale thought from my brain. I was thinking.

'Solvitur ambulando,' says St Augustine. It is solved by walking. One might set out constrained by the most tightly knotted problem, and all at once, as if its loose end had been tied to one's boot, find oneself, with the merest tug of final disentanglement, following the course of its certain solution. Thomas Hobbes, who in the event he had a brainwave en route had an inkhorn installed in his walking stick,[3] objected to Descartes' famous statement 'I think, therefore I am', on the grounds that you might substitute 'walk' for 'think' and make as much sense. With typical *hauteur* Descartes responded that although 'I walk, therefore I am' was a perfectly valid proposition as far as it went, it wasn't *très utile*, as while you could doubt you were walking, you could by definition never doubt you were thinking, doubt being a cogitative faculty in and of itself.

If Descartes was ever unsure he was walking, I doubt in turn that he had ever ascended Penny Widow Hill in a hailstorm, but that aside, I

---

3. To much the same purpose I keep my trusty Olympus WS-311M digital voice recorder gaffer-taped to the shaft of my carbon duolock walking pole. Half a plastic vending cup serves as an effective rainhood/windguard.

wonder if his and Hobbes's squabble might have been resolved had the walking/thinking distinction been erased altogether. *Ambulare est cogitare*. Walking *is* thinking. I have often 'thought', scouting the walks for this guide, that I am not so much 'walking' as mapping the paths of my mind, or, conversely, 'thinking with my body' much as Wordsworth extemporised 'Tintern Abbey' while taking the walk it describes – even if, to do that now, you'd have to walk along the A466, which despite following the course of the Wye, the poet's beloved 'wanderer thro' the woods', is let down by poor verging and frequently so busy with lorries taking a short cut to the M48 that you'd need a pair of Boots' excellent Muffles Wax Earplugs to extemporise so much as a shopping list.

After Black Hill the path descends steadily before veering right to rejoin West Malvern Road. At the junction of this ancient salt route with the often heavily congested A449 you might like to stop for a formal lunch at the Malvern Hills Hotel, where the chef and his team offer such imaginative dishes as 'Grilled halloumi cheese set upon a fennel, watercress and pear salad', or alternatively, pop across to the refreshment hut opposite for a flapjack or a piece of fruit. Warm Cornish pasties are also available, as are bacon baps, but on perusal of my stool Sunita has pronounced me borderline gluten-intolerant, so when peckish I tend to stick to more tolerable grains such as oats or the spelt found in Dr Karg's delicious seeded krispbreads. Cross the road, and to the right of the car park pass through a gate to ascend steeply through trees, noting on your right a stone tablet commemorating, among other things, William Langland, 'the famous 14th Century poet' who 'at a spring nearby . . . slombred in a sleping' and 'dreamt his vision of Piers Plowman'. The spring in question is called Pewtriss Well, just north of British Camp on the Herefordshire–Worcestershire border, where, had he been around today, Langland's dreamer Will would have been woken not by the sheer beauty of Christ's 'passion and penaunce', but by lorries the size of the sky delivering mineral water to the bottling plant, now owned by Coca-Cola, that blights the neighbouring hamlet of Colwall. Follow the stony path as it winds uphill to reach the top of the Herefordshire Beacon.

Legend has it that Caractacus, great chieftain of the Catuvellauni tribe based in modern-day St Albans, staged his last stand against the Romans here at British Camp. Tacitus casts doubt on this in his *Annals*, but Elgar was sufficiently taken with the myth to use the Beacon as the setting for his cantata *Caractacus*. And it was with something of the spirit of the ancient British warrior that I confronted David, of Photography by David, when he rode up that June afternoon on his mountain bike. David had, I admit, been somewhat on my mind, ever since, at a drinks party held by our neighbours Peter and Jasmine Agnew, Jasmine had sung David's praises with an intensity that may well, for all I knew, have owed as much to genuine feelings of admiration as the booze-fuelled compulsion to get on her husband's wick.

'David Redfern?' she had sighed. 'So talented. So good-looking. So *manly*.'

They had known each other since the sixth form at John Masefield High School. Difficult as it may be to imagine, Jasmine was once a flat-chested, bespectacled brunette, and had nursed a crush on the budding lensman at once aggravated and soothed by the entirely requited devotion he felt for Karen, then his girlfriend, now his wife.[4] David and Karen were – and remained, as Jasmine stressed to the increasingly rigid-lipped Peter – the local golden couple. Knowing David as I do, which admittedly isn't very well, I had to suppress a frown of cautious scepticism. Sunita and I were married under the arboretum at Eastnor Castle nearby, and there's a photograph David took of us kissing, framed in the raised bows of two violinists poised on the opening notes of Brahms's String Quintet in G ('The Water Vole'), that captures the joy of that day with something close to eloquence. But talented? Manly? I had my doubts. Certainly, that afternoon at British Camp, manly talentedness did not, it seems,

---

4. Aggravated, so Jasmine explained, because if only she had been as pretty and confident and generously busted as Karen she might have had a chance with David. Soothed because she just wasn't, and even the most jealous and mean-spirited person would have to admit that David and Karen were made for each other, and there was no point in pretending otherwise.

equate to basic consideration for others, as not only had he left a deep tyre-track in the carefully maintained turfing between the summit and the bridleway, but he insisted on telling us, in exhaustive detail, about his new 'passion project',[5] a coffee-table book entitled *Holes*, in which photographs of the eponymous absences – tree cavities, the hollow hearts of bamboo canes, see-through gaps in seaside rock formations – would sit alongside 'evocative texts' he had the gall to suggest Sunita might help him compile.

I lost little time in making our excuses. Turn sharp left at the summit and keep going for roughly three-quarters of a mile until you reach a circular stone waymark like a frozen wheel of fortune. Follow the arrow marked 'Gullet Quarry'. The path takes you through scrub and huddled hawthorn before tending left into the louring gloom of News Wood. Here the sky flits in dark shoals amid the sea of green, and bushes seem to whisper as you pass. Go through a metal gate or its neighbouring stile – it really doesn't matter which – and hopscotch the inevitable puddles as the route lures you down through oak, ash, lime and the sporadic unwelcome blaze of exotic conifer, mounting like the layers of David's hair in bands of nodding gold. Turn left at a crossing of ways, descend to the quarry, strip off all but your underpants and dive into a deep, glassily green pool whose spring-fed freshness is guaranteed to put paid to the most galling of earthly concerns – even if only one of you is brave enough to take the plunge!

To be fair to Sunita, the water *is* exceptionally cold, and as the numerous information boards and warning signs indicate, 'can cause sudden cramps which could lead to drowning'. Nothing on God's earth can compare to the feeling, emerging from a 'wild dip', that the very essence of you has been renewed, and to swim in the

---

5. As distinct from what he called the 'gas-bill-paying b****cks' of his day-to-day photography business. Realising his faux pas he began with the most glutinously smooth change of gear to single out our wedding as an enchanting exception – 'some jobs turn out so magical you almost forget you're there to earn a crust' – which slippery stuff Sunita to her discredit tipped back her head and swallowed like a sea-bird's meal of mackerel.

embrace of the quarry's curving rockface, with the strata of schist and gneiss rising above you like a crystalline history of the universe, is to feel, for all the billion tiny needles in your blood, tantalisingly close to what it means to be alive. On our honeymoon in California, Sunita and I drove up from Cambria, where we watched juvenile elephant seals chest up the beach like escapees still bound at the ankles and wrists, to San Francisco, stopping on the way to walk in Big Sur, that relentlessly beautiful stretch of wooded coastline south of the Carmel River. Following the course of a swollen creek we came across a canyon whose honey-coloured walls enclosed a swimming hole, still as the sky it reflected, and shaded by willows in the imperceptible process of falling into the water. And swimming in that knife-cold, silent pool, as Sunita looked on from a rock, I felt a happiness that could only have been more intense had my new bride been persuaded to join me.

But I *am* an experienced swimmer. Every year, scores of people lose their lives entering or walking near uninvigilated waters. The Gullet, for example, is not only cold, and serviced by a notoriously slippery footpath, but littered at its deepest points with treacherous quarrying equipment, such as derricks and squirrel-cage conveyors, on which the unwitting diver, blinded by the murk, could all too easily snag a foot or groping hand. For every hapless swimmer pulled lifeless from the lake, several more have never been found, wedged (so it's said) between the weed-beribboned rotor units of a crane or long-forsaken granite crusher. Wild swimming, as I say, is a potentially joyous activity, but like walking it poses very real dangers, and when one adds in certain factors like Sunita's tachycardia it's hard not to have some sympathy with those who, like the venerable members of the Malvern Industrial Archaeology Circle, think swimming at the Gullet is 'both extremely foolish and dangerous' and should be 'discouraged at all costs'.

Leave the Gullet by retracing your steps to the waymark at the crossways. Continue straight on through a metal gate, and of a crow's foot of possible paths choose the middle one, uphill to a view over Eastnor Park where, that summer day, a gust of warm, grass-sweetened wind swept up the hill and tousled our hair. Follow the well-made path to the right of an obelisk erected to the memory of Edward Charles Cocks, whose family own Eastnor Castle, the neo-Gothic pile to your left in whose charming gardens we were married last May. The grounds are open to the public, except during the annual 'Big Chill' music festival in August, when you may find your path blocked by poker-faced security guards in fluorescent jackets. The Big Chill is designed to appeal to the older, more family-oriented drug-taker, who rejects as false the choice between continuing to enjoy 'nu jazz' and 'viscous trancecore' on the one hand, and having three kids and a Vauxhall Zafira on the other. I have every sympathy for the Cocks, who from the size of their invoice last May clearly have a pressing need to defray the cost of running their estate by any means necessary. But it would be nice if they could do it without restricting the right to roam to dance-music enthusiasts with £130 to fritter on tickets. Still, it has to be said that the festival's 'Leave No Trace' outdoor-ethics policy, whereby revellers are incentivised not to strew the countryside with plastic beer cups and ethnic-food containers, is some recompense for the yearly diversion.

Descend to a lake – lit up during the festival to resemble a 'faerie dominion' – surprise the resident spiders by crossing a clanking foot-bridge, and swinging a sharp left, head diagonally uphill in the direction of the castle. Cresting the field, veer right towards the spire of Eastnor Church. The 'nor' in Eastnor is derived from the Anglo-Saxon *nearu* or *nearwe*, meaning 'narrow', 'confined' or 'oppressive';[6] *Éast-nearwe*, or the 'Oppressive place to the East', may have been a term coined by the citizens of Ledbury, two miles west of the village, in reference either to an actual prison-house (*nirwð*) or to the vaguely swampish air of quarantine that adheres to the place to this day.

Cross the main road and hurry down an avenue of limes. Turn right at the church, and just before a pokey cottage[7] half-asphyxiated

6. From *The Anglo-Saxon Rune Poem*, l. 27: 'Nyd byþ nearu on breostan', 'Trouble is oppressive to the heart.' As true now as it was in the eighth (or possibly ninth) century.

7. Owned, incidentally, by David. When he's not renting it out to Londoners on a short-break basis, David sometimes uses the cottage as an alternative 'think-space' to his spacious if glibly inauthentic mock-Regency villa in Ledbury.

in wisteria, turn left at a footpath sign into open, rolling farmland. In fallow years these fields have an almost corporeal quality, brown and finely furrowed, sweeping in sensual curves to meet at the soft V of Eastnor Hill Wood. It was amid these 'fields and coverts' that Ledbury's John Masefield set the famous fight scene in his long narrative poem 'The Everlasting Mercy', in which to the 'laughter of the whimbrel' the dissolute, promiscuous Saul Kane hands out a pasting to his rival Billy Myers, before undergoing a timely conversion to Christ. Passing through a gap in the trees, you may feel a similarly pious urge as you strike north-west towards Dead Woman's Thorn, a shapeless copse whose inexplicable eeriness, even on sunlit afternoons, is as palpable as a cold raindrop on the back of the neck. Grey shrikes can sometimes be heard here, mourning the eponymous woman, said to be a milkmaid murdered by the husband she cuckolded. Strike on, fearing no evil, to enter Coneygree Wood via a path that soon becomes a steep sunken track.

As Robert Macfarlane points out in his deeply comforting book *The Wild Places*, these 'holloways' constitute a hidden map of Britain. Or the south-east of it, in any case: draw a line between the mouth of the Tees, between Redcar and Hartlepool, and the mouth of the Exe in Devon, and to the north of it you'll find the harder, igneous and metamorphic rockscape that has over the centuries proved impervious to the passage of feet, the clatter of hooves, the grinding revolutions of the cartwheel. In the soft south, however, what began as superficial footpaths were worn down, like the depressions on the threshold of churches, by centuries of travel into man-made ravines, deep enough to hide a priest or couch a sudden habitat. Descending this cool tunnel, immured in sedimentary rock from which bouquets of hart's tongue and broad buckler ferns spring, I felt as if Sunita and I were alone at last, sunk in the earth, unmapped, uncontactable, invisible to satellite technologies, and if I didn't suggest we threw off our clothes, and ran naked through the deepwood towards its silent green infinities, it was only because Sunita slipped on a patch of mud and in correcting her fall slightly pulled a muscle in her back. Keep on where the path gives way to a metalled track and turn left at a T-junction to enter Ledbury proper, where our walk ends.

Turn right at Ledbury Books & Maps, where for sundry senseless reasons you are unlikely to have purchased this guide, and continue down the Homend, passing the fine timbered Market House on your right, whose noteworthy 'bressumers' or supporting beams are described by the local historian Robin Entwistle as 'attractive if somewhat niggardly in their chamfering'. While its south-western outskirts leave a good deal to be desired, at its heart our home town lends weight to Goethe's felicitous description of architecture as 'frozen music'.[8] And if Ledbury strikes the rambler as a place in which commercial interests and the built heritage work not, as they so often do, at cross purposes, but to *invigorate* each other, that is in large part down to the selflessness of civic-minded public servants like Alan Oakeshott, whose tireless representations to the town-centre management committee have done so much to retard the Homend's degeneration into a soulless, identikit high street. Not everyone sees things the same way, of course: the Ledbury Business Forum, chaired as it happens by our neighbour Peter Agnew, favours a more laissez-faire approach to the usurpation of our historic town centre by parasitic chain stores. I have nothing but the highest regard for Peter – not least for his key role in the establishment of the East Herefordshire Diversity Panel, a dedicated support framework for local ethnic-minority businesses – which is why I'm sure he'll forgive me for generally having taken Alan's side in their frequent, frank, but never less than good-natured debates over Ledbury's future.

'Greedy little petit-bourgeois toilet salesman' was how Alan put it, after Peter suggested – no doubt solely to wind Alan up – that if a 'retail giant' were to bid for the lease on his high-street premises[9] he'd sell up 'like a shot'. Peter, in turn, has been known to refer to

8. Does this, I often wonder, make music 'defrosted architecture'? Listening to Bach's *Goldberg Variations*, as I often do on walks when motorway noise and other auditory intrusions preclude the music of silence, it strikes me that it might.
9. Peter Agnew Interiors, suppliers of bespoke hand-crafted bathrooms and sanitary ware.

Alan as a 'drunken old has-been' and 'drag on the local economy'! That the two of them are, in reality, the best of friends, and only having a bit of fun, should not obscure the fact that a genuine ideological difference obtains between them, and that it's exactly this diversity of opinion that helps to keep the local democratic process alive. Like many provincial English towns, Ledbury, however handsome, suffers from its fair share of alcohol-related crime and disorder, and it stands as testament to the vigour of the town's 'big conversation', as the council puts it, that there should have been such vocal disagreement as to how to tackle the problem. Either way, it's fair to speculate that, were he alive today, John Masefield would have been taken aback to find the streets down which his gin-soaked anti-hero staggered now designated an alcohol-free zone enforced by blanket CCTV coverage! Plans are also afoot to build a relief road to the east of the town, effectively turning the bypass into a ring road, and tempting revellers currently lured into Ledbury to urge their designated drivers further on, to the vaster drinking barns of Hereford or Gloucester.

On the other hand, the proposed new route passes within twenty yards of my garden, blundering through meadows that are home among other things to yellowhammers, linnets, voles, skylarks, weasels and deer. Furthermore, as an 'environmental measure' the council proposes erecting twenty-foot baffle boards that in deflecting the road noise can only ruin the view. Small as it is, the garden my father planted is one of my chief delights, crowded with tall grasses, cyclamen, my mother's favourite rambling rose, cream-pink Adélaide d'Orléans, and those wildflowers that have drifted in like welcome refugees: rosebay willowherb, lesser celandine, foxglove, white campion. To sit by the pond on a summer evening, looking out beyond the garden's whispering fringe of aspen to the Malverns beyond, is a pleasure whose loss no amount of compensation could redeem. In lighter moments Sunita calls this our chance to sell up now and move to London, but anyone party, as I am, to the disconnect between environmental and planning departments at the local-authority level will realise how serious a threat this development poses. It is, at least, something that Peter, Alan and I all agree on.[10] We can only cross our fingers and trust that, if the big conversation is as big as it's cracked up to be, common sense must surely prevail. Meanwhile, continue up the Homend to the station if you plan to catch a train back to Malvern, or, if time is *not* of the essence, stop in at the Retreat for a pint (or three!) of well-kept Wreakin's Hammerblow (6.6%) and a plate of chef Colin's tasty if arguably over-buttered tuna-salad sandwiches.

10. Peter I know for a fact is concerned about his passing trade; Alan that pubs will close.

Walk 2: The Slad Valley

Five valleys congregate on Stroud, the 'Notting Hill of the Cotswolds', and the least ruined of these is the 'bird-crammed, insect-hopping sun-trap' in which hard-drinking ladies' man Laurie Lee enjoyed 'Cider With Rosie' in the years before motorised transport shattered England down the faultlines of its A roads. The odd eyesore aside, however, there is much to enjoy on this walk, even if the route is sometimes tricky to follow, and the valley's capricious weather patterns can leave the best-prepared rambler longing for the comfort of the hearth. Rain, shine, or horizontal blizzard of sleet, two robust ascents, and a lengthy tiptoe through a permanent mudslick will ensure your post-walk pint of Pig's Ear is well-earned!

If walking is what makes us human, then a potent symbol of our humanity has surely to be the *gluteus maximus* – the main muscle in our buttocks. A scrawny, unimportant scrap of flesh in apes, in humans the largest of the three gluteus muscles has developed, via millennia of repetitive exercise, into the largest muscle in the body – rock of our

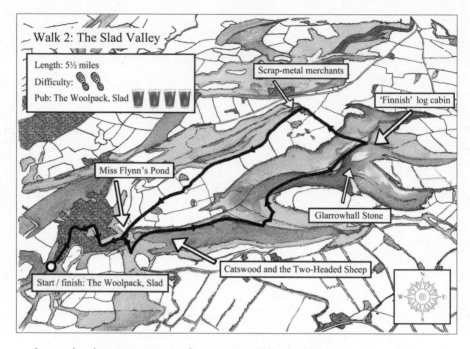

Walk 2: The Slad Valley

Length: 5½ miles
Difficulty:
Pub: The Woolpack, Slad

Scrap-metal merchants

'Finnish' log cabin

Miss Flynn's Pond

Glarrowhall Stone

Start / finish: The Woolpack, Slad

Catswood and the Two-Headed Sheep

lower backs, guarantor of our verticality, bold, Ionic volute of our thighs: the backside. There are those who claim that man stood up and walked so that his penis, no longer hidden under the table of four-footed deportment, could be brandished as a 'threat display organ', the better to demoralise rivals, and that the male organ of increase thus stands as humanity's totem. But there have been times, bestriding the landscape beside, and frequently behind, Sunita, when I have so marvelled at this masterpiece of biomechanical engineering that the matter has seemed settled beyond argument. *In posterior*, as the Romans might have said, *essentia*. In our fundaments, our fundament.

I have a feeling Laurie Lee would have agreed. This walk, which would have been as familiar to him as the sensation of walking itself, starts at the Woolpack, his local for eighty-three years, where the newish landlord now keeps a variety of appetising local ales, including Uley's potent Old Spot and Pig's Ear, as well as a good choice of international lagers such as Stella. Turning right out of the pub I was reminded of the author's famous ramble from Slad to the jittery fishing villages of pre-Civil War Andalusia, the famous account of which may as well, I've often felt, have been called *As I Walked Out One Midsummer Morning and Bedded Half the Women in Spain*. Revisiting chapter eight, 'To the Sea', in which the incorrigible old troubadour recalls his whistlestop tour of Valdepeñas, where the youngest of a group of girls 'in their early teens' softly loosened 'knots' in his 'flesh' before 'tying them up again', I was reminded how an aptly chosen lyricism can help bridge the gap in comprehension between Lee's more innocent, less hysterical age and ours, where having your knots loosened by a thirteen-year-old prostitute would as likely have you placed on the sex offenders' register as the GCSE syllabus. How times have changed.

Continue along the main road through the village, until a fork by an information board takes you right along Steanbridge Lane, whose exposure to the winds funnelling down the valley may help to displace any vapours left over from lunch! The likes of Cabbage-Stump Charlie, Percy-from-Painswick and Willy the Fish, who frequented the Woolpack in Laurie Lee's day, 'drinking hot-pokered cider' as they watched 'their wet boots steam', are long gone, of course, replaced as the 4x4 must follow the haywain by an eclectically minded, well-spoken, fleece-wearing crowd, as like to be just back from Goa as the sheepfold or half-loaded wagon. Just as well, when one recalls the incident in *Cider With Rosie* where an unwitting punter is kicked to death by the so-called 'colourful characters' at the bar. These days a warmer – if often no less raucous – welcome is extended to all, and the chief danger you are likely to face (other than never starting the walk!) is the prospect of losing your wife to the vexingly handsome barman, Seb, who once played a dashing but sadly unnamed cardiothoracic consultant in *Casualty*.

Follow the road as it bends sharply right at a charming, seventeenth-century mill house recently acquired for £2.2 million by a Mr Maqbool Al Qatari, a property developer from Dubai. Opposite a telephone post at the bottom of the hill, turn right to pass the pond where the mentally dishevelled Miss Flynn meets her Ophelia-ish end in *Cider With Rosie*. You may like to picture her pallid, watery outline as you throw bread to the pond's resident ducks, coots and moorhens. Through the trees to your right lies Steanbridge House, once owned by *Cider*'s benevolent

Squire Jones, whose passing marks not only the end of the book but of a thousand years of not entirely unenviable social stability. Note the elegant Georgian façade, although students of architecture should be aware that the perimeter fence is electrified, and pressure sensors are said to be buried in the outlying pastures. Climb a stile to ascend a steep, muddy field, admiring meanwhile the complex interaction of the quadriceps and gluteus muscles that obtains during hill-walking. Much has been written about the decline of the wild in this country, but it only takes a close examination of parts of the human body to be reassured of our proximity, whether walking in a green valley or the anaesthetic confines of a shopping centre, to what the incomparable American novelist Willa Cather called the 'brutal triumph' of dirty, untameable nature:

I am here still, at the bottom of things, warming the roots of life; you cannot starve me nor tame me nor thwart me; I made the world, I rule it, and I am its destiny.

Pause to catch your breath before mounting a second stile into Redding Wood. Follow a winding path uphill, passing on your right a large badger sett with an entrance like a moan from underground. The Western European badger, *Meles meles meles*, is distinct from its American and Asiatic cousins not only in its rather insistent, if not 'badgering', classification – the name means 'badger badger badger'[1] – but in its relatively peaceable nature. Where the ferocious honey badger of southern Iraq will do battle with porcupines, puff adders, leopards and even man himself,[2] the domestic badger, immortalised

---

1. Signifying, presumably, its extreme 'badgeriness': it is the badgeriest of all badgers.
2. Reliable sources claim that shortly after the invasion in 2003, British forces released a swarm of man-eating honey badgers into the insurgent stronghold of Basra in southern Iraq. A local housewife, Suad Hassan, told Agence France-Presse that she had been attacked by one of the creatures as she slept. 'My husband tried to shoot it but it was as swift as a deer,' she explained. 'It is the size of a dog but its head is like a monkey.' Coalition officials rushed to deny the claims but have remained conspicuously quiet about them since.

by Kenneth Grahame as a kindly if gruff figure who 'simply hates society', is content to grub around for earthworms, bulked out by the occasional nut. All of which makes its historical persecution at the hands of callous 'badger-baiters' all the more despicable. Under the Protection of Badgers Act 1992, it is now – as is only right – an imprisonable offence to harm one of these enchanting creatures, or even to damage its sett, and it is one of contemporary Britain's small triumphs that the practice of flushing out badgers with powerful lamps, only to be torn to shreds by slavering Staffies, is as obsolete a part of country life as driving under the influence or anti-immigrationist bigotry.

At the top of the bank, keep a drystone wall on your right, and continue in a north-easterly direction until a wide path crosses yours at right angles. Turn right here, and climb a gentle incline between beech trees. In *The Secret Life of Trees* the redoubtable Colin Tudge notes that beechwood infected with fungus is particularly valued by turners, the fine black lines of decay beautifying the timber in much the same way that penicillium moulds transform dull curds into Roquefort, or noble rot concentrates the flavours in a Château d'Yquem. Walking these woods in late autumn, when the paths galosh your boots in red-brown leaves, I am often filled with a musty melancholy at this falling away of things, the corruption at the heart of renewal, and the sweet if nearly unbearable sadness in every step of these walks, which must all of them end – even if, in the case of circular routes like this one, I sometimes fantasise that on returning to the starting point, I might simply start again, and walk around and around until my legs can carry me no further. In 1968 the British adventurer Donald Crowhurst set off in a trimaran of his own devising to circumnavigate the world single-handed, an attempt which was to end in his mental breakdown and suicide, but for my money the more compelling story is that of his forcefully eloquent French rival Bernard Moitessier,[3] who dropped out of the

3. 'You do not ask a tame seagull why it needs to disappear from time to time toward the open sea. It goes, that's all.' Imagine it in the French accent. Forceful stuff.

race – eventually won by the dependable if unglamorous Robin Knox-Johnston – not because he got into difficulties but because he'd gone round once and wanted to do it again. 'In my end is my beginning,' says T. S. Eliot, and if Sunita says this is a typically male refusal to accept the finiteness of things (parties, drinking sessions, swims in disused quarries) I can only extend the weary hand of sympathy to Moitessier, who would have completed his second full circle had his wife not insisted he pull in at Tahiti for a cuddle and a cocktail in a coconut.

Where a higher path sweeps in from above, take a sharp left, and continue through a brief clearing to reach the northern edge of Catswood. Here, among the larches, according to a local myth recorded in *Cider With Rosie*, dwells the dreaded Two-Headed Sheep, which speaks in a double voice and, if pressed, will tell you the date and nature of your death. Having recounted this to Sunita, in a fit of admittedly boyish inspiration I pretended to stop for a pee, switched on my walking-pole voice recorder, and recorded the words 'December the 5th, 2090, smothered by rose petals', before jogging up behind her, and in sheepish tones repeating the prediction at the same time as playing back my recording. Granted, it was a gloomy afternoon, and a certain otherworldliness inhered to the forest's shadowed thickets. But considering that Sunita would be a hundred and seventeen in 2090, and of ways to go death by rose petal was surely custom-designed to appeal to my beloved's often endearingly flaunted sensuality, you'll understand my surprise when she pushed me away, citing her 'special horror of suffocation' of which I was apparently all too aware, and plugging her ears when, a full ten minutes later, I caught up with her and (as a slate-cleaning change of subject) began to share my thoughts on the primeval origins of bipedalism.

That put paid to that. But imagine that first walker! Imagine what heady dream inspired him to climb up his knees and straighten his back! Imagine the thrill of it! Imagine how much it must have *hurt*! Imagine the mockery, the Neanderthal frowns, the sneers of the stolidly quadrupedal in the face of such avant-garde impulsiveness! Imagine the embarrassment! The *guts* it must have taken, in that

African valley unlike, and yet also *not* unlike, the secluded valley that stretches below you, to have stood and with hairy, flailing arms taken those first small steps for man! That first unsteady wobble with the sun on your front! Strolling from A to B with the unconscious ease that attends our most elementary functions, we all too easily forget the sacrifices made by that original hiker, whoever he was – that pedestrian pioneer, the ur-rambler – whose astonishing advance was, in terms of raw angles, the equivalent of our bending backwards through ninety degrees – and staying like that for four million years.

Follow your nose along this exquisite woodland path for just under a mile, keeping an eye out for roe and mottled fallow deer in the valley to your left. Scooped from the Cotswold escarpment by a lumbering glacier, the Slad Valley can feel almost detached from the mainland, with its ancient oaks, its island biology,[4] the sunken isolation enforced by its high ring of hills. Heavily crested with beech wood, the lip of the valley was the limit of Laurie Lee's world, at least until 'distances crept nearer' with the coming of the motor car, and the moon no longer 'rose from our hill' but 'from London . . . in the east'. Ignore paths to the left and right to plunge down the narrow, slippery path to the valley's tender cleft. If your companion happens to be walking far ahead of you, it can be fun to close one eye and hold her frail form between your thumb and forefinger, taking care to move in time with her in case she slips from your grasp or, conversely, you crush her altogether!

Leap a stream, mount a cellulitic field flank and dodge a cottage to climb the metalled path behind it, before taking the second of two paths springing back like a lapwing's crest-feathers from the eastward thrust of a nasty bend. It was around about here, stopping for a timely leg-stretch beneath the lightless picture windows of an isolated bungalow, that I began to worry that Sunita might be seriously annoyed with me. In slow traffic on the way to Slad we had passed an ash tree whose heartwood had rotted away, leaving a deep hollow whose entrance could be said without too great a stretch of the

---

4. Several unique species of snail make their home among these fields.

imagination to resemble a D. Quite casually I remarked that this might make a good cover for David's *Holes* book, expecting at the very least the expression of mildly interested assent that usually attends such observations on car journeys. To my surprise, however, Sunita said nothing, opening the glove compartment to extract a Fox's Glacier Fruit, before slamming it shut without offering me one.

'I don't know why you have to be so snide about David,' she said.

I slid my fingers down to grip the wheel at the unrecommended, but hopefully less snide-seeming, position of twenty-five to five.

'I wasn't being snide.'

A pause. A clacking noise as Sunita tongued the sweet around her teeth.

'You're just worried he'll find a publisher.'

I sighed. 'Not true.'

'Well, you can stop fretting. He's given up on *Holes*.'

Apparently he and Karen were trying for a baby. True friend that she is, Sunita had offered to help them prepare themselves spiritually, reminding Karen that a child is actually born the moment the desire to have it enters either parent's mind: it's no accident, as my wife so wisely points out, that we use the word *conception* as a synonym for the creation of new life. While it was entirely typical of Sunita to have met Karen's initial resistance to this powerful idea with such patient understanding, in private she admitted to a certain frustration. For years David had waited while Karen built up her career in events management. Now her business was beginning to falter, and David's pick up – all the more so after a shot he'd taken of a corn bunting peering at a golf ball had made the front page of the *Ledbury Evening Star* – she was pressurising him to procreate.

'It's *so* selfish. And then when I try to help them deal with the situation Karen's neck gets all tense.' Grimacing, Sunita had made her neck tendons stand out like the buttresses on a tropical tree-trunk; among her many other talents my clever darling was a cruelly accurate mimic. 'I mean, I would say, fine. If that's how you want to play it: your loss. But it's David I feel for.'

The upshot was that Karen was demanding David spend his

weekends at home with her. Even without the extra pressure of *Holes*, his photography business left scant time to devote to a marriage soon to be tested by the responsibilities of parenthood. And so after the umpteenth Sunday left to her own devices, Karen had laid down an ultimatum: something had to give. And that something was *Holes*.

'Pretty rich when you consider how much time Karen sets aside for what *she* wants to do. David's not allowed to spend so much as an hour working with me on *Holes* and yet what does Karen do every Sunday? Takes Robin Entwistle's dog for a three-hour walk. It's completely outrageous.'

Robin Entwistle, incidentally, is a prolific amateur historian and naturalist whose series of bird-fancier's walking guides, *Ornithological Rambles in East Herefordshire*, *West Worcestershire*, etc., I had recently been taken aback to find stocked in the 'Local Interest' section of Ledbury Books & Maps – where, as I say, due to a preposterous altercation over muddy hiking boots ramblers will have been unable to purchase this guide. In recent months Robin had begun conducting guided walks in person, and we would occasionally cross on the paths between Coneygree Wood and Eastnor, I alone, Robin leading a congregation of twitchers, stopping now and then to point out a mistle thrush or some such with his rather ostentatiously knobbly walnut walking stick. Clearly, dogs and birds don't mix, at least for the purposes of hushed observation, and it had become a standing arrangement between Robin and his next-door neighbour Karen that on the days he was off with his birds Karen would dogsit his beloved black Labrador, Smoky.

As to David and Karen's marital difficulties, I had privately to admit to some sympathy for the distaff position. Unlike David, I have always tried my hardest not to let my artistic ambitions get in the way of my private life, preferring to see them as integral rather than extraneous to it. But I could see that Sunita's temper, that morning on the way to Slad, might have been a coded plea for a little more 'we-time'. For there *had* been evenings when, in the grip of inspiration, I had turned to my watercolour brushes at the expense of conversation, or a nature documentary we might enjoy together; I had to concede that if David could subordinate his private passions to his marriage, so could I. Taking a secret vow to treat Sunita to a weekend away, then, I issued a non-specific apology, confident that would settle the matter. But now, wincing as I pushed against the tension in my hamstrings, I wasn't so sure that it had.

Briefly after a path joins yours from the left, descend rotten steps to vault a stile at the edge of the wood. You are in a field. Call out your companion's name if need be. Continue at pace along the field edge to vault a second stile back into the woods. Gloucestershire County Council tends to favour the standard post-and-rail stile, with a maximum distance of 450mm between the top step and the top fence rail. This in turn favours the basic 'lazy vault' ('*passement paresseux*') familiar to practitioners of *parkour*,[5] whereby one hand is placed on the highest part of the obstacle to be vaulted, and the legs swung over at an angle of ninety degrees. Here the path can get marshy, and if for one reason or another you are keen to make ground, you may feel your light treatment of the Two-Headed Sheep has come back to haunt you, as you slip and slide in a mudslick that is at once permanent and mysteriously slipperier than any mud you've ever slipped and slid in before.

Try not to lose your temper. The Slad Valley is by and large a majestic, inspiring place, and a gratifying sense of achievement awaits the rambler prepared to put up with a small number of trying interludes. What treasure isn't guarded by dragons? At the end of your boggy slog a pebbly path provides a welcome opportunity to declog your boots. Turn left here, downhill to a crossing of ways overseen by a tumbledown structure that may remind you of the hangman's cottage in *Cider With Rosie*. Here the hapless executioner, discovering

5. Traditionally confined to urban areas, the radical French art of 'free running' or '*l'art du déplacement*', wherein the practitioner, or *traceur*, clears obstacles by means of a system of jumps, rolls, vaults and precision landings, is increasingly in evidence on the footpaths and bridleways of rural England. On a recent stroll along the River Evenlode from Adlestrop – immortalised by Edward Thomas in his poem of the same name – I saw a wiry Asian teenager effect a stunning *saut de chat* over a trio of tubular-steel vehicle barriers.

that in the darkness of a 'storm-black evening' he had dispatched his own son, hanged himself from a hook in the wall, whereafter the cottage fell into ruin. Still, spookiness is a contextual matter, and with a zero-tailswing excavator to clear a larger patio, there'd be nothing to stop an enterprising self-builder taking advantage of the fundamentally sound Cotswold stonework to knock up an attractive, if isolated, starter home or holiday cottage.

Pass this 'ruin with potential' on the right, and ascending a steep path to climb a stile into High Wood, call out your companion's name at the top of your voice. (Walkers whose companions remain closer at hand may prefer to omit this last step.) In a clearing a few yards to the north-east of the stile stands the Glarrowhall Stone, a slender, rather gravestone-like monolith overshadowed by an oak reputed to be over seven hundred years old. Standing stones have long been associated with fertility, and it's said of the Rollright Stones, some thirty-five miles across the Cotswolds on the Oxfordshire–Warwickshire border, that young maidens would come at night and press their breasts to them, ensuring thus the fruitfulness of their wombs. 'Glarrowhall' is derived from the Old High Norse *glearwe*, 'glory', and *heol*, 'hole', referring to the round, two-inch aperture it may no longer interest David to note lies at roughly waist-height near the apex of the stone. Local legend has it that should a furtive lover be sufficiently well-endowed to conceive *through* the 'glearwe-heol',[6] his offspring will grow up to be champions, although until they in turn achieve issue through the hole they will never know the true identity of their father. One variation on the myth, itself a variation on the 'questionable paternity' motif found in the *Epic of Gilgamesh* and the twelfth-century romance-poem *La Pomme Épineuse* ('The Thorn-Apple'), sees a 'hole-child' return to avenge his cuckolded stepfather by slaying his mother; while in another, admittedly reported by Robin, the stone itself bears offspring in the form of a circle of smaller, holeless (and therefore barren) stones. In any case, unshockable walkers of an engineering bent might like to make a detour to

6. The stone is roughly four inches thick.

the stone, and puzzle out what contortions the woman would have to go through, to receive what small portion of male organ would protrude!

Strike on, quite possibly alone, and climb a stile to join a drab route that runs parallel to a farm track a hundred yards to your left. Listen out for woodpeckers, who drill in these woods, and for the cry of the common buzzard, a sound so mournful it might be in pre-emptive lament for their prey. Below a bungalow whose front elevation, in stubborn disregard for the local architectural idiom, is

The common buzzard

got out like a Finnish log cabin, slalom the posts of a non-existent fence and, two hundred yards later, ignoring a steep deviation to your right, pick out a path downhill to a high-quality, poplar-wood stile. Here on that overcast November afternoon I found Sunita standing in the adjoining meadow, head down as if scanning for worms, withstanding the pit-pat of an oncoming downpour with her fists clenched and her feet set indignantly apart. She was crying.

'What's the matter, pumpkin?' I asked.

'I've had enough,' she said.

It was a quarter to four. According to the website I'd consulted before we started out on the walk, we had just under half an hour left of daylight, and at least an hour and a quarter left of the walk, assuming a steady walking pace of four miles an hour. Now, as any lover of the outdoors will know, roughly half an hour of twilight will remain to the walker after sunset, which in our case would mean the last fifteen minutes of the walk would be conducted in pitch darkness. A problem, potentially, if you're dragging a broken leg down a glacier in the Peruvian Andes, but in a light shower three miles from Stroud, on a route whose last section keeps to a recently remetalled B road, I felt confident we'd make it out of the valley in one piece. By unfortunate coincidence, however, at this point the report of a shotgun echoed over the trees, and although I was able cool-headedly to point out that this was the tail end of the grouse season, and if Sunita was afraid of the dark she could avail herself of the powerful Maglite D-Cell I had thought to stow in my ramble-sack, she began to cry even less controllably.

The problem as she saw it was to do with the route. Before setting out on any walk I sketch out a rough map, gleaned from the Ordnance Survey and any number of online resources, and make photocopies for both Sunita and me with the intention that any changes can be pencilled in en route, before the authoritative map is rendered in watercolour. In the case of the Slad walk, the tenant of nearby Snow's Farm had seen fit, no doubt for sound land-management reasons, to remove a fence whose rightmost stanchion bore a fairly crucial waymark, towards which Sunita was clearly no longer able to strike across field. Like character, like love, the countryside is always in flux, and with the exception of a tiny minority of rapacious money-grubbing vandals the nation's farmers are only ensuring the landscape's vitality by removing hedges and fences, altering field boundaries, and, regrettably if sometimes unavoidably, blocking public footpaths with barbed wire or agricultural waste. Still, it can be distressing to find yourself disoriented all of a sudden, and to cheer her up I reminded Sunita of the amusing story wherein Words-worth, in his cantankerous later years, kicked a hole in a drystone wall that was obstructing an ancient right of way.

'F**k Wordsworth,' said Sunita, before striding off in what was, incidentally, the right direction – north-east across the field, then left over a brook towards an aluminium farm gate whose dropped hinges can, but in this case didn't, make the latch hard to budge. Sunita loves Wordsworth, incidentally, although she reserves her greatest admira-tion for Shelley, a 'more romantic' Romantic, and a favourite of mine, even if, in contrast to his more robust precursor, he set out on *his* grand walking tour with the admirable purpose of 'reading in greater depth from the Book of Nature', only to get as far as Calais and shack up for the summer with the wife of a local customs official.

No, there was something else at stake, even taking into consideration our argument in the car. For her thirty-second birthday I had taken Sunita to Venice, and finding ourselves momentarily lost in the backstreets of Dorsoduro, the left thumb and wrist in the clasped fists of the island, I had scarcely consulted my popout map before Sunita had clacked across the *campo* to deposit herself, iron-eyed, in a bar from which it took several pricey cocktails and an elaborate if not entirely justified admission of incompetence to extract her. When Sunita was six, her mother Amrita had run off with a wealthy, Harrow-educated lawyer from Bombay, only to be cast aside and die in childbirth before Sunita and she had the chance to be reunited. Soon after, her father Raj rented out the family apartment in Calcutta, moving with Sunita first to Riyadh before a succession of decreasingly stable job opportunities took him to the Highlands of Scotland, High Barnet and back – this time without his now-teenage daughter – to Calcutta again. And if her inadequate parenting had left her with anything it was the compulsion to walk away – witness any number of our trifling disagreements! – frustrated, once she had, by a rather contradictory unwillingness to be lost, even for a moment. In any case, that overcast afternoon outside Slad, her fractious mood might have continued indefinitely had I not had the good fortune, flailing through the mud to catch up with her, to pass a woman heading in the opposite direction, wearing an expression of such terminal contempt it made my bowels set to meet her eye. Half a minute behind her, making no obvious effort to close the gap, came her husband, yomping downhill with an aggressively ostentatious cheerfulness. Having taken one look at Sunita, he leant in as he drew level with me and, with a clubbable lift of the eyebrows, said, 'I've got one like that.'

Opinions are divided as to the etiquette of addressing strangers on footpaths. An exchange of 'hellos' is fine, even required, but anything more elaborate risks, at one extreme, redundancy ('Lovely day for it'), and, at the other, assuming complicity in what may well turn out to be a strictly private outlook on the world. In this case, as luck would have it, the presumptuous passer-by got my attitude to women so precisely wrong that I was able to convert a misapprehension on his part into an exculpating bout of comic indignation on mine. 'I've got one like that,' I said, repeatedly, as Sunita and I climbed a stile to labour uphill through dense tree cover. Compared to Sunita, I'm no mimic, but something in the constriction of my voice caught the man's Pooterish misogyny, and – friends at last – Sunita and I laughed like ducks until a stone stile gave way to open farmland, and a blast of icy wind whipped the breath from our mouths.

Continue along the field-edge to your right. In poor weather you may like to deploy the stowable hood of your kagoule, as even short-term exposure to a horizontal sleet-storm can have a paralysing effect on the face. In a short while the path becomes a broad, stony track, leading north-west to skirt the entrance to Down Barn Farm, a thriving mixed agribusiness whose setting amid tummocky pastures, handsome Georgian outbuildings and barnyards bustling with Wyandottes and Rhode Island Reds is marred only by the hideous scrap-metal merchants that blights the north-east corner of Longridge Wood, where you turn left at a footpath sign.

Keep straight ahead. One of Laurie Lee's last public appearances was to protest against plans to build ninety houses on a stretch of the valley that had failed to win protection as an Area of Outstanding Natural Beauty. Arthritic, partially blind, and already suffering from the bowel cancer that would carry him off aged eighty-three, he stunned a meeting organised by the developers by giving a speech, white stick held aloft like a poultryman guiding his geese, in defence of the 'rabbits, badgers and old codgers like me' who should, in his opinion, retain eternal custody of the 'small tight valley' he held so close. Sure enough, the plans fell through, and walking this lovely tree-lined path, which as night falls gives a view over the lights of Slad, pin-pricked in the blackness like an answer to the sky, you may feel a shaming urge to protect your own small corner of the planet. Which in my case, after an initial ecological-impact assessment, now seemed all but certain to be split down the middle by the eastward extension to the A417. Other ill-conceived schemes have been proposed for the Slad Valley in the decade since Laurie Lee's death – most recently a plan to create an artificial lake near Dillay Brook[7] – only to be rejected by a local planning authority committed not only to the health of the local economy, but to the same, apparently 'irrational' attachment to the land as is borne out by the words on Laurie Lee's headstone, across the road from the pub in the graveyard of Holy Trinity Church: 'He lies in the valley he loved.' One can only hope their equivalents at Ledbury Town Council achieve a similar enlightenment.

Follow the path as it descends gently through beech and suet oak. You may feel a magical stillness as the storm stirs the treetops above you, lamp-black against the watery wash of the sky. Walking in tree cover at dusk, with the lights of home in view, instils a special excitement that comes as far as I can tell from an intimation of the spirit of wildness that Willa Cather evokes, the half-frightening, half-reassuring thrill you feel knowing that warmth, and light, and food, and company, lie no more than twenty minutes' walk away, but that if anything should happen, if your legs gave out, and your mobile phone lost its signal, you might as well be in the depths of an irretrievable wilderness. Incidentally, Vodafone users should be assured of reliable reception in all but the most thickly wooded parts of the route, but if, like Sunita, you subscribe to the T-Mobile network, and have problems connecting, you might like to check their handy online 'coverage map' before you embark on this or indeed any of the walks in this book.

Keep ahead at a clearing on your right, where a red gate opens onto a faint path through the woods. This leads to Bulls Cross, a desolate saddle of heathland where the village gibbet once stood, and, as Laurie Lee tells it, is visited each night by a silver-grey coach pulled by a team of spectral horses. That said, it's just a hill, and unless you're particularly keen to try your (newly appeased) companion's patience in the hope of seeing an ectoplasmic pile-up, ignore

---

7. Which would, incidentally, have placed my 'spat' with Sunita several tens of metres underwater – appropriately enough for a couple one of whose rare points of difference is their respective love and hatred of the stuff!

the diversion to keep on where the trees begin to thin, the track becomes a tarmac path, and, on the night we did the walk, the rainclouds drew back to reveal a smear of buttery moonglow in the west. Pass the pond where Miss Flynn drowned to make your way back into Slad, stopping at the church to pay torchlit respects to Laurie Lee before retracing your steps to the Woolpack.

Reports of the death of the English country pub have been greatly exaggerated, at least if this fine – if sometimes rowdy! – example is anything to go by. Meals on offer include a traditional fish and chips, or you can opt for the bar menu, which features a wide choice of continental-style open sandwiches such as crab or cheese and pickle. The night we were in, however, the regulars seemed more interested in us than the food, possibly as a result of the tempting range of Cotswold bitters barman Seb was busy tapping direct from the casks! At one point I nipped to the loo, quaintly situated outside in a Type-V Portakabin, and on my return heard gales of raucous laughter that stopped as if extinguished by the rusting iron thumb-latch on the door – and then started again as I took my place near the hearth. Visitors especially from America may find the atmosphere somewhat 'salty', but the odd good-natured and, all things considered, complimentary reference to a certain area of your wife's anatomy is a small price to pay for an experience that, when so much about the English countryside has changed, harks back to a simpler, freer, less puritanical time. A fine, unspoilt community local. Recommended.

Walk 3: The Brecon Horseshoe

Now we're talking. The three peaks that 'nail' the Brecon Horseshoe to the hoof of the Beacons – Cribyn, Pen y Fan and Corn Du – offer some of the finest walking south of the Lake District, without the hordes of tourists that afflict the better-known slopes of Snowdonia. That said, this is a strenuous walk, beset with very real dangers, and every year 'fair-weather friends' of Britain's wilder landscapes take it upon themselves to climb these peaks without adequate preparation, or mindfulness of weather conditions that can change on a quicker and more careless whim than the idiots who choose to ignore them. Injury and death are often the result. Inexperienced ramblers, unable to navigate in mist or blinding storms, might prefer to sit out less meteorologically propitious afternoons in the excellent pub that marks the beginning and end of this walk.

Start at the Boar's Head pub on Ship Street in Brecon. Many walkers prefer to mount their assault on the Horseshoe from the Storey Arms, four miles south of Brecon nearer the foot of the climb. Indeed, this

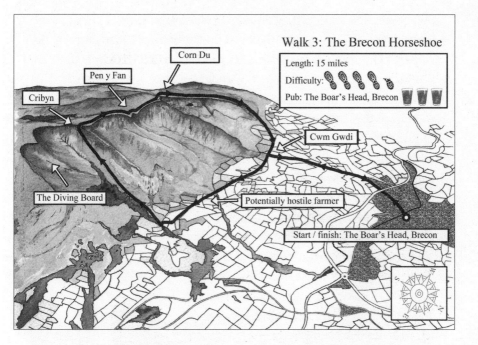

is one of the starting points for the infamous 'Fan Dance', part of the initial Fitness and Navigation phase of selection for the SAS, where candidates undertake a 15-mile march, or 'tab', up Pen y Fan, down the other side and back again, rifle in hand and with a 35-pound rucksack or 'bergen' on their backs. As Andy McNab recalls in *Immediate Action*, his incidentally rather superior follow-up to *Bravo Two Zero*, no cut-off time is specified, although when he 'did the Fan' an officer running alongside him said, 'If you keep with us, you're all right. If you don't, you're f***ing late' (my asterisks). Regrettably, despite its name the Storey Arms is in fact an Outdoor Education and Mountain Rescue Centre, not a pub, and although starting at the Boar's Head adds a good hour and a half to the walk, the malt / biscuit undertones of landlord Barry's well-kept Ramblers Ruin (5.0%) constitute ample compensation for the lost chance to pit yourself against the hardy recruits to the Special Air Service!

Turn left out of the pub to cross the gushing River Usk. Keep ahead, mindful of the oncoming traffic – especially if, like me, your eyes take a while to adjust to daylight after the comforting gloom of the pub – as

Ship Street first seamlessly slides into Bridge Street, then Orchard Street, Church Street, Newgate Street and finally, at a fork just short of the (superb) Drover's Arms, the scarcely pronounceable Ffrwdgrech Road.

Pinch your nose to navigate the underpass beneath the thrumming A40. It's hard to believe this is essentially an extension of London's Oxford Street, some hundred and eighty miles to the east, although the stocky pong of urine, down here amid the buckled cans and hijacked shopping carts, brings the spectre of urban squalor rather closer. Ignoring the industrial estate to your right, continue down a steadily more countrified lane for just over half a mile. Keep on at a fork amid sweet chestnuts, and fifteen yards later, at another fork, veer left to hug the treeline as, looming before you, the bosomy profile of Tyle Brith and

Sweet-chestnut stem with open fruit husk

Pen Milan precedes the smoothly pubic mound of Pen y Fan beyond.

This is a favourite spot of Sunita's and mine. On a day-trip we took to the region last year we pulled up not far from here and rolled down the windows to breathe in the mountain air. Suddenly it was as if the dirty veil of engine noise, of petrol smells and arguments in the car, had been drawn back to reveal a deeper reality. Sun slipped through the branches of the lay-by's fringe of sessile oaks, coaxing wisps of vapour from the tarmac, ghosts of the rain that had until its abrupt cessation fallen steadily since we crossed the border into Wales. Not three feet from the Prius's steaming bonnet a small, copper-breasted bird landed on a branch, cocked its neckless head and, as if to greet us, called *veest!*

'Brambling,' I conjectured, but at this point Sunita had turned onto her knees to reach the two-compartment picnic cooler on the back seat, and the impulse to ornithological speculation somewhat dwindled in me. Reclining our seats we gazed up at the voluptuous skyline, lost for words as we speared Bengali specialities from the Snap 'n' Lock food containers nestled stably in our laps. That day's walking might, on the debit side, have been confined to an amble round the antique shops of Merthyr Tydfil, but I remember the swell of gratification I felt, pulling back onto the B4558, when Sunita turned to me and, the fragrance of fenugreek still sweet on her breath, admitted that day-trips like these almost made up for not living in London.

Keep on for just over a mile to reach the car park at the old Cwm Gwdi training camp. You are now cradled in the cleavage of Tyle Brith ('Mottled Hummock') and Pen Milan ('One-eyed Mound'). And there *is* a sense of safety here, between the jostling slopes of tender grassland, a deep and almost maternal intimation of shelter that anyone who's seen one of the area's regular hailstorms sheet in from the south-west knows is completely illusory. For this is serious walking territory. Preparation is vital. Clearly, compared to the Alps, or even the Grampians, the Brecon Beacons scarcely register on the scale, but I have simply had too many conversations with too many furious search-and-rescue personnel, called away from their families to pluck an idiot in light trainers off the side of a mountain a child could have told him cried out at the minimum for solid ankle support, not to feel justified sounding a bit of a bossy-old-grandpa note of exasperated caution. The Beacons *aren't* the Andes, but the false sense of security this can bring is exactly what leads impetuous amateurs to bite off more than they can chew. Remember – this is nature we're dealing with, and as attractive as it can be at times *it doesn't give two hoots about you.* So please. Stay safe! Something as simple and widely available as a sturdy pair of walking boots could save your life, and ramblers embarking on the more ambitious walks in this book might also consider coming equipped with a GPS device, whistle, torch, signal mirror, first-aid kit, thermal survival bag and – best (and cheapest!) safety net of all – a partner to do the walk with.

Unfortunately on the morning in question Sunita had to pull out at the last minute. After the success of our car tour last year, and my long-standing vow to steal some special 'we-time' for the two of us, I had planned to treat Sunita to a surprise mini-break at the Felin Fach Griffin, a justifiably renowned pub-with-rooms just off the A470 north of Brecon. The idea was to 'bag' the Horseshoe before a slap-up supper in which pints of nutty Thomas Watkins OSB might have been paired with roasted diver scallops, or a terrine of chicken confit with hazelnut mayonnaise. Allowing seven hours for the walk, at that time of year (mid-Feb) to return to the starting point with daylight to spare meant leaving the Boar's Head no later than 10.15 a.m. Brecon is a good fifty miles from Ledbury, and knowing how long it can take my better half to get ready, I'd set the alarm for ten to six, switching it to vibrate and hiding it under my pillow so I could get up first and prepare Sunita's breakfast tray. In her defence, my wife is *not* at her best on less than nine hours' sleep, and if I was a little stung by her reaction to the tray, behind whose stripey egg-cups was propped a scrolled printout, tied with a red ribbon, of the automated email confirming our reservation at the Griffin, I can only blame myself for not insisting we go to bed earlier the previous evening, even if I'd been forced to say why and spoil the surprise.

The boiled egg and soldiers seemed to soften her mood. But then, rooting about in several jackets for her phone, she picked up a text message, sent early the previous evening by David, and from its cluster of expletives and typographical errors either in a state of drunkenness, high excitement or both. It seemed that *Holes* was back on. Sunita had recently attended a nature-writing workshop at the Walnut Tree Hotel in Great Malvern. There she had taken the card of Malcolm Thorne, the senior, and indeed only, editor at the Ptarmigan Press, a small but highly respected publisher of mostly local-interest books, based in Ludlow. Clearly, Sunita had grander plans for *Motherless in Calcutta*, but on the offchance Ptarmigan might be interested in *Holes*, she had taken the liberty of emailing Malcolm a two-page outline and ten sample photographs. That they *were* interested – 'vv intrssd', according to David's text – had come as all the more of a surprise for David, as Sunita, soberly judging it a long shot, had neglected to tell him she'd sent out his material in the first place. Still, interest was interest, and they now had until Monday to write the thirty pages of accompanying text Sunita had misled Malcolm into thinking were already written.

'But what about Karen?' I said. 'What about their plans to get pregnant?'

Sunita stared at me in disbelief. 'David might have a *publisher*, Graham. How do you think his child would feel? When it found out it had prevented its father from realising his dream?'

And so it was that I set off for the Beacons *tout seul*, my inevitable disappointment set off by the knowledge not only that Sunita was prepared to forgo a weekend of pleasure to help a friend in need, but that in supplying David's text she might get the chance to revive her own career as a writer. Besides, walking alone in remote places, one begins, like the hero of the medieval Irish saga *Buile Suibhne*,[1] to be reconciled to one's exile by the rhythms of nature, the 'clean, fierce wind', the 'yewiness' of 'yews', the 'fragrance of hazelnuts'. Studies have shown that of all means of treating depression walking is by far the most effective, and climbing a stile in the fence at the Cwm Gwdi car park, before crossing a footbridge and ascending steps, I felt the black dog of Sunita's absence recede into the verdant hillscape around me. Not only does walking stimulate the production of serotonin and norepinephrine, the neurotransmitters whose reuptake is inhibited by modern antidepressants, but immersion in natural environments is known to have a tranquillising effect, as what we perceive as 'green' derives from light with a medium, unhurried wavelength, lapping at the shores of our brains. Much as Sunita and I would have enjoyed the woodland path that curves off from this point, its verges loud with trumpet bands of daffodils, I was consoled, as so often, by the thought that via the simple act of placing one foot in front of the other I would soon, like Sweeney, be quite happy in my utter desolation.

Keep ahead until you reach a footpath sign. Confusingly – and, to the lazier among us, no doubt a little temptingly – this points in only one direction: straight back to the car park at the start. Sturdier ramblers may prefer, as I did, to treat themselves to a fizzy cola bottle and the thought that nothing so conditions the lungs to stiff walking as stiff walking itself. The mountain ahead of you, Cribyn,

1. Translated by Seamus Heaney as *Sweeney Astray*, although I prefer *Sweeney Demented*.

is an impressive, haughty prospect, its proffered foot poking out below horizontal bands of carboniferous limestone, mounting to the cinched waist of its summit like the flounces on a flamenco dancer's skirt. Turn left after the gate, and after the short if slippery negotiation of a field-edge, climb a stile. In twenty yards, turn right at a T-junction to saunter through a farmyard whose owner, if he's in anything like as bad a mood as he was the day I did the walk, may resent your presence to the point of active scowling. Ignore this – bearing in mind, massive subsidies notwithstanding, the hardships of farming in these harsh hillside conditions – and, climbing another stile, further aggravate the farmer by crossing his field to its south-eastern corner. In his latest collection, *Esgyrn* ('Bones'), Rhodri Thomas, perhaps the most promising of the group of young Welsh poets known as Y Saith ('The Seven'), addresses the deep communicative divide between those who work this land, and those, like Thomas himself, who have become estranged from it. This is perhaps most powerfully evoked in the closing poem, 'Dannedd' ('Teeth'), in which the poet describes his return to the family farm near Ystradgynlais after three years working as an oral hygienist in Prague:

> Brwnt, hanner-gladdwyd yn y ddaear
> Mae gwên ddafad yn gwawdio fy nigywilydd-dra
> *Dirty, half-buried in loam*
> *A sheep's grin mocks my impertinence*[2]

A gap in a row of lonely hornbeams gives onto a second, higher field. Take a deep breath. You should be out of range of the farmer's shotgun by now! Keep to the right-hand edge here, by an unsightly fence, before climbing first one stile, then, after a short jog downhill, another, and then a third at the far end of a field whose oddly narrow proportions gave me an unpleasant sense that something bad was

2. My translation. You might arguably substitute 'cheek' for 'impertinence'. Incidentally, it's common practice in this part of Wales to bury dead sheep where they drop – hence the 'grinning' skull Thomas is horrified to find poking from the soil.

about to happen, or was happening already, only reinforced by the hackneyed but no less eerie rasping of a crow. Turn left onto a gloomy footpath, where, hearing an odd trickling noise – despite the fact that, according to my map, the only stream hereabouts was several hundred yards away and muffled in trees – I stopped and to my simultaneous annoyance and relief discovered that my Platypus hydration pack had developed a puncture and was leaking all over my waterproof trousers. Turn right onto a metalled path and leap Nant Sere ('Sportive' or 'Mischievous Brook') to continue your long ascent to the summit of Cribyn.

Something in this uphill slog reminds me of the walks I took with my father as a boy. Every Sunday after church we would climb Penny Widow Hill overlooking Ledbury from the north. It's no more than six hundred feet – scarcely more than a hummock to me now – but from a six-year-old's perspective the unscrolling entirety of green seemed as endless as the tug-downable towels to which my father would lift me in the washrooms of motorway service stations. As devout as he was a keen rambler, shortly before his seventy-second birthday he took part in a Good Friday ascent of Leckhampton Hill outside Cheltenham, in which participants had to carry a seven-foot cross whose construction from medium-density particle board detracted less than you might think from its weight. My father was a small man, scarcely to scale with his cross, and I remember thinking, as I watched him struggle out of the Sandford Lido car park, that a less cussed spirit would have dumped the pesky thing on the pavement and taken whatever divine punishment was coming to him.

But we Underhills are an obstinate lot! Where the metalled path becomes a broad, stony track, show similar faith in your salvation by keeping on at a National Trust sign marked Cwm Cynwyn. Shortly afterwards, bear right onto the clear path that leads inexorably to the summit of Cribyn, which, at 2,608 feet (795m), ramblers should be warned is exposed to the sort of freezing winds to make you feel the shape of your skull. In mid-Feb I was all too glad of the hundred-weight microfleece – lightweight but surprisingly warm – I had on under my windsmock. Still, the views are spectacular, taking in the distant Black Mountains, Llangorse Lake and the Usk Valley, as well as the sweeping, shadowed corries clawed from the sides of Corn Du and Pen y Fan. Bear right to breast the saddle. As has been noted, the Brecon Beacons provide relative sanctuary from the crowds, at least compared to the top of poor Mount Snowdon, whose regrettable accessibility by rail has led to its year-round annexation by quick-fix summiteers, oblivious to the fact – self-evident to the rest of us – that the pleasure of being at the top *might* have something to do with the effort expended in getting there! Nonetheless, of all stretches of this walk, the ascent to Pen y Fan is perhaps the most trodden, and care should be taken where the path along the ridge has been eroded, largely by 'rambling groups' that insist on walking five or six abreast where a single file might better have preserved the verging. Fans of unusual flora might like to keep an eye out here for clumps of mountain kidneywort, a rare species of bryophyte whose tiny, mud-brown leaves are scarcely distinguishable from the thin earth that sustains them. Bryophytes are among the simplest and most ancient organisms known to man, their name deriving from the Greek φυτόν (*phyton*), 'plant', and βρύω (*bruo*), 'to be full to bursting', as, lacking both flowers and seeds, they reproduce via vast explosions of spores – an all-too-understandably frustrated response given the barrenness of the mountain conditions!

'Pen y Fan' means 'Summit of the Hill', which isn't particularly helpful when you consider how many hills there are around here. Viewed from the ridge its profile is not, in my opinion, unlike a good-quality wooden coathanger,[3] the Welsh translation of which, 'Cambren Cot', might have proved a useful and indeed rather euphonious clarification to the Celtic shepherd confused as to exactly which hill you were talking about. The cairn which marks the summit stands at 2,907 feet (886m) above sea level, meaning that you are now the highest human being south of the three hundred tourists queuing for Cornettos on the summit of Snowdon. The view

---

3. Without its hook.

from Pen y Fan is one of the most breathtaking in South Wales, encompassing in its north-easterly sweep Waun Fach and the brooding Black Mountain, and, closer at hand, Llyn Cwm Llwch, whose name, 'The Lake of the Valley of the Lake', is as impenetrably reflective as its surface, gleaming like a fallen sequin at the foot of Corn Du. Pause here to listen to the wind, carrying the mewls of distant buzzards like driftwood on a gentle tide, although the day I was last there a disparate crowd of three dozen ramblers, who from the relative emptiness of the paths seemed to have been airlifted onto the summit by helicopter, were milling about like press-ganged friends at a must-see exhibition, one father of five matching his youngest's piercing screams with barks of irritation as she was lowered, legs protesting, into the steel-frame baby carrier he had on in lieu of a ramblesack.

I was about to cut my losses and head for Corn Du, when, passing into range, my Nokia N78 announced the arrival of a voicemail. It was Sunita, and I'm not ashamed to say my heart pinked like an overheated engine when, as I pressed 'Show', her name came up in the list of missed calls. The voicemail, however, turned out to be one of those interminable eavesdrops on the sound someone's outer garments make when moving. Like as not she had sat on her phone, and if the message she left was accidental, I was still touched – and, in truth, somewhat troubled – by its intimacy, indecipherable as it was against the rustling of her raincoat. Listening to her voice, unmistakably hers (the fluting vowels) yet abstract in its muffled faintness, was a little like looking at the black-and-white photograph she kept in her leather-bound *Collected Works of Shelley*, of her by the Seine with her previous boyfriend Xavier, the evidence of a life lived independently of mine as incontrovertible as the chemicals that had darkened on the paper. I phoned back, but the call went directly to voicemail, throwing open the grimly ironic possibility that while I was trying to get through to her, she was, several hours on, still leaving me a message, unwittingly recording (at considerable expense!) the whispery sonic fringes of what I imagined was now a hard afternoon's labour at David's kitchen table.

   Leave Pen y Fan by the broad track that leads down and then gently
up to Corn Du ('The Black Horn'), the third and final summit on our
walk. A sure foot is necessary here, as erosion has loosened the rocks
on the descent from Pen y Fan. Again, irresponsible rambling practices are to blame, combined with the alternating droughts and
flash-floods of summers deranged by climate change. Still, as a teenager, at least when my father was in more liberal mood, I would
apply what the French call *'l'esprit du bouquetin'* to rocky, loose declivities like this, switching off my brain and trusting to the instinctive
'spirit of the mountain goat' to guide me as I ran, leapt and skidded
through the scree. Unfortunately, on this occasion a lone woman
rambler was walking fifty paces ahead of me, and even watching my
step I dislodged a jagged fragment of sandstone that with just a little
extra momentum might easily have bounced up and vaporised her
skull. Descend even more steeply after the brief climb to the cairn
on Corn Du, passing on your way a small obelisk dedicated to the
memory of little Tommy Jones, a five-year-old miner's son who in
August 1900 lost his way and died at this spot of exposure. It's worth
remembering, even on cloudless afternoons, how quickly these
mountains can turn on you, and the sheer human suffering caused
by hypothermia, splintered bones, and the sort of head injury I so
nearly inflicted on the woman walking below me on the ridge. In
1860 the pioneering photographer Eadweard Muybridge suffered
severe head injuries when a stagecoach lost control in the hills of San
Francisco. Some fourteen years later, suffering from mood swings
consistent with damage to the frontal lobes of the brain, Muybridge
discovered that his considerably younger wife Flora had taken a lover,
one Major Harry Larkyns. Confronting his rival, he said, 'Good
evening, Major, my name is Muybridge, and here is the answer to
the letter you sent my wife,' and shot Larkyns dead. Put on trial for
murder, Muybridge was acquitted on the grounds of justifiable
homicide, although Flora, unable to forgive him for killing her
lover, sued for divorce before losing her mind and dying at the tender
age of twenty-four. All of which only goes to show what fragile
shells encase us, and what a duty of care we owe ourselves, walking

these mountain trails, or even lower-altitude but equally hazardous routes like the slippery path to the quarry described in Walk 1.[4]

Pass to the left of Llyn Cwm Llwch as the path continues to descend into the valley. Here, as a Welsh mountain pony ambled over to me, Sunita rang, and quite without thinking I began to scratch behind the pony's ear, causing as I fumbled to answer the call the animal's lower lip to decouple from its jaw and release a glistening filament of drool.

Sunita was understandably annoyed to learn about the voicemail. She and David had been for a walk, to 'shake loose' some ideas for a piece of text accompanying perhaps Sunita's favourite picture of David's, a dramatic yet somehow intimate close-up on a blowhole in Cornwall, erupting in an ecstatic geyser of spume. They had stopped at the eastern end of Cut Throat Lane – only yards, incidentally, from the proposed route of the new A417 – where an insect had nibbled a hole in a dandelion leaf. Sunita's phone had been in the front pocket of her jeans, and she would in all likelihood accidentally have called me while kneeling to assemble David's tripod. All very irritating, especially as she and David might just as well have 'shaken loose' their 'ideas' here in Wales, which, I can vouch, is as full of holes (crannies, eyries, the coronal openings of daffodils) as the semi-rural outskirts of Ledbury! Still, the Horseshoe walk *is* a little longer than Sunita is used to, and agreeing that what with the traffic, and it getting dark so early, I might as well stay over at the Griffin after all, we elected to save our 'proper chat' for another time, as David's wife Karen had just laid the table for lunch.

'I'll miss you, my honey bee,' I said.

'Me too,' said Sunita. 'But you watch yourself now. You know what those gastropubs are like. Full of randy divorcées!'

---

4. Muybridge's famous stop-motion photographs of naked figures running, walking, climbing steps, etc. are collected under the title *The Human Figure in Motion* (London: Chapman & Hall, 1919). Fascinating to speculate that the loss of impulse control associated with brain injuries of his type might have been what gave him the monomaniacal application to create this landmark in our understanding of the mechanics of movement.

Exceptionally attractive, the Welsh mountain pony is distinct from other wild and semi-wild breeds in its combination of surefootedness, vast intelligence, and the even temperament that has for many centuries made it an ideal choice for the underage equestrian. This friendly little palomino trotted after me for half a mile, and it was only when I bore slightly left to join the path by Nant Cwm Llwch that I noticed *quite* how keen it had become on me! Forgive the unruly animal – for it knows not what it does – and continue beside the stream to enjoy outstanding views in all directions. The metaphysical poet Henry Vaughan, who lived less than two miles from here in the charming (if publess!) village of Llansantffraid, saw an image of the resurrection in the streams that fret these valleys, and even shorn of its religious context his unjustly neglected poem *Silex Scintillans* (1650) offers despairing ramblers a comforting vision of death as part of the natural cycle of decay and rebirth:

> Dear stream! dear bank, where often I
> Have sat and pleas'd my pensive eye,
> Why, since each drop of thy quick store
> Runs thither whence it flow'd before,
> Should poor souls fear a shade or night,
> Who came, sure, from a sea of light?

As the stream nears the bottom of the valley, ramblers will be further cheered to pass between hedgerows that in summer months are blowsy with foxgloves, harebells and a rare, red-speckled perennial known as *bys y dilledydd* or 'Haberdasher's Finger'. You are not yet, however, entirely 'out of the woods', as these paths are frequented by mountain bikers, hurtling off the higher ground lost in a reckless dream of unimpeded speed. Most will, to give them their due, sound a warning tring on their bells before mowing you down. If, like me, you ever find yourself tempted *not* to step out of the way, it might be in everyone's interests to remember, as I try to, that nothing human is alien to me – except perhaps for illegal offroading on motocross bikes, which quite apart from churning up the paths is going

48

to get a walker killed or seriously injured one of these days. Brecon Beacons National Park Authority, take note. There are ramblers' lives at stake.

Climb a stile, turn right, and climb a second before following the course of a mossy stone wall on your right. You may find at this late stage in the walk that your hands have swollen to the size of clown's gloves. Don't be alarmed. Manoedema or 'Puffy Hand' is very common in ramblers, as the 'hanging swing' to which the hands are naturally subject during walking forces blood to pool in the fingers, causing them to swell. There's not much you can do but wait for the swelling to subside, although an effective pre-emptive measure can be to walk with your hands up in the air, as if surrendering at gunpoint. (It's at times like these that walking alone can have its advantages.)

Follow the course of Nant Cwm Llwch to cross a footbridge. At a car park, pass through a gate and follow your nose as rough, impacted earth gives way to metalled blacktop. Nearing the end of a walk, I infrequently submit to a momentary gloominess the walk itself has helped to keep at bay, in this case prompted by the threats to the Beacons posed by climate change, the Welsh Assembly's determination to open them up to gravel extraction, and the nagging worry that I might never be a good enough husband to my wife. Ignore this, if you feel anything similar, and turn right at a crossroads onto a charming, sunken B-road, in summer months pausing to pluck white bindweed flowers from the hedgerows, furled tight like umbrellas or splayed like the horns of old gramophone players. Squeezed at the plump nub where the sepals meet the stem the flower will spring out with a satisfying if barely audible pop, at speed if the flower has yet to open, or with a magical floating parachute-action if fully in bloom. As children we called this game 'Granny pop out of bed', and on an evening stroll in Ledbury, the summer Sunita and I were newly married, I remember sending a succession of white flower-heads soaring over her shoulders to float down in front of her face, and her collecting them, one by one, in the hollow of her half-lifted blouse.

As you turn left at Cwm Gwdi, to retrace your steps to the Boar's Head, take a last look at the mountains behind you. The Beacons are named after the practice, under brave Llewellyn the Last, of lighting signal fires on their summits, to alert the Welsh resistance to impending attack by invading Anglo-Norman forces led by Edward I. And it's not so hard, late in the day, as darkness begins to obliterate the skyline, to imagine its high peaks picked out by bright points of fire, warning of grave dangers ahead.

Walk 4: Regency Cheltenham

Cheltenham has been called 'the most complete Regency town in England', and a stroll round its elegantly proportioned streets will imbue the walker with a sense of well-being dispelled with relative infrequency by the reminder that to qualify as the most complete Regency town in England is hardly an arduous task. Save for an optional detour into parkland, this route keeps to well-maintained stone, concrete-flag and bituminous pavements, but ramblers considering wearing 'ordinary' shoes might bear in mind that the desirability of proper internal cushioning is increased, if anything, by urban walking surfaces. Besides, advances in walking-boot design have been such that even the most style-conscious visitor to this resurgently fashionable spa town might be proud to have a pair of Gel-Trek Vindicators poking out from their jeans or plastic over-trousers!

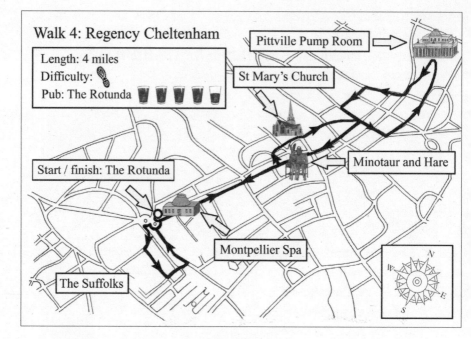

When Desert Orchid won the Cheltenham Gold Cup in 1989 I was underneath my recently acquired second-hand Honda Concerto, tightening what subsequently proved to be a persistently thunderous muffler. My late first wife was watching the race in a room adjoining the garage, and when in the final furlong Desert Orchid, to whom as ramblers will remember the heavy going was not at all suited, yearned past the mud-loving Yahoo, Anne let out a scream of such ragged release that I sat up with a start and gashed my brow on the manifold gasket. When, as coincidence would have it, I most recently attended Cheltenham Racecourse, earlier this May, I did so not only following a precipitously ill-tempered argument with 'wife no. 2', but with a similarly nasty cut to the head and neck region – although in this instance, owing to its precise location, I was able to conceal it from my companions with a stylish if predictably derided cravat.

Still, the Rotunda Tavern on Montpellier Street is a fine place to 'kick back and relax', even if your wife has forcibly excluded you from the house, you've lost £25 on the horses, and your 'friends' seem to derive inexhaustible amusement from likening you to a

lecherous Edwardian cad! Cheltonians will protest the abundance
of fine pubs nearer the racecourse, but Alan knows the landlord at
the Rotunda, and the pub's situation near the famous Gordon Lamp[1]
gives easy access to the glories of Suffolk Square, with its intricate
ironwork balconies, and the impressive if somehow melancholy
Regency terraces of the Lansdown Estate. I was, naturally, in favour
of walking from the racecourse to the Rotunda, but Alan was impatient to get 'strapped in', as he put it, to a proper drinking session,
having won £90 on Bengal Lancer, a horse I had deliberately *not* bet
on, for fear of the inevitable ridicule. In any case, Steve Reed was
by this point too drunk on warm lager to stand, let alone walk three
miles, and we ended up ordering a cab, Steve and Alan's interminable mocking of my neckwear preventing me from admiring, let
alone commenting on, the flamboyant Greek Revival villas over
which our cab gave fleeting vantage. Sometimes I wonder if your
friends are merely the people you've been too polite to leave behind!

   The Rotunda serves a good selection of cask-conditioned ales and
fine wines. Sunita and I had been enjoying a late supper of quinoa
linguine simply tossed with artichoke hearts, walnut oil and raisins
when the conversation turned to the tax breaks available to freelancers who, like Sunita, worked from home.

   'We could be claiming back *far* more of the mortgage,' she said,
with an encompassing flourish of her fork. We had been out for a
fact-finding stroll along the proposed route of the new A417, and the
first glass of wine, on top of the lateness of supper, had made Sunita
light-headedly forthright. 'Which would mean we could afford a

1. Erected to the memory of General George Gordon, doomed hero of the siege
of Khartoum (1884–5). Despite holding out for ten months against the marauding
Sudanese, Gordon was held in such indifferent esteem by the citizens of Cheltenham
that when asked to stump up the £200 for the memorial lamp, they raised £20. The
base is made of fine red and grey 'strawberry roan' granite, but the three drooping
stems from which the lamp-heads are suspended succeed only in memor-
ialising the flaccidity of the public response to Gordon's self-sacrifice, and indeed
the rather damp West Country gloom I've never felt Cheltenham's honeyed stonework entirely succeeds in dispelling.

bigger place. Or the same-size place in a more expensive area. Do you see?'

I did.

'But poppet,' I said, after a lengthy if not altogether comprehending examination of the tablecloth. 'In what sense is this tax deduction justified? As I understand it you work on *Holes* at David's place. And as to *Motherless in Calcutta*, well. Forgive me, but I was under the impression you'd put that to one side while you rethought the narrative structure.'

Sunita laid her fork down. 'I didn't realise you had such a low opinion of what I do.'

'Sweet pea,' I said, laying my hand on top of hers, with the mildly unfortunate consequence that the tines of her fork pressed sharply into the veinous underside of my wrist. 'I'm *incredibly* proud of what you do. And I think your suggestion is intriguing. But you know pedantic old me. I just wanted to make sure I understood.'

Sunita shrugged, and withdrew her hand. 'I was looking online, is the only reason I brought it up. And there were a couple of one-bedroom flats that seemed surprisingly good value for west London. But it doesn't matter. Forget it.'

I turned to look through the patio doors into the deepening blue of the garden. Above the pond I could make out the stands of lesser bulrush, *Typha angustifolia*, nodding narcoleptically; further off, in the more complete darkness cast by the aspens at the foot of the garden, a single, puzzlingly early glow-worm moved in loops and sudden circles, as if an unseen child were writing its name with a sparkler. Sunita had pushed her half-eaten linguine aside, and, crossing to the store cupboard, helped herself to a slice of her favourite gluten-free sticky ginger cake. When I spoke again I was surprised to feel my throat croak open, to its peatiest depths, like the hollow ash we'd seen outside Slad.

'Would you really want to live in the city? Away from all this? I honestly feel if all I could see from my window was rooftops and cars I . . .'

'You . . .?'

'I might feel as if I were missing out on something.'

Sunita laughed, not particularly kindly, I have to say. 'Not something you'd *ever* say of the semi-rural outskirts of Ledbury.'

I smiled. Sunita was right, of course. Ramblers of all people will recognise the tensions inherent in what the Edwardian naturalist W. J. Arbuthnot called 'the siren call of the hedgerow': between aloneness and loneliness, noble isolation and misanthropy, adaptation to the slower rhythms of nature and straightforward, soul-corroding boredom. Nonetheless, I was alive to these tensions, and ramblers can rest assured that if life at Foxglove Cottage ever fell short of what someone of Sunita's temperament deserved – well, I had my plans.

'There's one thing we have to remember about living here,' I said, taking Sunita's hand again. 'We're *stewards*.'

'Oh, f**k off.'

'No, I mean it. My father built this house. Is it really so ridiculous to want to pass on his legacy intact to our children? And possibly even their children after them?'

'If we *have* children.'

'Well, I didn't mean *our* children, necessarily. I meant children in general. Future generations.'

'No you didn't. You meant our children.'

'If there was any such nuance or undertone to what I said, well, so be it. You know my feelings on the matter. But I'm not suggesting we go upstairs and procreate this minute.'

'*That's* just as well.'

I stood up and moved behind Sunita with the intention of massaging her shoulders. 'Let's stop this, shall we, peaches? Why don't we go through to the living room? You can tell me more about these tax breaks while I rub what must be a *very* sore pair of pixie-feet.'

I had just positioned my thumbs on the upper fibres of Sunita's trapezius muscles when she raised her hands off the table, let out a scream of a length and unselfconscious intensity to make me glad I'd submitted to her earlier demand I shut the patio doors, and ran upstairs to the bedroom. Knowledgeable readers will have noted my passing reference to the aspen trees in the garden, the flatness of whose petioles – the short stalks attaching each leaf blade to its stem – causes the leaves to tremble in even the gentlest of breezes, giving the tree its Latin name, *Populus tremula* ('trembling' or 'chattering poplar'), and the leaves their colloquial name of 'ladies' tongues'.[2] Unfortunately, or fortunately, depending on which way you look at it, *my* lady's tongue was most un-aspen-like in its stillness, as I rapped softly on the bedroom door, at once careful not to upset her further, and desperate to atone for my crass insensitivity. At thirty-three, Sunita's 'body clock' was ticking, and quite apart from the fact that mine might well definitively have tocked, to have brought up the subject of children so casually was a mistake I had the opportunity to regret at my leisure, sitting outside the Rotunda banned from so much as giving her a call.

Montpellier Walk is a shopper's paradise, its fashion boutiques, cookware shops and delicatessens mingling with a laser hair-removal clinic and a branch of Sketchley's, the dry-cleaner's, whose green-and-white corporate branding walkers will be pleased to note is sensitively subordinated to the neoclassical aesthetic of the parade. The outdoor smoking area of the Rotunda gives out over Montpellier Walk, and although on this occasion, having waited twenty minutes for a table under the patio heater, Alan and Steve were now well and truly strapped in for the afternoon, I well remember walking here during visits to my grandmother, fascinated by the thirty-two armless female figures that separate each shop-front from its neighbour. Note the slenderness of their necks. Like the tribune of caryatids at the Erechtheum in Athens, the figures are designed to support the great weight of the entablature above them while remaining alluringly feminine in form, a combination of daintiness and surprising strength they share with Sunita, who towards the end of one of the Agnews' regular 'lasagne on laps' parties once challenged

2. As they're never still. An imputation matched in its obsolete misogyny by the old Herefordshire name for the oak tree: the *yedder*, a corruption of 'yes, dear', the response of the long-suffering woodsman to the constant creaking or 'nagging' of mature oaks in high winds.

me to an arm-wrestle on a corner of Peter's prized glass coffee table, supported in its case not by caryatids but a tribune of bronze golfers discussing a shot.[3] I won, but only just, and for weeks afterwards suffered from mild tendonitis offset, if not alleviated, by Peter's large-hearted refusal to accept compensation for the hairline crack my final heave had left in the glass.

Cheltenham's renown as a 'place to take the waters' dates back to the early eighteenth century, when Samuel Beecham, a notorious rogue, naval captain and arable farmer from Spalding in Lincolnshire, married Frances, daughter of the late Sir Henry Tattershall of Cheltenham. Along with his wife's considerable fortune, Beecham acquired a well, about a mile west of Montpellier Walk on the current site of the sports-nutrition specialists Cotswold Muscle. As recorded in his journal for 1714, excerpts of which are on view at the Cheltenham Museum, on first tasting the water Beecham suspected his 'sheepe . . . hadde beene wont to use the well as a p*sse-pot'. The prominent physician Dr Isaiah Crabtree had, however, recently published a treatise on the purgative properties of iron-rich 'chalybeate' water, and although no evidence exists that Beecham had read Crabtree's seminal text, that the wily old 'Father of the Spas' quickly realised he was on to something might be surmised from his subsequent land-grab. Between 1716 and 1740, the year of his death,[4] Beecham, whose ancestors had for centuries eked out a threadbare existence growing root vegetables on the Fens, used the Tattershall name and economic clout forcibly to purchase over a hundred and fifty orchards, smallholdings and farms, extending as far east as the peaceful hamlet of Montpellier, where in 1809 Beecham's great-great-nephew Henry Thompson built what is in my view the finest of all

---

3. The table was a wedding gift from his former father-in-law, prized not because Peter is an astonishing philistine, or because he feels any particular attachment to his first wife Eileen, but because golf is his sole means of meaningful contact with Tobias, his and Eileen's rather sullen sixteen-year-old son, now residing with his mother outside Bristol.

4. Ironically, from a gastric haemorrhage probably arising from just the sort of acute peptic ulceration the spa waters he found so disgusting were claimed to prevent.

Cheltenham's surviving neoclassical spa buildings. It's now a branch of Lloyds TSB, and if the underground well has long since dried up, ask one of the mostly helpful customer-service representatives for permission and you might instead direct your attention upwards, at the interior of the rotunda, designed by the celebrated J. B. Papworth in 1826, and as ethereal in its concentric pale-blue panels or *lacunaria* as the conversation outside the eponymous pub that afternoon was down to earth.

'Missus sling you out then, did she?' This was Alan, tucking into his fourth pint of citrusy, wholemeal-toasty St Austell's Tribute (4.2%). 'What you do? Smack her one, did you?'

'That's right, Alan,' I said, with a sportsmanlike smile. 'I often find physical violence a useful fallback position when words elude me.'

'Words? Elude you? That'll be the day.'

A snigger from Steve here: his first sign of life for at least half a pint. 'Perhaps it was her gave *him* a smack.'

'Well, you couldn't blame her, could you? If I had to listen to him bang on about trees all day I'd be pretty f***ing tempted. Is that why you're dressed up like Lord Peter Wimsey? To hide the throttle marks?'

'No.'

'Look, Reedy,' said Alan, pointing. 'He's blushing! You hold his arms while I get the cravat off.'

I rose from my chair. 'I really wouldn't do that if I were you.'

'What are you going to do?' said Alan. 'Slap me with a glove? Whip me with your watch-chain?'

Quite a hard punch in the thigh here, followed by a tiresome ten seconds while Steve and Alan rolled around in their chairs, wheezing like slow-punctured basketballs. Drunk or sober, Alan has always been a tease, but now that Lucy, the youngest of his three daughters, has married and moved to Cardiff, I have noted alongside the marked increase in his drinking a harder, more insistent edge to his sarcasm, as if his discharge from fatherly duties has absolved him of the responsibility to be polite. Still, to give him his due, the occasional roughness of his remarks is tempered, to those that know him, by his unerring egalitarianism: he finds everyone ridiculous, himself included. I am, as I think ramblers will agree, someone who 'enjoys a joke' myself, but can only defer to a man who calls himself 'Ledbury's healthiest octogenarian 52-year-old'. After all, if laughter is the only fitting response, other than unappeasable terror, to death, then it stands to reason that someone who smokes and drinks as much as Alan is going to have a proportionately inflated sense of humour.

Steve, on the other hand, is an altogether more withheld sort of figure, and it always comes as something of a surprise when, around the five-pint mark, his tongue begins to decouple from his usual sense of propriety. In his younger days, or so I'm led to believe, Steve had a well-earned reputation for 'wild behaviour', but since his spell at HMP Hewell,[5] and subsequent divorce from Christine, restraint has for the most part been his watchword. Granted, his weakness for powerful 'skunk'-type cannabis *is* a little unbecoming in a 37-year-old father of two, but we all have our poisons, and in recent months Steve has shown a new maturity in moving into a caravan on his younger brother Jason's land. Being passed over, even in favour of someone far more qualified, competent and temperamentally suited to farming three hundred acres, could scarcely have been easy, and it's testament to Steve's strength of character that he should have come to so workable an accommodation with the brother he once vowed to dismember and feed to his prize-winning pigs. Three generations of Reeds have farmed at Nettlebed, and although Steve has chosen to plough a different furrow, as an odd-job man and occasional gardener, his attachment to the place was evident the time I flailed down the rutted farm track to pay him an impromptu – and in hindsight perhaps ill-advised – visit after dark, and he only lowered his pump-action shotgun once I'd stepped out of the Prius and convinced him it was me!

In any case, in the six months since Steve started helping out in

5. For setting fire to an eight-mile run of speed cameras between Ross-on-Wye and Much Marcle.

the garden I have not only had the pleasure of recommending him, in the professional sense, to David and Karen, but of coming to think of him as a friend, to myself, and to Sunita on the long afternoons when I'm at work and David is busy with his photographs. A more unlikely pair you'd be hard-pushed to imagine – the weatherbeaten, peat-scented, pony-tailed man of few words, and my exquisite, cosmopolitan, intellectual Sunita – but for one reason or another they have formed a mutual fan club so staunch I have sometimes had cause to fear for my marriage! Seriously, though, that Steve and Sunita should have developed such an easy, albeit socio-economically unconventional, intimacy is a source of quiet satisfaction, and if Steve and Alan subjected me to a bit of a ribbing that afternoon outside the Rotunda, I was privately rather flattered they were taking her side.

Had Alan not been buying, I might at this point have struck on past Imperial Gardens to the Promenade, home to the Municipal Offices of Cheltenham Borough Council. Note the statue of the Cheltenham-born physician and water-colourist Dr Edward 'Bill' Wilson, whose extraordinary bravery on Scott's ill-fated expedition to the South Pole is belied by the oddly camp attitude of his effigy in bronze. The offices of Herefordshire County Council are housed in a perfectly serviceable, and notably well-insulated, converted police headquarters dating

Dr Edward 'Bill' Wilson

from the mid-1960s, but I can't walk past the offices of my borough-council counterparts at Cheltenham without experiencing a pang of not altogether edifying envy. What a privilege to benchmark the authority's per-capita CO_2 reduction against national performance indicators behind arguably the most coherent Regency façade outside Bath! Clearly, tackling climate change in Herefordshire brings its own satisfactions, but to tackle it beneath an entablature, or between the Ionic columns of a rusticated portico, would be to imbue this vital effort with a measure of dignity unfurnished by precast-concrete window casements.[6]

Continue down the Promenade to the far end of Long Gardens, where the Promenade becomes pedestrianised, and ramblers may be surprised if not actively nauseated to find a minotaur sitting on a wrought-iron bench with his arm around a hare. The great era of English neoclassicism, between the publication of Colen Campbell's *Vitruvius Britannicus* in 1715, and the regrettable embrace of Gothic modes later in the nineteenth century, constituted a conscious and in my view laudable effort to reject the clotted convolutions of the baroque in favour of 'the noble serenity' Matthew Arnold so revered in classical Greek architecture. Somebody, however, might have had a word with whoever made the minotaur sculpture, its playful figuration and roughcast textural qualities providing eloquent proof that to borrow from Greek antiquity is no guarantee against making an absolute mockery of it. The minotaur, of course, was the offspring of a bull and the refreshingly open-minded adulteress Pasiphaë, who in order to get the bull in the mood had a special wooden cow-suit made by the Athenian artificer Daedalus, father of Icarus, and the descendant, incidentally, of the mythic king Erechtheus, whose temple on the Acropolis is supported by the chorus-line of caryatids reproduced on Montpellier Walk. The slaying of the minotaur by Theseus represented the final liberation of the (civilised, patriarchal) Athenian city-state from (barbaric, matriarchal) Minoan Crete, where a bull-cult existed alongside the worship of the *labrys*, or double-headed axe, wielded by bare-breasted Minoan priestesses and familiar today as a symbol of female homosexuality. As a wedding present my sister Barbara, who, living in New Zealand with her partner Danielle, was unable to attend the actual ceremony, FedExed us a labrys in the form of a novelty door-stop, whose handy reversibility means that either

6. Although it has to be noted that the difficulty of properly insulating Georgian and Regency buildings invariably has a drastically limiting effect on their energy efficiency.

blade can be stepped on in order to wedge the other up to the requisite width beneath the door.

Unfortunately it was exactly this ease of use that was to lead to my banishment from the house the night before the 'boys' trip' to Cheltenham. As I say, Sunita was refusing to answer my soft entreaties at the bedroom door, at least until I made the admittedly incautious suggestion that I enumerate – for the second time that evening – my reasons for wanting to stay at Foxglove Cottage.

'For Chr*st's sake, Graham,' came Sunita's response. *'They're going to build a f***ing road through it.'*

I am, as the few of you I've had the honour of meeting will know, a man of even temperament. And so it gives me no great pleasure to recall what I did next – kick the carpet, with little or no regard for the consequences, before returning downstairs, where I regret to say I grabbed a 35cl bottle of Rémy Martin and went out to regain some semblance of self-composure in the garden. With the backrest of my recliner set to maximum horizontality I lay and watched a moon like a fingernail-paring fall through fast-moving clouds. An easterly wind was up, and as the aspens chattered, the rushes hushed themselves, and a newt or small frog broached the pond's surface with a percussive *plop*, I became aware of the natural world not as substance but as process, an ongoing thing at joyously oblivious odds to the deadening stalemate of petty human disagreement. And despite the chill in the air I began to doze off, lulled by a tentative sense of my own place in the natural scheme of things, although that may equally I admit have been down to the half-bottle of cognac.

I was woken a few minutes later by a high-pitched, mournful puling. A fox! I thought. How magical! But then the noise became a word: help. *He-e-elp*. I turned in my recliner. Sunita was leaning out of the bedroom window, pawing at the brickwork beneath the sill, her lustrous black hair haloed by the pale shine from the bendy reading lamp behind her. 'Somebody please help me!' she was saying. I was struck by her beauty even as my heart barged past my tonsils.

'I'm coming!' I yelled, dashing into the house with that strange mixture of instantaneity and aching slowness that attends all emergencies, as mentally I rehearsed my pitched grapple with the intruder, all consciousness of my natural limitations in strength and fearlessness flushed from my mind by a not altogether unpleasant flash-flood of adrenaline. Clearing the last three stairs in a single bound I aimed my shoulder at the bedroom door.

It didn't budge. I tried again. Stuck fast.

'Help!' I could hear Sunita crying. 'He's locked me in! *I don't know what to do!*'

It was then that I realised what had happened. In my *petit mal* of anger at Sunita's (actually perfectly justified) pessimism re Foxglove Cottage v. the A417, I had accidentally kicked Barbara's labrys door-stop with such force that it had wedged itself immovably between the bottom of the door and the raised walnut edge-strip separating the laminate floor of the bedroom from the landing carpet. Luckily, I happened to have my Swiss Army knife in the chest pocket of my wrinkle-free expedition shirt (cotton-polyamide mix, stone-grey, now ruined), and simply by using the nail file to sand away at the bottom of the door, I was able in under two minutes to free the labrys and gain access to the bedroom.

It was all quite amusing in retrospect. *Stay away from me*, Sunita was screaming, still labouring under the absurd impression that in the few minutes between our last cross exchange and her discovery that the door wouldn't open I had somehow silently chiselled a hole in it, fitted a mortise lock and turned the key.

'It's all right, my sweet,' I explained, with a chuckle. 'You see . . .'

'Help me! Please, God! *I'm being attacked!*'

Man-and-wife rambling teams who have ever 'got their wires crossed' will be tickled to learn that as I moved towards Sunita, arms outstretched, she sprang at me, digging her fingernails into my neck before running downstairs to arm herself, as I was later to discover, with my Kitchen Devil knife-sharpening steel. All a ridiculous misunderstanding, of course, although by this stage matters had reached such a bewilderingly high pitch of violence and hysteria that I had the conversely reassuring sense that from now on they could only get better. This sense came too late, unfortunately, for Peter Agnew, who as a good friend and neighbour felt it his duty to walk the few hundred yards from his enterprising if architecturally illiterate barn conversion in his dressing gown and tartan slippers. I *didn't* invite him in, as it was late, but despite the fact that I was bleeding quite profusely from the neck Peter was quickly satisfied that it had all been just 'a bit of a domestic', and that I wasn't about to murder my wife! Although he had, as he meekly admitted, already called the police.

Royal Crescent is accessed via Crescent Terrace, a short street on your left as you recoil from the minotaur sculpture. Yates's Wine Lodge is housed in a fine, double-fronted Regency villa, complete with wrought-iron 'beetle-brow' window-crestings and a pedimented quadristyle loggia, and especially on the nights when the legendary DJ Mushy is in residence caters to an eclectically minded, 'up for it' crowd of twenty- and early-thirtysomethings that has seen Cheltenham dubbed the 'Ayia Napa of north-eastern Gloucestershire'. On reaching the crescent, note the characteristic rustication on the lower storeys. The edge of each stone is bevelled or 'chamfered' to give the onlooker a greater sense of its depth and, consequently, its mass, visually anchoring the airier upper storeys to the ground. This sense of solidity is extended by the elegant curve of the crescent itself, its half-embrace gifting the rambler a comforting feeling of permanence undone at a stroke by the unspeakable 1960s bus terminal to his left.

Preferring to 'cool off a little' following my largely very friendly interview with the two officers from the West Mercia Constabulary, I decided against calling on Alan to put me up for the night, instead booking into a single room at Ledbury's justly famous Feathers Hotel. Now, of course, Sunita and I can look back on the whole ludicrous episode and laugh, but at the time I thought it best, before subjecting myself to the scrutiny of my friends, to gather my thoughts, lest I blurt out something I'd have been better advised to keep to myself. So easy – especially when drink is involved – for the flabbiest misapprehension to harden into fixed belief!

Turn right down Crescent Place to pass between handsome John Dower House and 'D-Fly', a stylish new venue offering fusion cuisine as well as spacious conference facilities. Yes, I was given a caution. Yes, we were given a leaflet reminding Sunita and/or me that we have the right to live our lives 'free from fear and violence' and that 'help is available'. Rightly precautionary as the police response was, however, it had all got preposterously out of hand, and it was a measure of how upsetting Sunita had found the whole experience that as soon as PCs Cox and Onions had left she ran out of the house, climbed into the Prius, and ignoring my entreaties drove off and crashed into a beech tree on the corner of Saxifrage Lane. Sunita was, thank goodness, unharmed, the damage being limited to a nasty crack to the Prius's front-bumper assembly, and the hefty fine that will no doubt accompany her mandatory twelve-month disqualification from driving.[7] This, as far as I was concerned, was the end of the matter, and while it took an actual physical tussle, the next afternoon outside the Rotunda, to prevent Alan from removing my neckerchief, I was able to put a stop to his playful questioning by agreeing that whether or not I 'knocked the wife about' I deserved my banishment from the marital home just for 'dressing like a t*at'.

At Clarence Street you might take a brief detour to inspect the papers of Samuel Beecham, on view at the Cheltenham Art Gallery and Museum, left. Other notable exhibits include the original furs worn by Bill Wilson on his Antarctic adventures, and a fascinating collection of early twentieth-century beer bottles. Alternatively, turn right then immediately left to enter Well Walk, the remnant of a grand promenade once lined with lime trees, horse chestnuts and yews, between which fashionable ladies, chaperoned by beaus in high collars and cravats not unlike my own, would stroll refreshed by spa waters to chatter inconsequentially in the back pews of St Mary's.

---

7. It emerged when Sunita's case was brought before the magistrate that PC Onions, a sometime participant in Robin Entwistle's bird-fancying walks, had stopped the squad car to draw PC Cox's attention to what he was 'fairly certain' was a juvenile barn owl, perched on a postbox on the far end of Saxifrage Lane. The officers were thus well within earshot when a 'cracking noise, as of smashed plastic' went up behind them, and caused the owl to take off from its perch with a long, unhurried beat of its wings.

Note the church sign in the graveyard, where the key aims of religious observance are handily rendered in bullet points:

• To respond to God's love
• To reflect God's goodness
• To renew God's world.

A similarly refreshing openness to modern means of delivering content is shown by Nigel, the vicar of St Bridget's, our local church in Ledbury, who has been known to give his sermon in the form of a PowerPoint presentation. Either way, I like to put in an appearance now and then, even if Sunita's spirituality, influenced as it is by various forms of animism and yogic thought, quite understandably resists conformity to the narrow confines of organised religion. St Mary's is the last surviving trace of medieval Cheltenham, and history-loving ramblers might like to take a peek inside, not only for the fine lierne vaulting[8] in the baptistry, but the many interesting memorial plaques, including one dedicated to the memory of none other than Captain Samuel Beecham, whose 'greate Regularitie & Probitie' ramblers might like to consider in the light of the observation in his journals, viewable on special application to the museum director, that man 'profitted more by his pr*cke than his pietie'.

A narrow alley in the north-east corner of the churchyard leads to the unremarkable High Street, and beyond it, Bennington Street, where I believe Guy Gosling, a recent new acquaintance of Sunita's, has invested in a local renewable-energy consultancy through his green venture-capital fund, Planet 2.0. Not long before our silly quarrel Sunita had attended another of her 'wild-writing workshops' in

8. Simpler rib-vault patterns radiate from a central point or 'boss'. Lierne vaults have additional ribs *spanning the primary ribs*, and in their web-like complexity are characteristics of grander ecclesiastical buildings like the cathedrals of Chester, Gloucester and Ely, and the church of St Pierre in Caen. Firm evidence, then, of Cheltenham's historical importance – and a happy rejoinder to Sunita, who, if she could ever be persuaded to come 'church-sniffing' with me, might revise her opinion of the town as a 'dumping-ground for second-rate Sloanes'!

Great Malvern. Personally speaking, I consider myself a compiler of walking guides first, a watercolourist second and a 'wordsmith' a very, very distant third, and would never presume that anyone outside my small and highly specialised readership – i.e. you, dear rambler! – might be in the least bit interested in my amateur scribblings. Sunita, on the other hand, being the real writer in this relationship, had leapt at the chance 'to explore wild narratives in a creative, non-judgemental environment'. From the little I'd seen, *Partition* (as *Motherless in Calcutta* was now called) contained several very beautiful evocations of the West Bengal landscape, and if the workshops proved worthy of the overwhelmingly positive write-up they had received in the *Ledbury Evening Star*, I hoped they might take Sunita's writing in a less florid direction than, if I'm entirely honest, I felt it had gone since she fell under the professional influence of David.

As it happened, also present at the workshop was the local historian Robin Entwistle. I believe Sunita only spoke to him briefly, but in the space of a few minutes he not only suggested the new title for her book, but gave her sound advice on the 'necessary warping of reality' that obtains in any 'shaped narrative', fact *or* fiction. Robin and I have had our differences, but on this I couldn't agree more. Neither, incidentally, could Guy Gosling, whose impatience to butt in on the conversation, Sunita recalled, was 'as palpable as a swelling balloon'. (A little swell of pride here, if you'll forgive me, at my wife's way with words.) Gosling is a writer, environmentalist and prospective parliamentary candidate whose family have lived and farmed at Alder Hall, between Malvern and Stratford near Pershore, since long before Sam Beecham drew that first fateful bucket from his well. Formerly employed in the PR department of a major petrochemical company, Gosling was inspired to write his prize-winning travelogue, *The Nineteenth Word for Snow*, by the ecological catastrophe wreaked by his own employers, strip-mining for oil in the tar sands of the Canadian Arctic Archipelago. I once had the honour of meeting Guy, at a signing of *Nineteenth Word* at Ledbury Books & Maps, and was struck by how his youthful appearance belied a deep and serious-minded commitment to reconciling the interests of free-market capitalism and the environment. In jeans and battered Converse, with a scuffed scooter helmet beside him on the signing table,[9] he may have *looked* like a boy caught scrumping apples, but he sounded like a Secretary of State – or at least like a boy who, having *been* caught scrumping apples, convinces the orchard owner to stop using synthetic pesticides and cultivate his apples in a more sustainable way. Since his decision to seek selection as the Conservative candidate for Worcestershire West, Guy had invested in a modest flat in Great Malvern, above the outdoor-clothing retailer on Maidenhair Road, and to get to know his likely future constituents had inaugurated a 'community dog walk' in which, on the first Sunday of each month, local dog owners were invited to discuss their concerns with their would-be MP as he walked his greyhound Rosie near the Worcestershire Beacon. It was with the same ethos of down-to-earth approachability that Guy had agreed to speak at the wild-writing event, and although I was a *little* miffed that Sunita should have been so taken with his elegant blend of natural history, self-examination and concern for the future of the planet, when there was something not dissimilar available rather closer to home, I was of course delighted that someone of Guy's stature should have taken so keen an interest in my as-yet-unpublished wife.

The massive car park at the northern end of Bennington Street serves as a sobering reminder of the bomb damage inflicted on Cheltenham by the Luftwaffe. Where Clarence Road meets Winchcombe Street, a hundred yards to your right, wrought-iron gates to your left announce another monument to thwarted hopes, the ostentatious Greek Revival 'village' of Pittville Park, intended by the eponymous speculator Joseph Pitt as a 'more exalted' rejoinder to the whore-mongering Beecham's developments in the south of the town. In 1801 an Act of Parliament was passed allowing over a hundred acres of common land to be enclosed and awarded to the highest bidder.

---

9. As described in *Nineteenth Word*, Guy went everywhere by scooter, 'loving the low-maintenance, park-anywhere freedom to get up and go' as much as its desirability from an emissions point of view.

The hapless peasant farmers thus displaced, Pitt set about his plan to have five or six hundred villas constructed in the latest Doric style, crowned to the north by a majestic domed Pump Room set amid thirty-three acres of landscaped pleasure gardens.

The Pump Room stands to this day and, if they insist, ramblers may still draw a plastic thimbleful of tepid, musty spa water from the original marble and scagliola pump. But by the time the first domestic building lots were offered for sale in 1824, Cheltenham's popularity as a spa resort was on the wane, word having conceivably gone round that the water did indeed taste as if a flock of diabetic sheep had urinated in it. Pitt was ruined. And walking these incomplete streets, I can't help but wonder if the sadness I invariably feel, returning to Cheltenham, has to do with the sense it embodies of wasted effort, briskly forgotten and covered over. Boxing south, round Wellington and Clarence Squares, then on through the centre of town back to the Rotunda, I think of the pig farmers and horny-handed orchard men turfed off their land by greedy speculators; of hubristic Pitt, who like Icarus overreached; of the grand terraces that were completed, but are still only piles of stone, grandiose façades concealing jerry-built jumbles of crumbling brick and rusted pipe-work.

But enough of the gloomy stuff! The plot of land on which the inexcusable Eagle Tower was built in 1968, just to the east of the Rotunda near both Bill Wilson and Guy Gosling's alma mater, Cheltenham College, was previously occupied by Wilson's childhood home, 'Westal', an attractive Regency villa demolished in the blackened name of 'progress'. It's a source of astonishment to me that, scarcely twenty years after the Second World War, during which Cheltenham suffered extensive bomb damage, more care was not taken to preserve what architectural heritage had escaped unscathed. On the cloudless, beautifully moonlit night of the 14th of November 1940, when the notorious raid, nicknamed 'Moonlight Sonata', was to obliterate the medieval heart of Coventry, eighty-one further raids took place all over central and western England. Bombs fell on Dowdeswell, just outside Cheltenham, and a few weeks later a huge device narrowly missed the town centre to destroy half of Stoneville Street, where my grandparents had moved only six months before. Ramblers will, however, be relieved to hear that the house in which Edward 'Bill' Wilson was born still stands, a few yards further down Montpellier Terrace on the opposite side. An epigraph on the façade reads:

EDWARD ADRIAN WILSON
ANTARCTIC EXPLORER
Born here 1872
Died with Scott 1912

The watercolour landscapes and wildlife studies Wilson painted in the Antarctic, some of which are on show at the Cheltenham Museum, are notable for helping to raise public awareness of a continent whose very strangeness has made it all the more vulnerable to exploitation. Not only that, but in their amateurishness they embody an unassuming, unselfconsciously direct response to their subject matter they have in common with Wilson's prose. Having lost Evans, then Oates, the surviving members of the expedition, Scott, Bowers and Wilson, were within eleven miles of a cache of supplies when a blizzard arrested their return from the Pole. '[We] are fit to go on,' wrote Wilson, 'only God seems to wish otherwise as he has given us quite impossible weather and we are now clean run out of food and fuel after a long period of very short fuel and intense cold and headwinds.' Lying down in their tent to die, the men addressed themselves to their final letters, Scott his formal, self-justifying 'Message to the Public', Wilson a more personal, touchingly unpunctuated farewell to his wife, Ory, in which he recorded his 'absolute faith and happy belief that we shall merely know nothing till we are together again and if God wishes you to wait long without me it will be to some good purpose'. He ends by repeating a phrase that in its calm simplicity invests the letter with the quiet of his closing hours, now the storm had passed, but left an insurmountable barrier between the three men and the lives that had now been denied them: 'all is well dear . . .'

You may choose to end your walk at the Rotunda. Sunita broke the silence some time towards eight that evening, after Steve had given up and walked to the station, and Alan had become engaged in such an increasingly testy argument with the organiser of Cheltenham's annual Poetry Slam that I had to step away with one finger in my ear to make out what Sunita was saying.

'I've been with Peter Agnew,' was what I eventually heard.

'Really?'

'Yes, Graham.' A sigh that blustered in my earpiece. 'I went round to apologise.'

'For what?'

'Oh, please. What do you think? For disturbing his evening, obviously. I can't tell you how embarrassing it was. Poor man thought you were murdering me.'

'Well, it was very thoughtful of you to go round. But you really shouldn't have, pea. It's *me* that owes him an apology.'

'But you're not *here*, are you? You're out on the p*ss with your loser friends.'

'Only because you said you wanted some time alone, my darling.'

'Anyway, Peter was very understanding. Why don't you have more friends like him? Instead of those two drunken low-lifes.'

'I thought you liked Steve.'

'Yeah, and I like the milkman too. Doesn't mean I'm going to have a f***ing drink with him.' A slurping noise here, as of herb tea. 'Anyway, I was just calling to say that if you wanted to come back to the house that's fine with me.'

'Really? I'm so happy you feel that way, my darling. I'll get on a train this minute. We can have a late supper, talk about things. I've been wanting so much to say sorr–'

'No, you don't understand. *I'm* not going to be there.'

'Oh.'

'David's over in Eastnor for a few days and he's invited me to stay with him.'

'In Eastnor? But how will you get there, my poppet? I hope you're not planning to use the car.'

'I'm not stupid, Graham. David's picking me up in the Audi.'

'Well, good. Just make sure to call me when you get there.'

'I don't know, Graham. I'm not sure I can make that sort of commitment. I just need some time to process what I feel. Within a *supportive* framework. It didn't bode well, what happened last night. It didn't bode well at *all*.'

I spent a moment reflecting on Sunita's assessment of our little spat. Ramblers might, as I did, wonder what my love for Sunita *was* but a 'supportive framework', and/or who other than her husband was better able to assemble one at short notice. Nonetheless, we *had* argued, and I had to concede that a 'fresh pair of ears' might be beneficial in this instance. Either way, I felt the will to spend another minute in the pub desert me – which was timely, as it turned out, as only moments before Alan and I had both been barred for life. The cause being Alan's scornful pastiche of John Cooper Clarke ('The bloody slam / In Cheltenham / Is full of c***s / Who think they're Keats') and the subsequent shoving match that caused the Poetry Slam organiser to stumble and nearly knock over a patio heater. Alan, who I have to say seemed rather pleased with the turn events had taken, was all for making an evening of it, even if he'd spent all his winnings and forgotten his PIN number.

'Come on, you boring b*st*rd. Just one more. Two at most.'

'I'd really rather not.'

'Yeah you would. Quick one at the Salisbury.'

I sighed. Both the Salisbury and the Montpellier Wine Bar boast an eclectic range of wines, cask ales and spirits. But the spirit had gone out of me, and unwilling to grapple any further with Alan's indomitable alcoholic will, I resorted to a white lie: that all was forgiven, and Sunita was back at Foxglove Cottage, waiting impatiently for my return.

'Gagh,' said Alan, with a contemptuous swipe of the air. A mile to the west of the Rotunda lies Cheltenham's only partially ruined Regency railway station, and withstanding Alan's emphatically mimed accusations that I was under Sunita's thumb, I was able with some expenditure of effort to push him into a cab, and thence onto the 21.33 to Great Malvern. Once aboard, he began vociferously to complain about the lack of buffet facilities, before abruptly falling asleep, leaving me to stare out at the blackness beyond the whistling window, relieved at whipped-past intervals by blurs of distant light.

Ramblers with more time and/or energy to spare, however, might like to continue past the station for roughly a mile to visit the tautological headquarters of GCHQ. Here, in 2004, a staff translator called Holly Beecham uncovered evidence that the government had authorised the illegal wiretapping of an organisation campaigning against oil excavation in protected areas, including Melville Island in the Canadian Arctic Archipelago. Ms Beecham was charged under the Official Secrets Act after going to the newspapers, but was cleared at the Old Bailey when the Crown decided not to offer any evidence. Like Bill Wilson before her, and Guy Gosling today, Beecham sacrificed her own self-interest to draw attention to the grave perils faced by the world's most environmentally sensitive areas. In doing so she brought honour on the questionable legacy of her ancestor Samuel Beecham, whose name has echoed like a cry on an ice field throughout Cheltenham's history, not least on the night when Hermann Goering's raid threatened to destroy everything he had worked so hard to build. Had he been in the habit of reading up on his targets before flattening them with incendiary bombs, it may have amused the *Reichsmarschall*, devising his 'Moonlight Sonata' at the Air Ministry Building on the Wilhelmstrasse in Berlin, that Beecham is a corruption of an old French peasant farmer's name, derived from *betterave*, 'beetroot', and *champ*, 'field', which in German would be rendered as *Beet-hoven*.

Walk 5: Stiperstones

Ker-rackk! Seams of aeon-hardened quartzite shatter as the ice retreats. Hurtling fragments cleave the yellow mist and detonate on impact like the death-cries of mastodons. The scree settles. Axe-heads are chivvied, livestock grazed. Candle-men descend with picks to reap the lead. Modern land-management practices reconcile the interests of agriculture, heathland preservation and leisure activities such as rambling. But the stones remain, stubborn-grey under answering skies, repositories of myth in an unpoetical age. 'Occasional' walkers attracted by the shortness of the route should note that the ridge path is exceptionally rocky, and thus next to impassable without the sturdy footwear they might otherwise be tempted to spurn in favour of trainers or skimpy ballet pumps. More experienced ramblers, by contrast, may like to extend the walk to include the convivial 'watering hole' their ill-equipped or less energetic companions will prefer to reach by car.

Directions: from the Stiperstones car park, just off the A488 twelve miles south of Shrewsbury, pass through a kissing gate by an information board. Follow a broad, grassy track uphill to Cranberry Rock. Pass some cairns, and Manstone Rock, with its identifying triangulation pillar, before reaching the Devil's Chair, and retracing your steps to the car park. Ordinarily I would have started on the other side of the ridge, at the Stiperstones Inn, a traditional Shropshire hostelry

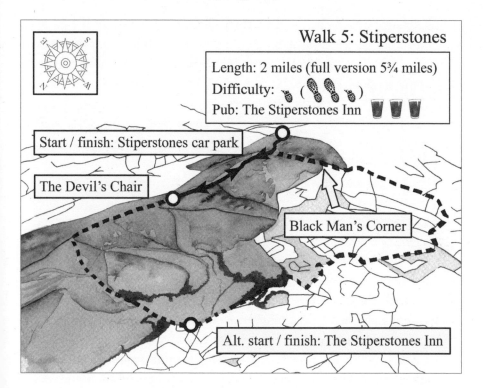

Walk 5: Stiperstones

Length: 2 miles (full version 5¾ miles)
Difficulty: 👣 (👣👣👣)
Pub: The Stiperstones Inn 🥃🥃🥃

Start / finish: Stiperstones car park

The Devil's Chair

Black Man's Corner

Alt. start / finish: The Stiperstones Inn

with Three Tuns XXX on tap, a wide range of tasty lunch options including Aberdeen Angus Lasagne, and a tranquil pub garden whose proximity to the hills gives the outdoor drinker a comforting feeling of enclosure. But it was Sunita's weekend, and if restricting the walk to a two-mile 'tour of the highlights' meant she got to see a fascinating rock formation she might not otherwise have been able to fit into her busy 'pamper schedule', that could only be a good thing for all concerned.

But oh, Stiperstones! How oft have I yearned for thy astral peaks, 'blue-purple as a flower of hound's-tongue'? Walk the three miles from Stiperstones village to the windswept hamlet of Shelve, its stocky rubble-stone church hunkered against the onrushing easterlies, and you stand poised at the head of a valley over which the ridge lumbers with the ponderous menace of a stegosaurus, its famous quartzite tors arrayed against the sky like horny back-plates. To experience this astonishing landscape at its best, there's really no alternative but to descend into the valley, as I did with Anne briefly before her accident, and, boxing round through lowland pastures festive with fairy flax and dotard's purslane, attempt the long, mildly strenuous slog up the ridge from Black Man's Corner.[1]

But not *this* weekend. Ramblers who have been following these routes in consecutive order – and it *is* advised, for reasons that will shortly become clear – will remember Sunita's disappointment in February, less, if we're completely honest, at missing out on the Brecon Horseshoe walk than the night at the Felin Fach Griffin it was intended to legitimise! It had, I must admit, long been on my conscience that Sunita's failure ever to get a break from her writing, and the occasional fits of temper that proceeded from it, were essentially my fault. Had I, for example, not presented the trip to Wales as a surprise, which with the benefit of hindsight I see now was designed more for my own egotistical gratification than any pleasure it might bring her, Sunita might have been able to arrange her work on *Holes* around it and get the weekend away with her husband she so richly deserved. Happily, since the misunderstanding over the door-stop, and the subsequent five days she spent staying at his cramped cottage in Eastnor, Sunita's relations with David seemed to have cooled, although she was characteristically far too generous of spirit to acknowledge that the man was and always had been a drain on her creative resources. With work on *Holes* suspended, in all likelihood indefinitely, Sunita had time and 'psychic space' to spare, and suppressed what might well have been a whelp of assent when

---

1. Not, thank heaven, as straightforwardly 'un-PC' as it sounds: volcanic activity has made the Stiperstones area rich in mineral deposits, and until the 1920s men would emerge without warning from mine-shafts or 'setts' hidden from rival companies amid thickets of bracken and fern. It's likely that the 'B.M.C.' toponym arose when a passer-by was surprised by a miner emerging from the undergrowth blackened from head to foot with lead sulphide or 'galena', and hurried to the nearest inn for a bout of ale-fuelled speculation. It's ironic that galena, a natural semiconductor, was the 'crystal' used in the early crystal radio sets that did so much to dispel the sort of ignorance that would immortalise a drunkard's tall tale in an insensitive place name.

I suggested we take advantage of the special 'Loony June' weekend rates available at the Mulberry Court Hotel in Church Stretton. And so to south Shropshire! To see Sunita so carefree, so *relaxed* – especially after the petty humiliation of her driving ban[2] – was something in which I admit to taking some selfish satisfaction, and if I *was* a little disappointed not to do the full six-mile Black Man's Corner route, we wouldn't have had time to do it anyway, what with the eye-openingly expensive half-day spa treatment to which it was my resolute pleasure to treat her after lunch.

To be fair the Stiperstones All-Ability Trail does give excellent views of both the ridge and beer-gut undulations of the Long Mynd to the east. Low marks, however, go to the 'wind-up sound boxes' with which the Shropshire Hills AONB Partnership has seen fit to line the route. 'Wind-up' is right. No one would dispute the transformative effect a little knowledge can have on one's appreciation of a natural landscape. But extending the scope of 'All Ability' to include visitors whose mental capacities shy at the concept of metamorphic rock formation, at least without extended recourse to analogies involving cake batter, is surely to fall prey to the nannyishly condescending impulses able-bodied ramblers and wheelchair users alike come to Areas of Outstanding Natural Beauty precisely to escape. Lunch at Impressions, the more formal of the hotel's two dining areas, included Dressed Cornish Crab, Glazed Shropshire Duck with a cherry-balsamic reduction, and a Warm Pear Frangipane for which Sunita was prepared temporarily to suspend her gluten embargo.

'Are you sure, my pumpkin?' I said. 'You know how bloated it makes you.'

'F**k it!' she exclaimed. Her mouth was crammed with walnut bread. I'm not sure I'd ever seen her so happy.

The fact was Sunita had grown tired of David's conservatism. It was a peculiarity of her greater talent that she mistook its reflected light for an original source in others; she made David seem better

---

2. And £500 fine, which I was able to settle via the Court Service's admirably user-friendly online payment system.

than he was, to herself included. For months she had pushed him to surpass his limitations, to ask himself the question: what *are* these holes? Why the fascination with them? To Sunita, it seemed as if they represented the gap between the photographer and his subject, the gulf they yearned to breach, but never could, filling the picture plane with an unfulfillable longing that if strong enough could transfer itself to the viewer, wherever he was, flicking through the glossy prints with the spine in his crotch and biscuit crumbs in the well of his pyjamas. But to David they were just holes, pictures of holes, holes: *Holes*.

'I take photographs,' David would say. 'I don't *talk* them.'

To him the artist was someone unusually at the mercy of his instincts, there to ambush passing morsels of actuality with the unthinking instantaneity of a hermit crab seizing a sand flea. If *this* was the hole, this helpless acquiescence of the true artist to his own powers of intuition, so be it: David couldn't say. The vatic silences with which any 'intellectual' questions about his work were invariably met were proof not of the hole between his ears but the philistinism of the questioner. In the end Sunita's patience, which exists in greater quantities than in anyone I've met, simply ran out. A few days after her return from David's cottage I found a pink Post-it note, scrawled in her hand, stuck to the sole of her ballet pump. 'D – PLEASE DON'T BE ANNOYED WITH ME,' it read. 'YOU KNOW I LOVE YOU.' Below this was inscribed an alternating sequence of hearts, stars and kisses, three lines deep. The note had been crumpled, then opened out again, and from the grimy pointillism of the adhesive strip I inferred that it had lain on the floor for a while before Sunita had unwittingly stepped on it. For a moment, I have to admit, I entertained the horrifying possibility that the note was a genuine, or even inappropriately ardent, expression of affection. Not to be conceited, however, but I think ramblers will agree one of my few endowments is an above-average faculty of insight, and I had soon come to a clearer-minded conclusion: that Sunita's 'apology' amounted to a sarcastic comment on David's failure to apologise to *her*. How else to read the excess of hieroglyphic endearments, so rich in reproach? Tossing the note in the composting bin, I chuckled at the thought of David reading it, angrily screwing it up, then opening it again for a final peek before throwing it aside with such warmth of feeling that he missed the wastepaper basket. Nonetheless, I thought no more about it, or David's volatile temper, until the incident, some four or five days later, when I bumped into him in the cleaning-products aisle of Tesco's in Ledbury.

'Graham,' he croaked, clearly thrown off his guard. 'How *are* things?'

I smiled. 'You imply by the stress on "are" an assumption that "things" aren't going as well as they might be.'

'Do I? I didn't mean to.'

'Things are fine, thank you very much. Sunita and I are treating ourselves to a little "mini-break" this weekend.'

'Anywhere nice?'

'Shropshire.'

'Perfect.'

'Yes.' My eyes narrowed. 'Why do you say that?'

'Oh, no reason. Just that it's peaceful there. You know – relaxing.'

For a slowed moment David and I stood there examining each other. Atop his trolleyful of shopping lay a spray gun of antibacterial bathroom cleaner, and as he prepared to explain quite what it was about my wife and me that made a 'relaxing' mini-break destination so 'perfect' for us, I saw him instinctively reach for the trigger. He needn't have bothered – the safety nozzle was turned to the OFF position. At that moment, however, any further elucidation was forestalled by the appearance of Peter Agnew, who, seemingly at the sight of David, brought his trolley to an abrupt halt and turned an alarming shade of fuchsia.

'Peter,' I called out. 'Are you all right?'

Without responding, Peter swung his trolley round and sped off in the direction of Dairy, Eggs and Cheese. There he was met by Jasmine, his wife, who after a brief exchange ran weeping past Fresh Produce to the exit.

'What's going on there?' I said, after a pause.

'I don't know, Graham,' said David, irritably. What was *wrong* with everybody? 'You'll have to ask Sunita.'

Cranberry Rock is the smallest of the three large outcrops of quartzite that punctuate the ridge. Exactly what light Sunita could shed on Peter Agnew's behaviour was something I would have to wait to find out. That said, supermarkets are, of course, highly alienating environments, and one might satisfactorily have attributed David, Peter and Jasmine's odd reactions to the influence fluorescent striplighting, and the unnatural superabundance of food, have on our animal brains. I myself have felt unexpected depressions descend while shopping for everyday necessities. A brisk walk will, I find, generally shoo the black dog, although for specific reasons ramblers suffering from dark feelings are advised to save Stiperstones for another day. Just short of 600 million years ago, Shropshire would have lain at the edge of the precursor supercontinent Gondwana, some sixty degrees south of the equator, or, if you prefer, thirty degrees north of Scott and Wilson's final resting place, roughly where the sub-Antarctic South Shetland Islands lie today. Gondwana comprised almost all the landmasses now situated in the southern hemisphere, as well as a sizeable chunk of northern Europe, and where Oswestry, for instance, sits at the junction of the A5 and A483 was a coastal outpost as remote as the old Soviet fishing ports crumbling into the Sea of Okhotsk. Plopping coastal swamps harboured toads the size of bulldogs on the outskirts of Shrewsbury. Plesiosaurs barked within earshot of Wem. Over hundreds of millions of years, as the continents were prised apart like clinched boxers, immense orogenic ('mountain-generating') forces compacted the coastal sands into strata of glittering quartzite, hard as hatred,[3] drawing them up and away into vast, buckled ridges as vertically distant from the seas that had formed them as man is[4] evolutionarily superior to microbial slime. And there *is* something displaced, something chillingly

3. Or, to be exact, a 7 on the Mohs scale of mineral hardness (diamond is 10), which I suppose would make it roughly as hard as active dislike, if 1 was indifference and 10 the urge to murder as protractedly and painfully as possible.
4. (Arguably!)

anomalous, about the 'primeval outline' of Stiperstones, as the admittedly borderline-hysterical local author Harriet Pike (1880–1928) described it. At its highest point the ridge stands at 1,758 feet (536m) above sea level, and alternating one's gaze between its ominous, swarthy crags and the inoffensive, sheep-flecked hillscape that surrounds them, the mind does recoil at the contrast, as if one were toeing a deliberate line into hell when the rolling lowlands of normality lay to either side.

Normality

Lucky that our trip to Shropshire found Sunita and me in such high spirits! Many interesting species make their home amid the common heather or 'ling' that beards the ridge. As connoisseurs of game will recall from the bird's flavour, heather is the staple diet of red grouse, recognisable by its clownish scarlet eye-hoods and galling habit of starting from the undergrowth with great explosions of feathery effort. Hassock Moths abound, in sorry contrast to Beckmann's Lax Fritillary, a once-common butterfly whose precipitous decline can be attributed to the dispersal of its habitat: the long, grey, 'tired-looking' wings that make this subtly gracious species so unmistakable can only carry it so far, between sprays of milk violet that grew in uninterrupted expanses until modern heath-management techniques – beneficial to so many other species – confined it to disparate patches the fritillaries literally can't be bothered to reach. Like birds, butterflies are biological indicators: canaries in the coal mine of global sustainability. In 1513 the Shrewsbury-born herbalist and mathematician Dr Robert Burdock recalled walking into a 'swarme of bluwe flutter-byes so thicke' he thought 'the skye hadde shatter'd', going on to speculate that if each was 'liberallie grogg'd with mandrake' and its 'waist tye'd with threde', when the butterflies came round 'they myght beare a man alofte as far as Bermingeham'. Today, of course, the so-called 'Common Blue' to which Burdock was probably referring has declined in such

numbers you'd be lucky to drug and harness enough to bear a bee
to Church Stretton, that's if you could *find* a bee, the catastrophic
collapse in whose colonies being yet another early sign of what
environmentalists like Guy Gosling are calling the 'sixth great extinc-
tion event'. It was a shared love of butterflies that helped to keep my
first marriage together, Anne's rather crispy manner falling away, like
a pupa, at the sight of a Painted Lady or the common Small Tortoise-
shell, *Aglais urticae*, she would forgivably if dogmatically misidentify
as a Red Admiral. As Anne knew, butterflies teach us to look at nature
differently, more *naturally*, their seemingly haphazard flight-paths leading us, if we choose to follow them, on voyages of discovery
inaccessible to our pedestrian, map-reading selves, glued to our global
positioning devices and lists of things to see. It was, unfortunately,
while following the wayward divagations of a migrant Clouded Yellow,
on holiday in north Devon eight years ago, that Anne strayed from
the clifftop path and fell to her death on the unforgiving rocks of
Hartland Quay. Walking, as ever, at least twenty paces behind, I had
momentarily lost sight of her, but as I pointed out at her lamentably
under-attended memorial service at St Bridget's, our best guess is that
she went the way we'd all want to go: doing something she loved.

We're all familiar with the legend of Boudicca. Less well known
is the story of Æthelflæd, or 'Wild Ethel', the daughter of a Saxon
lord who held lands around Stiperstones in the years before the
Norman Conquest. Ramblers are often surprised at the degree of
freedom afforded to Anglo-Saxon women. As Sunita delighted in
hearing, while I helped her negotiate the gradual but trickily uneven
ascent from Cranberry Rock, Wild Ethel certainly lived up to her
name, leading regular and audacious attacks on the Norman garrison
at Ludlow under the notoriously pompous command of Roger Fitz
Neil. One of Sunita's main complaints against David was his compla-
cency, his 'sheer sense of entitlement', as she so eloquently put it,
and it wasn't, I have to admit, entirely without design that we reached
Manstone Rock – the second, and far more impressive, quartzite
formation, from which Wild Ethel would once boldly have surveyed
her father's lands – just at the point in my narration where she lays

siege to the arrogant Norman's fortress and sets fire to his private quarters.

Wild Ethel! My wife, as some of you will know, is an extraordinarily gracious creature, elegant, urbane, *contained*, but capable now and again of acts of abandonment so life-affirming they put one's simultaneous embarrassment to shame. I well recall the occasion, attempting a spine-tingling 'Wraiths and Ale' walk from Covent Garden tube to Holland Park, when our way was barred by a 'Gay Pride' procession on Regent Street. Revellers dressed as air hostesses and broccoli florets paraded to deafening electronica. Banners handily segmented the march by profession: Gay Tax Inspectors, Gay Employees of the Crown Prosecution Service, Gay Environmental Engineers. Two men in fluffy angel's wings bore placards that between them read WE'RE GAY – GET OVER IT. We had, but the problem was getting past it, or even *under* it, the pavements being so crowded with onlookers that we stood no chance of pushing through to Oxford Circus underground. Naturally, I was concerned for Sunita's safety, and was checking the crush for escape routes when I saw my wife rise in the air, hoisted over the interlocking steel barriers by a muscular man in gold hotpants. Next thing I knew she was aboard a flat-bed truck got up like a jungle paradise by the Douanier Rousseau. The parade couldn't have been moving at more than two miles an hour, but try as I might to squeeze through the crowd the truck and its writhing menagerie pulled away towards Piccadilly, my last sight as it disappeared round the graceful neoclassical curve of Lower Regent Street a tableau of Sunita with her hands entwined high in the air, her shapely rear burnishing a gorilla's thankfully featureless crotch as a Gay Housing Energy Officer, dressed as a leopard, festooned her neck with a yellow feather boa.

I was at once horrified and deeply proud. Just over a week later she called me from a phone box on Praed Street. I need money, she said, but I knew a plea to be brought home when I heard one. Reading her ostensible demand, that under no circumstances whatsoever should I come to London to find her, for what it truly was – a demand that I come to London to find her – I boarded the next train to

Paddington and intercepted my poor, confused sweetheart at the hotel to which she'd requested I wire the cash. And seeing her emerge from the lift at that Bayswater flophouse, her bedraggled feather boa trailing on the carpet behind her, I felt the same golden giving-way I did opening the door on her that rainy Wednesday evening she came back from David's. For my part, I had just returned from a rather tiresome 'community-outreach' open day at which local residents were invited to voice their concerns re the council's sustainable-energy initiatives. A man mostly obscured by a pillar, but whose voice I thought I recognised, asked in contemptuous tones what I thought the point was of handing out free energy-saving lightbulbs when a chunk half the size of Scotland had just fallen off the Antarctic ice shelf.

'It may seem absurdly out of scale,' I replied, hearing the wind go out of my voice. 'But cumulatively even the smallest actions can make a big difference.'

The room fell silent. It wasn't as if I'd said anything they hadn't heard a hundred times before. It was just – or so it seemed to me – that the abject lack of conviction in my voice amounted to an admission of something everyone in the room knew, but at the same time expected a man in my position unflaggingly to deny. But I had flagged. An elderly lady broke the silence by announcing that her niece had recently purchased ten chickens, and my momentary embarrassment, if not quite forgotten, was at least free to lose its heat unlagged by close attention. But a sense of defeat, of a necessary fiction exploded, followed me home, and I realised as I tossed my car keys on the kitchen table that another story I had been telling myself – that Sunita staying at David's was all for the best – was equally far-fetched. I wanted her home.

And then the doorbell rang. It was actually a good deal later, but with the help of several cognacs the two hours that had crawled past collapsed to a single point in retrospect. It was raining hard, and pasted to her face Sunita's black hair looked so beautiful that before I knew it I'd stepped into the wet and cupped her head in my hands. Her occipital ridge felt as fragile as a wren's egg. A chunk fell off my ice shelf. The waters might have risen there and then and I wouldn't have cared.

'Let me in, then,' she said. 'I'm f***ing drenched.'

We sat discussing David's character while Sunita dried her hair, and I mulled what nice dinner I could make of the rather bachelor-ish bits and bobs in the fridge.

'I mean, compared to you, for example,' said Sunita. 'David's just so *uptight*.'

I felt the compliment spread in my chest like a swig of brandy. 'How about a risotto? I could pick some radicchio. And there's some Gorgonzola here that seems' – sniff sniff – 'perfectly edible.'

'I've eaten. For example: the first night I was there. We were sitting downstairs, having a cup of mint tea, just chilling basically. And I started saying how understanding Peter Agnew had been. Especially given how badly *his* marriage is going. And David says, out of the blue, Will you *please* stop going on about Peter Agnew all the time? I don't *care*.'

I shook my head. 'Just incredibly wrapped up in his own concerns.'

'Just incredibly self-absorbed, exactly. I mean, he was annoyed with me anyway, for wearing his T-shirt. But there was really no need to fly off the handle like that.'

'You were wearing his T-shirt?'

'I didn't have my nightie with me. I mean, I suppose I might have asked. But it's not like I'd been rooting through his *underwear* or anything. But he takes one look at me and says, in this *tight* little voice, Actually I'd prefer it if you didn't wear that. "It's my favourite." And I say, Uh, okay. I'll take it off if you insist. But I'm not wearing anything underneath.'

'And where was Karen at this point?'

'At some event somewhere. Edinburgh, I think. And he says, Oh come on, Sunita. "It's not as if I don't see you naked all the time."'

'What?'

'Oh, you know. He meant spiritually. Apparently I'm always baring my soul to him. The fact is he feels threatened by me. Plain and simple. Men are such little boys, aren't they? Particularly the good-looking ones.'

'So did you give him his T-shirt back?'

'Of course I gave him his T-shirt back. And please don't look at me like that, Graham. I've had enough male insecurity to last me till next f***ing Christmas. He averted his eyes, all right? I slept in a towel. Looked a sight better than I did in his precious T-shirt. It's baggy on *him*. And he's got pecs like paving slabs.'

Later I lit a fire, and Sunita reclined on the sofa while I attempted to comfort her. Quite apart from her disappointment over his artistic limitations, Sunita had been deeply upset by the ingratitude David had shown in accusing her of 'going on' about Peter Agnew. This was, of course, several days before my discovery of the Post-it note, and subsequent encounter with David in Tesco's, but even then it came as no surprise to hear that when Sunita had suggested David show his portfolio to Guy Gosling, who often had need of photographers on his various projects, David had shrugged and said he'd 'think about it'. *Think* about it? The audacity of the man! The sheer arrogance! Compare Gosling himself, who despite an almost prime-ministerially crowded diary had offered not only to meet David, but to mentor Sunita in her redrafting of *Partition*. Such is the generosity of spirit afforded, it has to be said, by a roomier allocation of talent, and as I began to administer an Underhill Footrub I was able to remind Sunita that, upsetting as David's behaviour might be, with Guy's help she could be about to embark on a period of greater fulfilment than she could ever have hoped to experience with a small-town wedding photographer.

'Do you really think so?' she said, drowsily. Once the foot is warmed up I like to make long, firm strokes along the arch with my thumbs.

'I know so, my darling. By the way, how are you fixed the weekend after next?'

'Mm. Fine, I think. No plans. Harder.'

'Good. In that case I'll book the hotel. I'm taking you on a special weekend!'

'Actually, hang on. Ooh – that's nice. Bit harder. *Ah*. I said I'd pop along to Guy's dog-walking thing. Come on. Harder. Give it to me.'

'But sweet,' I said, giving it to her as best I could. 'We don't have a dog.'

'So what? It's me he wants to see. *That's* more like it. Oh, *yeah*. Yes. *Yes!*'

'Well, I suppose we could put it off to the weekend after.'

'No, it's okay. There'll be too many people there anyway. Further up. Just there. Harder. Oh, yeah. That's good. That's *very* good. Mmmm.'

A sigh, a twitch and a slackening of the jaw: the touching spectacle of my loved one passing out from sheer pleasure.

'That's settled, then,' I said, rounding off the U.F. with the sort of gentle, sleep-inducing strokes to the upper foot known in massage circles as *effleurage*. 'The weekend after next it is. I'm sure *someone* we know will be going to Guy's thing. Karen, for instance – she'll have Robin's dog that day, won't she?'

Sunita's eyes snapped open. 'What did you say?'

'That Karen would probably be attending.' Frowning, Sunita withdrew her foot. 'Guy's thing. So she can tell you all about it.'

Clasping her knees to her chest Sunita lay staring at the ceiling.

'Darling?' I said, after a pause. 'So is that settled, then? The weekend after next?'

'Yeah,' said Sunita, to the ceiling. 'That's settled.'

Note the forbidding human 'faces' embedded in the craggy flanks of Manstone Rock. It's a function of the crystalline structure of quartzite that the rock splits into complex, interlocking patterns more amenable to anthropomorphic interpretation than the vaster granite boulders of the Lakes and Brecon Beacons. One only has to glance at the doleful head at the rock's northern extremity, staring from what appears to be the bow of a warship, to understand how worrying early Saxon settlers must have found this landscape. I didn't tell Sunita, but far from dying for her noble cause Wild Ethel actually ended up *marrying* the loathsome Roger Fitz Neil, disappearing thereafter from the historical record, but re-emerging in myth: it's said that as punishment for sleeping with the enemy she is imprisoned for eternity in the lead mines that run for miles beneath the ridge.

Only when England is returned to the English – i.e. the ragbag of Germans and Danes that had the run of the place before the French came and conquered them – will Wild Ethel be allowed to rest in peace.

In the meantime she serves as a convenient 'poster girl' for the local branch of UKIP, whose pink placards urging NO TO MASS IMMI-GRATION can be found cable-tied to many farm gates and fences in this most peaceful and underpopulated corner of England. As the story of Wild Ethel goes to show, it's a short leap from an innocent folk tale to the sort of proprietorial over-attachment to a landscape that leads to place names like Black Man's Corner, or, indeed, the community tensions that Peter Agnew's work on the Diversity Panel has done so much to dissipate. Sunita and I were, as it happens, talking about Peter as we approached the Devil's Chair, the third and final outcrop on the route. Sunita had, once again, been extolling Peter's sensitivity, and although she would never be so judgemental as to call Jasmine a hard-hearted, ignorant vulgarian, her penetrating analysis of the Agnews' 'differing personal philosophies' made sudden sense of the odd comment David had made, after we'd witnessed Peter and Jasmine's quarrel in Tesco's a few days previously. 'You'll have to talk to Sunita.' Why? Because she understood the Agnews' marriage *as implicitly as if it were her own*.

'Jasmine only wants a husband so she can be unfaithful to him. What else could be keeping the marriage together? Peter likes military histories and updating his wine journal. As far as I can tell Jasmine's interests extend to dieting and hair extensions.'

'He has money.'

'Yeah, but he keeps such a tight hold on the purse strings that she'd be better off divorcing him. No, it's not the money. And I very much doubt Peter is a demon in the sack. She just wants the stability. It makes the sleeping around more exciting. After all, you can hardly experience the thrill of adultery if you're single, can you?'

I saw Peter's face redden in the cleaning-products aisle. 'Not David.'

'No,' laughed Sunita. 'David wouldn't be interested in Jasmine. Peter blushed because he's in love with *me*.'

'He is?'

'Of course. Can't you tell?'

'Why would that make him blush at the sight of David?'

'Because *he* thinks *I'm* in love with *David*. Obviously.'

I stopped in my tracks. Ahead, the Devil's Chair rose up from its jagged bed of scree like a giant awakening from a nightmare. 'And are you?' I said, toeing a fragment of quartzite.

'Oh, Graham,' said Sunita, turning. 'Don't be ridiculous. I'm taken!'

And with a twirl that made her kagoule rustle, Sunita ran off towards the outcrop. Ridiculous, as I say, the over-ascription of meaning to a patch of land, whether it be at the service of UKIP-style xenophobia or, marginally less objectionably, the sort of pathetically fallacious, morbid ruralism Stella Gibbons so gleefully satirises in *Cold Comfort Farm*. Sombre as the Stiperstones may be, personally I'd find it hard to get too worked up about a landscape in which my beautiful, talented, graceful young wife had just pledged her undying love to me! Here's Harriet Pike, for example, getting all significant about the Devil's Chair in her preposterous first novel, *The Waning Brook*, published in 1922:

Nothing could dissuade Violet from the notion that evil dwelt in those stones. Charles had laughed when she told him that Gabriel Finch refused to go up there after dark. But Violet had seen the fear in the old shepherd's face, and had felt it herself that morning when, under glowering skies, the Chair had lain there like a pile of broken bones, an immense, baleful rejoinder to all human hope and pride.

I was clambering over those 'broken bones', chuckling to myself about this very passage, when I heard Sunita cry out from somewhere beyond my immediate line of sight. Heart thumping, I vaulted over a jutting mass of quartzite onto a narrow, sloping ledge, only to slip and in preventing a more serious fall ram my coccyx against a fist of rock that sent such a judder up my spine I half expected a bell to ring in my head. I sat for a while, comprehending the pain. Nothing broken. But it was one of those injuries that beyond a certain age the experienced rambler knows will niggle at him for years, taking a small but significant edge of pleasure off each walk. As Andy McNab would have said: *D*mn.*

Sunita was sitting on a hummock in a sunken clearing below the summit of the tor, her upper body quivering with tears. As I hobbled, hand in the small of my back, to a ledge that gave onto the clearing, she turned her mascara-blackened face to meet mine, then, turning away again, reached for and like a tired child effortlessly grasped a startlingly higher level of misery.

'Where have you *been?*'

'Walking behind you, my petal. I fell. But what's happened? Have you hurt yourself?'

'No.'

Sunita gripped the cuffs of her waterproof and pulled the sleeves taut. Against the yellow polyester her fingernails showed an angry red. Then a single large raindrop fell, and, disappearing into her hair, seemed to activate something in her. She stood.

'Get me out of this awful f***ing s***hole, will you?'

'What's the matter? You seemed so happy just a moment ago.'

'Well, I'm not now, am I?'

'I suppose not. But don't you like it here? It's only a spot of rain. And look – *there*, darling. A stonechat! See? With the orange under-parts? Isn't he lovely?'

'I don't see anything. And no, I *don't* like it here. These stones have such . . . I don't know. *Negative energy.*'

'Oh, sweetheart. Stones can't have "negative energy". They're stones!'

'Graham. How many times do I have to ask? *I want to go back to the hotel.*'

The drive to Church Stretton took us close to the route of the following day's walk on the Long Mynd. As we descended into the Carding Mill Valley the sun came out, engulfing the heather in a tide of golden light that made the sullen mood in the car that little bit less easy to sustain. I placed a tentative hand on Sunita's knee. She didn't flinch. And although at this point we met a sports-utility vehi-cle occupying, typically, more than its fair share of road, forcing me to remove my hand and change down to second, I realised we'd come to a tacit understanding that – to my considerable relief – I had been wrong not to capitulate more quickly to Sunita's change of mood. We drove on, in a sunnier silence, with the visors down.

Walk 6: The Long Mynd

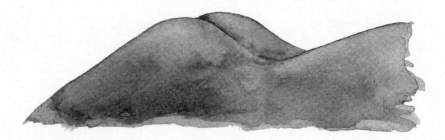

'What are those blue remembered hills?' asks A. E. Housman in 'A Shropshire Lad'. Answer: Wenlock Edge and the Long Mynd, part of the Shropshire Hills Area of Outstanding Natural Beauty. As if he'd forgotten! 'Mynd' is a corruption of mynydd, the Welsh for mountain, and although the Long Mynd is neither that long, a mountain, nor blue, for that matter, ramblers seeking a moderately energetic 'yomp' with very pleasant, if not outstanding views, could do worse than penetrate the inviting valleys or 'batches' that part its tender flanks. As a bonus, Church Stretton, where this walk begins and ends, was the first town in the West Midlands to be awarded 'Walkers are Welcome' status, which aside from the impeccable condition of the local footpath network, and the well-presented 'superloo' situated in the main car park, is evident in the indefinable 'rambleriness' that pervades this old-fashioned place – the kindly shopkeeper, tolerant of mud, the echoing clump of hiking boots on tarmac – even if its long-standing nickname 'Little Switzerland' applies as much to a certain insularity in its residents as the attractions of its hilly terrain.

Sunita was still feeling a little wobbly the morning after the incident on Stiperstones, which in retrospect she put down, at least in part, to the deleterious effects on her immune system of 'all that toxic

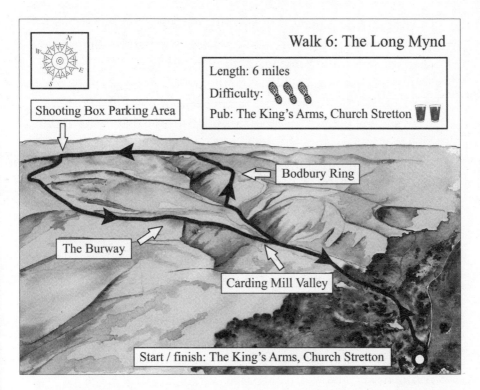

Walk 6: The Long Mynd

Length: 6 miles
Difficulty:
Pub: The King's Arms, Church Stretton

Shooting Box Parking Area

Bodbury Ring

The Burway

Carding Mill Valley

Start / finish: The King's Arms, Church Stretton

cr*p' she'd had for lunch. This placed me on the horns of a difficult dilemma. One of the reasons for coming to south Shropshire in the first place was the balance the landscape struck between attractiveness and accessibility, and I was loath to take to the hills without at least trying to persuade Sunita what dividends a modest investment of effort might pay. On the other hand, she *didn't* seem well, and had expressed such sincere regret for her outburst on the Devil's Chair that I couldn't in all conscience object to her spending the morning in bed.

'I'm sorry, Graham,' she had said, from her hidey-hole amid the pillows. 'I've been a spoilt little girl. Sometimes I wonder why you put up with me!'

Why indeed! Even to have thrown the matter open to question was proof positive that Sunita wasn't herself, and if a lazy morning, followed by (a healthy!) lunch, and the lymphatic drainage massage offered by the hotel spa, meant paying for a whole extra night, it would at least go some way to repairing the damage done by the sort of 'abusive eating patterns' Sunita had, as she rightly pointed out, asked me 'time and time again' to help her avoid. In the end we reached a compromise: I would do the walk alone, and on the drive back to Ledbury we could take a brief detour along the Port Way, an ancient but perfectly motorable drover's route that passes within three hundred yards of the Pole Bank, at 1,693 feet (516m) the third-highest point in the county. Clearly, I'd have preferred to spend the day in the company of my wife, but as we had in fact already *seen* the Pole Bank, albeit from considerably further away, on the previous evening's drive over from Stiperstones, I'd have been an ungrateful so-and-so not to appreciate the concession!

By 10.45 I was admiring the fine close studding on the side wall of the King's Arms, a short stroll downhill from the hotel on Church Stretton High Street. A late start, I'll grant you, but after breakfast in bed at the hotel, as I was waterproofing my boots over the *Observer* magazine, an article about 'green pin-ups' had caught my eye, not least because one of them was Guy Gosling, naked but for a liberal coating of tar sand.

'Peaches,' I ventured. Sunita was deep in *Observer Woman*. We all know how annoying it can be to have our reading interrupted, and in the circumstances I was grateful for the leer of only moderate hostility revealed as she lowered her magazine to the duvet.

'Listen to this,' I continued. '"I've always been struck by something Roald Amundsen said." Oh, for pity's sake.'

'Roald Amundsen said, "Oh, for pity's sake"?'

'No, no,' I chuckled. '*I* did. See here? In brackets after "Roald Amundsen" they've put "the Norwegian explorer who beat Scott to the South Pole in 1911". As if we needed to be told.'

'Can I go back to my magazine now?'

'No, listen. "Since childhood Amundsen's ambition had been to reach the North Pole. And yet it was the *South* Pole he conquered – in other words, one of the most remarkable feats in the history of exploration was achieved by a man walking as far as humanly possible *away* from where he wanted to get to. 'No human being,' he said, 'has stood so diametrically opposed to the goal of his wishes as I did on that occasion.' And in a similar way I've spent a lot of time in the far north when the area that's really fascinated me has always been Antarctica."'

A pause, while I reckoned the weight of his words. 'Who do you think that is?'

'I don't know. Leonardo DiCaprio? I'm really not very interested.'

'It's Guy Gosling.'

Sunita went back to her magazine. A woman on the cover was clutching her naked breasts and laughing. With the integral sponge applicator I blotted a muddied droplet of waterproofing fluid from the small part of Gosling's thigh not plastered in bitumen deposits. 'It says here that he's applying for a grant from the Antarctic Artists' and Writers' Program. To study the effects of climate change on the Wilkins Ice Shelf.'

A sigh from behind the magazine. 'Look, I know all this, Graham. Guy *told* me. Now will you please leave me in peace? I'm *trying* to relax.'

Removing the strong cheddar, honey-roast ham and squeezy bottle of small-chunk sandwich pickle I had left to chill in the minibar overnight, I assembled my lunch bap as quietly as possible, sweeping the crumbs into the gutter of the *Observer* magazine before gingerly folding it in four and stashing it in the rather ungenerous oval waste bin by the writing desk.

'What are you doing?' said Sunita, putting her women's supplement down.

'Getting ready to leave, my cabbage leaf. Are you sure you won't be persuaded to come?'

'Where's the magazine? You didn't throw it away, did you?'

'I'm afraid I did. You said you weren't interested.'

'How can I know how interested I am until I've read it? J*sus, Graham. You can't leave anything alone, can you? Will you get it out for me, please?'

I retrieved the magazine and emptied its gutter of breadcrumbs. A small chunk of pickle had got stuck to Guy Gosling's forehead, and although I flicked it off soon enough, and the stain it left was in any case indistinguishable from the clots of oily sludge adhering to his face, I had inwardly to admit to a thrill of guilty glee at my invisible act of defacement.

Some forty yards further north up the High Street from the King's Arms, a narrow alley between the Buck's Head Hotel (note the heavy stone quoining) and the adjacent building gives onto the churchyard of St Laurence, worth a detour for the frankly 'top-shelf' fertility symbol or 'sheela-na-gig' above the north doorway. As we know from the story of Wild Ethel, women before the Norman Conquest were afforded freedoms that seem generous even by today's standards. But be warned. Ramblers expecting the homely idolatry of a traditional parish church may be shocked to see a grinning female figure holding her swollen vulva open as if to invite us back inside.

Opinions are divided as to the significance of this 'gargoyle with a difference'. Scholars such as Professor Maplewood of the University of Hebron, North Dakota, ascribe an 'apotropaic' or 'warding-off' function to the figures, noting that of all things on God's earth the Devil cannot bear the sight of female genitalia. Others see a distaff version of the wodwo, or Green Man, a pagan goddess assimilated into Christian iconography by virtue of the same wild, irrepressible potency that, for women like my sister and her partner Danielle, has sustained the bare-breasted Minoan priestess as a symbol of female non-cooperation. During the nineteenth century, in what local historian Robin Entwistle amusingly calls 'a *lapidary* instance of late-Victorian censorship', a pebble was placed in the vagina of the Church Stretton figure, by all appearances a somewhat counterproductive attempt to make it look less rude. Similar figures can be found in many parts of Britain and Ireland, and in her fascinating paper 'Sheila-of-the-Unspeakable: Early Christian Iconography and the Myth of the Uncontainable Female',[1] Professor Maplewood notes that were one to 'join the gigs' on a map of Britain, a pattern would begin to emerge that at first glance bears an intriguing resemblance

---

1. Prof. Roxy Maplewood, *Journal of Medieval Gender Studies*, Vol. LXIV (2002): 38–65.

to a ram's head. Recent research has suggested that in the early Romanesque period it was not uncommon for female stonemasons to be employed in the construction of churches, and it's having studied the distribution map more closely that Maplewood makes her most audacious claim: that the pattern of sheela-na-gigs does not in fact constitute a ram's head, but a representation of the female reproductive system, even if the paucity of carved figures in the west of Ireland and East Anglia means both Fallopian tubes are disconnected from their ovaries, and the unruly, joyfully subversive female principle hidden in the landscape is ultimately – if only just – infertile.

Leave the churchyard by the small gate facing the west door. Not a hundred and fifty yards to your right the notorious Burway Road leads left, uphill, towards the National Trust estate of Carding Mill Valley. As noted by the late Michael Raven in his excellent self-published *Guide to Shropshire*, the Burway is 'very, very dangerous', traffic on an unwalled stretch further up the valley being 'allowed, unbelievably, to travel in both directions'. Indeed, I had cause only the previous evening to share Raven's incredulity, when, passing this nauseatingly precipitous spot downhill, Sunita pulled up her skirt and asked me to examine a bruise she thought had 'turned a funny colour'. I couldn't see any bruise at all, the paradoxical effect of which was I spent far longer staring at her inner thigh than if the bruise had been plain to see. At this point, as ill luck would have it, a modified Vauxhall Corsa came hurtling round the corner, and it took my steeliest reserves of willpower to override the natural urge to veer left and plunge to our deaths in the delightful heather-clad valley below. Note the sky-blue sprays of wood forget-me-nots that cheer these hedgerows between April and July. German folklore has it that a valiant knight, reaching to pick a posy for his lady, was pulled into the river by the weight of his armour; as he sank beneath the surface, he threw the posy onto the riverbank, crying *vergißmeinnicht!* – don't forget me! Whatever the truth behind the myth, these delicate if persistent little flowers have for centuries symbolised enduring love, even unto death, and contrary to the claim that during the Second World War they stood as totems of resistance to Nazi occupation,

Luftwaffe pilots were given forget-me-not lapel pins by their wives, lest they were fated not to return from raids like the *Mondlicht Sonate* that visited such destruction on Coventry.

Pass the laminated sign exhorting dog owners not to let their pets 'deficate the footways [sic]'.[2] Steve Reed, who keeps Staffordshire bull terriers, is incensed by these signs. Dog 'poo', he argues, is a bio-degradable and indeed nutritive substance, which left on open grassland will be gone in days, if not hours. Instead these 'note-leavers', as he calls them, motivated by a neurotic obsession with their own excreta,[3] insist that the mess be scooped up and bagged, with the result that drystone walls the country over are plugged with plump parcels of polythene that will potentially sit there for centuries. He can get quite heated about it. Steve's sudden passions, all the more shocking for his habitual inwardness, have been a contributory factor not only in his problems gaining access to little Callum and Lee, but his failure since his divorce from their mother to settle for anything steadier than a series of 'flash in the pan' relationships. It was only a shame that we were unable to be there for him that afternoon. Steve's brother Jason had just won a contract to supply pork to a major supermarket, and to celebrate was throwing a barbecue to which Steve had somewhat grudgingly been allowed to invite a few friends of his own. And had it not been for the more pressing necessity of treating Sunita to some much-needed downtime, we would most likely have popped round for half an hour, if only to help guide Steve through the conflicting feelings provoked by the prospect of seeing his younger brother's self-satisfied face on a packet of Taste the Difference sausages.

The Carding Mill Valley derives its name from a stage in the manufacture of textiles, for which Church Stretton was widely known in the eighteenth and nineteenth centuries. Before it can be spun, wool

2. Or, indeed, [sic sic], 'defecate' not being a transitive verb last time I checked. What entanglements proceed from our zeal to flee from Anglo-Saxon frankness! Incidentally, 'deficate', if the word existed, would mean 'to clear of figs', which would of course have the ironic effect of making your dog de*fec*ate more.
3. Not quite how he put it.

or cotton must be 'carded', or detangled, much as in the present day a lady might brush out the knots in her hair after washing and/or vigorous activity. The last and indeed only time I tried to do this for Sunita she grabbed the brush from my hand and thwacked me on the forearm with it, accusing me of 'pulling her hair out in clumps', even though I'd been extra-careful to hold it above the area to be brushed, thus alleviating the strain on her follicles. Luckily for me she used the flat side of the brush as the striking surface, which is more than can be said for the children, some as young as two, who were employed as carders as recently as the early twentieth century. At Carding Mill, which has since been converted into luxury flats, carders worked twenty-hour days, and were punished for 'claggy' or incompletely detangled wool by having the iron-toothed carding brush dragged across their bare flesh – a form of torture incidentally first recorded in Minoan Crete, where saffron thieves were carded to within an inch of their lives, before being beheaded by one of the aforementioned priestesses wielding a labrys.

Child labour, at least in this country, is thankfully a thing of the past. That said, judging by the behaviour I witnessed that morning on the Long Mynd, a return at least in part to the disciplinary rigours of old is surely overdue for consideration. A green minibus I later saw was marked WEST COSELEY YOUNG LADIES' CLUB had parked outside Carding Mill's well-appointed gift shop and visitor information centre. I was approaching the centre on the high path above the road, and from my vantage, as swifts shrilled in circles below me, a group of roughly twenty figures, identically attired in green, were arranged around the minibus in attitudes of instantly readable disobedience.

At this point a rambler can do one of two things. Either he hangs back, allowing the party he wishes to avoid to open up a distance ahead of him, or he quickens his pace and, overtaking, opens up a distance behind. The problem with the first strategy is that he will likely be forced to adopt a slower-than-natural pace; with the second, a faster one than is comfortably sustainable.

After some deliberation I plumped for strategy B. As I passed the minibus I'm afraid to say I suffered the indignity of being asked for my telephone number. The group, which I now saw comprised girls aged between roughly twelve and sixteen, was in the care of a young woman whose bulbous Black Country accent did little to compensate for her natural lack of authority. With all the self-possession I could muster I began my gentle ascent to the National Trust car

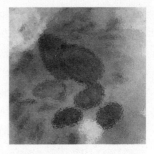

Underwater trail mix

park, and was traversing a shallow ford when I felt a succession of small objects strike the back of my kagoule. I looked down at the water. Foundered on the ridged concrete bed of the ford were a half-peanut, two almonds and three sultanas: trail mix. Fearing further attack, I turned and ran.

From behind me the valley filled with mocking laughter. My plan had been to bear right at the confluence of two streams, ascending to the plateau via an ancient wool track known as Mott's Road. But in my haste to escape the young 'ladies' of West Coseley I found myself plashing through a stream and struggling uphill much earlier than I'd intended, through pathless expanses of heather to the univallate hill fort of Bodbury Ring. 'Univallate' means 'bounded by a single rampart', and as I sat catching my breath at the centre of the ring, I thought of 'The Circular Ruins', the story by Jorge Luis Borges in which a sorcerer comes to such a place to dream a man into existence, only to discover that he himself has been dreamt by someone else. And sitting there, looking out over the grassy weal of the rampart to the valley below, listening to the shimmering, metallic echo of the children's voices, so innocent – melodic, even – now they were hidden from sight, I wondered who in their right mind might ever have dreamt me.

Unzipping my kagoule I leant back on my elbows and, realising that I was shaking, breathed the warm, heather-scented air. The sun had come out, shooing the shadows of stout-bottomed clouds across the hills towards Church Stretton. Ahead, as if erupting from the earth, a meadow pipit shot over the brow of the hill, goading on its own frenzied wingbeats with small, insistent shrieks, *sfee*, *sfee*, *sfee*, *sfee*, before stiffening in mid-air and, gliding groundwards, exhaling in euphoric release, *sfiahhh*. According to the OS map I had completed scarcely more than a quarter of the walk, but my unplanned scramble up Bodbury Hill had put me ahead of schedule, and it was turning into such a beautiful day that I thought I might extend the walk to the Elizabethan Zoo at Whittingslow, where Sunita and I could meet for lunch before a stroll around the mandrill enclosures. 'Everything happens for a reason,' as my wife so wisely says, and it was with a nod to my unwitting allies at the West Coseley Young Ladies' Club that I extracted my phone from its designated internal pocket and pressed 1 for Sunita.

It rang, and rang, and went to voicemail. Fair enough: she was trying to relax, and, trusting to a second go to carry its own implication of importance, I rang again. Still no answer. Concluding that after the trials of the previous day she must have dozed off, I left a voicemail, suggesting that when she woke she might charge a cab to my credit card and meet me in the zoo's ample parking area. If the weather held out we could walk the four miles back to Church Stretton after the mandrills.

Satisfied that the offer of a chauffeured lunch would draw even my luxurious darling out of bed, I struck to the north-west, soon joining an easily discernible path after my brief detour into wilderness. Like the Stiperstones, the sandstone formations of the Long Mynd were formed when coastal mudflats were buckled skywards by tectonic activity. Amateur palaeontologists may be interested to note that fossilised raindrops have been found beneath the heather that swathes the plateau; it was oddly comforting, bearing half-left at a junction of three paths to join the ancient Port Way, to think that inches below my hiking boots lay evidence not of early hominid tool manufacture, or skeletal adaptations to bipedalism, but a miserable afternoon by the seaside, 600 million years ago. The Port Way, quite apart from providing an excellent walking surface, gives fine views towards Stiperstones to the north-west; to the south-east, Housman's beloved Wenlock

Edge the other side of Church Stretton; and, to the south-west, the Pole Bank, towards which I was discouraged to see the green-mantled members of the West Coseley Young Ladies' Club approaching from the east.

Without thinking I sprang from the path and hunkered grouse-like in the heather. My options were limited. The girls had stopped, no doubt for a landmark or beginner's common species to be pointed out to them ('skylark', 'harebell'), and for a moment, strung out along the skyline at irregular intervals, they appeared incongruous as conifers, a species introduced against all better judgement to a landscape that baulked in its wake. Were I to wait, or take a detour that would intersect with their trajectory at a safe distance, crucial minutes would be added to the walk, when I was already cutting it fine if I was to reach the Elizabethan Zoo before its award-winning organic restaurant closed. I had no choice but to quicken my pace, and reach the Pole Bank far enough ahead of the girls for them not to recognise me by my walking pole or regrettably high-vis tri-climate jacket.

I started out at a running crouch. A few yards short of the Burway, which cuts across the Port Way at right angles, a burial mound or 'disc barrow' known as the Shooting Box[4] swells from the heather on your right. Disc barrows, recognisable to the expert eye by the unbroken earthworks around their circular or ovoid ditches, are rare in this part of England, and are thought to have been set aside for distinguished Anglo-Saxon women like Wild Ethel. Parking is available nearby, for 'whistle-stop' sightseers lacking the energy or inclination to walk up to the barrow, from which panoramic views extend over the Shropshire Hills and, on clear days, as far as the Brecon Beacons. I had just passed the barrow when, checking left and right for traffic on the Burway, I caught sight of what seemed like a familiar vehicle half-obscured by a horse trailer in the nearby parking area. The West Coseley contingent was no more than four hundred yards from the Pole Bank, but an obscure sense that my life

4. Named after an insensitively sited grouse-shooting amenity removed, not before time, in 1992.

was about to crumble like a cliff-edge drew me as if magnetised to the car, which on closer inspection turned out, as I had suspected, to be David's ice-white Audi TT.

I peered in through the tinted windows. A half-eaten packet of extra-strong mints lay in the coin tray between the ergonomic 'bucket-style' front seats. On the passenger seat, a roadmap open to south Shropshire. I cast a glance to my right. The West Coseley girls had gained the tumulus near Boiling Well, and were beginning their final descent before the gradual, 300-yard climb to the Pole Bank. I fished out my phone and dialled 1. Atop the National Trust information board near the entrance to the car park, a magpie had landed, and greeting it with as cheery a 'Good afternoon, Mrs Magpie' as I could manage, I failed at first to notice that not only was Sunita's phone ringing in my earpiece, but that a phone with an identical ringtone to hers – the 'Habanera' from *Carmen*, as it happens – was ringing from inside David's car.

I cancelled the call. So did Carmen. I rang again: *L'amour est comme un oiseau rebelle*. Leaning in to examine the interior more closely, I visored my eyes with both hands, and as the chopping edge of each little finger touched the glass of the passenger window, fifty bugles blared in unison, sending the magpie flapping into the sky, and me starting back from a sight it took a second, timorous peek to confirm I'd seen: Sunita's phone, juddering on the back seat, its lit screen displaying 'U'.

My mind eddied. Had Sunita left her phone at David's? Eastnor was over fifty miles away. Would he really have driven over specially to give it back? Or had – no, surely not – Sunita been understating the extent of her relationship with David? I needed time to examine all the possibilities, but the car alarm, which showed no signs of abating, had attracted the attention of the West Coseley girls, several of whom had now diverted from the Pole Bank and were skipping through the heather towards me.

'Hey, mister!' one was shouting. 'Are you a dogger, mister? Are you having a w**k?'

I had run half the length of the Burway before my legs would carry me no further. Slumping on a tussock it struck me that I'd run out of puff only yards from the dangerous bend in the road where the Corsa had almost sent me and Sunita to our deaths the night before. It was getting on for one, and in the early afternoon light, soft-filtered by cumulus, the hills from my vantage point looked so smooth, so tender in their gentle succession, that it was as hard to imagine anything cruel happening in their midst as the sheep, dotted in their dozens on the flanks of the Carding Mill Valley, looking up from their puddles of shadow and baring their teeth in a snarl. A car passed – an emphysemic Ford Cortina – and then another – a Saab – before my heart had returned to its resting rate. The injury to my coccyx I'd sustained on Stiperstones had, in the early stages of the walk, proved unexpectedly ignorable, but as I pushed myself up on my knees it was obvious that the run on hard tarmac had inflamed it, and instinctively guarding my spine from extra pressure I stumbled into the road at the very moment a car came careering downhill. As it swerved to avoid me, skirting the precipitous edge in a peacock's fan of grit, I recognised David's number plate, if not the car's inhabitants, tinted to faint silhouettes behind its receding rear window.

My coccyx was the dot in an exclamation mark of agony. I was, to say the least, impatient to get back to Church Stretton, but lacking the will to hitch a lift, I had no choice but to limp there on tip-toe, hoisting my buttocks aloft with one hand in a questionably effective attempt to cushion the jolt each step dealt to my spine. As it leaves National Trust property to enter the outskirts of Church Stretton the Burway is shaded by oaks and rare service trees, and crossing a cattle-grid I heard a blackbird break out in song, the fluting, glacial-runoff joyousness of which worked in inverse proportion to the shaft of molten pain rammed up my rear end. Still, in not much more than an hour and a half I was sitting in the foyer of the Mulberry Court Hotel, washing down two painkillers provided by the receptionist.

'You've been extremely kind,' I said. 'But I couldn't ask you to call my wife, could I? It's just she never answers when she sees it's me.'

'Doesn't she, now?' As she wedged the receiver between jaw and shoulder a shadow of amused recognition passed across the receptionist's face. 'I wonder why that could be. What would you like me to say?'

'Just that I've sustained a further injury to my coccyx and am waiting here for her.'

A bit lip. 'Your wife's name?'

'Sunita. Bhattacharya.'

'The Asian lady? With the feather in her hair?'

'That's her.'

Smiling, the receptionist replaced the receiver. 'In that case you can tell her yourself. She's only across the road at the King's Arms. I saw her go in half an hour ago.'

The main bar of the King's Arms was sunk in stubborn gloom. Near the window, which seemed to repel as much light as it admitted, sat the pub's sole customer, a tawny-faced man in huge glasses, whose subaqueously slow soliloquy on supermarket beer promotions was having, by all appearances, a steadily liquidising effect on the landlord, propped fist-to-cheek on the bar by his elbows.

'Course you've got the vouchers now,' said the tawny-faced man. 'You see the *Sun* today? They got a three-for-one voucher that lasts all week. So I bought forty *Suns*.'

The landlord's fists had slid up his cheeks to the extent that his eyes were half-closed. A good selection of bitters including Wells Bombardier (4.3%) was available, but I took advantage of the landlord's inattention to back very quietly towards the exit. Either the smiling receptionist had got her pubs mixed up, or Sunita had taken one look at the place and turned on her heel. It was only when I had my hand on the doorknob that I noticed the sign: TO THE BEER GARDEN. Temporarily rousing the landlord from his stupor I bought a pint of Bombardier, with its toothsome hints of caramel, scone and ripe fig, and made my way towards the open door at the back of the pub. This gave onto a cracked concrete patio surrounded by crumbling outbuildings, and from somewhere beyond I heard the characteristically strident display-call of Sunita's laughter.

My mouth was dry. I took a sip of Bombardier. Steeling myself, I turned right, then left at the corner of the outbuildings, and arriving in the garden found myself as drowsily deficient in understanding as I had been standing at the foot of the stairs, in my Thomas the Tank Engine pyjamas, the night nearly thirty-five years ago that I saw my mother, nominally the hostess of that month's women-only reading group, passed out on the carpet clutching a bottle of my father's special-occasion sloe gin. Sitting at a picnic table, by a bottle of wine tipsily embedded in an ice bucket, was David's wife Karen, watching from the shadow cast by her broad-brimmed straw hat as Sunita, barefoot, ran laughing towards a big black dog I recognised as Robin Entwistle's Labrador Smoky – who, running towards her, swerved at the last moment and barked in sheer exultation at his uncatchability.

'Karen,' I said, as brightly as my confusion would allow. 'What are you doing here?'

Karen smiled at me tightly as I set down my pint. 'I don't know.'

'Isn't it *great* she could come?' This was Sunita, arriving breathless at the table. Pinned to her hair, as the receptionist had indicated, was a purple feather, which made a typically quirky contrast with the informality of her summer dress. As she sat down and put an arm around Karen, a single drop of perspiration ran down Sunita's throat, and in my mixture of perplexity and relief at having found her, it was all I could do not to lean forward and blot her tender breastbone with my index finger. But I sat there, transfixed, as the droplet disappeared into her décolletage, and a frown stole over Karen's features.

'Wonderful, yes,' I said. 'I didn't realise you two had a lunch date.'

'We didn't,' said Karen.

Sunita squeezed Karen close. 'I saved you from that ghastly barbecue. Didn't I?'

'Not really,' said Karen, looking away towards the foot of the garden, where Smoky was lying on his back, twisting and pedalling his paws in a patch of dappled sunlight. 'I probably wouldn't have gone anyway. Not with the dog.'

'Whatever.' Sunita threw her arms back and addressed the time of year. 'Far too nice a day to be doing anything very much, isn't it? Apart from having lunch with friends.'

Karen made no response.

'And is David well?' I said, after a pause.

'Fine.' It had, I realised, been our wedding when I had last seen Karen, and in the two short years since that happy day her face had narrowed, revealing in its sharper lineaments a quick, sad womanliness that might have begun to approach Sunita's in beauty had she not also seemed so stern. 'He's in Wolverhampton. Taking the pictures at a christening.'

'God,' said Sunita. 'Where would you rather be less? Wolverhampton? Or Jason Reed's barbecue? Oh, by the way. Karen was really keen to see the view from the Pole Bank. So we popped up there in the Audi before lunch.'

'Keen's a little strong,' said Karen. 'But still.'

'You're my hero,' whispered Sunita, grinning as she reached over to grasp my hand. 'I *told* Karen you wouldn't mind.'

Suddenly the table lurched and it was only my quick reaction that saved Sunita from getting a lapful of white wine. I was, however, unable to save my pint of Bombardier, which fell with a crack and emptied its contents over my waterproof trousers.

'*No*, Smoky,' said Sunita, rising to chase after the Labrador, which had pushed off the edge of the table and embarked, drunk with the fun of it all, on a flat-eared circuit of the garden. Moments later Sunita was standing in the pool of dappled sunlight, where, slapping her thighs, she charmed just the latest in a long line of panting, abruptly docile animals into sitting up in the begging position, paws in her hands.

'Are you all right?' said Karen, as I stood to brush the bitter off my trousers.

'Fine, thanks. The waterproofing is actually integral to the fabric, so it'll repel anything from rainwater to a glass of red wine.'

'No, I mean: are you all right?'

I smiled semi-comprehendingly. 'I think so. Shouldn't I be?'

No response. For a moment we stood and stared towards the bottom of the garden. Sunita was kneeling to rub Smoky behind the ears, the back of her dress streaked with sunlight beneath an advisory council of willows.

'You know,' said Karen, lighting a cigarette, 'when Sunita first started helping David with *Holes* I was glad. He's never been very good with words. Always had a bit of an intellectual inferiority complex, although of course he's much too proud to admit it. And Sunita seemed so . . . well, fluent. Sophisticated. Imaginative.'

'She is.'

'Yeah, well, David was impressed. And told her as much. Which was maybe a mistake, because that was when she started getting the wrong end of the stick.'

'What makes you say that?'

'All this stuff about Peter Agnew, for a start. On and on about what an amazingly intelligent, sensitive, handsome man he is. As if she were trying to make David jealous.'

'This is David's reading of the situation, I take it.'

'Maybe.' Karen exhaled ruminatively through her nose. 'But I have my own reasons to be suspicious. Today, for instance. What's she playing at?'

'I was under the impression she'd invited you for lunch.'

'I don't know about you, Graham. But I'm not in the habit of driving fifty miles for a jacket potato and a glass of bad wine. I was meant to be taking Smoky to Guy Gosling's dog-walk thing. But Sunita said she had something important to tell me. And do you know what it was?'

'I have a feeling you're about to tell me.'

'That she thought I was a really nice person and she'd like to be my friend.'

'I'm sure she *would* like to be your friend.'

'Oh, come on. Wake up. It's not *me* she wants to be friends with.'

'I'm not sure I know what you mean.'

'I'm sorry, Graham. You probably don't want to hear any of this. But if she does want to be friends I have to say asking lots of personal questions about my husband is a slightly odd way of going about it. That and telling me how incredibly great *her* relationship is with him. Other than preventing me from going on Guy Gosling's dog walk I can only think Sunita asked me here to get closer to David. Which is nuts, but it's like I say. Your wife has got a vivid imagination.'

Needless to say I preferred not to dignify this with an answer. In silence we turned to watch Sunita drawing Smoky ever higher on his haunches, rubbing her thumb and forefinger together as if sprinkling something irresistible on his snout. And it struck me how funny it was, and how sad, that someone as plainly intelligent as Karen could be so oblivious, to project qualities onto others without the slightest apprehension that she was describing herself. Another interpretation of the sheela-na-gig figure is that in being so grotesque, so confrontational, it served to neutralise the fear men and women alike feel towards powerful females, just as the mythic beast, from Beowulf to the modern horror film, tidies our primal fears into the comforting confines of narrative. And standing there that sunlit afternoon, I felt an almost infinite tenderness for Sunita, laughing as she walked the dog on its hind legs, entirely innocent of the fear she inspired, when the truth – even if certain people lacked the good grace to recognise it – was nothing whatsoever to worry about.

Walk 7: Undiscovered Birmingham

The post-industrial wastelands north of Birmingham might seem an awkward fit for a book that seeks to celebrate what scraps of wild country-side remain to the rambler in Britain. But as the great Roger Deakin says, 'There is wildness everywhere, if only we stop in our tracks and look around us.' This lengthy route is fascinating not only for the insights it gives into the part our inland waterways played, irrigating our hard little island as it flowered into Empire, but for the signs of life, both natural and cultural, that have sprouted from its ruins. Ramblers with 'flat' or pronated feet should note that it is often more taxing to the arches to walk on level than mountainous ground; discreetly inserted, inexpensive orthotic insoles can provide relief without emasculating the wearer or branding him as 'handi-capped'.

Guest of honour at the July meet of the Gloucestershire and West Midlands Saturday Walkers' Club. It is a source as much of amazement

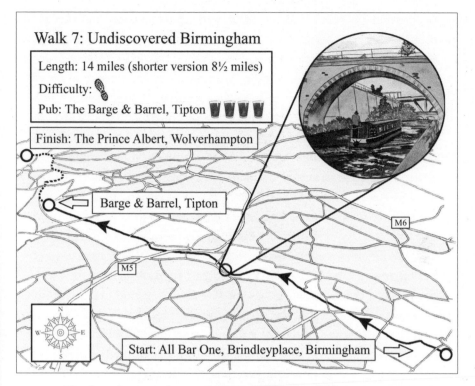

Walk 7: Undiscovered Birmingham

Length: 14 miles (shorter version 8½ miles)

Difficulty:

Pub: The Barge & Barrel, Tipton

Finish: The Prince Albert, Wolverhampton

Barge & Barrel, Tipton

M6

M5

Start: All Bar One, Brindleyplace, Birmingham

as pride that the members of GWMSWC should have come to use my humble little pamphlets both as guides for their monthly outings and as starting points for the ale-fuelled discussions that invariably attend their completion! Despite the drizzle, and reports of a chemical spill further up the canal towards Wolverhampton, all the 'usual suspects' were there, and it's a fitting tribute to Cozza, Ros, Geoff B., Brooke, Babs and the Clapster, to name only the most vocal of twenty-three attendees that day, that their enthusiasm for one[1] of the less obviously appealing routes in my six volumes of walks should be recorded for posterity in my seventh.

If only everyone were so dependable! No doubt it will all blow over, but I *have* been a trifle disappointed with Steve Reed's behaviour in the weeks since, for unavoidable reasons, we were unable to attend

1. Originally published, in different form, in *Pub Walks in Shropshire and the West Midlands*.

his brother's barbecue. What Steve gets up to 'in the ladies department' is his own affair, but ramblers will understand the demands
placed on my powers of forbearance when, returning home from
Hereford one evening, I found a) Sunita in tears, b) a residual smell
of cannabis smoke in the study, and c) a history of inappropriate web
browsing on my Compaq Presario. Having, hopefully without incrim-
inating myself, conducted my own discreet researches, I have been
reassured that to retain the services of 'www.FindLoveTonite.com'
is not to infringe an actual law. But to use a computer *I share with my
wife* to browse the profiles of members – and I beg the reader's indul-
gence here, in the firm if unhappy belief that only by full quotation
can the severity of Sunita's ordeal be conveyed – like 'Neglected
Housewife', looking, by her own admission, '4 a REAL man 2 meet
her currently UNMET NEEDS', without then observing the basic
courtesy of deleting the cache, is to be absent-minded to the point
of active negligence.[2] It was only Sunita's typically selfless intervention that prevented me from ringing Steve and telling him not to
bother coming round to weed the drive the following Tuesday.

One's friends are like a ring of hills, shielding the greater heights
of marital happiness, half-hidden in cloud, from the worst excesses
of the elements. And lately – although, as I say, it will doubtless all
blow over – it has been as if the movement of mountains had speeded
up a trillionfold, and in a moment, what had been a huddle of heavy
ascent had collapsed into a plain. Brindleyplace, across the canal from
the International Convention Centre in the historic heart of Birmingham, is named after James Brindley (1716–72), the engineer appointed
by the illustrious members of the Lunar Society to build a canal
through the coalfields of West Bromwich, Dudley and Tipton, halving

2. Incidentally, if the level of detail in my recall of Neglected Housewife's profile
seems to suggest an improper delay before the page was closed down, that is only
because the accompanying photograph, of a slim blonde in an orange bikini,
seemed in some way familiar. NH's given location being 'Heref/Worcs borders',
this was not beyond the bounds of possibility, but as the photo had caught her in
the throes of a supposedly verve-conferring dance move, in which her hair had
swung in front of her face, I suppose we'll never know.

the price of coal overnight, and igniting the inferno of invention and trade that would blacken the hills and singe a quarter of the world an angry pink. It's now home to a spacious branch of All Bar One, my rendezvous that morning with GWMSWC. And although one might feel a reflex contempt for a brightly lit, blond-wood chain pub that restricts its draught-ale offering to an insultingly invasive brew like London Pride, it was actually quite hard to maintain that contempt once I'd sat down with my pint, in the warm, on a comfy chair, watching the rain stipple the surface of the canal while I, and twenty-three shamingly patient members of GWMSWC, waited for Alan to show up.

He had insisted on coming. Shortly after the incident with Steve, Alan and I had attended another of the now-regular wild-writing events held at the Walnut Tree Hotel in Great Malvern. The timing was a little unfortunate, as the event coincided with the closing evening of the Ledbury Poetry Festival, where I had been looking forward to Martin Coote reading from his latest collection, *Hardy Perennial*, 'a lyrical meditation', according to the programme, 'on relationship breakdown, environmental catastrophe and death, redeemed – if only just – by the solace Coote finds in his garden'. Nonetheless, Sunita had been asked to read from *Partition*, and although I had my doubts as to whether the rather parochial scale of the Walnut Tree event was truly commensurate with her talent, it was reassuring to note she would be sharing the bill with Guy Gosling, speaking about his experiences in the far north, and the journey he planned to make to Antarctica.

Less reassuring was the fact that David had also been invited. As if Sunita's prose weren't visual enough, several of his 'holes' had been selected as counterparts to the readings, including a murky shot I was on closer inspection passingly gratified to note was a close-up of the hollow ash tree we'd seen outside Slad. Wines including an opinionated Rioja and an excellent, lemony Spätlese (13 and 11% respectively) were on offer after the readings, and it brings me no pleasure to report that both David and Karen, taking full advantage of the minimal mark-up, made considerably more of an exhibition of themselves than David had of his photographs. Having seen and heard quite enough for one evening, I had left ahead of Sunita and the others, and it wasn't until the following day that Alan rang to say he had a serious matter to discuss.

'We need to talk,' was all he would say.

The Lunar Society was so called because it met on nights when the moon was full, making the walk home, after an evening spent discussing the latest advances in natural philosophy, invariably over several bottles of cognac, that much less likely to end in one of the canals those discussions had helped to bring about. Between 1765 and 1813 the Society included among its members the theologian, political theorist and discoverer of oxygen Joseph Priestley, the incomparably brilliant James Watt, perfector of the steam engine, and both Charles Darwin's grandfathers, the potter Josiah Wedgwood and the physician and polymath Erasmus Darwin, who was to grow so fat a half-moon was cut in his dining table to accommodate his stomach. When Alan, who if nothing else shares a healthy appetite with the elder Darwin, finally hove into view, we were able to leave Brindley-place via the footbridge and turn left towards Wolverhampton, following a route that in the swathe it cuts through Birmingham and the Black Country both enacts, and reflects back on, a faith in scientific progress we have lost – and which, it struck me, the previous week's wild-writing seminar had been implicitly dedicated to repudiating.

First up had been Guy, who began with a brilliant if rather sombre account of the impact cruise ships were having on the fragile ecosystems off the coast of Antarctica. Between 1773, when Captain Cook was the first to sail beyond the Antarctic Circle, and the late 1950s, no more than a few hundred explorers and scientists had come within striking distance of the great *terra incognita*. Now upwards of 30,000 tourists visit every year, many on vast cruise ships, hastening the break-up of the sea ice already set in train by climate change, and introducing invasive species, like the voracious cuckoo mussel of Tierra del Fuego, which clings to the ships' hulls until it finds a more congenial substrate, such as the rocks, mantled in unique lichens and mosses, that strew the shores of the Antarctic Peninsula. 'What we know,' as Guy so wisely said, 'we destroy. In opening up this beautiful, savage landscape to tourism we have conquered the crucial last kingdom of the unfamiliar.'

Next Daisy Rux-Burton, a well-spoken if rather flustered ex-girlfriend of Guy's, flapped up, perched at the podium and spoke very rapidly on the subject of sparrows. It had, I admit, been a taxing day at work, and after the compelling eloquence of Guy's piece my attention began to wander, before being drawn back stagewards by the realisation that Daisy was softly but openly weeping, recalling her parents' garden in the Cotswolds, now almost entirely bereft of her favourite birds, where once they had squabbled in untold numbers over her mother's proffered plates of grated cheese. In appearance Daisy resembled not so much a sparrow as the eponymous bird in Thomas Hardy's 'The Darkling Thrush': 'blast-beruffled', her blouse, cardigan and plumage of middle-brown hair thrown into a confusion caused, judging by the stillness of the night outside, by a strictly local storm.

After Daisy, the local historian Robin Entwistle spoke at length – and passably well – on the nineteenth-century German ideal of nature, Weimar hiking clubs, and the structural similarities of the jackboot to the *Wanderschuh*. And then it was Sunita's turn. The speakers were seated at the edge of the stage, and as my clever darling brushed nothing from her dress and strode forward, I perceived the gap between us as a vacuum impelling me to fill it, and had to suppress the urge to stand up and clap. She looked beautiful.

'I was lost,' she began.[3] 'Uprooted. Afflicted by a restlessness that knew no compass. Like Odysseus, whose name means "the hated one", I felt my urge to wander as a curse, a punishment for some unknowable crime, compounded, paradoxically, by my urge to

---

3. Sunita's understandably jealous guarding of her manuscript has meant that I quote here from memory. Nonetheless, my recall of good prose is next to eidetic, and if certain phrases ('knew no compass', 'keener understanding') seem to strike a more Underhillian than Bhattacharyan note, that might as easily be explained by 'marital osmosis' as any licence on my part.

wander. Looking out over the endless, unbearable flatness of the Vale of Severn, I felt simultaneously hot and cold, claustrophobic and exposed, trapped in my freedom to go anywhere. And so when I made the decision to retrace parts of the journey my mother had taken as a child, walking the hundred and fifty miles from Dhaka, in what is now Bangladesh, to Calcutta, where I was born, it was not only to make sense of her abandonment of me when I was scarcely older than she had been at the time of Partition. It was to gain a keener understanding of that mass migration of peoples, the biggest in history, and how it had made my freedom, to which I had grown so indifferent, a living possibility. It was a long shot, but I thought that way I might gain the one thing I had never had: the desire to stay still.'

A pedant might point out that to undertake just under a quarter of the journey, by cab, is not *quite* to relive the hardships experienced by the fourteen and a half million Hindus, Sikhs and Muslims displaced after 1947. I had been on that trip, the purpose of which, as far as I understood it, had been to introduce me to Sunita's father, aunties, uncles and cousins. With one notable exception we hardly spoke of her mother. I got the sense that, twenty-five years on, the open wound caused by Amrita's desertion had hardened into a weal, still felt, but no more remarked upon than the apartment's surviving traces of femininity: a dusty perfume bottle here, a hand mirror there. When, shortly before our trip to West Bengal, Sunita had moved the last of her possessions into Foxglove Cottage from her rented house in Upper Wyche, I had found her upstairs in the bedroom, sobbing over an open keepsake box whose wooden lid was carved with a preening swan. Seeing me, she snapped it shut, turned the tiny key and despite all tentative inquiries refused to tell me what had so upset her. Later that evening, however, she relented, unlocking the box and showing me its contents. Among a jumble of old postcards and passports with the corners cut off was a photograph of her mother, shockingly youthful at twenty-six, with Sunita's indignantly straight nose, fine as bone china, and those alluring eyes, pinched into a downward curve at their inside corners like the repeating teardrops in paisley. Attached to the photo with a paper-clip was a letter from Amrita's lover Saif, dated 5 October 1980 and addressed to Sunita's father, informing him that Amrita had died of a blocked blood vessel giving birth to a stillborn baby girl. And that was that. The swan box was shut and stowed in the attic, and until the reading from *Partition* the other evening at the Walnut Tree Hotel, I never heard Sunita dwell in any detail on Amrita, her untimely death or her early experiences migrating on foot to Calcutta. On our trip to Bengal the month before we were married, it was only a chance remark by Sunita's cousin Suresh, in the cab back from a (fascinating) visit to an elephant orphanage near the border with Bangladesh, that revealed we were following the route taken by Hindu migrants half a century earlier. Coincidence or not, Sunita, hair snapping in the blustery heat of the open window, seemed unmoved.

But what did I know? Listening to her read, that evening in Great Malvern, I was made aware of a hinterland of high feeling beyond the Keep Out sign of her everyday self. For instance, I hadn't realised that it was only by leaving the 'intensively farmed', 'bland, denatured tidiness' of England for the 'steamy wildernesses' of West Bengal that Sunita was 'able to find' her 'true self: rampant, jungly, sensual. Alive.' So what if her account of our travels ever strayed from the literal truth, or almost entirely omitted me? All stories get twisted in the telling, and besides, to have revisited the pain of abandonment, by one's own mother, required a degree of honesty far in excess of any petty adherence to fact.

What canal walks lack in topographical variety they make up for in their ease of navigation. In large part the New Main Line from Brindleyplace to Tipton Junction follows a straight, well-signposted route in a north-westerly direction, the result of Thomas Telford's improvements, in the mid-1820s, to the rather wonkier course taken by Brindley's original. Indeed, Telford dismissed the Old Main Line as 'scarcely more than a crooked ditch', but for all his typically Scottish chippiness we need not take the younger man's words as a wholesale dismissal of the achievements of Brindley and his sponsors at the Lunar Society. They were, on the contrary, a continuation of the Society's founding belief, that through the application of reason, industry and will, the kinks in Nature's errant course might be straightened, and man's lot perpetually improved. I had been making a similar point as the group approached Telford's famous Galton Bridge, whose single span, once the world's longest, is supported by an arch whose lattice of criss-crossed girders lends the structure an airiness that belies its cast-iron solidity. Several members had stopped to stare up, take photos, marvel at man's ingenuity, etc., etc., whereupon I took the opportunity to suggest to Alan that we have our 'little chat'. At this point, however, Linda Birch, a fairly recent recruit to GWMSWC, started sneezing, seemingly without recourse to a handkerchief, and I had no choice but to offer her mine.

'Thank you *so* much,' said Linda, handing it back. Smiling off my irritation, I waved the handkerchief – a second-anniversary present from Sunita – away, as Linda had sneezed into it with such audible viscosity that my gorge rose even at the thought of stowing it in one of the several scrunched-up carrier bags I kept in my ramblesack. At the short introduction I'd given to the walk, back at All Bar One while we were waiting for Alan, Linda had been conspicuous by a sort of glazed eagerness that seemed to proceed from something other than what I was actually saying, and now, as she pocketed my monogrammed Egyptian-cotton love-gift, I found myself stepping dangerously close to the canal edge in an effort to impose some distance between us.

'Typical, isn't it?' she sniffed. 'Everyone else gets hay fever when it's sunny. I get it when it's raining. Goodness knows why.'

'Well,' I said, tipping an apologetic hand at Alan. 'It's quite interesting, actually. While these sorts of damp conditions do tend to "wash" the air of pollen grains, they also stimulate the growth of mould spores, which in certain people can induce rhinitic symptoms such as itchiness and mucus production. In the absence of any underlying health problems I'd say that was the reason.'

For a moment Linda stood there beaming. 'You must give me your home address,' she said, eventually.

'All right,' I said, without thinking. 'Why?'

'So I can post you your hankie, silly,' said Linda, dabbing one eye with her wrist. 'Washed and ironed, of course.'

Half hoping she'd forget, I promised to write out my address when we reached our destination,[4] and holding aloft my rain-jacketed copy of *Pub Walks in Shropshire and the West Midlands* I led the troops onward. Free of Linda, I was ready to give Alan my undivided attention when Geoff B. caught up with me, breathlessly brandishing his digital camera. On the screen was a close-up of a fine fluted pilaster Geoff had spotted through the trees on the nearside pier of Galton Bridge. I was torn. From the vaguely industrial noises Alan was making, it was clear he was struggling to keep up. But the pilaster really *was* quite an interesting find, and promising to attend to Alan in just a moment I fell into a discussion about the lost impulse for attractiveness in civic architecture, and its relation to our equally defunct pride in the achievements of human civilisation. That the pilasters were hidden in trees, thought Geoff, said everything about our modern priorities, and with certain reservations I had to agree. It was, ironically, exactly the sort of debate to which Alan would have delighted in applying his robust brand of scepticism, but by the time Geoff and I had reached a natural pause in our conversation, Alan had fallen so far behind that even GWMSWC's unrepentant slow-coaches Cliff and Warren had overtaken him.

I could only imagine Alan wanted to discuss Peter Agnew, and his seeming mental breakdown after the readings at the Walnut Tree Hotel. It had emerged that Peter, long a stalwart opponent of the eastward extension to the A417, was planning to speak in *favour* of the proposals at the forthcoming public inquiry at Ledbury Town Hall. For a supposed 'guardian of the town centre',

4. The Prince Albert on Railway Street in Wolverhampton. The rambling community is a broad church, and the fact that the Prince Albert is a gay pub is of as little consequence to the overwhelmingly heterosexual membership of GWMSWC as, for example, Cliff and Warren's habit of walking several hundred paces behind the rest of the group, hand in hand. That said, the 'Bertie' can get a little boisterous on a Saturday afternoon, and were it not so handily situated between the canal and the railway station, we'd probably go somewhere else.

let alone the owner of a property that, like Foxglove Cottage, would be affected to the point of uninhabitability by the plans, this was a striking *volte face*. Several hundred pages of evidence in support of the road had recently been submitted by a cartel of road-haulage contractors, and without wanting to repeat unsubstantiated and potentially libellous speculation, the fact that Peter's change of heart had followed so promptly had at the very least struck Alan as suspicious.

'Where he gets the b****cks to show his face here beats me,' Alan had said, as we milled in the Walnut Tree's conference suite after the readings. 'I should go over and knock his f***ing block off.'

Dismaying as Peter's betrayal may have been, I had my mind on other matters. Sunita had been deep in conversation with Malcolm Thorne, the publisher that had expressed an interest in *Holes*, and taking advantage of Malcolm's temporary indisposition – a brie and cranberry parcel, I think, gone down the wrong way – I begged Alan's pardon and went over to congratulate Sunita on her performance. Sunita, however, was more interested in what was going on behind me – Karen 'flirting outrageously' with Guy Gosling. After our chat in the garden of the King's Arms in Church Stretton I had come to think of Karen as something of a fantasist, but it was a surprise nonetheless to see such an undeniably attractive woman brazenly subordinate her dignity to a passing drunken fancy – albeit for an undeniably attractive man.

'Look at that,' said Sunita, shaking her head. 'And I thought we were friends.'

In an alcove at the far end of the room, Guy Gosling was standing with his elbow resting on the central meeting rail of the sash window. From where I was standing, I could see him slowly screwing and unscrewing its coronal brass fastener. After a quiet start the aftershow party had gathered momentum, and one had to raise one's voice to make oneself heard. Nonetheless, Karen could be seen actually *leaning away* from Guy, pressed against the wood-panelled walls of the alcove with seemingly no compunction as to how it might look. It was almost as if Guy were bearing down on *her*, so shamelessly was she forcing him to lean forward, and I said as much to Sunita.

'Bullsh*t. Look at her, pushing her t*ts out. She knows *exactly* what she's doing.'

And with that, Sunita was off, pausing on the way to the ladies' to drain an abandoned glass of Spätlese. Why should she, I wondered, be so exercised by the sight of Karen flirting with Guy? Was she jealous? Clearly, the innocent enjoyment of other men's attention – and, by extension, resentment at its deflection elsewhere – was by no means inconsistent with spousal constancy. We all like to be admired, and I would be a stern husband to feel threatened by so natural an impulse in my wife. But there was something in Sunita's outburst that hinted at a deeper, more primitive feeling, and it was a moment before I realised what it was: an offended sense of justice. Whatever had gone on between Sunita and David, to stand by idly while Karen made a fool of him would be to taint an evening that had, at least in the case of Guy's and Sunita's readings, proved an uplifting celebration of truth, memory and the redemptive power of nature.[5] I had half a mind to have a word with Karen myself. Not, however, being much of a 'butterfly' at social gatherings, I took a moment first to graze at the table of canapés, and had just helped myself to a fourth filo tartlet when I spotted Guy Gosling, momentarily alone as he transferred a drooping sliver of quiche to his green paper napkin.

'I'm so sorry to intrude on your evening,' I said. 'But I just wanted to say how much I admired your piece.'

'Oh,' said Guy, through a mouthful of quiche. 'Thanks.'

'We've actually met before. I don't know if you remember, but we had a very interesting chat at Ledbury Books & Maps. When you were kind enough to sign my copy of *Nineteenth Word*. You made the point that if an actual financial value were attached to the ice caps then it would be in the interests of the free market to prevent them from melting. Fascinating idea.'

---

5. Not to mention the effect Karen's behaviour with Guy was having on Sunita's new friend Daisy, who, judging by the unhappy zeal with which she was stuffing her cheeks with mini Scotch eggs, plainly still nursed feelings for her ex.

'Mm. Yeah. Sorry.' Taking his last bite of quiche, Guy wiped his hand on the napkin and shook his head. 'I sign a lot of books.'

'Of course.' I held out a hand. 'Anyway, I'm Graham Underhill. Sunita's husband.'

Guy's eyes widened, and I felt his bony hand flinch in mine. 'Really? Gosh.'

'How are your Antarctic plans coming along?'

'Still waiting to hear if we've got funding.' Guy flicked a glance over my shoulder. 'Listen, would you excuse me? I should say hello to David Redfern.'

'Charming fellow,' I said, as Alan, walking the cautious catwalk of one too many wines, took Guy's place beside me at the canapés.

'Who, Guy Gosling?' said Alan. 'Pfah.'

'You don't rate him.'

'I don't *trust* him. Old-fashioned slash-and-burn Tory dressed up as Jack in the Green. I could refreeze the ice caps single-handed if I had his sort of cash.'

Rather absent-mindedly I had poured a measure of white Spätlese into the glass I'd been using for red, producing a faux-rosé known to Alan, Steve and me as a 'Dirty Susan'. 'How are you, Alan? Enjoying the party?'

'No. I've never met such a bunch of self-regarding, pompous, *fey*, deluded f***ing w***ers in all my born days. Wild writing? These people are about as wild as afternoon tea. And there's not nearly enough to drink. It's *Thursday*, for crying out loud. You're meant to get four-fifths as p*ssed as you would on a Friday.'

I'd have been the first to admit that Alan's bluntness could be refreshing. At just that moment, however, it was merely drunk, and lacking the patience for one of his disingenuously affronted denials, I handed him my Dirty Susan and headed for the gents'.

'Where you going?' he called after me.

'Call of nature.'

'Good name for this event.'

I stepped out onto the landing. A grand flight of carpeted stairs swept up from the entrance hall below, and between the top step and the toilets to my right a mass of guests had gathered, seemingly in far greater numbers than the turn-out for the readings. Close your eyes and the hubbub of conversation might have been the roiling of an angry sea, trapped far below in a cove, or the tumultuous fuss of insects feeding from a lavender bush. And amid it all, moving through the crowd, was Sunita, identifiable even as she bent to kiss a cheek, or receive a compliment, by her elaborate fascinator of green, black and purple feathers, quivering above her head like the crest of a resplendent peahen. Beneath the stairwell's elaborate, if rather dusty, crystal chandelier, Guy was standing talking to David, and as she moved in to clutch them both by the hand Sunita said something to make their heads tip back in laughter. Flush with pride, I made for the toilets.

Leaning at a urinal with his forehead touching the wall was Peter Agnew. As male ramblers will attest, adjacency while urinating is unconducive to conversation at the best of times, and given the potential for warm words regarding the ring road I felt it best at least temporarily to hold my tongue. Experiencing some initial difficulty achieving urethral release, I trusted to the usual trick of visualising a gushing mountain stream, with near-immediate success.

'Hello, Peter,' I said, zipping my trousers and walking away towards the wash basins. I had pumped into my hand a puffball of hand-washing foam when it struck me that Peter hadn't yet responded. I looked to my left. He was standing in precisely the same position in which I'd found him, right hand loose by his side, brow pressed to the tiles above the urinal. For a cold moment I feared he might be dead.

'Peter? *Peter?* Can you hear me?'

Stiffly, as if still tangled in the spider's silk of a dream, Peter stood upright, buttoned his fly and burst into tears.

A little over a minute later I had followed him back into the party. The poor man had, I regret to report, proved resistant to all attempts at consolation, and ascribing his sensitive mood to a combination of professional stress and too much alcohol, I took the liberty of putting to the test the Walnut Tree's recently installed, and commendably energy-efficient, new 'Airblade' hand-drying technology. The sheer *sharpness* of that gale-force blast! Stepping out onto the landing, palms parched as pressed leaves, I was, however, taken aback to see Peter, still heaving with sobs, clutching my wife by the elbows.

'But I'm in *love* with you,' I heard him wail, as, much to the amusement of a pair of teenage waitresses, standing by hugging their round metal trays to their chests, Alan tried his boozy best to intervene. By the time I had begged passage through the crowd, Peter had let go of Sunita, and shrugging free of the feeble half-nelson in which Alan had eventually succeeded in placing him, retreated weeping in the direction of the conference suite. Desperately concerned for her well-being I placed a soothing hand on Sunita's arm.

'What happened?'

'Don't touch me there! I'm *covered* in bruises.'

Alan cleared his throat. 'Seems like Ledbury town centre isn't the only thing Peter Agnew is determined to f**k.'

'Alan, please,' I said. 'What was Peter *saying* to you, my pumpkin?'

'Oh, just the usual stuff,' said Sunita, rubbing her bruises. 'That he couldn't live without me. That he was thinking of emigrating to New Zealand and wanted me to come too. That my reading was the most beautiful thing he had ever heard in his life.'

'And so what did you say to him?'

'"Yawn" was my opening gambit. Then "Let me go, you f***ing psycho." But that just seemed to get him *more* excited. So I told him I couldn't have an affair with him because I was already having one with David.'

'What?'

'Relax. It was just to get rid of him. Where *is* David, by the way? And Guy – where's he?'

Alan scanned the crowd. 'I think they must have gone downstairs to the bar.'

'Thank f**k for that,' said Sunita. '*So* embarrassing.'

Alcoholism is a disease, and as such Peter can no more be blamed for his actions than Alan be taken to task for his off-colour sense of humour, or Sunita her occasional bouts of cardiac arrhythmia.

Nonetheless, my poor darling had suffered quite a shock, and I was grateful to Daisy Rux-Burton for stepping in and giving her a much-needed hug. Calm was soon restored, and it seemed as if the party's tidal patterns of indifference had washed over the incident with Peter – until, to my alarm, he was spotted talking to Karen outside the ladies' toilets. From the colour rising in Karen's chest – a terrible palette of nauseous grey and vengeful red – it seemed likely that Peter was passing on the misinformation that Sunita had been sleeping with her husband.

At this point Guy and David arrived back on the landing, holding pints of Wye Valley's extremely sessionable Butty Bach (4.5%)[6] they had carried upstairs from the bar. And coolly, with serene clarity of purpose, Karen strode across the landing and dealt David a slap that caused his pint to be sick on the stairs.

All at once I felt a presence by my side. It was Daisy, cheeks flushed a winter pink. At the head of the stairs, Sunita was stroking David's arm, engaged in an apparently underappreciated attempt to comfort him. Peter had left. Karen had tried to, but been intercepted by Guy, who had overtaken her on the stairs and was now blocking her way with one hand to the banister. Alan was walking around muttering to himself in tones of seeming self-recrimination. And slowly, with a sort of helpless familiarity, Daisy collapsed tearfully into my chest, transfixed by the sight of her beloved ex-boyfriend Guy with his arm around a sobbing Karen. It was at times like these, it struck me, that the idea of giving up drink seemed abruptly less unthinkable.

The Coseley Tunnel was built in 1837 to straighten the circuitous route the canal had previously taken around Coseley and Wednesbury Oak. Thomas Telford had died some years earlier, in September 1834, and the tunnel, over 357 yards long, is a testament to the spirit of continuous improvement that not only informed the canal project, but imbued the age. Local legend has it that the tunnel is haunted by the ghost of Hannah Johnson Cox, the 'White Lady',

---

6. Instantly recognisable by its mellow copper tone and generous head.

who when the mood takes her will rise shrieking from the waters and stab unsuspecting ramblers in the back, just as she was stabbed by her alcoholic husband Phillip in 1901. Penetrating the depths of the tunnel, it's certainly easy to see how such ghoulish folk tales arose, as within a few dozen yards the grainy darkness, the slippery cobbles underfoot, the steadily melancholic drip from the slimy, algae-covered bricks overhead conspire despite one's better judgement to tease up the hairs on the back of one's neck. Funny that this monument to reason should inspire such irrational fears! It didn't help that halfway down the tunnel a pair of teenage girls were leaning against the bricks, sullenly smoking, their faces periodically lit an infernal orange by the embers of their cigarettes.[7] We were, of course, strong both in numbers and *esprit de corps*, but as the girls' expressionless faces loomed closer I felt the sure constriction of a panicking hand on my arm. Too anxious to turn round and see who it was, and too polite to shrug them off, I led on, avoiding eye contact with the smokers, overruling my own groundless if persistent fears until a vast sneeze exploded behind me, identified the hand on my sleeve and set the tunnel echoing with ironically rather spectral laughter.

Once everyone was out the other side I thought it best to do a head-count. Twenty-two: three short. Then Cliff emerged from the tunnel, leading an ashen-faced Warren by a firm, maternal hand.

'Your friend Alan had to stop,' said Cliff, clasping Warren's shaven head to his chest, where the latter began to sob. 'Said his feet were killing him.'

I sighed. 'Where is he?'

'There's a pub about a mile back. He said to meet him there.'

The Barge & Barrel, featuring the Ace of Spades Rock 'n' Blues Bar, is set back from the canal where it meets Brindley's meandering

---

7. Not so brightly, however, for the colour of their rainwear to be discernible. Astute ramblers may nonetheless wonder, as I did, whether daylight might have revealed the green livery of the notorious West Coseley Young Ladies' Club. I fear we shall never know.

Old Main Line at Tipton Factory Junction. To tell the truth I was not best pleased to have to retrace my steps. It's not every day I get to walk with such an enthusiastic, informed and indeed like-minded group of ramblers as the members of GWMSWC, and quite apart from the personal frustration of not completing the walk, I had to contend with their obvious, if in most cases decorously suppressed, disappointment that I wouldn't be taking part in the post-ramble discussion at the Prince Albert. Linda Birch was perhaps the most unguardedly upset, to the extent that I actually began to see the *upside* of going my separate way, and to fill an awkward pause in which I feared for a hot second that a kiss might be expected, I succumbed and wrote my address on the inside cover of her copy of *Pub Walks in Shropshire and the West Midlands*.

Tipton, like many formerly industrial towns in the Black Country, has in recent years fallen on hard times, something to which the acres of despoliation to either side of the canal bear uncomfortably eloquent witness. A little further up towards Wolverhampton, the canal-side site of a former car-parts factory is now a vast, rubble-strewn wilderness, stretching back to the stacked hoops of two gas towers a quarter of a mile to the west, and it's a bitterly ironic reminder of how far the area has fallen since the heyday of the Lunar Society that the bricks that lie in weed-choked heaps beside the towpath, cairns to the memory of a more confident age, should of all things be branded UTOPIA.

But wildflowers grow from them. Along the length of the canal, in cuttings strewn with smashed concrete and twisted machine parts, daisies thrive in near-laughable abundance. Prickly dewberries grapple with wire-link fences. Abandoned toilets make impromptu pots for lady's bedstraw. From the windows of derelict factories showers of brilliant-yellow birdsfoot trefoil

Discarded toilet seat

fall, their lower petals like tongues, stuck out as if in answer to the most misguided, and indeed dangerous, idea the enlightened men of the Lunar Society ever had: that nature should or could be contained.

I found Alan rubbing one bootless foot near the back of the Barge & Barrel. As well as a wide range of beers including Banks's toothsome Original (3.5%), proprietors Andy and Penny lay on a bostin'[8] backdrop of blues, hard rock and heavy metal. Having nurtured such ground-breaking acts as Led Zeppelin,[9] Black Sabbath, Deep Purple and Judas Priest, Birmingham and the Black Country have as much right to be called the crucible of heavy metal as the Mississippi Delta does the birthplace of its progenitor, the blues. In his excellent band biog, *The Story of Judas Priest: Defenders of the Faith*, Neil Daniels suggests that the 'soot, pollution and general grimness' of the industrial West Midlands had a profound effect on the metal mentality – literalised, one might argue, in the case of Tony Iommi, guitarist and founding member of Black Sabbath, who lost the tips of his right middle and ring fingers working in a sheet-metal factory, and developed the 'power chord' as a way round the lack of sensation he felt in his stumps.

And it's this spirit of survival, this refusal to be bowed, that earns the blighted wastelands north of Birmingham their place in what is

8. A local term. Like the flamenco term *duende* (≈ 'soul', 'authenticity'), *bostin'* is hard to translate satisfactorily. 'Fantastic' or 'brilliant' will do, but miss the wry but indomitable note of resistance enacted in the opening plosive, *bǒ*. Things might not be bostin' in the slightest, but the term stands as shorthand for the belief that, against enormous odds, they might be one day, as in 'Wouldn't it be bostin' if Walsall beat Villa?' or 'I'm afraid we're going to have to let you go.' 'Bostin'.'
9. Interesting to note the centrality of rambling to early Led Zep. Witness 'Ramble On' from *Led Zeppelin II* (Oct. 1969), and the lyrics of their cover, on the band's debut album *Led Zeppelin* (Jan. '69), of the traditional folk song 'Babe I'm Gonna Leave You': 'I ain't jokin' woman, I got to ramble'. The 'speaker' of the second song, given such ardent voice by Robert Plant, is of course torn by the contradictory impulses to stay with his beloved ('go walking in the park every day') and to walk away from her ('really got to ramble'), a theme that extends back through the English and American folk-music traditions to the mythic leave-taking of Odysseus from Penelope. We must walk away, it would seem, from what we love.

for the most part a celebration of mountain, wold and stream. They are wild, in the truest sense. And besides, which is more disheartening? A ramshackle backstreet reclaimed by unruly vegetation? Or a lovely valley ruined by a rubbish dump? I leave it to the rambler to decide. Walking back, alone, through the Coseley Tunnel, I found the underage smokers still there. 'Hello,' I said, rather stiffly, and in their reply – *Yow awlroight* – I heard not only ordinary warmth, where I had expected hostility, but traces of Anglo-Saxon pronunciation that have weathered nearly a thousand years of steady homogenisation to persist in the modern-day Black-Country accents of two fifteen-year-old girls. Judging by the grimace elicited by the removal of his second boot, Alan was clearly in some pain, and although I was curious to hear what he had on his mind, I thought it polite first to press him on his repeated failure to invest in a pair of orthotic inserts.

'I'm not a f***ing cripple, you know.'

'Alan,' I laughed. 'That's an absurd overreaction. *Millions* of people suffer from biomechanical foot disorders. In fact I'd go so far as to call it a silent epidem–'

'Look, just give it a rest, will you, Graham? J*sus.'

I returned my attention to the several cardboard beer mats spread out on the table. 'PUT AN END TO DOMESTIC VIOLENCE,' they said, below a picture of fists bound in white ribbon. As I say, after the fracas at the wild-writing event I had gone home ahead of Sunita. I was all for her coming with me, but with typical – and, for certain people I could mention, instructive – self-sacrifice she felt she should stay behind and apologise to Guy on Peter's, Karen's and to some extent David's behalf. What had happened was, I agreed, a shoddy way to thank one's guest of honour for sparing his valuable time, and I was only glad, having entrusted Alan with her safekeeping, that Sunita had returned home confident that the situation had been rectified, albeit at four o'clock in the morning. Quite what point there was in discussing the matter further I had no idea. But Alan was a martyr to his arches, and seeing as he'd walked eight and a half miles in the rain just for a pint and a chin-wag, I thought the least I could do was to hear my old chum out.

'F***ing health Nazis,' said Alan, turning as the afternoon threw a bucket of rain at the window. 'How much does the pub get fined if I have a cigarette? Two and a half grand? I'll pay it.'

'We could stand out under the bridge.'

'No, you're all right.' A deep drag on an imaginary fag. 'Look. What I'm about to say you have to promise not under any circumstances to mention to Sunita. She'd have my b*ll-s*ck for a bathing cap.'

'I promise.'

'I'm not having an affair with her.'

'With who?'

'Sunita.'

'I didn't think you were.'

'Good.'

'Never in my wildest dreams would I even have *suspected* it.'

'All right, all right. Steady on. It's not *that* unlikely, is it?'

'No, I mean, you're a *friend*. I'd never suspect you of doing that to me.'

'Yeah, well.' Alan picked up a beer mat and started making little tears along its edges. 'I just thought, what with all that nonsense the other night at the Walnut Tree, it was worth making one thing crystal clear. Adultery: not my thing. Not cut out for it. Absolutely zero action going on between *me* and Sunita. You can rest assured of that.'

I took a long draught of Banks's, noting, by the by, its quenching hints of hop and burnt chocolate. There is nothing on God's earth – apart from time spent with Sunita – to compare with the pleasures of a good pint, in a good pub, with a good friend. And Alan, I realised, *was* a good friend: a true friend. Not only had he walked himself ragged just to put my mind at rest, on a matter that had never even *occurred* to me, but to protect my precious darling from the very idea that she might be thought unfaithful – exactly the sort of baseless speculation that had so ruined the Walnut Tree event – he preferred we keep his admission of innocence between ourselves. And it's only, my dear rambler, to demonstrate that innocence (and my trust in Sunita) that I share it with you.

Walk 8: Shakespeare Country

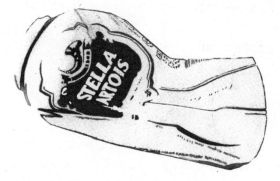

'The English are all Shakespeare,' wrote Delacroix. 'It is his influence that we see in all the things most characteristic of them.' One might question how Shakespearean it is to deface a footpath sign, or build a caravan park across a public right of way, but many parts of this ultimately rewarding walk do indeed give an insight into what Warwickshire was like in Shakespeare's time, and what remnants of his influence have survived the transformation of the Forest of Arden into a featureless 500,000-acre agribusiness. Like many a mid-sized market town in England, modern-day Stratford-upon-Avon has its fair share of ugly, soulless retail and housing developments, and it should be noted that the early part of this walk passes through a council estate of singular cheerlessness. Nonetheless, a final stroll downhill rewards the patient rambler with pleasant views over the Avon Valley, and a return to the starting point via a rather more salubrious part of town!

Start at the Dirty Duck pub a hundred yards down Waterside from the Royal Shakespeare Theatre. In summer months you may take your drinks across the road and enjoy them in the oak-shaded gardens that abut the river; while Flowers Original (4.4%) is *not*

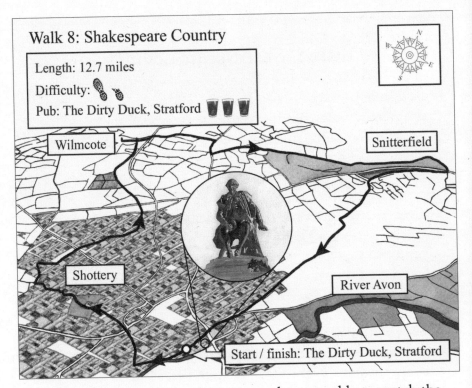

Walk 8: Shakespeare Country

Length: 12.7 miles

Difficulty:

Pub: The Dirty Duck, Stratford

Wilmcote

Snitterfield

Shottery

River Avon

Start / finish: The Dirty Duck, Stratford

ideally served in cloudy plastic, it can be agreeable to watch the narrowboats pottering by, allowing the hard-working folk that frequent the famous Actors' Bar the quiet pint they both crave and deserve. Some months ago I had the honour of meeting the actor playing Duncan in the current production of *Macbeth*, set in Nazi Germany, and in rep with *The Winter's Tale*.[1] Between his chilling final appearance in Act I ('Conduct me to mine host: we love him highly') and reincarnation as Old Siward in Act V, Brian liked to 'steal a few cheeky ones' down the Duck, and having just completed a particularly invigorating eighteen-mile stroll along the Avon from Evesham, I felt bold enough to ask him if I'd seen him receiving

---

1. In which Brian plays a touchingly enfeebled Antigonus: much hilarity, on the night we saw it, when the pursuing bear paused, looked at the audience and looked back at Antigonus again, as if assessing the effort-reward ratio of dining on such a scrawny old bird.

emergency surgery for a ruptured aorta on *Casualty* the previous week. I had. Not only that, but the actor playing his cardiothoracic surgeon was none other than Seb, part-time barman at the Woolpack in Slad, from whom, as it turned out, Brian had heard all about Sunita! Quite extraordinary. To hear, like Petruchio of fair Kate, Sunita's 'virtues spoke of', and (of course) her 'beauty sounded', by a *professional actor*, was a pleasure of such rare note that, for fear of having too much of a good thing, I have on subsequent visits given Brian as wide a berth as possible.

Some four hundred yards south of the pub, Southern Lane meets Old Town under the cruciform invigilation of a First World War memorial. Ramblers may consider the chancel of Holy Trinity Church, left, *vaut le détour*: here Shakespeare's bones lie buried. Having assiduously collected all six vouchers from the *Ledbury Evening Star*, I had been lucky enough to secure tickets for *The Winter's Tale* at the very reasonable price of £12.50, plus £2.50 booking fee (per transaction), thus quelling the guilt I might otherwise have felt treating ourselves to a pre-theatre dinner at Trinculo's. Sunita *adores* Silvio's monkfish – as well she might, at £18! – but I hadn't expected her gratitude, when I told her over breakfast where we were going that evening, to extend as far as agreeing to accompany me on the twelve-mile walk with which I planned to fill the afternoon.

'Are you sure, my blossom? You could get the train and meet me there.'

'No, thanks,' said Sunita, sullenly pushing her egg to one side. 'Train's full of yobs.'

'Or we could get Steve to – ah, well. Maybe not. What about the bus? I'm sure if you changed at Worcester –'

'Is this meant to be some kind of joke?'

'No, of course. Silly idea. I suppose we could hang the expense and order a cab.'

'Look. Do you want me to come on this walk, or don't you?'

Smiling, I stowed the shiniest of a particularly fine batch of apples in the mesh compartment of my ramblesack. 'Of course I do, my darling. I was just making sure you were coming because you *wanted* to.'

And so the matter was settled. Odd, Sunita's reluctance to take the train to Stratford, as since her disqualification from driving she had happily disappeared for days on end by rail, most recently, dear girl, to check the route of Walk 2 preparatory to its inclusion in this guide. ('Flawless,' she had pronounced it, I'm pleased to report.) Not that I minded, if it meant I got not only to drive her, but to spend the entire day in her company! Heading north-west, Old Town passes Hall's Croft, luxurious home to Shakespeare's elder daughter, Susanna, and her Cambridge-educated husband, the respected physician Dr John Hall. Nothing so demonstrates the divergence in the fortunes of Shakespeare's three children as the handsome half-panelling of this stunning five-bedroom townhouse. Hamnet, of course, died of uncertain causes at the age of eleven; his twin sister Judith survived into adulthood only to marry a whoremongering vintner, and outlive the last of *her* three children by twenty-two years. It was Susanna, always her father's favourite, that made it into the middle class, bagging a nice doctor and raising a daughter, Elizabeth, who would marry a knight.[2] On the rare occasion I have managed to raise the subject of children without instantaneously scaring Sunita away – the knack, like coaxing an ambivalent cat with the tips of your fingers, is to remain very still and very quiet – she has alluded, movingly, to her fear of taking on the responsibilities of parenthood when our own future seemed so uncertain. Not uncertain as far as *I* was concerned, but as much as I hoped that one day I might have a smaller Underhill to walk the slopes with, I respected Sunita's circumspection. It was, paradoxically, a measure of how seriously she took the idea of having a family that, for the time being at least, she was refusing point-blank even to consider it as a possibility.

2. Sir John Barnard, knighted by Charles II in 1661. Elizabeth had been married before, to the wealthy landowner Thomas Nash, but neither union bore fruit. With Elizabeth's death in 1670, the direct line of descent from our greatest poet ended only fifty-four years after his own death.

In *Shakespeare the Thinker*, the much-lamented scholar (and keen rambler) Tony Nuttall recalls following the route from Stratford to Anne Hathaway's cottage at dusk, 'the idea of re-enacting Shakespeare's walk' becoming 'gradually less fatuous' as the 'shadows gathered', erasing the impedimenta of the intervening centuries. Much as I admire Professor Nuttall's rejection of the pretentious excesses of modern Shakespearean criticism, in favour of a more commonsensical reading of the plays, I've tried his 'walk with Shakespeare' trick more than once, each time to no avail. Even as the suburbs give way to the cool enclosure of oaks, I find it hard to forget that I've just walked through a housing development of singular insensitivity. Here Shakespeare, popping round to Anne's, would have walked on common land, his breeches brushed with bold oxlips and the bobbing heads of trollop's fescue. Needless to say, Shakespeare of all people would have been passionate in his advocacy of low-cost community housing, but given the acreage of proximate brown-field site and irredeemable scrubland, to lose several dozen acres of any wildflower meadow – let alone one that may well have informed Perdita's famous flower speech[3] in *The Winter's Tale* – to a brutal development of dishcloth-coloured boxes is to squander a priceless treasure that belonged to us all.

No wonder violent crime is on the increase. To make matters worse, as Sunita and I emerged into the estate from a path between high fences, there loomed into view an end-of-terrace semi whose thuggishly brusque front elevation was furnished with a pair of Victorian-style – and no doubt motion-sensitive – carriage lamps.

'Look at that,' I said. 'If you're going to live in a discredited socialist experiment then you could at least have the good grace not to be snobbish about it.'

---

3. 'Here's flowers for you: / Hot lavender, mints, savory, marjoram, / The marigold, that goes to bed wi' th' sun / And with him rises, weeping: these are the flowers / Of middle summer, and I think they are given / To men of middle age.' Shocking when one has always identified with the play's romantic lead, young Florizel, to find oneself, without quite knowing where the years have gone, a suitable recipient of marigolds!

Sunita laughed. 'Who's the snob? And it's not as if Foxglove Cottage is anything to write home about.'

This was uncharacteristically unkind. But before I had the chance to respond Sunita's phone rang, and she raised a finger to silence me. Then, glancing at the screen, she seemed momentarily to lose her composure, before switching off the unit altogether.

'Who was that?'

'Nobody.' Smiling under unaccountably wide eyes Sunita held out her hand. 'Let's just walk, shall we?'

We reached Anne Hathaway's cottage in silence. Little is known about Hathaway, other than that she was, at the time of her marriage to Shakespeare, twenty-six to his eighteen, pregnant, and in possession of six pounds, thirteen shillings and fourpence, a goodly enough sum in those days to compensate for what seems, on the scant evidence available, to have been a less than happy match. 'Do you think,' says Steven Dedalus in *Ulysses*, 'the writer of *Antony and Cleopatra*, a passionate pilgrim, had his eyes in the back of his head that he chose the ugliest doxy in all Warwickshire to lie withal?' Dedalus is, of course, speaking for effect, but certain things must surely be inferred from Shakespeare's twenty-year absence in London, and the fact that as one of a number of beneficiaries to his will poor Anne was left with his 'second-best bed'. Ramblers may wish to take a short detour to visit the house, with its original fireplaces, enchanting if completely anachronistic cottage garden, and seventeenth-century bread oven, all for the fully defensible price of £8. Sunita, on the other hand, refused outright, citing no interest whatsoever in the 'f***ing socks-and-sandals Shakespeare experience', and began to drag me towards a hedge at the far end of the coach park, by all appearances meaning me to profane, in the words of the Bard, her 'scarlet ornaments'.

'Sweet pea,' I protested. 'There are people watching.'

'Who cares?'

Of course I realised in an instant what my clever darling was up to. Pretending to 'make love in a ditch' while a coachload of Japanese tourists looked on was Sunita's response to the deadening effects of international heritage tourism: exactly the sort of joyously bawdy subversion of which, one feels, Shakespeare himself might have approved. While we're on the subject, I am broadly in favour of *al fresco* lovemaking, as long as genuine privacy is guaranteed, and the ground checked for hazards such as dog mess and/or biting insects. What Sunita meant by murmuring 'This'll show him,' as she laboured to remove my plastic overtrousers, remained, however, a matter for conjecture, although chances are she was referring to the elderly Japanese gentleman frowning at us through the tinted windows of the coach. Under the improvised awning of its open luggage hold the coach's driver was standing stone-still in his Polaroids, smoking a cigarette, and, concerned lest he think we were actually about to take our clothes off, I pulled free of Sunita's clutches and broadcast a nervous laugh.

'Agh,' said Sunita, throwing up her hands. 'You're no fun.'

Whereupon she stormed out of the car park in a deftly realistic show of high temper.

Two hundred yards further up Cottage Lane a commendable 'CYCLING PROHIBITED' sign points right down a narrow leafy track. For some reason, in the few minutes since our show of high jinks in the coach park, Sunita's simulated ill-humour seemed to have shaded into the real thing, and refusing my offer of a morale-boosting Fruit Pastille she remained submerged in a sullen silence, lagging unchar-acteristically far behind as I turned left at the end of the track and followed Church Lane up to its junction with the Alcester Road. Ramblers are advised to take greater care crossing this busy A-route than I did when, anxious that my sulky sweetheart might not have realised that a cycle route stood between her and the safety of the central reservation, I stopped and turned, failing to notice the blue Isuzu van turning right out of a hidden side street, at speed. Its driver might, in my opinion, have restricted himself to a single short parp on his horn, as opposed to the vigorous masturbatory mime with which he felt it necessary to express his displeasure. Still, it *was* quite funny, and if I was a little bemused by the hard edge to Sunita's laughter, as she passed me on the opposite pavement, better that than to have risked her being mown down by a negligent cyclist.

From Sidelands Road to the Stratford-upon-Avon canal the route follows the course of a brook some scholars believe may have been the model for the place of Ophelia's muddy death. No willow grows aslant it now, and so reduced is its flow, as a result of the disastrous impact on natural drainage systems of unsustainable urban sprawl, that you'd have a job drowning a kitten in it these days, let alone a fully grown woman. Unless, of course, she'd tripped, smacked her head and fallen face-first into the water. Sunita had by now pressed so far ahead as to slip out of sight; crossing Drayton Avenue, and following the course of the brook as best I could, I was pleased to find separation a spur to my navigational instincts. Turning left, between tall spruce and the north-eastern fringes of a housing estate – built, incidentally, on land in which Shakespeare once held a share of the tithe – I emerged through the trees to join the towpath, where I found Sunita perched on the semi-erect balance beam of a lock. She was eating a large red apple, and looked so captivating in the rippling light reflected off the water that I was nearly glad of having lost her momentarily, for the joy of seeing her anew.

'Your hand, my Perdita.'

'P*ss off, Graham. I'm eating.'

A fair cop, even if a slightly less violent swatting-away would have made the point with equal eloquence. Incidentally, her apple *did* look good, and shrugging one arm free of my ramblesack I reached round to extract my own apple – only to find it missing. I was in the midst of retracing the steps I'd taken that morning, quite certain I'd trans-ferred a firm, shiny Braeburn from the fruit bowl to the mesh compartment of my ramblesack, when, pushing off the balance beam, Sunita threw her apple half-eaten into the canal, and I realised that my stealthy sweetheart must have pilfered mine without my feeling it. Served me right for not packing one for us both! Besides, if Sunita was fretful that day I could scarcely hold it against her. It had been, I regret to reveal, a difficult few weeks *chez* Underhill-Bhattacharya. After a series of delays the full public inquiry into the proposed ring road had been held at Ledbury Town Hall. Ramblers will be able to guess at my feelings, but matters were complicated by the conflict of interest inherent in a council officer objecting, as a private individual, to a scheme advanced as a core improvement lever for the local economy. Indeed, my reservations about the destruction the road would visit on a patch of land I loved second only to my wife were tempered by the inconveniently compelling argument, put forward by my colleagues at Highways and Transportation, that the displacement of through-traffic eastwards would improve air quality not only in Ledbury town centre, but along the A417 corridor as a whole.

As a county-level Environmental Sustainability Officer I had been called to give evidence on the fifth day of the inquiry. Time, as ever, was limited, but I was able in reasonably meticulous detail to take the panel through my 86-slide PowerPoint presentation, assessing the loss of biodiversity along the proposed route as benchmarked against the key environmental 'wins' for the areas the scheme was designed to relieve. Ramblers may recall the minor barracking I received at the community-outreach open day I attended in May. Coincidentally, or not, a man with much the same voice was present at the inquiry on the morning I gave evidence. While I'd be the first to defend the indispensability of free and fair debate not only to the local democratic process, but to our collective response to the threat posed by climate change, I question how constructive it was to interrupt me halfway through what was, in all honesty, one of the less consequential sections of my presentation.

'Armed revolution,' he called out.

'Excuse me?'

'The only hope we have – the *only* hope we have – is the violent overthrow of the global capitalist system.'

Legitimate as this point of view may have been I had no choice but to note it and move on to 'Considerations relating to roadside vegetation maintenance and weed control'. Scarcely less impassioned, if rather more to the purpose, were the reactions to Peter Agnew's contribution to the inquiry. I had to get back to the office, and could only catch the first twenty minutes or so, but it was clear from the outset that his decision to support a scheme liable to draw business *away* from the town centre was viewed as inconsistent – to say the least – with his responsibilities as chair of the Ledbury Business Forum. I had, in fact, bumped into Peter that morning, buying a bottle of hydroactive sports drink from the newsagent adjacent to the Town Hall, and from the readiness if rather rigid formality of his nodded hello it might have come as a surprise to an unacquainted third party to learn that less than three weeks previously he had been pleading with my wife to elope with him to Auckland. A little of Peter's emotional side, however, was exposed briefly before I had to absent myself from the inquiry, when, responding to a question put by my old friend Keith Frampton, a reporter from the *Ledbury Evening Star*, regarding Peter's links to the road-haulage lobby, his voice cracked like bracken underfoot. 'With respect,' he said, prodding the ring-road feasibility study with his index finger, 'my father lived in Ledbury. As did his father before him. I can assure you, Mr Frampton, that any decisions I take on its behalf are mine and mine alone.'

After the sixth day the inquiry was adjourned while the panel reviewed written objections to the compulsory purchase orders proposed by the Highways Agency. As things stood, only a small number of properties, two of which had been unoccupied for years, were earmarked for demolition. However, for a short stretch the route passed to the east of Coneygree Wood, within eyeshot of Eastnor, and a concerted effort by such part-time residents as David Redfern had seen an alternative route tabled, a few miles to the west on the Ledbury side of the wood. For a short while in 1914 the great Robert Frost lived in Ledbury, and in 'The Road Not Taken' he pokes fun at his friend and fellow poet Edward Thomas, for fretting, at forks in the woodland paths they walked together, over what might have happened if they'd taken the other way:

> Two roads diverged in a yellow wood
> And sorry I could not travel both
> And be one traveler, long I stood

And looked down one as far as I could
To where it bent in the undergrowth

And so, in its way, the planning committee stood, at the divergence
of two as yet inexistent roads – one, as originally planned, that would
displease the residents of Eastnor, and another that wouldn't, in
exchange for the demolition of a few 'architecturally insignificant'
properties on the north-eastern outskirts of Ledbury, our very own
Foxglove Cottage among them.

'You know I've been thinking,' said Sunita, the day after my appearance at the inquiry. After weeks of heavy rain the last few days of
August brought a spell of dry weather, and arriving home in variable
states of despondency I had derived some comfort lying out on the
sustainable teak recliner, sipping from a bottle of something nutty
as the dusk snuffed the garden inch by inch. Earlier that evening
Sunita had popped out for a quick drink with her new best friend
Daisy, and had returned three hours later touchingly incapable of
quite forming a consonant.

'You love this place, don't you?'

In relationships as close as ours it's not always necessary to verbal-
ise a response.

'Well then,' she went on. 'Why don't you put up more of a fight?'

I sighed, and took Sunita's hand in mine. 'Because, my sweet pea,
the residents of Eastnor have as much right to protect their landscape
as we do ours. Besides, aren't you glad? In a few months we could
have sold up and be living in London.'

'Oh, b*lls to London. I like it *here*.'

'You do?'

'Well, no. Not exactly. But the point is, *you do*. And I realise now
how selfish I've been not to respect that.'

She was all for mounting a counter-attack on the 'self-interested'
residents of Eastnor. The Stratford-upon-Avon Canal was built at the
turn of the nineteenth century to link the Warwickshire Avon – made
navigable within twenty-five years of Shakespeare's death by the
construction of a series of locks and weirs – with the Worcester and

Birmingham Canal in the south-western suburbs of Birmingham. By the mid-twentieth century the Stratford canal had fallen into disuse, and but for the efforts of a local team of waterway enthusiasts ramblers would be denied the opportunity, crossing a road bridge at Bishopton Lane to continue up the right-hand side of the canal, to admire the harlequin colours of the narrowboats moored alongside, or chuckle at the often marvellously irreverent names with which their owners have chosen to broadcast their inimitably 'boatie' sense of humour! In the two miles between Bishopton Lane and the Station Road bridge, where Sunita and I left the canal to turn left into the village of Wilmcote, I counted a 'Moody Cow', a 'Grounds for Divorce' and – my favourite – a 'Sir Osis of the River', which, Sunita being her usual score of paces ahead, I would have photographed for her amusement, had the couple on its geranium-crowded deck not been patently on the point of murdering each other.

Among the several attractions on offer in the mainly charming village of Wilmcote are two excellent pubs, the Mary Arden Inn and the Mason's Arms, where ramblers may feel themselves entitled to a pint or two of appley, sour-doughy Otter Ale (4.5%), depending on how long it takes their partner to 'powder their nose'! Mary Arden, of course, was Shakespeare's mother, and while Sunita predictably refused to go anywhere near it, ramblers with a stomach for historical reconstruction[4] may like to visit Palmer's Farm, the nattily preserved, half-timbered farmhouse where Arden spent part of her childhood, and out-of-work actors in authentic Tudor smocks now palp the teats of rare cows. Knowing at first hand the formidable pressures of public service I am not, as I hope my regular readers will acknowledge, in the habit of criticising my counterparts in other local authorities. It is more in the spirit of fraternal concern that I draw attention to the state of the footpath network between Wilmcote and Snitterfield. Whether or not your interests extend to Elizabethan ox-washing techniques, or cheese-making as Mary Arden might have

4. And £8.

practised it, dismay will inevitably be your guide, attempting to retrace the route the poet's mother must have taken, visiting her 'bit of rough', yeoman's son John Shakespeare, in his modest home three miles to the east. Return to the canal, turn left, and turning right three hundred yards later, through an incongruous wrought-iron gate in lieu of a stile, it is possible at least to *begin* one's journey east through open countryside – although I use the term loosely, the 'countryside' hereabouts being more akin to a post-nuclear blast zone than the 'unfrequented woods' immortalised by its greatest son.

Beyond the thunderous Birmingham Road, however, the route becomes impassible. Footpath signs, where they haven't been ripped from their stanchions, point towards impenetrable thickets of bramble strewn with crumpled lager cans. Compelled temporarily to trespass, ramblers hoping to pick up the path further on will find their way definitively barred by a concreted-over caravan park built for the local traveller community.

Defaced footpath sign

Scientific studies have shown that walking, at least in the sort of 'nethermercies' or loose-fitting trousers that Shakespeare's father might have worn, can help to maximise male fertility, as the temperature of the testes, swinging free from the clammy adjacency of the abdomen, drops to a level most propitious to the production of sperm. Is it, therefore, too much to assume that the sperm that made Shakespeare was made in its turn *on this walk* – this walk that John Shakespeare might well have taken *every day* over that hot, joyous summer of 1563, when his higher-born wife was found to be with child? In Ireland, travellers are referred to as *an Lucht Siúil*[5] – 'the walking people' – and with their centuries-old tradition of nomadism, let alone their endearing passion for poetry and song, one can scarcely believe they'd mind being asked to 'budge over' a

---

5. Etymologically related, as keen-eared ramblers will have noted, to *Suibhne* – Sweeney, the wandering king.

little, if they knew what a significant right of way their cheap-but-not-so-cheerful 'mobile homes' were blocking![6]

Cutting our losses we walked east out of Wilmcote along Featherbed Lane, turning right after three-quarters of a mile to tramp resentfully, for three hundred vergeless yards, beside the hurtling Birmingham Road. With Sunita's encouragement I had decided to write a letter formally objecting to the alternative route proposed for the ring road. Needless to say, I was careful to acknowledge both the difficulty of my position, as a council officer, and the many undoubted benefits, particularly to the people of Eastnor, of building a dual carriageway directly through my house. Having posted the letter – to have sent it by internal mail would, I judged, have been a misuse of council resources – I experienced a sense of liberation akin to divesting oneself of one's clothes on a hot summer's ramble. It was only a shame that Sunita seemed incapable of sharing in this remission from anxiety, however brief; if anything her mood seemed to worsen. Truth be told, after the embarrassment with Peter at the Walnut Tree event I had been looking forward to a period of intimate calm with Sunita, and it hurt that this feeling seemed not to be reciprocated. One morning she might be tearful, begging forgiveness for her 'snappish behaviour' and 'all the stress' she 'must be' putting me through; later that day she might be sullen and withdrawn to the extent that she shrank from my touch. Clearly, Sunita attached as much importance as I did to our cosy way of life, and I could at least in part attribute her fretfulness to the worry that our objection to the ring road might not fall on sympathetic ears. Other than that, I was at a loss as to why her mood should be proving quite so intractable; I could only cleave to the hope that her

6. Although it's not clear when travellers first came to Britain, Shakespeare mentions them on several occasions, most notably in *Antony and Cleopatra* (prob. 1606), when Mark Antony, in bitter reference to his lover's dusky charms, calls Cleopatra 'a right gipsy' (IV.xii.28). Tantalisingly, some scholars speculate that the famous 'Dark Lady' of the sonnets may have been of Romany origin; whatever the exact truth of the matter it seems the Bard – like certain other authors I could mention! – may well have had a thing for 'healthier' complexions.

agreement to come on the Stratford walk was a sign that she was emerging from it.

A sign for 'Stratford Armouries and Snitterfield' leads left off the Birmingham Road onto Gospel Oak Lane. Road walking, as I have often explained to Sunita, has its advantages, and raising my walking pole to 'Freddie Mercury' position – noting, by the by, that my voice recorder was working loose from the shaft, and badly needed a fresh binding of gaffer tape – I made a note of the basic mutual courtesies it is the duty of both ramblers and motorists to observe. First, unless you're approaching a bend, always walk on the right-hand side of the road. This allows the rambler and oncoming motorist to establish eye contact in good time for the pass. Second, practise empathy. Ramblers should remember that behind the wheel *they* might find brightly coloured rainwear, sudden movement or partial nudity distracting to the proper operation of the vehicle. Third, ramblers are *not* horses. Depending on the width of the road, and proximity of oncoming traffic, motorists should of course give the rambler a respectful berth, while remembering that he / she is highly unlikely suddenly to fall over, or rear up and plunge boot-first through their windscreen. We're walkers, remember: we *can* walk! Slowing to a crawl, or executing an exaggerated swerve into the outside lane, is as likely to be read as sarcasm as a safety procedure. Aside from the obvious benefits of a bituminous walking surface, many minor roads, roofed like Gospel Oak Lane in ancient trees, offer an equally if not more attractive natural environment than the fields to either side, and given the proper fulfilment of the motorist–rambler contract there's no reason to think of roads as anything more hazardous than exceptionally well-maintained footpaths.

Snitterfield is approached via a narrow metalled track signposted left off Gospel Oak Lane. But for a pair of slumped cottages his father John may have visited, few traces of Shakespeare remain in this unremarkable village. Perhaps worth adding, apropos of Sunita's recent mood, that when I say I was at a loss as to what might have been adversely affecting it, I am neglecting to factor in the difficulty she was having contacting Guy Gosling by phone. Graciously – given the Walnut Tree fiasco – Guy had agreed to cast an eye over the latest draft of *Partition*. Eager to hear his response, Sunita had waited a fortnight before leaving him a series of voicemails. No doubt he had been busy, but shaving in the bathroom one morning last week, I overheard Sunita in the garden, leaving Guy a message to the effect that his failure to call her back was unacceptable. 'Just because you're a famous f***ing author doesn't mean you can treat me like sh*t.' She had a point, of course, but hastening downstairs to find Sunita's mobile phone implanted in the euphorbia, I was moved to remind my hot-blooded sweetheart not to take things so personally. Guy would read *Partition* just as soon as he could set aside the time.

At the burnt-down remains of a pub, the 'Monarch's Way'[7] leads south-east out of the village to cross the teeming A46 via an ugly concrete viaduct. Such are the inauspicious beginnings of what soon becomes perhaps the most attractive section of this walk, through orchards baubled in autumn with festive red apples, and acres of sensitively kept parkland marred only by a golf course and hideous neo-Jacobean mansion turned four-star hotel. Footpath signs marked 'Monarch's Way' line the two-and-a-half-mile path downhill into Stratford, a boon for all ramblers, save those who rely on their partner's ignorance of the route to keep them close at hand! In Shakespeare's day, the hills hereabouts were enclosed by the usurious Combe family; by the turn of the sixteenth century, up to a sixth of Warwickshire's population had been divested of their lands, leading to the sort of desperate banditry personified in *The Winter's Tale* in the form of Autolycus. By the time I caught up with Sunita, however, by the car park of the hideous neo-Jacobean hotel, she was chatting to the handsome young owner of a convertible BMW, and I might as well have engaged a tree in conversation as address her on the problems faced by Elizabethan peasant farmers.

7. The monarch in question being Charles II, who fled this way after his defeat by Cromwell's New Model Army at the Battle of Worcester in 1651. Shakespeare would have been eighty-four at the time of Charles I's execution – not such an outlandish possibility when you consider that his sister Judith, for all her misfortunes, lived to seventy-seven – and it's spine-tingling to speculate what he would have made of this most dramatic of royal tragedies.

Nonetheless, if we were to get to the pub before dinner, we would have to press on, and aiming an amiable nod at the young sportscar enthusiast, I took Sunita by the arm. *Jab!* went Sunita's elbow, into the soft flesh between my bottom rib and the knob of my hip bone. *Oof!* I replied, bending into an involuntary stoop, and making a noise that no doubt sounded more alarming for my attempts to make it less so.

'Don't you *ever*,' said Sunita, 'grab hold of me like that again. Understood?'

It was. Understanding, in fact, was the order of the evening – especially in the case of the charming young man in the BMW, who, tactfully offering us the opportunity to 'cool off' in each other's absence, suggested he give Sunita a ride into town.

'Yes please,' she said, before turning to find me with my hands on my knees, struggling for breath. 'I suppose you'll be wanting a lift too, won't you?'

'No, it's okay,' I gasped. 'I'll walk.'

With a wink, then, and the cocking of two pistol fingers, Sunita's dashing new friend gunned his engines, and the two of them sped off towards Stratford in a cloud of atomised gravel. 'Being winded', or 'diaphragmatic spasm' as it's more properly known, is a cramp like any other, in which the diaphragm responds to blunt injury by popping up like the foil lid of a fermenting yogurt pot, thus limiting the lungs' capacity to fill with air. Distressing as this may be, the spasm should pass relatively quickly if the sufferer is encouraged to remain calm. In the circumstances, then, I had thought it best to walk it off, even if Sunita's soothing presence might have helped prevent the sort of painful 'aftershock' an injudicious breath or jolting misstep might so easily, and indeed on several occasions did, provoke. Later, as we took our seats in the Upper Circle, I turned to Sunita, anxious lest she were disappointed by the distance I hadn't quite realised our special-offer tickets would impose between us and the stage. That said, when the chap in the BMW had finally dropped Sunita off outside Trinculo's – the traffic had been 'a nightmare', apparently – dinner had been conducted in a similarly uncomfortable silence, so it may have been something else entirely.

'You all right?' I whispered. 'You're awfully quiet.'

Before she had the chance to answer, however, the house lights went down, and to a ripple of genteel amusement a voice on the PA reminded us to switch our phones *on* again – *after* the play had finished! Commendably, Sunita had kept her phone *off* for the duration of the walk, and absent-mindedly pressing the power button, she accidentally switched it on. Seconds later, as the actors took their as-yet-unlit positions on stage, the phone emitted a pair of loud beeps, signalling the presence of a voicemail, and causing a woman in the row in front to turn round and give Sunita a glare of such scandalised contempt that it took me a good two scenes to suppress the urge to make a comment in return.

The Winter's Tale, as ramblers will recall, concerns the consequences of the unhinged conviction of Leontes, King of Sicilia, that his beautiful wife Hermione is having an affair. This production was set in an indeterminate time and place where royalty eschewed silk doublets and furs in favour of casual linen-wear, and rooms of state resembled nothing so much as enormous tilted cheeseboards furnished with scatter cushions. 'Solid' was the best word I could find for it, although at times I found myself unable to concentrate on the verse for the sheer amount of *walking* with which the actor playing Leontes had chosen to emphasise his jealousy.

Too hot, too hot!
[*Walks to centre front of stage*]
To mingle friendship far [*walks downstage left*] is mingling bloods [*back to centre*].
I have *tremor cordis* on me [*walks halfway downstage right then swivels, clutching heart, and walks halfway downstage left*]: my heart dances,
[*Walks centre stage, cocks head at Hermione and Polixenes 'paddling palms' on scatter cushions*]
But not for joy [*walks upstage, swivels, strolls downstage, shaking head gravely*] – not joy.

And so on. The poor chap must have covered several miles by the time he realised that Hermione was innocent. Still, Sunita seemed to be enjoying herself, near-choking with laughter when dear old

Brian, as Antigonus, replied to Leontes' accusation that he was incapable of staying his wife Paulina's tongue:

Hang all the husbands
That cannot do that feat, you'll leave yourself
Hardly one subject.

It was only after the interval – when, ironically, the play takes a turn for the comic – that Sunita's mood seemed to deepen. Having taken the trouble to pre-order drinks – a glass of Laurent-Perrier Rosé for her, a pint of rather average Marston's Pedigree (4.5%) for me – I was a little frustrated to glance through the plate-glass windows of the bar and spot Sunita talking on her phone outside the theatre, when she had purportedly just popped to the ladies'. The interval was short, and before Act IV began there were several matters I wanted urgently to discuss. As Nuttall reminds us, the pastoral mode in plays like *The Winter's Tale* is riven by internal contradiction: all very well to sing the artless virtues of the shepherd, but in doing so the poet is by definition distancing himself from those virtues, being art-*ful*, analysing the green world in a way its inhabitants would find no more meaningful than the bleatings of the sheep they tend.

But the desire is still there; the poet still yearns to enter the green world, and it's from this unfulfillable longing that the poetry derives its power to move us. The bar was busy with the chatter of smartly dressed couples, quickened by their evening out, and filled with a longing of my own I secreted Sunita's glass of champagne behind the breast of my tri-climate jacket. Managing to spill not much more than a quarter of it down the front of my technical T-shirt, I tip-toed downstairs to the exit just as Sunita seemed to be wrapping up her phone conversation.

'Well,' she was saying. 'You're welcome to her.'

'Was that Guy?' I said, as Sunita, cheeks streaked with mascara-darkened tears, cancelled the call.

'Yes. I . . .'

'Don't say anything.' For a moment, I admit, I had been unpleasantly surprised to find my wife in floods of tears on the phone to another man. But if *The Winter's Tale* teaches us anything it's to think before we speak, and as I handed Sunita her glass of champagne – apologising the while for spilling a bit – it came to me what must have upset her.

'It's Karen, isn't it?'

Sunita stared at me, then, in one abrupt gulp, knocked back the champagne.

I smiled. 'You think she and Guy are having an affair.'

'Uh, yeah,' said Sunita. 'Possibly. I mean – well. You know what she's like.'

'My sweet, silly girl,' I said, enfolding her in my arms. 'You're a very gifted writer. But you've got to remember the enormous *pressures* people like Guy are under. You think, Wait a minute. If he has the time to carry on with another man's wife, why can't he spare a moment to read my book? Well, two things. One, he has to let off steam. Two, you know what? They're probably *not* seeing each other. Look at Polixenes. Is he really cuckolding Leontes? No. Why? Because he's the King of Bohemia! He has *important things* to be getting on with. Just like Guy! Poor chap scarcely has time to walk his dog let alone indulge in a petty affair with Karen Redfern. So if he can't always give you the help you need, you must-must-*mustn't* take it as any sort of reflection on your talent.'

'No,' sniffled Sunita, into my tri-climate jacket. 'You're probably right.'

The two-minute bell rang, and I decided to save the lecture on the pastoral mode for another day. Retaking our seats, I feared for a moment that Sunita's quarrel with Guy had left her too exhausted to sit through another ninety minutes of Shakespeare. But how wrong I was! How quick I am to judge her! Long before the climactic transformation of Hermione's statue into living, breathing queen – without doubt Shakespeare's most audaciously beautiful *coup de théâtre* – my sensitive sweetheart, tenderised already, was in floods of tears at this timeless tale of loss and redemption. In time she set me off, and we were still crying, softly but surely, when we arrived home two hours after the lights had gone up.

Walk 9: The Slaughters

The handsome Gloucestershire village of Bourton-on-the-Water, where this walk begins and ends, is known as 'The Venice of the Cotswolds', on account of the five stone bridges that vault the River Windrush as it ambles through the green. Like Venice, however, Bourton has fallen victim to its attractiveness, and ramblers whose stocks of shortbread and ceramic moons are sufficient are advised to leave the crowds behind as soon as physically possible. The neighbouring settlements of Lower and Upper Slaughter, no strangers themselves to the tourist's glazed gaze, are nonetheless a safer bet for a soothing afternoon's stroll, not least because the open fields between them, mounting from the sleepy River Eye in billows of dreamy green, constitute what this humble rambler considers classic Cotswold country. An alternative route, largely staying within the bounds of Bourton, is given for occasions when constraints of time or temper demand a substantially shorter walk!

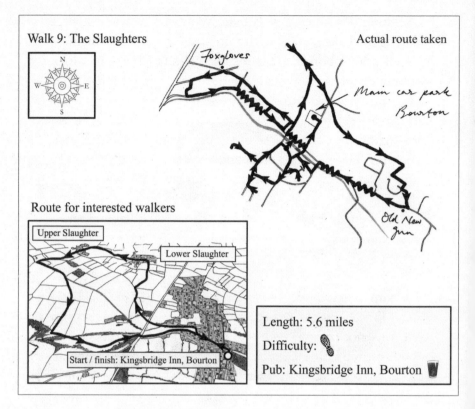

Walk 9: The Slaughters

N W E S

Foxgloves

Actual route taken

Main car park Bourton

Route for interested walkers

Upper Slaughter

Lower Slaughter

Old New gun

Start / finish: Kingsbridge Inn, Bourton

Length: 5.6 miles

Difficulty:

Pub: Kingsbridge Inn, Bourton

'Bourton' as a place name derives from the Anglo-Saxon *burh*, 'fort', and walking (or trying to walk) its thronged streets on a Sunday afternoon, the rambler will be struck by the notion that everyone here, himself included, is imprisoned in a sort of fortress of the mind, the maximum-security paradox that by his very presence he is destroying the charming-Cotswold-village ambience he had come here to imbibe. For decades brave men have campaigned for greater access to the land, and with the passing of the Countryside and Rights of Way Act in 2000, ramblers previously robbed of their natural heritage are now free to roam over their rightful share of mountain, moor, heath and down, let alone the less spectacular but equally indispensable network of footpaths across more intensively cultivated farmland. And yet on fine summer afternoons great swathes of the countryside are deserted, while a handful of hills and winsome villages are condemned by their celebrity to slow and undignified suffocation.

Nothing new in this, of course. Wordsworth was criticised for bringing the Lake District to the attention of the sort of sightseer he himself pooh-poohed in poems like 'The Brothers', in which the 'homely Priest of Ennerdale' decries the moping tourist, 'Perched on the forehead of a jutting crag', scribbling pale platitudes in the time a real man 'might travel twelve stout miles / Or reap an acre of his neighbour's corn'. A hundred and seventy-five years later, the celebrated fellwalker and guidebook writer A. Wainwright was voicing similar grumbles to his pen-pal Margaret Ainley:

Lakeland is utterly lovely and charming, a heavenly paradise on earth – but oh the crowds! There is no fun in walking in procession, not even in delectable scenery.

This from the author whose *Pictorial Guides to the Lakeland Fells* were shortly to sell their millionth copy. Ramblers need not doubt my reverence for – nor obvious debt to – the great man, but it is an irony I myself escape only by virtue of my obscurity that in popularising certain walks Wainwright helped to destroy the very thing he loved most.

Sunita had agreed to accompany me on the Slaughters walk despite being in far from peak condition. The day after our trip to Stratford she had become ill with tachycardia, the delayed effect, in her opinion, of the strain put on her heart by the excess of exercise. I need not emphasise the distress I felt, seeing her laid so low, and if that distress ever shaded into frustration, ferrying boiled eggs upstairs and lukewarm hot-water bottles back down them again, it was only because, when convalescence demanded she forget about her worldly concerns, on more than one occasion I found my diligent darling fast asleep with her mobile phone clutched tightly to her chest. At around the same time a letter had arrived from the council, informing residents whose properties might have to be demolished that a decision on the precise route of the ring road would be made by the first week of October. That was now less than a month away, and I had to admit to a sense of mounting anxiety only held in check by the need not to retard Sunita's recovery. If she was brave enough to come out walking as early as the following weekend, it was the least I could do not to jeopardise her health by sharing my feelings of anger and crushing despair. Granted, I might have forewarned her that Bourton was liable to be crowded that day, but as the route whipped us swiftly off the village green into open countryside, I was confident we would soon be enjoying the peaceful stroll we both needed and deserved.

'I'm having a panic attack,' said Sunita.

It's perhaps worth noting that we had the care of Robin Entwistle's Labrador that day. Yet again an excursion of ours had coincided with Guy Gosling's monthly dog walk, and it was doubly unfortunate that on the very Sunday Sunita had arranged to relieve Karen of her usual Smoky duties – i.e. the very day Sunita was in possession of a dog! – she would once more be prevented from accepting Guy's long-standing invitation to join him, his greyhound Rosie and his would-be constituents for an 'issues-focused' ramble in the hills. Still, she didn't seem to mind that much, perhaps because, in her convalescent state, she shied at the prospect of walking with what was, in effect, a forty-strong pack of hounds. Indeed, that afternoon in Bourton, I was concerned that the responsibility of Smoky alone might be proving too much for her fragile constitution. We were crossing to the eastern flanks of the Windrush from the Kingsbridge Inn, where ramblers might enjoy a well-kept pint of Wadworth 6X (4.3%) in reasonably pleasant surroundings. Smoky and I had stopped to examine a trout, static in the current like a walker leaning into a gale, and I was about to point this out to Sunita when I saw her standing in the middle of the bridge, clutching her chest as a very old lady in a mobility scooter waited, stooped at the handlebars, to resume her crossing.

'It's all right, my chestnut,' I called out. 'See the church? We turn right off the High Street there. Within a matter of minutes it'll be as if there's no one in the world but you and me.'

'And that f***ing mutt. Tell me, Graham. Why have you brought me here?'

'To go for a walk.'

'A walk? How can we go for a walk? You can't move for old biddies in wheelchairs.'

'I beg your pardon, madam.' Cupping Sunita's elbow I eased her aside, and as she passed the old lady raised a hand in thanks – but not before Sunita had twisted free of mine.

'Get your hands off me. How many times do I have to tell you? I have *bruises* there.'

'Please, keep your voice down.'

'Why? Everyone's deaf here. Look at them, shuffling along. It's like a zombie movie. I *hate* this place.'

'Well,' I said, kneeling to stroke Smoky, who had begun to whimper, poor thing. 'That's why I'm suggesting we leave it as soon as possible.'

'I don't *feel* well.'

'Don't you? Well, why don't we sit down for a little while? Over here, on the grass.'

'I'm not sitting on the f***ing grass. It's covered in duck sh*t.'

'On that bench, then. You sit there, I'll pop across to the supermarket for some water.'

'I don't want water. I don't want to sit down. I want to *leave*.'

'Fine. I'll get the car.'

Sunita frowned, and began to pat the belly of her dress. 'What about lunch?'

Ramblers of a less even temperament may find nothing out of the ordinary in the sensation I experienced at that moment. Nevertheless, I hope never to experience it again. Originating somewhere around the upper respiratory tract, it quickly became so overwhelming that the person I understood myself to be seemed momentarily to be displaced by it, pushed to one side where I could watch words emerge from this other, redder rambler's appallingly distorted mouth.

'You're being selfish and unkind, Sunita. And I want it to *stop*.'

A long pause, as Sunita's expression of stern incredulity thawed into a smile.

'*What* did you call me?'

'Selfish,' I mumbled.

'Selfish and . . .?'

'Unkind.'

Sunita seemed to exult in this admission. 'How dare you?' she said. Around us a steady procession of sightseers passed by as heedlessly as a river splits to skirt an island. 'How *dare* you speak to me like that? You little man. You pathetic, pedantic, *boring* little man.'

And with a final exclamation of contempt – *Ha!* – Sunita turned and walked off in the direction of the Kingsbridge Inn, soon disappearing from view behind the blue-and-yellow parasol of an ice-cream cart. It would have been difficult to overstate how profoundly I reproached myself at that moment. My wife – my beautiful Sunita, more precious to me than mobility itself – was unwell, and if her behaviour on the bridge had erred on the side of petulance, she had only been driven to it by the same feelings of claustrophobia that had caused me to succumb to such unforgivable temper. I was so disgusted with myself, in fact, that it was a moment before I realised that Smoky and I should abandon all thought of the planned walk[1] through the Slaughters, and set off in search of Sunita instead.

1. If you're interested: heading north-west up the High Street, turn right at the handsome Georgian church of St Lawrence, then left onto School Hill. Follow the path, marked at intervals by rather inadequate stickers on fenceposts, for one and a half miles, crossing a field, a busy A road, and two more fields before turning right at a cowpat-splattered B road, then right again at a footpath sign, heading for Lower Slaughter along a field-edge where, entomologists will be interested to note, the rare cruet wasp has been known to build its nest: look out for the tell-tale pattern of three black dots on the female's thorax (or one on the male's). Your three-quarter-mile path to the neighbouring village of Upper Slaughter follows the course of the Eye: keep one of yours out for it and you cannot miss your way. Keeping the Norman church of St Peter on your right, walk gently uphill to a junction, cross the main road and continue uphill to a copse whose isolation may strike a melancholy note. Skirt it to its rightmost edge and turn left onto a road that in half a mile keeps on as your path yearns off to the right, along a field-edge that soon coincides with the route of the Macmillan Way, a long-distance walking route named in honour of the famous cancer charity. Worthy as this may be, personally I prefer not to be forcibly reminded of the inevitable during an activity one of whose functions is to relegate it to the back of my mind. At a nest of signs turn left to follow, for one mile, the course of the Windrush back into Bourton-on-the-Water.

Incidentally, since Robin Entwistle's talk on the subject at Sunita's wild-writing seminar, I had taken the liberty of looking more closely into the workers' hiking movement in pre-Nazi Germany. I was, it goes without saying, more than familiar with the parallel development of a 'rambler consciousness' in Britain in the years before the Second World War. Since the late eighteenth century, when Brindley and Watt were presiding over the rapid industrialisation of the economy, working men had escaped the cramped, insanitary conditions of the city to breathe the fresh air of the Peaks, Lakes and Dales. Wainwright himself was born in the grim Lancashire mill town of Blackburn, and in his autobiography *Ex-Fellwanderer* (1987) he recalls his impressions on first visiting the Lake District as a young man of twenty-three:

There were no big factories and tall chimneys and crowded tenements to disfigure a scene of supreme beauty, and there was a profound stillness and tranquillity. There was no sound other than the singing of the larks overhead. No other visitors came.

Later, of course, he headed to the hills less to escape industrial squalor than the company of his shrewish first wife Ruth. Nonetheless, it's a counter-intuitive but unavoidable irony that the origins of the rambling movement lie more in the towns than the country, where, if anything, the right to roam has traditionally been resisted by landed interests. And if that resistance is marginally harder to maintain these days, we have the stubborn courage of our rambling forebears to thank. On the 24th of April 1932, a group of working men led by Benny Rothman – the ramblers' Bolivar, our Che Guevara – perpetrated a mass trespass on Kinder Scout, a moorland plateau in the Peak District, in protest over the failure of the legal system to prevent landowners from denying access to ancient rights of way. A running battle broke out with a cohort of violent gamekeepers, and several of the ramblers received lengthy prison sentences, but the point had been made. Property might be nine-tenths of the law, but one-tenth isn't, and it was to lodge that sacred fraction in the public's mind that these humble men waged their hobnail revolution.

A similar re-engagement with the countryside was underway in Weimar Germany. Historians have tended to see movements like the *Naturfreunde* ('Friends of Nature'), which offered working-class Germans the chance to shake off, if only temporarily, the shackles of industrial capitalism by organising mass hikes in the mountains, and the *Wandervogel* ('Wandering' or 'Rambling Bird'), a youth group dedicated to the cultivation of an independent spirit through early exposure to the wild, as part of the fatally Romantic, reactionary attachment to the land that was to find its logical extreme in fascist nationalism. A barked command and, falling into line, the haphazard clatter of boots becomes the synchronised tramp of marching *Wehrmacht*. But as John A. Williams points out, this is an easy conclusion to draw in retrospect; working backwards from the diseased romanticism of the Third Reich, one can trace the lineaments of a diverse and often genuinely progressive movement, founded on the distinctly un-totalitarian idea that by engaging in nature you might become free.

Those among you fortunate enough to have visited modern-day Germany may have been taken aback by the habit of the native ramblers to take to the excellent footpath network (*Fußwegnetz*) wearing nothing but a pair of stout walking boots. I well remember a trip my late first wife Anne and I took in the Bavarian Alps, when, hiking the high trail between Osterfelderkopf and the Alpspitzbahn, I rounded a blind bend to discover Anne with her fist raised above a man splayed against the rockface in naked surrender, his hairy torso neatly anatomised by the chest, waist and shoulder straps of his thirty-litre ramblesack. Nude rambling, or 'freehiking' as it's increasingly known, has a long and noble history in Germany, and is in some senses inseparable from the history of rambling itself. In 1921 the poet, metalworker and unionist Josef Steubel founded the *Nackte Berge* ('Naked Mountains') movement, in the belief that only by escaping the *lebenslange Freiheitsstrafe* ('life sentence') represented by clothes could the rambler attain *befreiter Geist*, the 'liberated spirit' offered by immersion in nature. Again, celebration of the naked body was later to be hijacked by the Nazi cult of Aryanism, but it's clear both from the photographs and diagrams in his widely distributed pamphlet of 1923, *Warum Nacktkultur Betreiben?* ('Why Practise Naturism?'), that far from privileging any sort of body type over another, Steubel's socialist brand of nudism had room for all shapes and sizes. Anne's growing habit of stripping off on public rights of way had, if anything, been encouraged by her encounter with Matthias on the *Fußweg*, all the more so when her guilt at having threatened to punch him begot a lengthy correspondence in which Matthias, regretful himself for having surprised her, took the opportunity to enlarge upon the benefits of his 'lifestyle choice'.

Chief among them was the 'amazing feeling of freedom and pride in one's body'. From personal experience I can by and large testify to this, with the caveat that pride in one's body can evaporate remarkably quickly when the skyline, so emboldeningly smooth, is notched by the sudden silhouette of a wearer of clothes, or 'textile', as the jargon has it. It has taken nearly eight years, but with Matthias's continued letters of support – and my second wife's ability to see the funny side of it all! – I have come tentatively to accept it as a blessing that Anne and I were naked at the time of her death. In the event of chance encounter we had at the beginning of our 'boots-only' phase been in the habit of carrying clothes in our ramblesacks – an easily wrappable sarong in Anne's case, and in mine, a pair of khaki cargo shorts whose first leg hole was mysteriously transformed by the presence of approaching strangers into a target as habitually missable as a basketball hoop. But in the months leading up to our final holiday together, Anne made several trips to London, taking advantage of Matthias's frequent lay-overs, en route to business meetings in Lagos, to discuss their shared interests face to face, and under his influence began to insist we leave our clothes and indeed our ramblesacks in the boot of the car. Either we're naked or we're not, went her argument, and on arrival in north Devon, it was only after a lengthy debate that I convinced her that the peculiarly hazardous combination of flint, chert and quartz fragments underfoot made hiking boots a regrettable necessity.

I have often wondered what might have happened if it had been raining that afternoon. For Anne the chance of a good drenching was all the more reason to take off her clothes. Nonetheless, the butterfly that so tragically led her astray would not, of course, have been flying,[2] and even if Anne had fallen off the cliff for some other reason, the rain would most likely have won me grudging exemption from nakedness. Which would, in turn, have precluded the need for me to walk the three miles back to the car before alerting the authorities. Clearly, what was subsequently dubbed 'the missing hour', by the largely very likeable Detective Inspector Holyoake of the Devon and Cornwall Police, could only add to the suspicions aroused by the clotheslessness of Anne's remains on Hartland Beach, and had it not been for the providentially perverted snooping[3] of a distant bird fancier, the fact that I was several metres from Anne at the time of her accident might well have been demoted to fiction. Ramblers will understand if I prefer not to dwell too long on the subject, but if my release without charge failed to absolve me of a personal sense of guilt, I have in recent years begun to come to an accommodation with the feeling that I might have done something to save her. If one has to be transformed, in a wingbeat, into a widower and murder suspect, is there not a certain redemptive beauty in that happening naked before the eternal glories of the ocean, with the free play of salt breezes on the skin, encircled by butterflies? I leave it, as so often before, to the rambler to decide.

Sunita was proving frustratingly difficult to track down. Starting at the Mad Hatter on Riverside, Smoky and I made a comprehensive tour of Bourton's exhausting profusion of tea rooms. No better luck at Bits & Bobs, Arty Crafty, Elysian Days or the Bourton Basket. From what I had seen of *Partition* I knew that one of the few periods in her childhood Sunita remembered with much fondness was the six months she spent with her father in Spean Bridge, not far from Fort

---

2. Much like Sunita, butterflies refuse to go out in wet weather. To understand why, imagine trying to keep your arms outstretched if you were wearing a pair of canvas wings and raindrops the size and weight of bowling balls were landing on them.
3. (And powerful 10x50 binoculars.)

William in the Scottish Highlands. Raj had accepted a managerial position at a woollen mill there, and for the brief, happy spell before his redundancy put him and Sunita on the road again, he had been in a relationship with a woman called Carol Marsh, a barmaid at the Spean Bridge Hotel. And so I had always attributed Sunita's otherwise inexplicable indifference towards pubs to the pain she must have felt, when her father's relocation to north London meant the severance of contact with someone she had come tentatively to think of as a mother substitute.

Nonetheless, that grim afternoon in Bourton-on-the-Water, I popped in – just to be sure – at the Kingsbridge, the Duke of Wellington, the self-cancelling Old New Inn, the Coach and Horses, and the dog-friendly Mousetrap on Lansdowne Road, where Smoky lapped at a much-needed bowl of water, I at three and a half pints of Wickwar's moreish Cotswold Way (4.2%), whose upfront maltiness, followed by figgy, pruney notes reminiscent of Moroccan *tagines*, only added to its intense drinkability. Pausing, as we took a right down Mousetrap Lane, to let Smoky lift his leg against a lamp post, I was reminded that I should perhaps have made use of the conveniences before leaving the pub, and a few yards further on stopped to relieve myself in a crop of foxgloves, *Digitalis purpurea*, where the path slewed right at an ugly metal fence. It was the Shropshire-born physician Dr William Withering (1741–99) who first described the remedial effects of digitalin, extracted from foxgloves, on patients suffering from cardiac conditions such as congestive heart failure, or the arrhythmic episodes to which Sunita can fall prey after prolonged stress or exercise. Combined with other plant extracts, or 'simples', foxglove had long been used by folk herbalists to treat what was then known as 'cardiac dropsy'; Withering's achievement was in refracting that ancient wisdom through a more enlightened, scientific set of mind. And if Withering is relatively unknown today, that might in part be

Digitalis purpurea

down to the appetitive habits of his fellow member at the Lunar Society, Erasmus Darwin, who, after Withering had spent nine years identifying the safest concentrations of digitalin for use in cardiac cases, consulted him with regard to one of his own patients and promptly published a paper entitled 'An Account of the successful use of Foxglove in some Dropsies, and in the pulmonary Consumption', as if it were he and not Withering who had done all the work in the first place. It's worth remembering, then, that not only did Withering pinpoint the curative potential of foxglove, he was also the first precisely to record its almost laughable toxicity. Ingested even in tiny quantities the upper leaves of the plant can induce vomiting, dizziness, diarrhoea, visual disturbances, headaches, terrifying hallucinations, convulsions and cardiac malfunction often resulting in sudden death.

Where *was* Sunita? It had started to rain, and feeling a corresponding onset of damp inner weather I began the tramp back towards the village green. My plan had been to hunt Sunita down, prosecute a skilful and unanswerable apology, and waiving the walk drive her to what in any case would have been the highlight of the route, the enchanting village of Upper Slaughter. The amusing place name is in fact derived from the Anglo-Saxon *slothre* ('wet' or 'boggy place'); Slough in Berkshire has the same etymology. As I had been looking forward to explaining to Sunita, the fact that *slothre* should over the centuries have been corrupted into a synonym for wanton carnage is especially ironic given the pact the village seems to have struck with the Grim Reaper. Not only is Upper Slaughter one of Britain's thirty-two 'Thankful Villages', which saw all the men they sent to the Great War return in one piece, but one of the very select band to have lost no men to *either* world war. As if that weren't miraculous enough, no fatalities were recorded when, on the 4th of February 1944, the village was hit by an incendiary bomb of the sort that, just over three years earlier on the night of the *Mondlicht Sonate*, had killed my grandfather and consigned my grandmother Iris to a wheelchair for the rest of her life.

The thankful status of this lovely, if publess, village is commemorated in a modest tablet in St Peter's Church, reached, rather unnervingly, via a sunken path between high banks densely packed with gravestones. We are dead who walk in sin, says the Psalmist; treading these ancient flagstones laid six feet below the surface of the churchyard, it *can* be rather hard to escape the feeling of being buried alive! Nonetheless, with its uniquely happy history, and tranquil air of timeless Englishness, Upper Slaughter is surely the last place to reflect that at the end of the footpath of life stands the trailhead of oblivion, and that even as we walk its sunny middle stretches, the dead lie piled to either side. Reaching Bourton's main car park, off Station Road, Smoky picked up a scent, straining at the leash as his snout swept the asphalt in exploratory arcs. And sure enough, sitting on a plastic chair, by a kiosk dispensing chips in styrofoam trays to a queue of mainly elderly tourists, we found Sunita.

'Give me the keys,' she said, holding out a hand with an infantile straightness of arm.

'I've been so *worried* about you, peaches. Where've you *been*?'

'Having a drink.'

'How annoying. I looked in all the pubs. I must have just missed you.'

'I haven't *been* in the pub.' From behind her plastic chair Sunita produced a bottle of Laurent-Perrier Rosé, from which she took a declarative swig. 'Keys.'

'Are you sure that's a good idea? You *do* seem rather –'

'Look, just give me the keys, will you? I want to get my stuff.'

I gave her the keys. Gathering herself with a touching looseness of movement Sunita rose and lurched off between the cars. My heart was full, but I kept my counsel, judging that if my apology was to carry full weight, it would better be made from the naturally authoritative position of the driver's seat, arm hooked casually around the wheel. Scarcely had we come within range of the Prius's remote locking system, however, when Sunita had unchunked the doors and starting walking towards the driver's side.

'What are you doing, sweetheart?' I called after her, quickening my step. 'You're not planning to drive, are you?'

No response. Sunita had opened the door and was lowering herself into the driver's seat. Smoky began to bark, sensing trouble. I ran to the passenger side and let myself in.

'Sunita,' I pleaded. 'You don't have a licence. You're over the limit. They'll put you in jail.'

'If they catch me.'

'Please, darling. Be reasonable. Let me drive.'

'No,' she said, and inserted the ignition card. Smoky had squeezed behind the passenger seat and was sitting up in the back, panting expectantly. 'I need to get back home.'

'Well, then,' I said. 'Why don't we swap places and we can be on our way?'

'Because you drive like an old woman.'

'That's not strictly fair.' Surreptitiously my hand had crept in to cover the start button. 'I drive *defensively*. In accordance with the prevailing road conditions. But in any case, what's the hurry?'

'I'm going out.'

'With who?'

'A friend.'

'What about Smoky?'

'What about him? You can take him back to Robin's. I'm finished with him, anyway. It's the weekend. I want to have some *fun*.'

'All right, then.' I stared at the raindrops on the windscreen, each holding, upside-down and in miniature, a mesmerically sharp image of the beech tree under which we were parked. 'We could play a game.'

'AAAAAAGH!' Grabbing my walking pole from between my legs Sunita brought the voice recorder to her lips, and failing to notice how tenuously it was now gaffer-taped to the shaft, roughly switched it on. 'I'm going to record this. So you can play it back and *hear* yourself. So you can hear *me*. You know what living with you is like? It's like that thing where you're completely aware but you can't move or speak.'

'Locked-in syndrome,' I said, after a pause. 'Or pseudocoma.'

At this Sunita attempted to wrench my right hand off the start button. Without thinking I took her by both arms and pushed her back into the seat.

'Don't grab me!' she screamed. 'I told you never to grab me again!'

'I'm not grabbing you,' I said, in a tone whose attempt to sound reasonable was not helped by the fact that Smoky was now pawing the back of my seat and barking, loudly and without respite. Sliding my hands down to cup Sunita's elbows, I began to convert the hold into a hug. 'I'm just trying to stop you starting the car.'

'What's this, then?' said Sunita, nodding at my hands. 'If it's not grabbing? Don't try and teach *me* English, little man. Who's the f***ing writer around here? You or me?'

'You, my darling. It's just–'

'Help! *Heeeelp!* I'm being *grabbed!* SOMEBODY CALL THE POLICE!'

By this stage Smoky was barking so loudly that it was a moment before I noticed a muscular gentleman tapping on the passenger window. A small crowd had gathered to watch, and it was with the weary expectation of my trial by mob that I stepped out of the car. Naturally, this gave Smoky the opportunity he had been waiting for, and slinking through the gap between the passenger seat and the door frame he set off at pace across the car park to freedom. And who could blame him? Or Sean, the burly window-tapper, for requiring ten minutes of patient contextualisation before agreeing not to call the police? Ten minutes in which, I imagined, as Sean pumped my hand and assured me I was, as 'a bloke', 'all right', Smoky would have reached the main road and be galloping towards the A40? What if I *had* been trying to assault my wife? The thought of Sunita left to fend for herself by an uncaring public is almost too awful to contemplate. In the event, some hour and a half later, when, having found Smoky sniffing at the hindquarters of a cocker spaniel outside the Kingsbridge Inn, I returned to the car, I was grateful to Sean for the note he'd left behind the windscreen wiper, informing me that Sunita, 'being unfitt to drive', had accepted his offer of a lift to Moreton-in-Marsh station and would see me at home. It was just short of Cheltenham, on my way to the M5, that I realised, were matters to be settled between me and Sunita, something stronger than a simple apology might be called for.

Walk 10: Sunita's Way

A shorter alternative to the route given in Walk 1, this refreshing 'quickie' amid the stirring undulations of the south Malverns was devised especially for the author's wife, but will delight ramblers, swimmers and amateur historians alike, irrespective of marital status! Beginning on the open plain of Castlemorton Common, the walk climbs to 1,109 feet (338m), before descending to a water-filled quarry ramblers are reminded has been the site of more than one fatal accident. Most visitors to the countryside will be aware of the dangers posed by loose rocks, freak weather conditions, poisonous plants, anaphylactic shock brought on by bee, wasp and hornet stings, stampeding cows and stray ordnance from the huntsman's rifle. What is often underestimated, however, is the severe risk of death represented by objects submerged in fresh water, and ramblers who share the author's Labrador-ish fondness for a 'dip' should not forget to exercise that noble breed's instinctive alertness entering the lake, no matter how placid its surface may seem to the inexperienced eye.

To make up for our argument in Bourton I decided to organise something a little out of the ordinary. Ramblers will remember the special place the Malverns hold in our hearts; it struck me that were I to depart from our usual route and devise a walk that might truly be

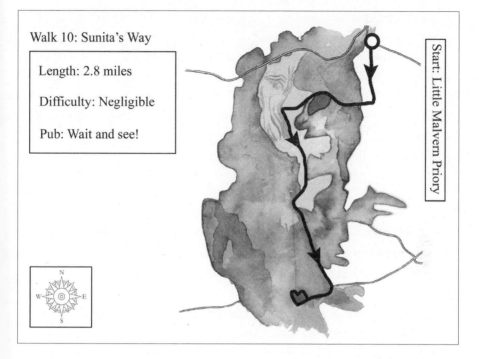

Walk 10: Sunita's Way

Length: 2.8 miles

Difficulty: Negligible

Pub: Wait and see!

Start: Little Malvern Priory

called Sunita's, it might go some way to atoning for the silly, vindictive behaviour with which I had undoubtedly caused her to seek solace in drink in the first place.

I chose a Saturday morning in late September to inaugurate the walk. Summer seemed neither to have started nor ended that year; June brought lightning and ripe blackberries, July sleet, August floods, and the first ten days of September a spell of such defeating heat that swifts were still circling the rooftops, screaming as if driven insane by the changes to their migratory patterns. Through the side passage of their barn conversion Peter Agnew's wife Jasmine could occasionally be seen washing her car in a frilly orange bikini. September the 29th, however, dawned as comfortably crisp as fresh bedlinen: reassuringly autumnal, and perfect walking weather.

We parked outside the entrance to Little Malvern Priory, a fine Romanesque church that once served the adjacent Benedictine monastery, dissolved by Henry VIII in 1534. Sunita had seemed particularly content in the weeks since our Bourton walk; having admitted how reckless it had been even to consider contravening the terms of her driving ban, she had turned her mind to serious things, spending long hours preparing the latest chapters of *Partition* to show to Guy Gosling – who, incidentally, I was delighted to hear had been accepted onto the Antarctic Artists' and Writers' Program for the coming austral summer. It had helped, of course, that to offset all her hard work Sunita had begun to make a greater investment in her social life – beginning, as it happens, that Sunday night she returned from Bourton, when she had gone out for a drink and not come back till lunchtime the following Tuesday. I would be lying if I claimed not to have been worried, but after by far our worst squabble since the mix-up over the labrys door-stop, I recognised the wisdom in our spending a short time apart. In the event, Sunita was in such subdued mood on her return that it would have been insensitive to press her on where exactly she had been.

'Well,' I said, toeing the as-yet-unrepaired crack in the Prius's front-bumper assembly. 'Here we are in Little Malvern.'

Sunita nodded softly, but made no other response.

'Would you like to know where we're going?'

Sunita shrugged. Ramblers will find the map I handed her reproduced above – sadly without the retaining red ribbon!

'Do you see what it is?' I said, after Sunita had stared at it a while.

'No.'

'It's an S.'

'Ah.'

'For Sunita. And sorry.'

'"Pub: Wait and see". You mean it's a surprise? Where you're planning to take me for a drink?'

I raised a mysterious eyebrow. 'Maybe.'

'Is it the Nags Head?'

'Mn?'

'It's the Nags Head, isn't it?'

'Where we first fell in love, my undupable darling!'

'What's this at the bottom?'

'A heart, see? Around the lake.'

'It's a bit jagged.'

'Yes, apologies for that. I could have made it smoother. But that would have meant straying from the public footpath.'

'And we wouldn't want to do that, would we?'

Something in Sunita's manner dissuaded me from answering. Consulting the map she set off in a westerly direction, turning left after seventy yards over a stile by a spreading oak tree that cast her hair in dappled shadow. I wavered for a moment before deciding to let her walk on alone. What, I wondered, was the matter now? That said, I knew from my own (far less ambitious) efforts how temperamental one could become during prolonged periods of creative endeavour. As Henry David Thoreau observes in his indispensable essay 'Walking' (1861), labouring indoors 'may produce a softness and smoothness, not to say thinness of skin, accompanied by an increased sensibility to certain impressions'. A 'good yomp', I reflected, was probably just what my industrious sweetheart needed. Turning right at a footpath sign, a few yards short of a farm it might have amused Sunita to know shares my surname, I began the steep, deeply shaded ascent of Tinker's Hill, feeling a heady swell of pride, as I gazed up at the rhythmical contractions of Sunita's heart-shaped hindquarters, that we were following the route of a walk named in her honour: Sunita's Way.

The path bends right as it approaches the tree-pipit haven of British Camp Reservoir, and as I paused to admire a particularly handsome specimen of the poisonous Cup and Saucer mushroom (*Agaricus poculum*), Sunita slipped momentarily from view. I found her sitting on a bench overlooking the reservoir, the wind fanning her hair into a blaze of black flame.

'We need to talk,' she said, as I sat down beside her.

'What about?'

'I haven't been faithful to you, Graham.'

'Well,' I said, after a pause. 'That's not necessarily a bad thing.'

Cup and Saucer mushroom

'J*sus Chr*st.' Sunita brought her fists down on the brink of her knees. 'Just for once. Can you *please* fail to see the bright side? It *is* a bad thing.'

Another pause. A very long one, in fact, in which I found myself examining the mountainous peaks and passes of my bitten middle fingernail. 'Who is it?'

'Are you really telling me you don't know?'

'No, no, of course not.' A squint into the distance. David? Peter? Seb? Robin? *Steve?* 'Yes, I am, actually.'

Sunita stood. 'This is pointless. I should go.'

'No, don't.' I rose, and held her elbow, and for once she didn't flinch. 'Don't leave.'

'This isn't making it any easier, Graham.'

'Please.'

Sunita sighed, and sat down again.

'You see,' I said, taking her hand, 'it *isn't* necessarily a bad thing. Plenty of marriages have been *saved* by infidelity. You've been under an immense amount of stress. It's no wonder you've sought an outlet in a "fling". So this is what I'm trying to say: *enjoy* yourself. *Be* with him. And then in six months' time, or even nine, you can come back and we'll start again. We've got the rest of our lives to get this right.'

Shaking her head, Sunita handed me the map. 'I don't love you, Graham.'

'But you see that doesn't *matter.*'

'I never did, and I never will. I'm sorry. I've been awful to you. And if I don't go now I'll just carry on being awful. So you see? It's over. For ever. It has to be.'

And she got to her feet and walked off.

I had often hoped, when Sunita and I had left this vale of tears, that (subject to planning regulations) a plaque might be affixed to one of these benches, 'To the memory of Graham Underhill and Sunita Bhat-tacharya, who loved these hills'. And sitting there, that blustery morning, clutching Sunita's crumpled map as I looked out over the concentrically ridged remnants of British Camp, I felt I might go one better: 'To the memory of Graham Underhill, who died on this bench'.

Sunita had walked off in the direction of the Gullet. Without much idea of what I might say, or do, when or if I found her, I smoothed out the map and headed south. Taking the clear path nannyishly marked 'NO PATH' on the circular stone indicator, I descended through tall grass towards the Gullet car park. Above me, a pair of crows moved in leisurely figures of eight, crossing and re-crossing each other's flight paths as if trying, but never quite managing, to reach an agreement. Aside from a burnt-out camper van the car park was empty but for one vehicle: a white Audi TT whose ownership was confirmed in the half-step it took the number plate to sharpen into legibility.

I turned right onto the tarmac path that leads to the quarry. The sky had turned inky, and in a moment I felt the first cold harbinger of heavy rain on my face. All was quiet, save for the osteopathic crack of oaks awakened by the wind, until the sharp snap of a twig was followed by a rustling of leaves, and a clucking noise that might have been a frightened pheasant, or a stifled human laugh. I walked on, hood up, and as the rain gathered force I passed another rambler walking in the opposite direction, hoisting the hood of almost exactly the same tri-climate jacket as mine, head down and huddled against the wind.

By the time I reached the Gullet the rain was coming down hard, releasing a sweet, musty smell from the foliage underfoot, and springing off the lake in small explosions that turned its surface white. From somewhere in the woods a crow broke out in churlish croaks. Briefly consulting the map, I strained to make out the rocky and indeed scarcely existent path that runs above the western edge of the lake. My plan had been that Sunita and I trace one half each of the heart shape indicated on the map, meeting on the silty, rock-strewn beach that forms the cleavage between its upper curves. Sunita would have taken the easy path around the lake's eastern extremity, while I, partly I admit to impress her, would have edged round the narrow, crumbling, vertiginous shelf I hope ramblers will not consider it too pompous of me to say I attempted *only having successfully done so literally dozens of times since the age of thirteen*. Schist, while an attractive and versatile form of metamorphic rock, exhibits, like slate, a layered or 'foliated' structure, with the result that it flakes off into slivers or jagged slabs under even the lightest pressure from a hiking boot. Impossible as it may be to verify, ramblers eager to 'bag' all fifteen walks in this book can, come to think of it, consider themselves instantly disqualified should they be so foolish as to scale this deceptively hazardous rockface.

No sign, touch wood, that Sunita had attempted it. I walked round to the clearing above the eastern edge of the lake. On a low wall, beside an information board warning of the dangers of swimming, diving or climbing in or near the lake, a heron stood in frozen profile. At the foot of the wall what might previously have been an orderly pile of large, jagged rocks lay scattered, as if someone had been sorting through them. In the mud, as I approached the information board, I found a confusion of bootprints, some not inconsistent with the pull-on platform boots Sunita had been wearing that day, together with a similar number of larger, chunkily treaded tracks rendered less legible by the mess of Gel-Trek Vindicator prints with which I had rather injudiciously contaminated the scene. On closer inspection, however, something caught my eye, and getting to my hands and knees I was able to verify that amid the footprints there was indeed a different sort of impression, losing definition in the rain but still clearly discernible: a pair of single tracks left by a mountain bike, or conceivably a scooter, between them leading to and away from the Gullet in the direction of the car park.

Wiping the mud off my hands I retrieved my walking pole, in order to record a summary of the evidence thus far gathered, only to find my voice recorder missing. *Idiot.* £92-worth of kit! How long had it been working loose? Weeks! I might as well have thrown it in the lake. It goes without saying, like all my possessions over a certain value the recorder was labelled with a laminated sticker bearing my email address, but given its stylish looks, ample 512-megabyte memory and class-leading TruBass audio-enhancement technology, I had to be realistic about the likelihood of anyone returning an Olympus

WS-311M. Cursing myself as I extracted my phone, I was about to take a photo of the bicycle/scooter tracks when from somewhere to my right I heard a splash, and, turning, saw a head of glossy black hair swimming towards me. It was a dog: a black Labrador, not unlike Smoky, chin held high to clear the water, making good progress towards a stick doubtless thrown by the figure standing on the oppos-ite shore in a hooded green parka. It might, in fact, have *been* Smoky, but at this distance, in the rain, the only way to tell was to hail its hooded owner.

'Lovely day for it!' I bellowed, raising a hand, but the figure in the parka made no response. Like as not a rainhood of such cowl-like depth would have a severely limiting effect on one's peripheral vision, and although its wearer was not much more than fifty yards away, it would only have required a millimetric turn of the head to conceal me in fake fur. Either way, my observer, whoever it was – Robin? Karen? Someone else entirely? – certainly cut a fairly unnerving figure, obscure behind the empty frame of his (or her) rainhood, and I can't say I regretted it much when the dog, having retrieved the stick, swam back to shore, shook itself off in a momentary cocoon of spray and decamped with its owner in the direction of Eastnor.

I retraced my steps towards the car park. Ramblers whose lives have ever abruptly collapsed about them may be familiar with the unexpected, if not rather embarrassing, feeling of elation that came over me at this point, although in my case it may have had less to do with the efforts of my psyche to protect itself from the full horror of the situation than the growing suspicion that Sunita had not exactly left me, but been *taken away* – conceivably against her will. To have got the police involved at this stage would, clearly, have been an absurd overreaction, particularly given the precedent for false alarm we'd established in the wake of our silly squabble back in May. A degree of urgency was, however, appropriate to my own investiga-tions, and arriving back at the car park to find the Audi gone, I helped myself to a Glacier Fruit, and launched with renewed vigour into the two-and-a-half-mile hike back over British Camp to Little Malvern.

In less than fifty minutes I was in the Prius and on my way to

Photography by David. Passing the field maples under which I had first asked Sunita to marry me – and whose leaves, I noted, remained an unseasonal green, when they should by now have turned yellow – I parked in North Malvern Road and trained my binoculars at the glass frontage of David's premises. A 'CLOSED' sign hung at a slapdash angle from its rubber sucker. From personal experience I knew that David liked to take a 'top-button-undone' approach to his wedding photography, and shifting my focus I sat contemplating the vast portrait in the window, in which the groom, clearly a bit of a card, was captured blowing bubbles at his bride, shielding herself with a bare arm from what might otherwise have been a nasty burst of detergent in the eye. Fifteen minutes later I was peering through the kitchen window of David and Karen's cottage in Eastnor. A sign Blu-tacked to its lower pane read, 'NO TO THE LEDBURY RING ROAD'. The kitchen was dark, but on the marble countertop I could just make out a tea plate, scattered with crumbs, next to an object that looked suspiciously like a half-eaten packet of the Entirely Natural Food Company's Gluten-Free Sticky Ginger Cake – Sunita's favourite.

Finding the door locked (and, judging by the pain in my shoulder, securely bolted) I set off towards my final port of call, the mock-Regency villa David and Karen had the misfortune of sharing in the south-western suburbs of Ledbury. The rain had eased off to a dispiriting drizzle – or 'mizzle' as they call it hereabouts – and queuing at the lights where the road in from Malvern meets the Homend, I listened to the metronomic *squee-shump* of the wipers, musing as I did so how much quicker this journey would be once the ring road was built.

Outside the house a yellow Mini Cooper was parked next to a potted box tree, clipped into a perfect sphere and tethered to the tarmac by a chain. The Audi was nowhere to be seen. In my haste to retrieve my binoculars from the glove compartment, I had stupidly neglected to switch off the engine, and as I focused on the raindrops on the Redferns' living-room window, I was dismayed to see the net curtains quiver then part to admit Karen, no doubt alerted by the glare from my headlamps.[1] I shrank in my seat. Her presence at home certainly seemed to lessen the possibility that it had been Karen who had observed me at the Gullet. Which still begged the question: where was David? At this point a car swung out, headlights engaged, from a parking space directly in front of the house, drawing Karen's attention to the extent that I soon felt safe to retrain my binoculars on the window. Karen had scarcely moved a muscle, but her gaze had turned inward, and if I knew anything about women, and their touching inability to conceal their feelings, I'd say the poor, deluded wretch had spent the morning in tears.

On my way home to consider my next steps I made a short detour to Nettlebed Farm. It had been nearly two months since Steve Reed and I had spoken, and whatever had happened in the interim ramblers will understand if I harboured some resentment for the shoddy way he had abused both my, and more particularly Sunita's, hospitality. As the Prius thumped and jounced over the potholes, two visions of the rural economy juddered into view. To my right, Jason's jurisdiction: the neat, knapped-flint farmhouse, the scrubbed yard, the L-block of picturesque outbuildings backing onto a field populated, but by no means crowded, with plump pink pigs wallowing drowsily beside their miniature Nissen huts. Ahead, at the far end of the farm track, the Steve zone, a half-acre of wasteland strewn with broken lorry parts and dominated – inasmuch as so lawless a landscape could be – by a sag-roofed, listing Portakabin, grey-green with algal matter, and Steve's caravan, propped on bricks and resplendent in three shades of biscuit.

Rattling over the cattle-grid at the threshold of the zone, I slowed the Prius to a halt. Parked outside Steve's caravan was a vintage Mercedes roadster I thought I recognised. Around its wheels an assortment of chickens were pecking at the scrub, marking the silence with their curled squawks of contentment. Other than that, there

1. Automatically activated by the poor lighting conditions. A safety feature for which I would, in almost any other circumstance imaginable, have felt nothing but gratitude.

was no sign of life, at least until the door of the caravan burst open and Steve, hair loosed from its habitual pigtail, naked but for a pair of bright-yellow Y-fronts, ran towards me aiming a pump-action shotgun through the windscreen at my head.

'Don't shoot!' I exclaimed, putting my hands up as far as the Prius's rather limited head-room would allow. My chances of survival weren't helped by the fact that Steve a) had an enormous joint dangling from his lips, and b) was peering over the top of his half-moon glasses with an expression of discouragingly suspended rationality. 'It's Graham!'

Steve lowered the gun. 'F**k you playing at?'

'Sorry, Steve,' I said, opening the car door, and, still with my hands up, climbing out. 'I just wanted a word.'

'Stupid f***ing c**t gonna get yourself killed.'

'I didn't realise you had such stringent security measures in place.'

'Can't be too careful,' said Steve, turning and trudging back towards the caravan. 'Not with the way things are.'

'I was just wondering if you'd seen Sunita.'

'No,' said Steve, without turning round. Then, a little more softly, 'F**k off, then.'

'You're not going to let me in?'

'No.'

'It's raining, Steve. Please. Just for a second.'

'I said no.' By now Steve had stepped back inside the caravan. 'It's not convenient.'

And he shut the door behind him. Moments later, to a cudgelling thrust of thrash metal, the caravan began to rock on its rusting suspension, gently at first and then with increasing violence, and in a shimmer of recognition I recalled the Neglected Housewife on FindLoveTonite, dancing for the camera in the frilly orange bikini I had seen Jasmine Agnew wearing earlier that summer. She had, of course, been training her hose at the very gold Mercedes now parked outside Steve's caravan. Side-stepping an oblivious chicken, I turned and got back in the car.

At some point during the drive back to Foxglove Cottage the

stimulation of mind afforded by the events of the previous two hours gave way to a simpler, starker, if perhaps unnecessarily pessimistic hypothesis: that my Sunita had gone, for ever. Any hope of a quiet moment in the privacy of my own kitchen was quickly dashed, however, by the sight of Sunita's friend Daisy, sitting on the doorstep examining her fingernails under the shelter of a flowery umbrella.

'Oh, *Graham.*'

'What is it?'

'*Sunita.*'

'What about Sunita, Daisy?'

'Where *is* she?'

A pause. 'I'm afraid I don't know.'

With a gasp Daisy dissolved into tears. Unlocking the front door I ushered her through to the kitchen and offered her tea.

'That's very sweet of you,' she said, scrabbling in her handbag for a packet of tissues. 'But have you got anything stronger?'

'Scotch?'

'Oh, *God*, no. I was joking. Tea's fine. But don't let *me* stop you.'

I smiled stiffly, and turned to fill the kettle. 'I appreciate your concern, Daisy. But may I ask how you know that Sunita is missing? If indeed she is?'

'We were meant to meet for lunch. And she didn't turn up!'

'With respect. It's not exactly conclusive evidence, is it?'

'Well,' said Daisy, lustily blowing her nose. 'Where *is* she then?'

I made no response.

'You see? It's just not *like* her. Not once in over six months has she failed to turn up. Which I suppose wouldn't matter so much if we weren't all so *worried* about her.'

'Worried? What possible reason could you have to be worried about Sunita?'

'Oh, you know. I feel awkward saying it. Your marriage. All the *trouble* you've been having.'

'Trouble? We haven't been having any trouble. And what do you mean, "we"? Who is "we"?'

'We is we. I mean, us is. Her friends.'

'I fail to see what this has to do with *anyone* but me and Sunita.'

'Please don't shout at me, Graham. I'm under a *lot* of stress at the moment. I just want to know that my lovely friend is safe and well.'

'Of *course* she's safe and well,' I said, adjusting my tone as I served Daisy her tea and joined her at the table. 'She'll be back soon enough. You mark my words.'

'You had a fight, didn't you?' said Daisy, clutching at her mug with both hands.

'An adult exchange.'

'Oh, God!'

'She'll have gone somewhere to think things over. She's done it before. I'm embarrassed to admit it, but she's disappeared for days on end on more than one occasion. You know what she's like. Passionate. Impetuous, even. But also very caring. And a caring person won't just have upped sticks and abandoned the people she loves, now, will she?'

Through her tears Daisy allowed herself a wet chortle of acquiescence. 'Probably not,' she said. 'So you don't think we should call the police?'

'Absolutely not.'

'Just to be sure?'

'No. We must show Sunita the courtesy of letting her come back in her own time. Then if we've heard nothing in the next three, four, let's say five or six days, we'll review our options. All right?'

'All right.' Daisy sniffed. 'There was one thing, now I come to think of it.'

'What was that?'

'It's probably nothing. But she had recently been saying she wanted to travel more. For her book. You know, visit places and people that were meaningful for her? If that makes sense? Return to her old haunts?'

'Thank you, Daisy. I'll bear that in mind.'

Having refused a slice of Sticky Ginger Cake – and left all but the most birdlike sip of tea – Daisy stood, and, to my considerable relief, made her excuses. She had stepped outside and erected her umbrella when something else occurred to her.

'She was your second wife, wasn't she?'

'Is. My second wife. Yes.'

'And the first unfortunately passed away.'

'Yes. There was an accident.'

'Down in Devon.'

'That's right.'

'You poor, poor man.'

I nodded gravely, and Daisy walked off, raising her free hand in a solemnly faceless farewell. I closed the door, and succumbing, briefly, to a riptide of grief concerned ramblers will be reassured to hear a large brandy helped temporarily to hold back, I went upstairs to the study to consult my maps.

Walk 11: The White Peak

'It is not,' wrote Henry David Thoreau, 'indifferent to us which way we walk. There is a right way; but we are very liable from heedlessness and stupidity to take the wrong one.' Setting out from his home in Concord, Massachusetts, Thoreau would by natural inclination strike to the southwest; for me the 'right' way habitually lies to the north or the south. Whatever your instincts, this challenging tramp in the Scottish Highlands provides both nourishing views and a splendid sense of isolation. However, the risk of sudden, blinding snowstorms, together with the man-made perils associated with the deer-stalking season, mean that this walk more than any yet described in this book should only be tackled by fit, well-equipped ramblers temperamentally suited to withstanding disaster.

Brainwave! The Highlands! As I say, in *Partition* Sunita had written with great affection of her father's ex-girlfriend Carol Marsh, and if, as Daisy had suggested, my nostalgic beloved had succumbed to the urge to revisit her old stamping grounds, Spean Bridge – 452 miles

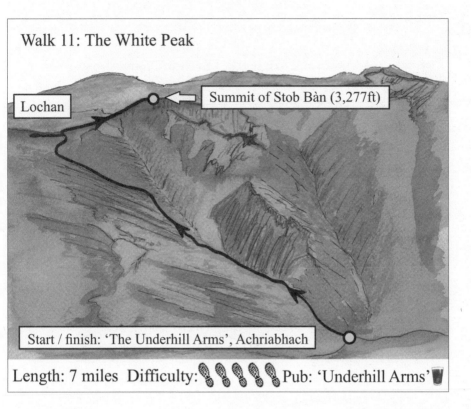

Walk 11: The White Peak

Lochan

Summit of Stob Bàn (3,277ft)

Start / finish: 'The Underhill Arms', Achriabhach

Length: 7 miles Difficulty: Pub: 'Underhill Arms'

from Ledbury according to Google Maps – would surely be high on the list. Three o'clock now. If I stepped on it I could be at the bar of the Spean Bridge Hotel in time for last orders. Stashing a change of underwear in my ramblesack, I inserted my Bluetooth and headed for the motorway. One thing, however, that ramblers may be surprised to learn is that I was born with exceptionally narrow ear canals, and somewhere between Stoke-on-Trent and Liverpool, the headset, tenuously secured by its bendable earhook, worked its way loose and fell into the maddeningly narrow gap between the driver's seat and the front central armrest. Sure enough, a few miles north of Paisley my phone began to ring. Did I answer the call, hand-held, and risk incurring a fixed penalty, let alone constitute a hazard both to myself and other motorists? Or let the call go to voicemail, and risk that the 'Unknown Caller' might neither leave a number, nor ever call again?

Fortunately – if illegally – at this point the large-panel van that had been preventing my access to the hard shoulder overtook me in the slow lane, and I was able to bring the vehicle to a controlled stop. *Unfor-tunately, however, the 'Unknown Caller' turned out not to be Sunita, but my old friend Keith Frampton from the *Ledbury Evening Star.*

'Lord Underhill.'

Keith I knew from a piece he wrote in the *Star* back in 2004, cover-ing my (ultimately vain) attempts to force a public inquiry into the unacceptable state of the towpath between Dymock and Hazle Mill on the Herefordshire and Gloucestershire Canal – whose course, incidentally, was originally laid out by a pupil of James Brindley's called Robert Whitworth. Quite apart from knowing his ales – argu-ably too well! – Keith was a natural newshound, with an infallible nose for a story, and ramblers will detect in our playful habit of ennobling each other in conversation the high yet easygoing regard in which we'd always held each other – apart, of course, from when it was Keith's round at the bar!

'Squire Frampton. How's the newspaper business?'

'Don't ask. What's this about your mate Steve Reed?'

'I don't know. What is it?'

'Where *are* you, by the way? Brands Hatch?'

'Just on my way to London. Council business, for my sins. What's Reedy done now?'

'He's been arrested on suspicion of attempted murder.'

'What? Of whom?'

'Peter Agnew. Shot him in the leg. Doctors say he may not walk again.'

Ahead, in the blackness, ascending and descending files of car lights described a rise in the road, and I began to imagine the motorway network given over to vast hordes of ramblers, organised into lanes according to walking pace, until the wake of a passing lorry buffeted me back to the matter in hand.

'That's awful.'

'Apparently,' said Keith, 'Reed was knocking off Agnew's wife. Know anything about that?'

'No.'

'Really? That's not what I heard.'

'What did you hear?'

'I heard that Agnew was head over heels in love with your missus. Which is why *his* missus ran off with Steve Reed.'

'Who told you that?'

'Sorry, your Lordship. It was off the record.'

I glanced at the clock. 20.42. Time to be on my way. 'Whether or not Peter Agnew had feelings for Sunita is something you'll have to ask him about.'

'I intend to.'

Promising to give Keith a call if anything occurred to me, I switched off my phone and slipped into the slow lane. It was gone ten to eleven by the time I reached the car park of the Spean Bridge Hotel. The Commando Bar, named in honour of the élite reconnaissance unit trained in the area during the Second World War, serves a substantial range of bar meals including Steak Sizzlers, as well as refreshing Scottish ales like Belhaven 80 Shilling (3.9%). Pulling up a stool, I ordered a pint, and with some perseverance managed to engage the barman in conversation. He was roughly my age, but the crow's feet at the corners of his mouth bespoke an older man's long practice at intransigence.

'Carol what?'

'Marsh, I think. Maybe Marshall.'

'Don't know her.'

'You're quite sure? She would have worked here in the late '80s.'

'I said I don't know her. All right?'

'I know Carol.' This from a portly, middle-aged man sitting at the far end of the bar.

'You don't happen to know if she still lives here, do you?'

'No, she doesnae live here. Moved to Inver-roy about fourteen, fifteen years back.'

'And how far is Inverroy?'

'About two miles that way.' The man jabbed

A Steak Sizzler

his thumb in what I deduced was an easterly direction. 'But I would-nae bother going there.'

'Oh. And why's that?'

'She's been deid for ten years. Drowned herself in Loch Linnhe.'

My visit to the area had, as it happened, coincided with the arrival of several coachloads of Japanese 'Munro-baggers', with the consequence that both the Spean Bridge, and the handful of other hotels and B&Bs in the village, were fully booked for the weekend. My amiable source of information was, however, fairly sure that for a small fee his sister Hazel could put me up, and if I gave him my name he could call and tell her who to expect. Politely declining the offer, I returned to the car, reasoning that while I was in the vicinity I might as well bag a Munro or two of my own. Heading back south, I turned inland at Fort William, and crossing the Water of Nevis arrived just after midnight below the castellated outline of the Polldubh Crags, deep black against a clear night sky lightened by the contrast. Sir Hugh Munro (1856–1919), who lends his name to mountains in Scotland over 3,000 feet, often chose during the gruelling task of measuring all 283[1] to climb them in the dark, less from a taste for the 'magical otherworldliness' Robert Macfarlane imputes to night walking, than from a measure of respect for the lairds, who, in the days before Kinder Scout, would have considered it well within their rights to blow his brains out for tramping across their mountains in broad daylight. These days, of course, the hills are open for the spiritual edification of all, and it's to dodge his fellow man, not the gamekeeper's bullets, that *this* Munro-bagger ever takes to the mountains

---

1. A Munro is defined as a *separate* mountain whose *autonomous* height exceeds 3,000 feet (914.4m). Munro himself argued for the inclusion of all summits in Scotland over 3,000 feet, whether or not they were deemed separate from other, higher peaks; this number runs to 538. Munro lost out, and the 255 lesser peaks are now referred to as 'Munro tops'. There are those who have accused Munro of monumental pedantry; I beg to differ. Having myself 'bagged' 45 Munros, I can well imagine getting to 283 and feeling an intense sadness, assuageable only by the prospect of bagging another, then another, and another, until my legs gave out, or there were no mountains left to climb.

at night! Nonetheless, walking in darkness has its own obvious dangers, and it was to steel myself for the ascent ahead that I reached onto the back seat, unzipped the two-compartment picnic cooler and 'opened the Underhill Arms': a can of (surprisingly complex) Tennent's Super (9.0%), enjoyed from the comfort of the driver's seat.

Suitably refreshed, I tucked a couple of emergency cans between my sleeping and bivouac bags, shrugged into my ramblesack and headed south, across the road bridge east of Achriabhach, feeling the fury of the waterfall that thundered underneath in a drumming on the soles of my boots. Reaching a wooden sign on my left, I switched on the 3-LED headlamp I had strapped to my brow, and read the words

MAMORE GRAZINGS
PLEASE
KEEP DOGS ON LEAD

Ever since I was a boy I had kept dogs, my most recent a beautiful blue-belton English setter called John Stuart[2] whose athleticism, high intelligence and deep-bred flair for pointing upland game birds made him the ideal companion on hilly terrain. To watch him run up Perseverance Hill, long coat cascading like water on rocks, was to marvel at an effortless grace in movement we hobbled, fallen walkers can only mourn in ourselves. At the summit, leaping up to meet my outstretched arms, he would often knock me reeling with the full force of his affectionate temperament. It was only unfortunate that Sunita was allergic to dogs, particularly hairy breeds like English setters, and when in his seventh year John Stuart developed mild

---

2. After John Stuart Mill (1806–73), author of *On Liberty*, and supporter of the Commons Preservation Society, which in its tireless if largely thwarted efforts to open up the countryside to all can be thought of as a precursor to the Ramblers' Association. Incidentally, 'blue-belton' setters are white ticked with black, with Dalmatian-ish black patches on the face.

arthritis in his hips, the decision was taken to put him down, rather than meet the expense of surgical intervention, or alleviate the symptoms by controlling his weight.

I switched off my headlamp and climbed the stile to the right of the sign. Ahead, the preliminary summit of Sron Sgùrr a' Mhàim, darkly breasting the sky, tallied with its name – 'The Spur of the Peak of the Round Steep Hill' – in the vague-verging-on-pointlessly-non-specifying way that for centuries has irritated ramblers attempting to navigate Welsh and Scottish mountain ranges.[3] My route lay between Sron Sgùrr a' Mhàim and the smaller hill[4] to its right, Sron Dearg ('The Red Spur' – just plain wrong), and followed the course of a burn, Allt Coire a' Mhusgain, which in capturing some of the landscape's sense of foreboding – Coire a' Mhusgain means 'Rotting Corrie' – at least sticks in the mind better than 'The Stream Near Some Trees' or 'The Burn of the Pass Between Two Moderately Large Hills'. Within a mile or so, when, opposite a waterfall, the path took a sharp left uphill, my eyes had begun to adjust to the darkness, and I was able without recourse to my headlamp to navigate by the light of the moon. Above and to the right, the dark shape of my destination loomed momentarily into view, before a cloud seemingly lit from within, like a paper lantern, obscured the double summit in drifting wisps; pausing for breath on a boulder I realised I had for one entranced moment succeeded in excluding from my mind what I'd done to Sunita.

I reached the summit in just over four hours. As a younger man I might have done it in three and a half, but by the time I'd turned right

3. Compare the memorable specificity, the sheer clear-sighted *appropriateness*, of the names given to England's finest mountains: Haystacks, Great Gable, and Skiddaw, from the ancient Cumbric *sgwiðow*, 'shoulders' – how unmistakably shoulder-like that mountain is!
4. [Highland hills between 2,500 and 3,000 feet are called 'Corbetts'. Those between 2,000 and 2,499 feet are, funnily enough, known as 'Grahams'. To a Scot the author's name would thus translate as 'a small hill under another one'. It's a sign of Underhill's self-estrangement at this point that he fails to pick up on such an intriguing coincidence. N.S.]

onto the ridge, between Sgùrr an Iubhair ('Peak of the Yew'[5]) and the false summit of Stob Bàn to the west, I felt a fatigue beyond the pleasant ache of exertion, compounded by the nagging back injury I'd sustained responding to Sunita's cry for help on the summit of Stiperstones. 'Stob Bàn' means 'White Peak': a fat lot of use in wintry conditions, when it's not as if all the neighbouring peaks won't be exactly the same colour, and highly misleading – even dangerously so – on nights like these, when close inspection with the aid of my headlamp revealed the scree on its uppermost flanks to encompass a pick-and-mix palette of sherbet yellows and greens. Still, it's a fine mountain, satisfyingly unrelenting in its ascent, yet bonnier in its varied rock formations and unsuspected burns than Ben Nevis, clearly visible to the north, up whose twelve-lane screeway ramblers must slog to experience the overrated thrill of briefly being the highest person in Britain. To get to the top is, of course, a natural human urge, and I count it the height of pretentiousness when certain of our number – naming no names, Geoff B.! – make a show of turning back five minutes shy of a thousand-metre climb, on the grounds that 'summits are banal'.[6] But it must equally be allowed that a sense of loss attends all high points we take the trouble to attain, and cracking a lager on the cairn at the flat-topped summit of Stob Bàn (3,277 ft / 999m), I thought of Sir Hugh Munro, driven on from peak to peak, top to top, until in his late forties arthritis put paid to his climbing career, five short of completing all 538 summits on the list he himself had compiled.

I switched on my phone to confirm the time: ten past four. To the east, beyond the barely discernible crests and corries of the Mamores,

---

5. Again: no yew.
6. Geoff's occasionally challenging personality is one of the reasons I have so far resisted his suggestion we film my back catalogue of pub walks – i.e. me walking them, and discussing various points of interest as I go – and upload the footage to a dedicated (and potentially paid-content) rambling website. Despite my continual demurrals, selective deafnesses, etc., etc., Geoff has rather presumptuously gone ahead and registered a domain name, underhillwalks.co.uk, on my behalf. Some people never listen!

the ten-mile ridge of which Stob Bàn forms part, the lid of night had lifted to admit a chink of cobalt morning touched with ochre. It was cold, but not, I judged, life-threateningly so, and I had begun to cast about for somewhere to sleep when my phone, finding a signal, alerted me, and an affronted-looking deer grazing a hundred yards below the summit, to the presence of two voicemails.

The first was from Alan.

'Graham?' it said. 'Graham?'

Then a good ten seconds of laboured breathing brought to a stop, protractedly, by Alan's attempts to replace the receiver. Legless as Alan would doubtless have been, the message having been left at a quarter past one on a Saturday night, it was unusually confused of him not to have realised it was my voicemail he had been talking to, and despite the ungodliness of the hour I thought it prudent to call him back. I was some way into leaving a message on *his* voicemail when a bleeping in my earpiece announced an incoming call – from Alan.

'Sorry,' he murmured, before I'd so much as said hello. 'I'm so sorry.'

'What for?'

'I'm so very, very *sorry*.'

'What are you talking about, Alan?'

'You're a good friend, Graham. Such a *nice*, f***ing . . . agh. Y'know?'

'Alan, it's good to hear from you. But shall we speak in the morning?'

Alan's breath blustered in my ear. 'You hear about Steve?'

'Yes. Have you seen him?'

''Safternoon. You know he could get life?'

'Well,' I said. 'He did try to murder somebody.'

'B****cks he did. It was self-defence.'

'Really?'

'Course it was. Agnew was coming down the track like his ar*e was on fire.'

'In his car?'

'Yeah. Steve thought he was going to ram the caravan. So he raised the gun just to slow him down. Even then Agnew got out of the car and came running at him waving his arms about. F***ing maniac.'

'It doesn't sound a lot like Peter.'

'Neither does crying his eyes out in public.'

I looked out towards Ben Nevis, its south face patched and streaked with snow, and realised I was shivering. 'It was you, wasn't it? That tipped Keith Frampton off about what happened that night at the Walnut Tree Hotel?'

I took Alan's silence for a yes. 'I'd have preferred you kept Sunita out of this.'

'I know, I know. It's just Agnew . . . he's such a f***ing . . . *toilet salesman*.'

I sighed. As far as Alan was concerned, this was, I realised, more about the ring road than anything: getting one over on Peter for going back on his word. There followed a long pause, in which I suspected from various faint gasping noises that Alan might have lapsed into unconsciousness. Then a grunt, a glassy tinkle, and the glacial crepitation of ice submerged in whisky.

'Nothing happened, you know. Between me and Sunita.'

'I know, Alan. You told me.'

'How is she, by the way?'

'I don't know. We've had a quarrel.'

'You haven't bumped her off, have you?'

'What makes you say that?'

'Only joking. Now if you'll excuse me I'd like to get back to drinking myself to death.'

Getting off the summit proved a good deal harder than getting onto it. Without warning a wad of nimbostratus had blown in from the north-west, and in an abrupt stroke of reduced visibility snow had begun to fall in muddled flurries. Clearly, everything would be fine, but it was with a nagging sense of alarm that I peered below the precipice for the ledge that had given me that crucial last leg-up onto it. I often feel, retracing my steps, that the landscape has been subtly rearranged by some mischievous sprite, but through the stereogram of swirling snow my pattern of descent was proving more than usually difficult to discern. With no choice but to sit on the precipice and lower myself down by my elbows, I began to use my right boot to 'read' the rockface, soon finding what I had trusted would be a Braille of safe footholds to be an inarticulate blank. Indiscreet as Alan may have been, he did at least seem to be unaware of Sunita's disappearance. Satisfied, then, that (bar Daisy Rux-Burton) the secret was safe with me, I slipped my elbows off the precipice and fell to my certain and not entirely unwelcome death.

As luck – or its absence – would have it, I landed on a saddle of rock whose soft cushion of moss did absolutely nothing to lessen the impact. Just as well, looking back on it, that there was no one but the deer to hear the yodel of agony that escaped from my mouth at this point, as it may have been couched in language I prefer on the whole to avoid. Automatically, as an amputee might grab the nurse's arm, I had reached out and gathered a handful of scree, and as the pain faded I opened my hand, letting the smaller fragments fall through my fingers, until a single, matchbox-sized rhombus of quartzite was left in the centre of my palm. In colour it was a very pale yellow – a whisper from white – and patterned like a Japanese fan with delicate blooms of grey and greenish lichen. Turn it and at certain angles the moonlight caught a secret, second pattern of rime ice, lacquering the lichen in glinting formations that recalled the flattened sprays in which cedar needles diverge from their stems. When people reason that, there being between thirty and seventy sextillion stars, each potentially with their own solar system, in the observable universe, the existence of life on other planets must be a mathematical certainty, they are surely doing lichen a disservice. Seventy sextillion equates to 7×10^{22}, or 7 followed by 22 noughts; there are fewer grains of sand on the surface of the Earth. But take a moment to look up at the sky, as I did that night, peering through the gaps in the canopy of clouds at what clearings of light-spangled blackness could be perceived. And consider the probability that, somewhere up there, a planet exists wherein conditions are sufficiently like our own for, say, amino acids to lurk in lukewarm ponds; multiply that by the probability that those basic molecules assemble themselves, quite by chance, into proteins, and that those proteins, over millions of years, with all their stupendously numerous opportunities for failure, evolve into proto-cell structures that evolve, in turn, if a stupendous number of other things go right, into a patch of grey lichen on a rock, and you end up with the sort of number to make 7×10^{22} look like a well-meaning start. You, dear rambler, like Sunita, and the lichen, and me, are a stupendous improbability, and it struck me, sitting on my rocky outcrop, staring at the almost certainly lifeless sky, that our seeming determination to put an end to life on Earth might come down, at some level, to a question of incredulity: we simply can't believe our luck.

With difficulty I descended to the ridge. Frenzied wraiths of snow reared up and gnawed at my rainhood. I was, I admit, in some considerable discomfort, each step sending a rivulet of pain up my spine, and it seemed an age before I reached the cairn where the ridge met the path leading down into the glen. Ignoring this, I pressed on, towards Sgùrr an Iubhair, in three hundred agonised yards reaching a small lake whose name, Lochan Coire nam Miseach – 'The Kids' Corrie Pool' – reliably fails to convey its unsuitability for children. Sinking to my knees, I broke the lochan's frozen surface with the nib of my walking pole and was bending to sup black water from the aperture I'd made when I remembered I still had a can of super-strength lager in my ramblesack. I drank greedily, and letting loose a belch that echoed round the glen, I unrolled my sleeping and bivvy bags in the lee of the corrie. The blizzard had, if anything, intensified, and worming into my makeshift bed I squinted through the entomological chaos of flakes in the direction of Ben Nevis, strangely comforted, despite the cold, and the dark, and the barren isolation of this high place, by the presence of a big thing I wasn't seeing.

I lay there, shuddering, for what may have been twenty minutes, hoping against hope that I might steal an hour's sleep before dawn broke and the first of the Japanese baggers crested the ridge. And I had, in fact, reached that pleasant point where one's thoughts begin to drift like errant snowflakes when it struck me that I hadn't yet listened to the second voicemail. It was from Keith Frampton, who, having spoken to Daisy, and a 'member of the public' who had been out walking their dog on Saturday morning, had established a) that Sunita had gone missing, and b) that around the time she had, I had been seen attempting to erase my footprints near the Gullet.

Walk 12: The Sea of Ice

La Mer de Glace, France's longest glacier, and the second-longest in the Alps, wends from its origins high in the Mont Blanc massif to feed the gushing meltwaters of the Arveyron. This walk, an old favourite of the author's, strikes south out of Chamonix, reaching the well-named Plan de l'Aiguille ('Plain of the Needle') via a demanding 3,936-foot (1,200m) climb. From here the glacier is approached on a 'balcon' whose spectacular views over the Chamonix valley, and ease of access by cable car, can make it frustratingly busy, and not just with ramblers: cyclists appear at these altitudes too. Many are courteous and responsible, but every year risk-taking 'speed freaks' force walkers off the footpaths, often to their deaths on the jagged rocks that jut from the escarpment. On a lighter note, refreshments are available year-round at the world-famous Grand Hôtel du Montenvers, from whose outdoor terrace Goethe once shuddered at the sublime violence of the glacier, groaning and cracking as it blundered through the valley below.

Static as it may appear at first glance, La Mer de Glace is of course constantly on the move, its middle section at a rate of up to ninety metres a year, or just over a centimetre an hour. Ramblers with an hour or two to spare have only to climb down to the ice and plant a

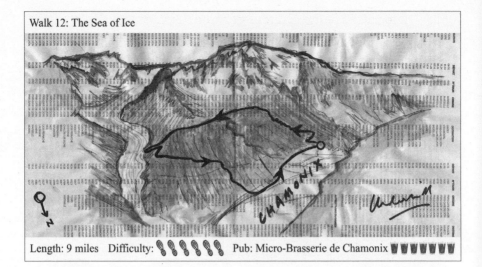

Walk 12: The Sea of Ice

Length: 9 miles   Difficulty: 🐾🐾🐾🐾🐾🐾   Pub: Micro-Brasserie de Chamonix 🍺🍺🍺🍺🍺🍺

stick (or other easily trackable object) in it, to get a sense of the implacable forces that carved the Slad Valley, or scooped corries from the flanks of Stob Bàn. In 'Mont Blanc' (1817), of all Shelley's odes perhaps Sunita's favourite, the glacier is figured as a pitiless, destructive force, creeping down the mountain 'Like snakes that watch their prey':

> vast pines are strewing
> Its destined path, or in the mangled soil
> Branchless and shatter'd stand; the rocks, drawn down
> From yon remotest waste, have overthrown
> The limits of the dead and living world,
> Never to be reclaim'd.

Only by confronting the supreme and indeed violent indifference of nature can we begin to understand our own. Today, sadly, the 'slow rolling' of the ice arouses subtly different feelings. Once clearly visible from Chamonix, the Mer de Glace is now shrinking by an average of thirty metres a year, and some climatologists warn that by 2037 the vast majority of Alpine glaciers will have disappeared altogether. 'Art itself is nature,' Polixenes reminds us in *The Winter's Tale*; to cut down a forest, or pump gigatons of carbon dioxide into the atmosphere, is part of the inescapably natural phenomenon of human stupidity. Nothing is unnatural. But some things *were* inhuman, independent of our influence: the great cycle from snowcap, to glacier, to river, to sea, and back to snowcap via the miraculous reversal of precipitation once set its own pace, before we swaddled the sky in impervious gases. We have conquered what to Shelley was unconquerable, and thus conquered ourselves, and it was the consequent sense of loss – the hole we have made at the heart of things – I could only imagine David had come here to document.

Incidentally, ramblers passing through Glasgow are advised to stop in at the legendary, if rather overlit, Babbity Bowsters on Blackfriars Street, where several pints of Inveralmond Ossian (4.1%) yielded peppery, malty notes, with subtle hints of banana Toffos, and the courage to give Karen a call. Reluctant for reasons I need not explain to disturb her or David at home, I first put a call through to Fleur, David's assistant at Photography by David, whose historically weak grasp of the principles of data protection I felt sure would quickly furnish me with Karen's mobile-phone number. In the event, Fleur was in such a chatty mood that within seconds of answering she had obviated the need to bother Karen at all, by letting slip, in tones of elated envy, that a friend of hers was getting married in Chamonix the following Saturday, and that David had flown out to take the photographs.

'It's going to be *so* romantic,' said Fleur, with a catch in her voice.

'I'll bet,' I said. 'Who's the lucky man?'

'Her snowboard instructor.' Then, quietly, as if it were contractual small print, Fleur added, 'He's French.'

'And will there be a church ceremony? Or just the civil?'

'Oh, yes. All the trimmings. I just can't believe I'm not going to be there!'

Unhappily for Fleur, her elderly Jack Russell had developed pneumonia, and fearful lest this were Lucky's final illness she would be spending the weekend keeping subdued vigil over his basket. I, however, having thrown a not entirely unjustified 'sickie' from work, was able to book myself on a cheap flight to Lyon. This was, of course, regrettable both from the point of view of my traceability by the authorities, and for environmental reasons, and I made sure to offset my emissions by investing £5.20 in a project to capture and combust methane emitted by the pork-production process in China. Impossible, nonetheless, to enjoy a flight entirely free of the drag factors of guilt and anxiety, compounded in this instance by the nasty cold to which I had succumbed after my night on Stob Bàn, and the nagging suspicion that I would be met off the plane by officers of the Rhône-Alpes police. In the event, bar the odd sneezing fit the journey passed without incident, and invigorated by the reliable pleasure of arriving in France, I put up at a serviceable hotel and spent the early part of Friday evening engaged in a leisurely stroll about Chamonix.

To my minor frustration, I found on application at the *office de tourisme* that Chamonix was home to two churches, one Catholic, one Protestant, and that marriage ceremonies were regularly conducted at both. Knowing the religious leanings of neither the snowboard instructor nor his swooning instructee, I took the trouble to visit both the Catholic church of St Michel, conveniently located near the tourist office, and the Église Réformée de la Vallée de l'Arve, tucked behind the war memorial on the Passage du Temple. Like Sunita's, my faith is a personal, non-denominational affair, owing much to Rousseau's conception of a natural morality, but I was able with what I was relieved to find was my still-operative French to pass myself off as devout to the custodians of both churches, ascertaining meanwhile that the Église Réformée would be closed to casual worshippers from 2 p.m. tomorrow, and St Michel from 2.30.

Well pleased with my researches I retired to the Micro-Brasserie de Chamonix, a little out of town on the Route de Bouchet, but well worth the walk for the very sessionable Blanche des Guides (5.0%), brewed on-site by a foursome of clued-up Canadians who saw in the glacial purity of the local waters a future for themselves in real ale. What with live music from the likes of Gary Bigham and the

Crev*ssholes,[1] the atmosphere was, in truth, a little rowdy for my tastes; nonetheless, pulling up a stool by the window I was quickly oblivious to all but the taste of the beer – banana again, clove, the inner tubes of old bicycle tyres – and the view across the road towards the skating rink, from where a pair of unhurried young lovers was strolling hand in hand, the girl's bright-red skates, hung around her neck by their laces, beating softly against her chest with each step. In Paris, not long before we were married, Sunita and I embarked on a walk in homage to Walter Benjamin, the great German-Jewish thinker whose unfinished *Arcades Project* did so much to extend Baudelaire's notion of the *flâneur*, or 'gentleman stroller of the streets'. Benjamin was born in Berlin, and as a student at Freiburg was a member of a youth movement connected to the *Wandervogel*. In later years, however, he devoted himself to the study of Paris, and its development as 'the Capital of the Nineteenth Century'. In its rapid expansion the city had become 'that ancient dream of human-ity, the labyrinth', among whose boulevards and shopping arcades the *flâneur*, that bourgeois Theseus, wandered in a state of contented aimlessness, 'botanizing', as Baudelaire has it, 'on the asphalt'. Benjamin observes that

In 1839 it was considered elegant to take a tortoise out walking. This gives us an idea of the tempo of flânerie in the arcades.

The trouble was a) that over any given distance Sunita's pace was liable to increase to a level inconsistent with the 'peculiar irresolution' of the *flâneur*, and b) when I *did* catch up with her, in the Place des Vosges, and started pointing out various features of the architecture,[2] my quick-witted bride-to-be, recalling a passage from Benjamin's *Selected Writings* I'd read to her that morning on the Eurostar, snapped back that such 'historical frissons' were 'all so much junk to the

1. My asterisk.
2. Specifically, the early seventeenth-century arcades that were to provide the model for the commercial developments of the nineteenth century.

flâneur, who is happy to leave them to the tourist'. And so under the wintry linden trees our 'Ramble in the Footsteps of W.B.' deteriorated into an argument all the more bad-tempered for the refreshingly acidic Picpoul de Pinet we'd enjoyed over lunch, and was brought to a peaceful resolution, ironically enough, only when I agreed to take Sunita shoe-shopping at La Vallée Village, exactly the sort of US-style out-of-town shopping mall that had proved the ruin of the traditional arcade.

Fortunately for the two wedding parties, Saturday in Chamonix turned out bright and clear as undisillusioned love itself. I, on the other hand, felt a little under the weather, the broad sample of excellent ales consumed at the Micro-Brasserie having definitively disproved the theory that 'drinking through' a cold might alleviate rather than violently intensify its symptoms. Lurking, then, in the shadow of the war memorial, I did my best to muffle my sneezes as the wedding party gathered at the Église Réformée. A mood of cheerful anticipation obtained, and I was almost beginning to enjoy myself when a beribboned black Daimler pulled up and disgorged the bride, all of seventeen stone in a blizzard of taffeta. By his middle forties, Walter Benjamin had himself put on weight, and developed a heart condition that made walking the streets of Paris a broken-winded ordeal. Similarly, our two-o'clock bride seemed to be having some difficulty mounting the steps up into the churchyard, and although in her way she looked lovely, huffing and puffing between the lines of smiling guests, one thing seemed beyond doubt: she wasn't a snowboarder.

I reached the moderately interesting baroque church of St Michel in good time for the 2.30 start. Guests had begun to gather in the Place de l'Église, the men uniformly suited, the women so distinct in their allegiance to tight silk, on the one hand, or flatteringly floaty viscose on the other, that it was as if they had walked down in opposing factions from the mountains that loomed over the church to either side. And there, strolling amid the crowd with, it struck me, something of the detached watchfulness of the *flâneur*, was David, in unseasonal linen, stopping now and then to loose off a shot that would, if our own album was anything to go by, come tantalisingly close to capturing the spirit of the couple's happy day. Arriving, rather the worse for wear, at the Hôtel Luxe the previous evening, I had been taken aback by the kindness of Mme la Patronne, who, taking one look at my rheumy eyes, bustled into the kitchen and came back with a chipped mug of *eau-de-vie*, hot water, honey and lemon, for which payment was vociferously refused. Tasty as it was, Madame's *bon vieux grog* had absolutely no effect on my cold whatsoever. But I had, at least, been left in no doubt as to the hospitality of the local population, and was therefore only moderately surprised, peeking from beneath the brim of my canvas rambler's hat, to see that David had been allowed to bring a friend with him, touching the arm of a handsome young guest with a graceful flirtatiousness that could only be Sunita's.

Heart thumping I began to walk across the square towards the church. At this point, however, I was taken unawares by a violent tickling in my sinuses, and unable to deploy my handkerchief[3] in time, released a sneeze that echoed round the valley and caused the entire wedding party to turn in my direction.

'Avalanche!' shouted David, and in the mirthful confusion that followed I was able to slope off to the relative safety of a café in the far corner of the Place de l'Église, having established, in the moment it took me to cover my face with my handkerchief, that the flirtatious Asian lady wasn't Sunita at all, but a much older woman, possibly of Burmese extraction, holding her white chiffon scarf to her chest as it flickered in the breeze.

The Catholic wedding mass is, of course, a rather protracted affair compared to the Protestant ceremony, or the dignified hurtle at which my and Sunita's civil ceremony seemed to pass. In any case, I was ordering my fourth café-cognac by the time the party emerged from the heavy oak doors of the church. From the foyer of the Hôtel Luxe I had picked up a copy of the excellent French-language rambling

3. To her credit, Linda had posted this back to me, clean and impeccably pressed, within three working days of the walk described in route 7.

quarterly, *Passion Rando*, and moving to a table under the awning I was able discreetly to peer at the procession of guests through the gap between my hat and a double-page spread on the under-appreciated footpaths of the Ardèche. No sign of Sunita. Settling my bill, I tailed the party as it made its way down l'Avenue Michel Croz[4] to the reception at the Hôtel Gustavia. It was, I had to admit, turning into an exceptionally tedious afternoon, but when David left the reception three hours later, I followed him to his hotel in the confident expectation that he would emerge soon afterwards, my wife on his arm, the two of them dressed for the sort of dinner I knew from long experience my discriminating darling would expect of him.

If only Redfern had been illicitly embracing my wife opposite the Micro-Brasserie! It's a mark of our enduring attachment to Chamonix that in 1770 the first inn anywhere in the valley to cater specifically for tourists was christened the Hôtel d'Angleterre, and in maintenance of that fine tradition, 'The Pub', which I had chosen for its clear view of David's hotel, was a replica of a proper English pub in all but the total absence of ale. I am not – unlike some 'beer snobs' who will for the moment remain nameless – entirely resistant to the charms of macro-brewed continental lagers, but have to concede that after five or six pints the excessively crisp mouthfeel and under-hopped malty sweetness *do* begin to get a little samey. Anyway, David and/or Sunita must have decided to get an early night, as no more was seen of either of them, and having depleted *Passion Rando* of its last driblet of interest I set about the task of retiring to my hotel. The first flight back to Birmingham left Lyon at 11.20 a.m., and allowing the stipulated minimum of two hours to check in, I calculated that if I rose at six and waited outside their hotel in my rental car, I would be in ample time to accost them before they jumped in a cab to the train station.

By half past nine I was beginning to wonder if David had decided

---

4. Named, incidentally, after one of France's greatest ramblers (1830–65), now chiefly remembered for falling to his death returning from the first successful ascent of the Matterhorn.

to make a weekend of it. From a *boulangerie* somewhere the smell of freshly baked pastry was drifting through the open window of my (surprisingly frisky) Kia Picanto, and, preferring to save for lunch the ham, Emmental and sliced-tomato baguette I had prepared before leaving the hotel, I was about to pop out for a sneaky *pain au chocolat* when David emerged from the lobby, alone, and wheeling his mountain bike. He was dressed in the serious cyclist's solemnly preposterous uniform, lime-green technical jersey over obscenely revealing black tights, with what later turned out to be a small camera attached to his helmet, and a tripod for a larger device lashed to the webbing on his ramblesack. Pausing for a moment to make sure Sunita wasn't bringing up the rear – I thought it unlikely, as not even the pep lent by an invigorating fling would convert my dainty wife to mountain biking – I started the engine and followed David through the south-eastern outskirts of Chamonix to the car park opposite the Aiguille du Midi cable-car station.

Leaving all but the lightest twenty-litre daysack in the car, I followed David into the forest at a sign for the Plan de l'Aiguille. My cold had partly abated, but my coccyx was bad, and after an encouraging start I began to drop behind a few feet with every metre or so of ascent. When the Nazis entered France in 1940, Walter Benjamin was forced to flee south, and as I watched David's raised buttocks inch away from me I thought of the incomparably greater pain Benjamin must have suffered, crossing the Pyrenees on foot,[5] overweight, unwell, and burdened with a heavy briefcase containing a manuscript to which he attached mysterious importance, and which has never been found. Arriving, exhausted, in Port Bou, Benjamin's party was refused entry into Spain, and unable to face hiking back over the mountains to Banyuls-sur-Mer, he took a fatal overdose of morphine.

It was past midday by the time I cleared the treeline and crested the Plan de l'Aiguille. It had been an ambition of Anne's, sadly unfulfilled, to freehike the Mont Blanc massif, and with what I knew to be the commendably *insouciant* attitude of the French to social nudity I

5. As Laurie Lee had done less than three years earlier.

momentarily considered stripping off in her memory. But it was October, and although the mountains were honeyed in autumn sunshine, I reminded myself that at this altitude, the sight of a limping, sneezing Englishman, naked when the season called for serious weathergear, might imprint itself on the minds of passing ramblers rather more than was strictly ideal. Having attained the relatively level terrain of the *balcon*, David had long since disappeared from view. I was, nonetheless, fairly sure I knew where he was headed, and with an exhalation of relief sat by a crop of still-flowering alpenrose and unpacked my lunch. A few yards above me, silhouetted against the brightness of the sky, a young mountain goat stood watching me askance, uncertain perhaps as to whether I represented a source of food or fear. Higher still, the snowcapped pinnacles of the Aiguille du Midi (12,602ft/3,841m) glittered like the spires of a crystal cathedral, and were it not for the interminable approach of a cable car, from several of whose window-seats tourists were engaged in the active assumption that I found their presence equally if not more impressive than the view, I might almost have forgotten how bitterly I longed for a glimpse of my Sunita. In 1728, at the age of fifteen, Jean-Jacques Rousseau returned to his native Geneva to find the city gates locked, and took the opportunity to escape its physical and intellectual confines by walking a hundred and fifty miles across the Alps to Turin. Almost fifty years later, near death, he began work on his *Reveries of a Solitary Walker*, inveighing in the ten walks that form the chapters of the book against the injustices of a society he felt had ostracised him for the courageous unorthodoxy of his ideas. Impossible in the space available to do justice to them, but I've often been tempted to speculate that the centrality of walking to Rousseau's career as a thinker must have informed his view, expressed with such force in the *Discourse on Inequality*, that the land belongs to us all – a view which, in turn, forms the intellectual backbone of the rambling movement today.

Cable car

Incidentally, ramblers ever 'caught short', as I often am, after rounding off a picnic with a coffee from their Thermos, should bear Rousseauian principles in mind by deviating at least seventy yards from the footpath – or fifty from any river, lake or stream – and digging a six-inch-deep 'cathole' which can afterwards be filled with soil and topped with a stone or small boulder. Hard work when the ground is as hard as it was that afternoon,[6] but if the delightful, three-mile yomp along the *balcon* to Montenvers is, as Rousseau would have wished, to be enjoyed by everyone, it would be an act of singular selfishness to expose other ramblers to the significant risk of gastro-enteritis, diarrhoea and even blindness faecal contamination can pose.

The Grand Hôtel du Montenvers is reached via a short walk down to the granite ridge that overlooks the glacier, and beyond it, the formidable peaks of the Grand and Petit Drus (12,316ft/3,754m and 12,247ft/3,733m respectively). From the comfort of the hotel's magnificent terrace ramblers and tourists alike may enjoy hot and cold snacks, as well as a good range of wines, beers and spirits, but having spotted David's bicycle on the ice I forwent both refreshment, and the cable car that embarks from the adjacent rack-and-pinion railway station,[7] to take the sturdy wooden staircase that leads down to the Mer de Glace. Every year a grotto containing furniture-shaped ice sculptures, and other moderately interesting ice-related items,[8] is excavated from the glacier's western flank, and as they near the mounds of lateral moraine ramblers will get a disquieting sense of the speed at which the glacier is melting from the increasingly wide spaces between the cave entrances carved in previous years. It was, as I had suspected,

6. In lieu of a trowel I make sure to carry an old stainless-steel dessert spoon in my ramblesack.

7. For a modest fee the elderly, the infirm and the plain lazy may skip the deathlessly beautiful walk described in this chapter and get the train from Chamonix instead. As they say in these parts, *chacun à son goût*.

8. Shovels, sledges and a St Bernard called Beethoven, after the St Bernard-based film of the same name, with whom, for another modest fee, tourists with a lively sense of humour may pose for a photograph.

exactly these 'holes' that David had come here to photograph, and as I reached the final flight of steps I saw the man himself bounding over the ice towards me – much like, at almost this very spot, the monster had approached Victor Frankenstein:

. . . his countenance bespoke bitter anguish, combined with disdain and malignity, while its unearthly ugliness rendered it almost too horrible for human eyes. But I scarcely observed this; rage and hatred had at first deprived me of utterance, and I recovered only to overwhelm him with words expressive of furious detestation and contempt.

'David! How nice to see you.'

As he clambered off the glacier onto the jumble of moraine and dirty snow it struck me that David's solemnly compassionate air had almost certainly been hastily assembled to disguise his guilt. It had been three months since I'd last spoken to him, at the fiasco that passed for the wild-writing event at the Walnut Tree Hotel, but his smoothly credible manner was immediately familiar to me.

'Graham,' he said. 'What on earth are you doing here?'

'I think you can guess.'

'Are you all right?' David reached out, then, registering my expression, withdrew a hand. 'You look *terrible*.'

'A touch of flu. But I seem to be bearing up, all things considered. Where is she?'

David looked down at his cycling shoes. 'I don't know.'

I was about to respond to this when I was overpowered by a sneeze.

'Bless you,' said David.

'Thank you.'

'I haven't spoken to her since – well. Since the morning she left you.'

'Ah,' I said, blowing my nose. 'Who's saying she left me?'

'I am. She told me, Graham. That it was all over between you.'

'So you admit it.'

'Admit what?'

'Don't mince words, Redfern. You know exactly what I'm talking about.'

'No, listen. Sunita called me that morning. To ask if I'd pick her up at the Gullet car park. She just wanted me for her driver, Graham. And I was all for saying no, but she pleaded with me. She can be very persuasive.'

'And where was it she wanted driving?'

'Malvern Link Station.'

'She was catching a train.'

'You'd have thought so. I don't know – she never turned up.'

'She wasn't at the car park?'

'No. We'd arranged to meet at eleven on the dot. I arrived with a minute to spare and stayed for at least half an hour. No sign of her. I tried to call, but her phone was switched off.'

'And did you see anyone else? In or around the car park?'

'No. Oh – apart from the guy on the scooter.'

'On a scooter?'

'Yeah. When I first arrived there was a guy sitting there on a vintage green scooter with the engine running.'

'And did you get a look at him? What did he look like?'

'I don't know. He was wearing a helmet. And he only stayed for five minutes before driving off.'

'And you didn't think to call me? After Sunita had pleaded with you and then failed to turn up? Weren't you worried about her?'

'Well,' smiled David, looking up the valley to where the glacier snaked south and out of sight. 'To be honest, it wasn't the first time she'd stood me up. Often when we were meant to be working on *Holes* she just wouldn't show. Or she'd turn up two days late. I got the feeling she devoted quite a lot of energy to making people wonder where she was. So no. I wasn't particularly worried about her. Should I have been?'

'No, I don't think so. I'm just – no. I'm sure she's fine.'

'Actually, I *was* going to give you a call. And then I talked to Karen about it. In the end, after all we'd been through with Sunita, we decided that if there was something funny going on it would be better if we kept our noses out of it. Maybe that was a mistake, in which case I'm sorry. For all concerned.'

'Hang on – all you'd been through with Sunita. What do you mean by that?'

David sighed. 'One thing you should know is that I love my wife and would never, ever do anything to deceive her. But Sunita has a powerful imagination. And there were times when she wanted certain things to be true so much that some people, Karen included, started to wonder if they were.'

With heavy heart I turned to face the glacier. Nineteenth-century accounts of the Mer de Glace make sense of its name: Mary Shelley speaks of its 'very uneven' surface, 'rising like the waves of a troubled sea', and in *The Mer de Glace, Chamonix, with Blair's Hut* (c.1806), now in the Courtauld Institute, J. M. W. Turner depicts the glacier as an ocean whipped into a tempestuous fury, the eponymous hut like a ship about to be foundered by a towering wave of blue ice. Now Shelley's 'tremendous and ever-moving glacier' has shrunk by almost a third, and from my perspective looked less like a sea than a silted-up river, clogged with moraine, skulking through the valley as if ashamed at how low it had sunk – at the sudden and unexpected smallness of things.

'Forgive me asking you this,' I said. 'But Sunita seemed to think that Guy and Karen were carrying on behind your back. It isn't true, is it?'

'Well,' said David. 'You never can know for sure, can you? Maybe it's deluded to think that my wife loves me as much as I love her. But there's one thing I am fairly sure of. Sunita liked to be the centre of attention. And she could get anxious to the point of paranoia about being upstaged. But let me ask you a question. As we're in an enquiring frame of mind. Did you love your wife?'

'More than life itself.'

'Did, or do?'

'Do. Always.'

'And you have no idea where she is?'

'No,' I said, quietly. 'I suppose I don't.'

'But you're quite sure she's fine.'

'I hope so.'

'Well,' said David, shrugging off his ramblesack and kneeling to extricate his tripod. 'I hope so too. I should get on.'

I nodded sadly, and at a loss for anything further to say climbed the wooden steps back to the Montenvers Hotel. Tending right at a footpath sign to the Musée de la Faune Alpine, and beginning my descent, I became aware of a painful swelling in my fingertips: Puffy Hand. Chamonix lay an hour and a half to the east, at the foot of the Mer de Glace, and, to ease the swelling, I had no choice but to take the path above the dirty, dying glacier with my hands held high above my head. When, near midnight, I arrived back at Foxglove Cottage, I was so exhausted that I put off reading my post until the following morning. Among it was a letter from the council, informing residents of the decision taken on the route of the eastward extension to the A417. Demolition work would begin shortly, and I was invited to vacate my premises any time between now and the 1st of February next year.

Walk 13: The Valley of Poison

As befitting the 'home of tea', the hills to the north of Darjeeling offer a soothing contrast to the enthralling, appalling tumult of Calcutta. That said, the Singalila Ridge, of which this two- to three-day trek provides a modest glimpse, is part of the Himalayas, and at elevations topping 11,500 feet (3,505m) ramblers will find themselves well tested as they climb up the walls towards the 'roof of the world'. Snows render the route inaccessible between December and February; the walk is best done in April or May, when the hills are ablaze with scarlet rhododendron. Hungry? Thirsty? Rice and chapattis will be your stalwart companions, and ramblers initially dubious about the local tumba *beer may find themselves 'getting it' in retrospect, after a long night laughing like madmen in one of the several rudimentary trekker's huts that line this scenic route.*

Linda Birch's comfortable if poorly designed early-1960s terraced house was situated in the Radford area of Coventry, which, having suffered extensive bomb damage on the night of the *Mondlicht Sonate*, had been rebuilt in the 'functional' style with which well-meaning town planners did so much to vandalise England in the decades following the Second World War. Indeed, on the very morning I

Walk 13: The Valley of Poison

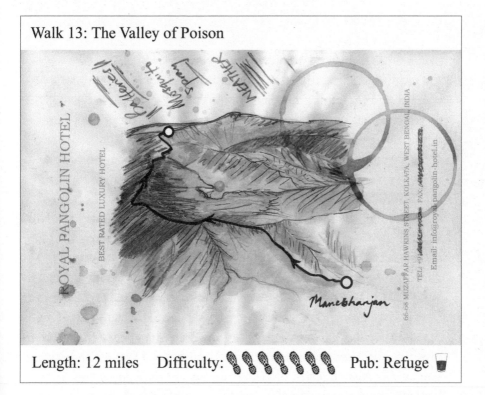

Length: 12 miles   Difficulty: 👣👣👣👣👣👣   Pub: Refuge 🍺

moved in, seeking simply to take a peek at Linda's mahogany-effect composite decking, I accidentally took the patio door off its hinges, and spent a glazed minute struggling to remount it before it pinned me to the conservatory floor.

'I hardly ever go out there,' went Linda's explanation, and as she tenderly, albeit needlessly, applied a Savlon-drenched cotton-wool ball to the superficial gash the rusted inside edge of the door had dealt to my hand, I inwardly marvelled at the sort of person who could leave a hazard like that unrepaired, whether or not they chose to squander their garden. Still, the incident with the door did at least furnish a partial solution to a problem I have to say I was beginning to find extremely embarrassing. Despite repeated efforts – ranging from a casual request over breakfast for Linda's bank details, to a farcical episode in which she imprisoned her hands in her armpits as I attempted to give her an envelope containing £200 in cash – Linda refused to take payment for the fortnight I planned to occupy her spare room, an arrangement I preferred to see more as a formal transaction than a 'favour', as she insisted on putting it, 'from a friend'.

On the morning, then, of my second Monday at No. 17, Honey-suckle Crescent, after Linda had left for work, I set about the actually rather satisfying task of replacing sections of her rotten door jamb with fresh timber before refitting the hinges. (*That* would show her.) After vacating Foxglove Cottage my hope had been temporarily to impose on my friends while I looked for more permanent accommodation. Jasmine Agnew, acting on Steve's behalf, had been kind enough to let me store my furniture, books and, most importantly, archive of walks, in the dilapidated but surprisingly roomy Porta-kabin next to his caravan. Meanwhile I had arranged to move into the guest room, until recently occupied by their daughter Lucy, at Alan and Heather's well-presented Victorian semi on Nightingale Lane.

Plans had changed, however, after I had been allowed to visit Peter Agnew at Ledbury Community Hospital. Peter had been refusing all visitors, not least Keith Frampton, who I knew from his frequent voicemails was eager to pin Peter down on his links to the road-haulage lobby. For much of the past three weeks the *Ledbury Evening Star* had been leading with the Steve Reed story – 'FREE THE NETTLEBED ONE,' went a recent front-page headline – and I had the sense, from a certain hectic constriction in Keith's voice, that he could foresee everything coalescing into a career-crowning exposé: Steve and Jasmine's affair; Peter's breakdown at the Walnut Tree Hotel; Sunita's disappearance; the shooting; and the murky web of relations between the Town Hall, the Ledbury Business Forum, and the cartel of road-haulage contractors that had so vehemently supported the ring road. I, of course, had my own reasons for evading Keith's inquir-ies, preferring to keep my marital difficulties as much to myself as was possible. Nonetheless, I suspected that, far from considering me a fellow victim of a prying local media, Peter would lump me in with the rest of a world he must, by now, have felt was out to get him.

And so it came as a surprise when the nurse on his ward returned with the news that Peter was willing to see me. Following her down a succession of corridors I was met with a slow cortège of suspended and failing ambulation: sad middle-aged children, pushing their parents in wheelchairs; ancient men clinging to their Zimmer frames; a desiccated woman, diminished by her dressing gown, trundling a bag of plasma on a stand. By the time we reached Peter, propped up in a private room, I was as self-conscious about each step I took, shrilly broadcast by the contact of rubber on lino, as one can sometimes get about breathing: offended by the miracle of continuance.

'Graham.'

Peter was lying with his right leg strapped in a plastic brace and hoisted in traction. He looked tired, of course, and older than his forty-seven years, but what struck me most, thinking back to the Peter I used to know, stiffly semi-present at Jasmine's lasagne parties, was how softened he'd been by the events of the previous few months. It was as if, without the system of pulleys and counterweights supporting his leg, he might collapse into a heap as shapeless as a beached jellyfish.

'How are you, Peter?'

'Oh,' he said, smiling. 'Not so bad. Doctors say I may walk with a permanent limp. But there are heavier crosses to bear.'

'I heard from Keith Frampton that you might never walk again.'

I watched Peter's eyes disown his smile. 'Not the first time that man could be accused of sensationalism.'

Glancing over my shoulder, I handed Peter the small gift I had picked up en route to the hospital: a bottle of Dorothy Goodbody's Wholesome Stout (4.6%). 'Won joint silver in the bottle-conditioned category at this year's Beer and Cider Awards. Should have been gold, if you ask me. Still, probably best to keep it under your blanket.'

'That's very kind of you,' said Peter, examining the label. 'But I don't know if I deserve it.'

'Well,' I said. 'No harm done. Apart from you getting shot in the leg, of course.'

Peter shook his head. 'You know why I was going round there, don't you?'

'To Steve's? No.'

'To give them my blessing. I was delighted for him and Jasmine.

Goodness knows, if Steve can make her happy, he's a better man than me.'

'But he thought you'd gone round to pick a fight.'

'That's right.' Peter pulled back the sleeve of his pyjamas to reveal a scrawny bicep. 'Mincemeat, I would have made of him.'

'I think Steve has been in a rather paranoid frame of mind recently.'

'Well,' said Peter, 'that's a shame. For all concerned. If only he'd let me get a word in edgeways I might have put his mind at rest.'

With a pang of understanding I saw Peter defending his position at the road inquiry. 'You're moving away, aren't you?'

'I'm not sure where yet,' said Peter, looking away towards the rain-patterned window. 'As long as it's nowhere near here. I'm afraid since everything that's happened I've rather fallen out of love with Ledbury.'

'Which is why you changed your mind about the ring road. You *wanted* your house to be demolished, didn't you?'

'Never liked it much anyway. Completely illiterate from an architectural point of view.'

For one reason or other I felt a little like crying. 'Keith Frampton will be disappointed. He thinks you're in the pocket of the road-haulage lobby.'

'Well, let him think that. Can't be much fun working for a local newspaper, can it?'

Peter's gaze had begun to turn glassy, and as he reached over his shoulder for the morphine pump I got up to leave.

'Give my regards to Sunita,' he said, closing his eyes and sinking back on the pillows. 'How are things, by the way?'

'You haven't heard? We're separated.'

'I'm sorry. Temporary, I hope.'

'We'll see.'

'Graham?' I had turned and walked out of the room when Peter called me back. 'Watch out for Alan,' he said.

'Why?'

Peter was lying with his fists clenched beside him on the mattress. 'That night I made a fool of myself at the Walnut Tree Hotel. Alan made a pass at Sunita. After you'd gone home. Nothing happened, of course. She was no more interested in an old drunk like him than she was in one like me. But it wasn't for want of him trying.'

It was his wife who answered when I rang Alan from the hospital car park.

'Heather,' I said, brightly, as the rain wheeled in white squalls across the tarmac. 'May I speak to Alan, please?'

'If I ever hear your or your b*tch wife's name again,' said Heather, 'I will kill both myself and that credulous old goat I have the misfortune to call my husband.'

By six the next evening I had moved in with Linda. Anyone seeking to understand the reactions Sunita provoked in people would be advised to look more closely at her cultural background. As I've mentioned, just over a month before we were married Sunita and I flew to Calcutta to meet her family, none of whom, sadly, were in a financial position to make it over for the wedding in Eastnor. Catching one of the city's trademark Ambassador taxis, as jovially rotund as saffron dumplings, I wondered as we sped from the airport whether this could be the Calcutta I'd read about, the seething hell of overpopulated humidity, built on a river delta whose appearance on the map corresponded to an idea I'd formed of the place as some sort of moribund swamp creature, half in and half out of the water, trailing its unspeakable tentacles in the Bay of Bengal.

And then: *whoomph*. Calcutta erupted around us. I was later to discover quite how exhilarating and, in places, tranquil the city could be, but turning right off Chittaranjan Avenue into a seemingly impenetrable mass of cars, cows, goats and (most of all) pedestrians, I succumbed to a fear for my personal safety exceeded only by my amazement at what violence was being done to the notion of space. And we, incredibly, *voluntarily*, had just driven into the middle of it. Our little yellow taxi was like a beetle overwhelmed by ants. Sunita was quite plainly enjoying herself.

Ambassador taxi

'Shall we get out and walk?'

I looked left to see shirt, *dhoti*

and trouser material pressed into frosted folds against the window glass. With glacial inevitability the taxi was sliding at right angles to its intended trajectory. 'No,' I said.

'Suit yourself. But it'll be quicker.'

This may well have been true. Calcutta is a walker's city – perhaps *the* walker's city – in the sense that its motor vehicles enjoy none of their accustomed privileges of access or speed.[1] In *The Arcades Project* Walter Benjamin conceives of pavement and roadway as parallel tracks in a race the pedestrian is predestined to lose: 'in the course of his most ordinary affairs, [the walker] has constantly before his eyes the image of the competitor who overtakes him in a vehicle.' In Calcutta the odds are more equal: even the cars are *flâneurs*. Somehow, drawing on reserves of near-transcendental obstinacy, our driver pushed through the crowd and out again, into the relative freedom of the southern suburbs, where cars were cars, and the pavements less busy with people than the perforated leaf-shadows of Chicken Pox Mahogany (*Swietenia varicella*). After his brief spell at the woollen mill in Spean Bridge, Sunita's father Raj had relocated to High Barnet and started an import–export business. When *that* failed, Raj moved back to Calcutta, leaving Sunita, then sixteen, in the care of Carol's equally hapless successor, and as we entered the modest neighbourhood Sunita hadn't seen since she was six, I touched her forearm, and found it hard, as if she were crushing a stubborn object in her fist.

'We'll only stay for an hour, okay? Just long enough not to seem rude.'

In my experience 'not seeming rude' was a social convention of which Sunita had always felt entirely free to absolve herself. In the year and a half since she'd first stopped my heart by the loans desk at Malvern Library, I had come to understand and indeed respect her occasional readiness to offend as a symptom of self-knowledge. Quite

---

1. Significant perhaps that in Calcutta the pavements are referred to as ফুটপাথ, *phuṭapātha*, 'footpaths': an urban environment infused with the language of rambling.

suddenly, however, the assurance I had considered an unalterable part of her personality appeared to have deserted her, and climbing the five flights up to her father's apartment she held on to my arm so tightly that aside from tender concern I momentarily felt a fearful thrill of estrangement: who *was* this woman? Ramblers with experience of subcontinental temperatures will appreciate the compromise my medley of loose-fitting linen attempted to strike, between comfort and the formality a conservative, if no doubt impeccably hospitable, Bengali family might feel entitled to expect. Sunita, on the other hand, had perhaps rather unthinkingly thrown together the sort of summer outfit that she had grown accustomed to wearing in England, and was thus all the more unnerved to find herself a few short footsteps from her family reunion wearing a denim skirt whose brevity erred on the side of airiness.

In the event, the instantaneous warmth with which I was received into the Bhattacharya family was such that it was half an hour at least before I had the chance to check if my anxious sweetheart was all right. Scarcely had I walked into the living room than my future father-in-law was taking me on a tour of it, introducing me to various relatives with a level of biographical confidence not in the least bit undermined by the fact that we'd met for the first time less than five minutes before.

'This is Mr Graham Underhill. He holds a first-class degree in Earth Sciences from the University of Birmingham. Is that right, Graham?'

'It was a 2:1, actually.'

'His many other interests narrowly prevented him from taking the academic honours that could so easily have been his. Today he is a senior local-government official responsible for maintaining Herefordshire's commitment to environmental sustainability. Aside from this he is a highly accomplished watercolourist and writer. On *nature*, Manisha.'

In her youth Sunita's octogenarian great-auntie Manisha turned out to have written a poem cycle about the birds of Bengal. Indeed, in the course of our short visit, I don't think I met a single member of Sunita's extended family that hadn't written, or wasn't writing, or

wouldn't like to write, a novel, or a book of verse, or memoir, or
short story, or pamphlet on the history of agro-industrial pollution
on the Indo-Gangetic Plain. There obtained in this averagely under-
privileged family an impulse to self-expression that might have
seemed pretentious in England, but here sounded as unforced a note
as a liking for cricket or food. Manisha and I got on particularly well,
and having spent a fascinating if rather one-sided twenty minutes
discussing the peculiar mating habits of the rare Himalayan Open-
throat (*Ephippiorhynchus oscitans*),[2] I felt as if sufficient conversational
elbow-room had been established to ask what Sunita's mother had
been like.

'Amrita? Very beautiful. Like her daughter. But not an easy woman
to be married to. The trouble for poor Rajeev was that she expected
life to be *interesting*. And as soon as it wasn't? She was off.'

'Do you think there was anything Rajeev could have done? To
keep the marriage together?'

Manisha thought for a moment. 'Not really. Amrita yearned for
stability – to be with a good, kind man. But then as soon as she had
it she didn't want it any more. I don't know. Maybe it reminded her
of the stability she'd never had as a child – she'd started life on the
move and so was condemned always to walk away from things. It's
maddening to think about, isn't it? You want something so badly,
even though you know perfectly well you won't want it once you
have it.'

I thought of what Manisha had told me about Sunita's mother
during the sad process, some two and a half years later, of packing
up Foxglove Cottage preparatory to its demolition. When my father
left home in the early 1950s, to take up his position as junior clerk to
the Treasurer at Ledbury Town Hall, he moved into digs near the
station while he formulated plans to build his own property, on a plot

2. Like the ostrich, and the elk, this stork-like bird, native to the sub-Himalayan
ranges north of Darjeeling, keeps a 'harem' of sexual partners; unlike them, and
indeed almost any other species on Earth, it is the *female* that does this, harbouring
up to twelve submissive males in specially adapted nests or 'boudoirs' constructed
of its own feathers fortified with jacaranda bark.

of land he'd chanced upon during one of the long walks he'd take to fill the lonely evenings after work, in the years before he met my mother. And although he never explicitly acknowledged it, I was certain that the effort of building his own house, brick by brick, was a response to the trauma of learning, from the safety of the Breconshire farmhouse to which he and his sister had been evacuated, that his childhood home had been hit by a German bomb, and, as far as he was concerned, simply disappeared, along with his father, and the happy, active woman his mother used to be. Iris died in her early sixties, when I was thirteen, but I have a memory of her sitting in the living room in her wheelchair, reminiscing about the strolls in the Cotswolds she and my grandfather enjoyed when they were courting, and bursting into tears with such girlish openness that I remember thinking how unthinkable it was that your life could stop without you dying, as hers had at the age of twenty-eight.

Clearly nothing in the dispiriting events of the last six weeks could compare to the devastating blow dealt to my grandmother on the night of the Coventry Blitz. But I had since my relocation to that city found myself uncharacteristically reluctant to move – indeed, after the patio door had been satisfactorily remounted on its hinges, even to get out of bed. I had the best human-resource practices of Herefordshire County Council to thank for the eight weeks' compassionate leave I had been granted, while, in the words of my departmental head, I recovered from the 'manifest strain' of separation. In my early days at the council a senior Community Housing Officer by the name of Iain Woodcock had been granted leave under what were rather sniggeringly rumoured to be similar circumstances. When after six months he had still failed to reoccupy his desk, it was generally agreed among the 'young Turks', of which I could then regard myself a member, that at forty-five he was considered past it, and had been bloodlessly if rather dishonestly 'let go'. At forty-nine, I liked to think of my continued employment *beyond* the age of forty-five as an implicit vote of confidence, and considering my excellent health, and more than satisfactory track record of meeting or exceeding my performance parameters, had no reason to suspect that my letter of objection to the ring road had prompted my employers to make a Woodcock of me. But with little to fill my days I was prone to black moods only, I regret to say, darkened by Linda's well-meaning attempts to lift them. Had I been less caught up in my own sorrows I might, for example, have predicted that the modest bit of DIY I'd applied to her patio door would have the opposite-to-intended effect – that is, to release me from her debt. So delighted was she, in fact, opening and closing the door with an ear pantomimically cupped to catch the squeak I'd oiled into inexistence, that she insisted on 'making a fuss' of me, and more for a quiet life than any appreciable desire to undertake what sounded, in all frankness, like a rather dull walk, I agreed to accompany her on a Sunday-afternoon potter around the grounds of Kenilworth Castle.

I had donned my kagoule, and was sitting on the hall floor lacing up my boots, when the doorbell rang, and an obscurely familiar face loomed into the snowstorm of Linda's frosted front door.

It was Daisy.

'Graham,' she wailed. 'I've *found* her!'

It wouldn't have taken a sleuth of genius to deduce that Linda had formed an immediate dislike to Daisy, and not only because our 'fun day out' had been interrupted. Something else was at stake – that I could tell from the audible force with which Linda was making the tea. As I showed Daisy through to the living room, there came from the kitchen the thump of a cupboard roughly shut twinned with the synchronous chink of startled china.

'You're not going to believe this.' Daisy had made fans of her hands, and was wafting her wet cheeks with them. 'She's in *Antarctica*.'

'Antarctica?'

'With *Guy*.'

'Guy Gosling?'

'Yes.' Daisy began to cry with renewed force. 'I'm so *happy*!'

At this point Linda came in with a tray of tea and fruit cake, and as I stood to relieve her of it Daisy's hands flew to her mouth. 'Oh, God. I'm *such* an idiot.'

'Tea?' said Linda.

'Milk. No sugar.' Unwrinkling her nose, Daisy turned to address me with maximum gravity. 'I meant I'm happy because she's safe.'

'Of course.'

'I'm also really *un*happy. Seeing as Guy's my ex and everything.'

'Yes,' I said. 'It must be very difficult for you.'

'Oh, but not *half* as difficult as it must be for you. I mean, Guy's just my ex. Sunita's your *wife*.'

'Quite. Cake?'

'Ooh, yes, please. Not that there's any actual evidence to suggest there's anything going on between them. In the romantic sense.'

'No.'

'Although,' said Daisy, subsiding into tears again, 'if there *was*, it may be some comfort to know that Guy is an absolutely *amazing* person.'

I reached out and patted Daisy's hand. 'That *is* a comfort.'

'So Guy contacted you, did he?' said Linda, handing Daisy her tea. 'From Antarctica?'

'Not exactly,' said Daisy, brightening. 'You know the wild-writing events at the Walnut Tree Hotel? Of *course* you do. God, what an evening that was! Anyway, I went the other night, and this chap Robin Entwistle was telling me about the *amazing* blog Guy has been writing. I'm *always* the last to hear about these things! So I had a look when I got home. And there was Sunita. Pictures, diary entries, everything.'

'There are pictures of Sunita on Guy's blog?'

'Loads. There's this *really* amusing one of her trying to shut her suitcase. The sheer amount of stuff you have to take! She's *sitting* on it and still it won't close. You should see the expression on her face. Absolutely classic!'

'Any of her actually in Antarctica?'

'Oh, God, yeah, awesome. You know Guy is out there writing about the break-up of this ice shelf?'

I took a nibble of fruit cake. 'The Wilkins?'

'The what?'

'The Wilkins. Ice shelf.'

'Yeah, and so there's this picture of them actually standing on a lump of ice that's floating out to sea? Sort of really beautiful and really worrying at the same time? If that makes sense?'

'It does,' said Linda and I, in unison.

'I don't know,' said Daisy, her voice rising on yet another tidal wave of despondency. 'On the one hand' – here the wave broke, foaming, on the shores of her next thought – 'I'm utterly, utterly devastated. And on the other, I'm really, really proud of them. I just think it's so *brave*, what they're doing. Even to withstand those conditions. I mean, brrr! But you just *know* they're doing it for all the right reasons. You know – for the *planet*.'

Later, as I showed Daisy to the door, she turned and grasped my hands in hers.

'I didn't mean to be so insensitive earlier. I'm genuinely sorry about you and Sunita.'

In the kitchen, Linda was filling the dishwasher, and to hear Daisy's voice above the clank and scrape of soiled teawear I was forced to lean in rather closer than I would have done otherwise. Daisy continued in a conspiratorial *sotto voce*.

'But it looks like you've landed on your feet. Linda's obviously a really cool woman. And *perfect* for you.'

And she was gone before I had the chance to correct her.

Our visit at Rajeev's apartment had come to a rather more abrupt end than appearances had led me to expect. Whatever her feelings about the rest of her family, Sunita had been looking forward to seeing her cousin Suresh, a lawyer, and in the course of my long talk with Manisha I was relieved to look over from time to time and find Sunita engaged in apparently agreeable conversation with him, his charming young wife Priya and even, for a brief spell, Rajeev. Ramblers will imagine my surprise, in that case, when the smile Sunita was wearing as she walked over with a foil platter of *chumchum*[3] turned out, on closer inspection, to be rigid.

---

3. A popular Bengali sweet dumpling made of cottage cheese, flour and sugar. These ones were alternately pale pink and yellow, and frosted with coconut. With the greatest of respect, *not* my cup of tea.

'You have to get me out of here.'

'Well, all right, my darling,' I whispered. 'But it's such a nice party.'

'Look. Do you want to cause a scene? In front of my whole family? Or do you want to be a man and get me in a f***ing taxi?'

We spent the ride back into town in a sweltering silence. Mark Twain, who had visited Calcutta in 1896, said that in India the phrase 'cold weather' was used merely 'to distinguish between weather which will melt a brass doorknob and weather which will only make it mushy'. This was doorknob-melting weather, and perhaps because of the effort required even to draw breath, it wasn't until we reached the air-conditioned cool of our hotel room that Sunita felt ready to talk.

'He's so *weak*,' she said.

'Who?'

'The cab driver. Who do you think? My father.'

'He seemed very nice to me.'

'Well, that's just it, isn't it? He *is* very nice. He doesn't care enough *not* to be. I mean, look at this.' Sunita plucked at her mini skirt. 'You know what he said to me? "You're looking good, Sunita."'

'That is conventionally understood to be a compliment.'

'I don't want a compliment from my father. I want him not to be *weak* for once. He was too weak to keep my mother. He was too weak to take care of me. Now he's so weak he can't even bring himself to disapprove when I come dressed as a call girl to his family reunion.'

It would be nearly a week before Suresh could spare the time from work to spend more in our company. In the meantime I was surprised and not a little delighted to find that Sunita could think of nothing more restorative than to leave the heat and sad associations of the city for the aerating immensities of the West Bengal Hills. Manebhanjan lay a short bus ride uphill from Darjeeling, itself some 6,950 feet (2,118m) higher than Calcutta, and as I began, after Daisy's visit, to research affordable passage to the Antarctic Peninsula, I was reminded of the heavenly drop in heat we felt crawling uphill between tea plantations. According to his blog Guy Gosling was based at a research station on Adelaide Island, off the east coast of the Peninsula, and if I flew to Ushuaia, at the southernmost tip of Argentina, I could join a cruise ship that launched expeditions to the island for as little as £8,000.

'You're not seriously thinking of doing this, are you?' said Linda, setting down a dimple mug of Adnams' moreish Broadside (4.7%) as, coincidentally enough, I clicked through to view the wide range of wines, beers and spirits available aboard the ice-strengthened *Oksana Antonova*.

'I don't see why not. I have the money.'

'From the compulsory purchase order?'

I nodded, perhaps a little meekly, and with a sigh Linda drew up a chair beside me at the kitchen table. 'That's for your new house, Graham.'

'Well,' I said, feeling an unwelcome warmth in my chest. 'I can buy a very slightly smaller house, can't I? It's only £8,000.'

'Plus flights. Plus expenses.'

'What expenses? "All breakfasts, lunches and dinners are included in the price. Deluxe packed lunches are provided for all peninsular excursions." And I'm hardly going to be bringing back a bottle of the local liqueur, am I?'

'And what if she's not in Antarctica? Where will it end? You're going to spend your father's legacy on a ridiculous wild goose chase. And then where will you be? In rented accommodation?'

'If it comes to it, yes. But it won't. You're being melodramatic.'

Linda made a disapproving face. 'Let's have another look at that picture.'

Switching windows, I scrolled down to the photo of Gosling and a female figure on the ice floe. It had been taken from a distance, in the feeble light of the austral spring, but ramblers would be as struck as I was by the woman's similarity to Sunita in complexion and conspicuously sensuous bearing.

'Are you even sure it's her?' said Linda, stolidly.

'Yes, Linda. Just as I'm sure it's her sitting on the suitcase.'

'But that picture was taken before they left. Look at the date on the blog entry. September the 26th. That's even before she disappeared.'

'Linda. The rigour of your scepticism is much to be admired. But I think I can be trusted to recognise my own wife.'

'But it's *Antarctica*, Graham. No one goes to Antarctica.'

'On the contrary, tourists in their tens of thousands visit every year. Why else would Gosling be giving talks on the impact of cruise ships on Antarctic ecosystems? There are no wildernesses left, Linda. For that, we shall have to wait for manned travel to Mars.'

Linda essayed a sardonic smile. 'Have you even *been* in contact with Guy Gosling?'

'I've tried. He won't answer my emails. As if we needed further proof that he has something to feel guilty about! But I've applied to the British Antarctic Survey for a visitor's permit. If Gosling is too ashamed to give me the common courtesy of a response I shall just have to take him by surprise.'

'For goodness' sake, Graham,' said Linda, reddening. 'This is *insane*.'

Failing to see the point of any further discussion I turned back to my laptop, and, with a series of ill-tempered clicks, navigated through to Customer Testimonials.

'Hang on a sec,' said Linda, touching my forearm. 'Go back.'

I clicked back to 'Dates and Rates', detailing prices according to the time of year and cabin type occupied.

Linda pursed her lips. 'So there are no single cabins.'

'No. They're all doubles or triples.'

'Gosh, so single occupancy is a very expensive way of doing it.'

'Well, yes. I suppose it is.'

'Look,' she said, tapping the screen, and leaving a fingermark it would undoubtedly take a lint-free cloth to remove. 'You save a thousand pounds each filling both berths.'

'Yes,' I said, and there followed a minute filled with the ringing silence of an ice field.

Engaging a guide in Manebhanjan, Sunita and I set off with eight other ramblers on the three-day, twenty-mile hike to the summit of Sandakphu, at 11,929 feet (3,636m) the highest point in West Bengal. In

Wild, the admirably unrestrained writer Jay Griffiths notes the common points in the vocabularies of mountaineering and the sexual subjugation of women: Western man *conquers* mountains, *penetrates* wild spaces in his mad race to subdue a force wiser indigenous peoples venerate as caring, maternal, and immeasurably greater than them. (One might add, in the Griffiths spirit, that man *assaults* wild spaces before *sticking his pole* in them.) Mind you, if anyone was harassing the mountain that cool morning as we climbed between spruce and giant magnolia, it was Sunita, leading our initially incoherent band of German, Japanese and English ramblers in a chorus of Bengali nonsense rhymes,[4] more than once drowning out our shy guide Lhakpa's attempts to discourse on the bamboo-grove habitat of the rare red pandas we probably now had zero chance of seeing anyway.

By the time we reached Bikhaybhanjang ('The Valley of Poison'),[5] at the end of our second day's trek, Sunita had supplanted poor Lhakpa as the *de facto* leader of the expedition. We had put up at a trekker's hut, where simple dishes of aloo paratha were washed down with *tumba*, the local 'beer' of fermented millet seeds topped up on an all-you-can-drink basis with warm water. Clearly, its alcohol content by volume decreased with each refill, but not by much, and drinkers were discouraged from shaking the wooden pot in which it was served, lest they ingest the sludge of millet seeds and risk being stretchered off the mountain hooting like a gibbon at the moon. Four or five pots and our polyglot assembly had achieved a faltering *lingua franca*, applied in the case of the male majority largely for the purpose of flirting with my wife. One of the German women turned out to be something of an authority on the *Naturfreunde*, and, engaged in as fluent a conversation as my German would allow, I was unaware of anything untoward until a shout went up, and I turned to see

4. For example, 'In the land of Dendrologica / The trees chop down the men. / To make a bed to rest their heads / They need no more than ten.' From *Rhudibudibarb*, by Mohit Chakraborty (1878–1917).
5. Named, it's said, after the locally abundant, and highly poisonous, flowering aconite 'Nilo Bikh', *Aconitum ferox*, although anyone who's sampled the local beer may beg to differ.

Sunita upending a pot of *tumba* over one of the English trekkers' heads.

'You presumptuous *pr*ck.*'

We had stopped for the night only two and a half miles short of Sandakphu. The plan had been to rise at 3 a.m. and undertake the brief but stiff climb to crest the summit at dawn, before beginning the journey back south to the trailhead with a stop in Bikhaybhanjang for breakfast. But there was still a band of turquoise at the horizon, and, although hiking on the ridge without a guide was officially prohibited, Sunita swore she wouldn't spend a night under the same roof as 'anyone who had the gall' to suggest she was out of her fiancé's league. It was the *tumba* talking, certainly. But there was no dissuading her. Slipping Lhakpa a few hundred rupees to turn a blind eye, we pressed on, and as the village receded behind us a crested goshawk began circling overhead, as if monitoring our progress. Quickly sobered by the cold, we reached the summit in a little under two hours.

In daylight this sacred place gives views over swathes of fir and blaze-red rhododendrons to four of the five highest mountains in the world: Makalu, Lhotse, Kangchenjunga and, at 29,028 feet (8,848m), great Everest itself. But there was no moon that night, and it was in near-total darkness that we approached the lights of the Sherpa Chalet, where a friendly welcome comes accompanied by excellent coffee prepared with sheep's milk, a basic meal of *dhal* and rice, and the intriguingly incongruous services of an STD clinic. Our room gave onto the valley, and quickened by the feeling, finally, that we were far away from everyone and everything familiar, we pulled the bed up to the window and looked out over the view we couldn't yet see.

'Never, ever leave me, Graham Underhill. You promise?'

'I promise.'

And we lay there, looking out, until the sun melted out of the highest places, and turned them orange, then yellow, then white.

Walk 14: The Worst Journey in the World

In the austral winter of 1911 Dr 'Bill' Wilson, 'Birdie' Bowers and the young zoologist Apsley Cherry-Garrard set off on a 67-mile trek across the Antarctic wastes to retrieve the enigmatic egg of the Emperor penguin. They barely survived, and it's to Cherry-Garrard's classic account of their journey, and the attempt on the Pole that was to claim Bowers's and Wilson's lives the following summer, that this walk owes both its inspiration and name. Ramblers reluctant to face five weeks man-hauling overburdened sledges in pitch darkness, ill-equipped and on starvation rations, at temperatures dropping below minus fifty degrees, will be reassured to note that the route is confined to the relatively temperate environs of the Antarctic Peninsula, where the worst privation they are likely to endure is the poor choice of ale aboard the cruise ships on which tourists to this blessedly hotel-free wilderness are required to spend the night. Nonetheless, this is Antarctica, and ramblers are advised to prepare themselves not only for the physical challenge of walking in sub-zero temperatures, but the emotional strain even the most cheerful of disposition can feel confronted with the continent's vast, spirit-crushing emptiness.

There came a point, not that many clicks south of Cape Horn, when I began to suspect that Captain Finch and Yuri, our Russian Officer

Walk 14: The Worst Journey in the World

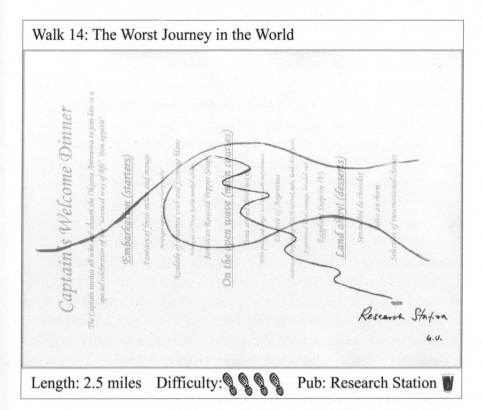

Length: 2.5 miles   Difficulty: 👣👣👣👣   Pub: Research Station 🍺

of the Watch, might be the same person. Considering its reputation for tempestuousness, our crossing of the Drake Passage had proved, so far at least, remarkably smooth, but with a regularity that would have been laudable, had I not been *trying* to watch a documentary[1] in the presentation lounge, Captain Finch's reassuringly matter-of-fact voice would emerge from the crackle of the tannoy to inform us that yes, we were still making good progress, that a fresh breeze of seventeen knots was still blowing in from the Southern Ocean,

---

1. *Titans of the Great Alone.* A sort of Wikipedia-level rattle through the Heroic Age of Antarctic exploration. Judging by the tone of unvarying hagiography, and rather incongruous soundtrack of synthesised dinner jazz, probably *not* intended for terrestrial broadcast. Nonetheless, perfectly watchable, if only for the archive footage: the main-mast of Shackleton's ice-clamped *Endurance* toppling like a felled tree, poor old Birdie Bowers feeding sugar lumps to his equally doomed pony, etc., etc.

and that a perfectly manageable swell of two to three metres, or six to nine feet in the imperial units, was still proving no match for the ship's twin 5,209-horsepower engines. Then Yuri would come on and say something like, 'Of course, the weather in the Drake Passage can change very quickly,' and although he was careful to reassure passengers that 'swells of up to fifty feet were, on balance, unlikely', I fell to wondering if 'Yuri' was, in fact, Captain Finch putting on a Russian accent, in order to give voice to his fear, or indeed secretly suicidal wish, that a freak wave would crash over the *Oksana Antonova*'s bows and send us see-sawing to the ocean floor.

Either way, there prevailed in the presentation lounge an atmosphere of hyperactive boredom, manifest in my new friend Janet's case in a frenzy of matrimonial intermediacy. Janet had come on the Discover Antarctica Cruise to celebrate her and husband Phil's ruby wedding anniversary, and to make up for Phil's conspicuous lack of interest in anything save the wooden spool with which he appeared to be French-knitting a vast, circular prayer mat, she had taken it upon herself to 'set me up' with one of the thankfully limited number of single ladies aboard the ship. Not for a moment would she believe that I had embarked on my 'solo cruise' for any other reason than to meet a 'special someone'. Somewhere along the line I had accidentally convinced Janet that I was an incorrigible tease,[2] and when a woman[3] she had a vicarious eye on walked into the presentation lounge and sat down on her own, my protestations that I was already taken imprinted themselves on Janet's consciousness no more indelibly than the last three times I'd made them.

'Go on, Graham. She's very attractive. For her age.'

'That's as may be,' I said, with a tolerant smile. 'But as you know,

---

2. Quite possibly when I made the mistake of filling a gap in the conversation with my suspicions about Yuri being a sort of irrepressible Mr Hyde-ish id-figure to Captain Finch's Jekyll. Janet had stared at me for a while, then, with a contemptuous expulsion of air between her teeth and bottom lip, slapped me on the forearm, as if I had actually been trying to have her on, as opposed to including her in a bit of self-evidently playful speculation.

3. A widow, apparently. Of at *least* sixty-five.

Janet, I'm on my way to Antarctica to meet my wife. What would she think if I walked off the boat with an attractive widow on my arm?'

'Phil.'

'Hn?'

'He's on about his wife again. The one in *Antarctica*.'

I took advantage of Phil's utter indifference to make my excuses and go for a mosey. About a year before she died, Anne and I had accompanied her parents on a 'Jewels of the Baltic' cruise aboard the sort of floating citadel whose unparalleled facilities[4] do little to compensate for the contempt they show for the world outside their walls. Vast SUVs of the sea, they are, of course, in the comfort and comprehensiveness of the environments they erect around their passengers, all the more able to induce in them the solipsistic notion that no other environment matters very much, or even exists. Signatories to the Antarctic Treaty of 1959 have, it must be said, agreed to a loose set of resolutions, imposing limits on the number of cruise passengers that can set foot on Antarctic territory at any one time, but operators regularly get around these by registering their vessels in jurisdictions not bound by the treaty, or by anchoring offshore in huge liners, accommodating as many as three thousand passengers, and launching staggered shore excursions that abide by the letter more than the spirit of the law. It's a commonplace that tourism destroys the very thing that attracts it, but nowhere is this irony more apparent, or literalised, than in the waters off the Antarctic Peninsula, where, like glazed onlookers at their own funeral, visitors granted ever easier passage through the disintegrating ice shelves are themselves directly contributing to that disintegration.

Still, needs must – and besides, the *Oksana Antonova*, I had been glad to find, was a modest vessel, in its dimensions, facilities and subtly acrid air of tired utilitarianism less like a luxury tourist resort than an ice-adapted Travelodge. Having on previous 'tours of

---

4. *Twelve* restaurants, *five* swimming pools, a putting green, a climbing wall, two *competition-grade* ping-pong tables, and a bar that served Craxton's hard-to-find Ostler's Promise (4.8%). I could go on.

inspection' looked in at the gym, and spent several hours thumbing through the polar-themed volumes in the ship's well if rather indiscriminately stocked library, I decided to treat myself to a box of milk-chocolate Lindor and pop round to the computer room to check my webmail. My most recent log-on, between the crab roulade and Argentinian meat-feast at last night's interminable 'Captain's Welcome' gala dinner, had afforded the rather disappointing yield of two emails. The first was from my old friend PC Onions of the West Mercia Constabulary, advising me that a member of the public had found my digital voice recorder in long grass near the Gullet, and been kind enough to hand it in. From its external condition it had evidently lain there for some time, but having replaced the battery, and played back some of the sound files, PC Onions was happy to inform me that it remained in full working order, and that when I got back from abroad I should 'definitely get in touch' to arrange its prompt return.

The second was from Linda. Alan, she regretted to say, had collapsed after an afternoon of heavy drinking and been taken to hospital. Distressing as this was, I have to admit to being more concerned with my own troubles – chiefly, that neither Guy Gosling nor the British Antarctic Survey had yet responded to my requests for a visitor's permit. This time, however, I felt certain that they would have, and it was with a sharp sense of disappointment that I logged on to my inbox to find it empty.

Out on deck the breeze had picked up and was teasing white crests from the waves. Like tightrope-walking, walking on board a moving seacraft demands of its practitioners a measure of relinquished self-scrutiny, of trust to their deeper instincts for uprightness, and although each step gave unpleasant intimations of bonelessness I was gratified, as a hand of spume shot up and slapped me in the face, to find my 'sea legs' in reasonable working order. I was, in any case, doing better than the couple on the aft deck, lurching and flailing and clinging on to each other with an intensity that might have been comic had it not been so enviable. Above us, eyeing my chocolates, a Wandering Albatross kept pace with the ship, the immense span of its wings, perhaps nine or ten feet in this instance, allowing it to glide for miles without so much as a single beat. And clutching the rail I thought of its breeding grounds on South Georgia, eight hundred miles to the east, where courting pairs of albatrosses preen, and sing to each other, forming monogamous bonds that often last for life. When the Ancient Mariner kills the albatross, his punishment, unlike his more fortunate shipmates, is to be claimed not by Death but by his spectral female superior:

> The Night-mare Life-in-Death was she,
> Who thicks man's blood with cold.

Now commercial fishing practices threaten to turn us all – or at least those of us who eat tuna – into Ancient Mariners. Attracted by the bait on the longline hooks used by Atlantic fishermen, the birds become entangled and drown, and ornithologists believe that an albatross is killed in this way every five minutes. Plucking a chocolate from the box, I threw it out to sea, and in an exquisitely effortless change of direction the albatross banked and caught it in its beak, free for the moment to enjoy it.

The next morning brought a lecture on the Belgian Antarctic Expedition of 1897–9, which, manned as it was by such future luminaries as Roald Amundsen and Frederick Cook,[5] was the first to spend an entire winter on the continent. Our lecturer was a young woman from New Zealand whose rather bespectacled manner was touchingly undermined by the fleshiness of her bottom lip, as softly plump as a wren's belly. Nonetheless, neither a plump lip, nor a mostly sound grasp of the facts, could excuse her failure to mention the single most significant *lesson* to be drawn from the young Amundsen's experiences sledging on the ice – namely, the catastrophic inefficiency of the man-hauling method[6] that was to put

5. Respectively, of course, the first men to conquer the South and, arguably, North Poles: arguably because Cook was a notorious liar, self-publicist and (later) convicted fraudster, who may or may not have reached the furthest point north a year before his fellow American Robert Peary, or indeed reached it at all.
6. i.e. dragging sledges yourself rather than getting dogs to do it.

Scott's *Terra Nova* expedition at such fatal disadvantage fourteen years later. Indeed, I was about to raise my hand to point this out, when Janet nudged me in the ribs and suggested I ask the nice young lady a question 'to show her how brainy' I was. This, I'm afraid, was the last straw, and pleading seasickness – the swell was topping fifteen feet that morning – I withdrew to my cabin and lay on my bunk.

'Miserable, utterly miserable,' wrote Scott, scarcely six weeks into his polar attempt. 'A hopeless feeling descends on one and is hard to fight off.' Depression walked beside Scott from the outset – even Apsley Cherry-Garrard, his great defender, described him as 'peevish, highly strung, irritable, depressed and moody' – and although by temperament I couldn't be more dissimilar, there were times aboard the *Oksana Antonova* when I wondered if travelling nine thousand miles to the Antarctic Circle might have constituted a marginal error of judgement. That morning, completing my fifth pre-breakfast circuit of the captain's deck, I had experienced my first sighting of an iceberg, and although it was a scrawny sort of thing, not much bigger than Foxglove Cottage, it was enough to raise the chilling prospect of reaching the Peninsula with no firm plan as to how I'd get to see Sunita. How much more keenly I missed her, now she was nearly in reach!

It was almost by accident that I picked up the email from Guy Gosling. By the afternoon of our third day at sea we had drawn level with the South Shetland Islands, the sub-Antarctic archipelago keen-minded ramblers will recall lies roughly where Walks 5 and 6 did 600 million years ago. Janet, Phil and I were disinfecting our boots for the cruise's first organised shore excursion, a trip by RIB[7] to see the chinstrap-penguin rookery on Deception Island, whose naturally perfect horseshoe bay is rendered tantalisingly inhospitable by the active volcano that seethes and belches inland. An argument had broken out between Janet and Phil over how unexpectedly warm

7. Rigid Inflatable Boat.

it was outdoors,[8] and to reassure Janet that she would indeed shortly be subject to the sort of miserable conditions a paying Antarctic cruise member had every right to expect, I kicked off my boots and popped back upstairs to the computer room to check the weather online. Absent-mindedly logging on to my email instead, I read the following at least twice before I'd quite realised who it was from:

Dear g
How extraordinary to find you in our humble little corner of the world – tell when and where and we'll come and meet you off the boat.
Best g

Chinstrap penguins are so called because of the narrow black band that delineates their faces like the strap of a soldier's helmet. To be addressed as 'g' by an environmentalist of Guy Gosling's stature was as deeply flattering as it was unexpected, and given the possibility, as laid out by Daisy, that his relationship with my wife was entirely professional, I felt no reason whatsoever simultaneously to consider it an unforgivably insensitive impertinence. And besides, what mattered above all else was the use of the first-person plural – '*our* humble little corner', '*we'll* come and meet you'. Alighting on Deception Island, I felt in those familiar parts of speech a proximity to Sunita that made a downy brown arm of the embrace of the bay, a lucid hazel eye of its waters, a décolletage of the mountains glimpsed beyond the coastal foothills. As we approached the rookery, a pair of elephant seals hauled out onto the beach, just as their northern cousins had on our honeymoon in California, and glancing south towards the Peninsula I felt what the great explorers of the Heroic Age must have felt: an impulse towards something so powerful that they would

8. From the 'Discover Antarctica' website: 'Contrary to popular belief Antarctica is actually a sun-worshipper's paradise. During the summer months (October to March) cruise members can enjoy between 18 and 24 hours of sunlight *every day* – so be sure to pack that sunscreen along with the blizzard-proof ice jacket!'

sacrifice their own lives to achieve it. No doubt Captain Scott had his faults.[9] But along with Wilson, Oates, Bowers and Evans he walked – lest we forget – *eight hundred miles* to the Pole, and over six hundred back, dragging a heavily laden sledge through blizzards of unusual and astonishing severity, to the camp where, heartbreakingly close to the supplies that might have saved them, the three surviving explorers succumbed to starvation and cold. It was without doubt one of the most exacting and courageous walks ever undertaken, and if there was a suggestion of self-forgetfulness, even destructiveness, in the way they went about it, there is surely something to admire in that too. When eight months after their deaths their bodies were discovered, frozen solid as Wilson's statue in Cheltenham, Scott was found with his arm thrown around his old friend Bill, and in the account, recorded in their respective journals, of the stoicism with which they faced certain death, they come back to life every bit as movingly as Hermione does in her *Winter's Tale*.

We reached Adelaide Island on the morning of our fourth day at sea. Through the mists it appeared as a long, low form, pale pink in

9. A tendency to depression, poor man. And irascibility. And stubbornness. And sentimentalism. Favouritism. Absent-mindedness. Self-pity. Taciturnity. Pompousness. Impatience with thorough preparation. Impetuosity, covered up and thus entrenched by a nervy sort of imperiousness that alienated his men, saw the most cautious and delicately framed dissent as insubordination, and approved against all advice and better judgement a) the use of ponies, which are herbivorous, and thus difficult and expensive to feed on a continent largely bereft of plant matter, b) the underuse of dogs, which are carnivorous, and better suited to the cold, c) the neglect of proper ski-training, d) the deficient marking both of depots and routes through heavily crevassed terrain, e) the fatally skimpy and nutritionally imbalanced rations stored in said depots, f) the inadequate sealing of paraffin canisters, well known to 'creep' or lose volume at very low temperatures, g) the inclusion of Petty Officer Evans instead of Lashly or Crean in the final polar party, despite explicitly voiced doubts over Evans's physical and mental fitness, h) the last-minute decision to take five men to the Pole, when there was scarcely enough food or room in the tent for four, i) a plan to provide relief on the return journey so complex and contradictory that the eventual rescue party under Cherry-Garrard turned back a week before the frostbitten, scurvy-ruined Capt. Oates crawled out of the tent to his merciful if entirely avoidable death by exposure.

the perpetual twilight, rising to a ridge of six peaks before descending gently to form a spit that reached as if yearning for the mainland. At 67° 15′ S the island lies within the Antarctic Circle, and aside from the pack ice through which the *Oksana Antonova* moved with a reptilian croak, the abrupt drop in temperature was evident from the expression of glacial indignation on Janet's face as we passed on the threshold to the observation deck.

'*Bl**dy* freezing,' said Janet.

'Well,' I said, resisting the temptation to point out that it had been too warm for her yesterday. 'It *is* Antarctica, Janet.'

'I know,' said Janet. 'But they could *warn* you, couldn't they?'

We had, in fact, been 'warned' over breakfast, although Janet, busy persecuting Phil for allowing a fried egg to disrupt his strict low-cholesterol diet, would doubtless not have caught Captain Finch's calm forecast of temperatures dropping as low as minus ten that afternoon, followed, inevitably, by a reminder from Yuri that the wind-chill factor could reduce that to minus twenty-five or thirty and cause instantaneous frostbite. Stepping out onto deck, personally I found the cold no less pleasantly bracing than a February morning in Ledbury, and although I was aware that blizzard-bearing winds could whip up without warning, I was comfortable in the knowledge that the trusty old tri-climate jacket I wore on autumn rambles in the Malverns had been specifically designed for extreme weather conditions. A low sun shone half-heartedly, as if exhausted by the effort of never setting, through a gauze of unbroken cloud, and as the thickening ice slowed us to a stop I saw the squat, pale-green form of the research station emerge from the generality of white like a lover's whispered wake-up call. I could scarcely believe all that lay between me and Sunita was a channel of freezing sea and a few hundred metres of barren, snow-covered rock.

We climbed into the RIBs. Fifty yards along-shore, a cluster of Adélie penguins, startled by

Adélie penguin

the splutter and growl of the boats' powerful outboard motors, poured like landslip off their lichen-mottled rock, surfacing in a vast repeating crochet-pattern of leaps and dives that made the sea boil and Janet clutch my arm. Passing an iceberg, our guide – a rather distressingly attractive young Argentinian named Paloma – cut the engine, and for an entranced moment we drifted past the exorbitant mass of white, listening to the fizz of a billion air bubbles released by its gradually thawing underparts, its colour beneath the waterline like the first blue of the horizon at dawn. And I would have been more interested to note its resemblance to the ruin of a Regency townhouse had a red speck not appeared on the island. A visit to a lemon-seal colony had been arranged for the landing party, whereas I, to Janet's indeterminately envious annoyance, had been granted special dispensation to pass a few hours at the research station as the guest of Guy Gosling. As Paloma restarted the engine, and shaped a course for the island's rickety wooden jetty, the red speck became an ice jacket, then a human, then a tall, lightly bearded man in wraparound sunglasses, moving through a sequence of basic stretching procedures as he pouted out to sea.

'Is that your friend?' said Janet.

'Well,' I said. '"Friend" is probably too strong a word.'

'Oof,' said Janet. 'If I was twenty years younger!'

'You'd still be ten years too old,' muttered Phil.

'Welcome to the worst place on Earth!' said Guy, giving a hand-up to Paloma, and causing Janet to emit a laugh of such ingratiating intensity that for a moment it was quite clear Phil was considering staying on the boat. Incidentally, it had been to my considerable relief and, I'm ashamed to admit, slight resentment that for the entire duration of the cruise Janet never once suggested I try my luck with Paloma. Elegant, quadrilingual and impressively know-ledgeable about Antarctic fauna, Paloma was also dark-eyed, full-hipped and deeply honeyed of skin, and as she pressed her head to the chest of Guy Gosling's ice jacket I experienced the oddly distancing sense that I'd seen her do something similar before. There followed a period of (not entirely unflirtatious) consultation between

Guy and Paloma, before it was announced that in three hours the party would reconvene outside the research station, for the launch of one of the helium-filled meteorological balloons with which scientists at the base monitored fluctuations in temperature in the lower reaches of the stratosphere. That settled, Guy turned to me.

'Gordon.'

'Graham. You probably don't remember me. We met at the Walnut Tree Hotel . . .'

'Yeah, yeah,' said Guy, with a waft of the hand. 'What do you say to a walk?'

Immediately to the north-west of the base, Reptile Ridge climbs to a height of 1,648 feet (502m). On a 'dingle'[10] day the arête gives excellent views over the Shambles Glacier, Mount Orca, and the spectacular ranges in the less accessible northern part of the island. Even at sea level it was clear that this was mouth-watering walking territory. Ahead, hiding the higher peaks behind it from view, a short but temptingly steep preliminary summit wore a uniform convexity of powder snow. More pressing matters aside, it was disappointing to learn that we would only have time to crest the ridge and walk back down again before the balloon launch later that afternoon. From Sunita I knew that Guy, like 'Bill' Wilson before him, had attended Cheltenham College, and hurrying to keep pace, as we crunched over firmer crust snow towards the foot of the escarpment, I was struck by the easy self-confidence evident in his happiness to say as little as possible without actively ignoring me.

'So,' I said, already a little short of puff. 'What is it exactly that you do here?'

'This and that,' said Guy. 'It's really not very interesting.'

'I'm interested.'

'Are you?'

---

10. British Antarctic Territory slang for fine weather. Bad weather is 'manky'. From the little I heard, much of the lingo peculiar to BAT settlements has a rather puerile ring of public-school inclusivity to it. Witness 'meats' for food, 'beast' for woman, and 'naize', a corruption of 'nice', as a general term of approbation. As in, 'Apparently it's going to be dingle tomorrow.' 'Naize.'

'Very much so.'

'Okay.' Guy stopped and turned. Behind him, against the bruised white of the sky, clouds of spindrift were moving through fluid mutations, like the starlings that mass at dusk above the Somerset Levels. The weather was changing. But Guy seemed unperturbed. 'Without wanting to go into too much detail. The guys on base are monitoring various things – temperature, humidity, carbon concentrations in the ice cores, variations in the Earth's magnetic field – to try and figure out why the ice shelves are melting so fast. And my job is to translate what they find into comprehensible English. Basically I'm the guy that sits there annoying everybody by asking stupid questions.'

'No, no,' I said. 'It's important work.'

'Yeah, well,' said Guy, brushing snow off his sleeve. 'Thanks. I certainly think it is. Part of the problem we have convincing people to do anything about climate change is the complexity of the data. As Arthur C. Clarke said, any sufficiently advanced technology is indistinguishable from magic. So the public is required to take the need for action on faith. But faith is irrational, which is exactly what the scientists are telling us not to be. No wonder nobody trusts them. We have to build the public's trust in these guys as a matter of urgency. At the moment it's just the ice shelves that are melting. Which as you know, won't actually directly affect sea levels, as floating ice displaces its own mass of water.'

'The Archimedes Principle.'

'Right, but when they all go, then the ice sheet over the West Antarctic landmass will start to melt, and we'll be looking at a rise of six, seven metres. Fifty if the whole continent goes. That's enough to turn Great Malvern into a seaside resort.'

Alarming as this prospect may have been, I was more urgently concerned with the turn the weather had taken. A familiar feature of Antarctic weather systems is the katabatic wind, a species of invisible avalanche caused by the build-up and sudden discharge of very large amounts of very cold, and thus very dense, air, high up on exactly the sort of elevated ice sheets that loomed over our position to the east. When the snow surface is loose, as it was that afternoon, blizzard conditions can obtain in a matter of seconds, and within a few yards of resuming our ascent it had become all but impossible to maintain a conversation.

'So is Sunita turning out to be any help?' I shouted.

'What?'

'Sunita. *Is she being any help?*'

Here Guy turned, and said something that the wind whipped from his mouth and threw into the distance. It sounded like, *She's not here, Graham.*

'*What?*' I shouted, quite sure I'd misheard him; this time, to make himself absolutely clear, Guy took me firmly by the shoulders, and bellowed in my face.

'*SUNITA'S NOT HERE!*'

No need to shout, I thought. Making a cut-throat gesture with one pudgily gloved finger – presumably to signal our abandonment of the ascent – Guy clapped me on the shoulder and started heading downhill. Visibility was soon down to a few feet, and anxious lest I fall behind I set off after his receding red jacket at pace. Ramblers will remember the mountain-goat technique I like to apply to steeper declivities, but unused as I was to the surface, it wasn't long before I'd lost my footing, slipped, fallen, and slammed my still-convalescent coccyx into a rocky outcrop barely covered in snow.

'The eternal silence of the great white desert,' wrote Scott, camping on the Ross Ice Barrier. Just my luck to let out a blood-curdling bellow of agony in the middle of a blizzard that would have silenced a mammoth. I lay in the snow for a moment, and would have lain there longer had the fear of losing sight of Guy not hauled me, crying out in pain, to my feet. I shouted his name, but the wind had risen to a vicious, twisting hiss that would have made a waste of breath of any further attempt. I peered into the distance, or tried to, and failed, as there wasn't any – only a faintly throbbing, tapioca whiteness that simultaneously had no depth and seemed to extend into infinity. During his legendary 36-hour crossing of South Georgia on foot, Ernest Shackleton reported feeling the insubstantial presence of an extra walker beside him, an experience recounted by T. S. Eliot in *The Waste Land*:

> Who is the third who always walks beside you?
> When I count, there are only you and I together
> But when I look ahead up the white road
> There is always another one walking beside you
> Gliding wrapt in a brown mantle, hooded
> I do not know whether a man or a woman
> – But who is that on the other side of you?

I, on the other hand, can report feeling the presence of no one at all, and for all that I cried out for Sunita, it was with a sense of my unfathomable aloneness that I stumbled onwards, into a wind that felt as if it were flash-freezing then smashing my face into shards. Distance having been obliterated, with every step I grew more horrified at the realisation that I might walk, and walk, and walk, and never get anywhere. In time, I stopped, and screaming out to gain, amid the infinite numbing whiteness, some sensory verification of my own existence, I thought of Anne, and that terrible day in Devon, raving on the clifftop like Lear, beleaguered by butterflies, naked but for a pair of old boots. Somehow, some flickering instinct for survival spurred me on, and I struck in what seemed to be a downhill direction until I put my foot out, found nothing and realised a moment before I would otherwise have fallen over it that I was standing on the edge of a precipice.

My memory of what happened next remains vague. I must have crawled into the lee of a snowdrift, and dug myself the rudiments of a cave, because when I came round at the sound of several voices what I saw was a roof of sparkling white suffused with an indescribably beautiful blue. How nice, I thought. I'm dead! And then to my considerable irritation I was dragged from my lucent cave of eternal rest, and wrestled onto a stretcher.

'Nonsense,' I recall saying, as I tried against more than one person's wishes to sit up. '*Please* let's not make a fuss.'

Whereupon I passed out for a second time.

At closer quarters the cluster of buildings that made up the research station had the temporary look of management offices on a massive building site. The blizzard had freshened the ground with snow, and the bay was busy with fragments of ice and larger 'bergy bits',[11] but it was hard to reconcile this ugly jumble of concrete and corrugated steel, surrounded by bare rock and swathes of muddy snow churned up by chunky tractor treads, with the immaculacy of the snowfields in which I might quite happily have died. In its small way, what lay before me was the most shockingly vandalised landscape I had ever seen. After a brief medical examination, in which a rather self-regardingly youthful nurse pronounced me 'healthy enough for my age', bar the second-degree frostbite on my cheeks, I was taken by Guy to the station bar, where I sat by a large picture window, swaddled in a blanket, nursing what I have to say was a very welcome triple measure of Highland Park single malt (47.5%). Outside, now the manky weather had given way to a dingle-blue sky, the party from the *Oksana Antonova* had gathered to watch the launch of the meteorological balloon. Drowsily curious as I was, I had nonetheless become inescapably distracted by a neatly bearded, stoat-thin man seated by the dartboard, aiming an unambiguous scowl at me.

'What's *his* problem?' I heard myself saying.

Guy glanced over his shoulder. 'Ash? Don't worry about him. He's spent nine months analysing air bubbles trapped in ice-core samples. Can tend to make you a little tetchy in human company.'

'A little tetchy? He looks like he wants to boil me alive.'

'Well, they're not mad about tourists here, it has to be said. Of course it didn't help that you got yourself lost on the ridge. It's like everywhere else: everyone hates a day-tripper. Except they hate them

---

11. Small icebergs, either reduced in volume by melting or 'calved' from larger fragments. A sense of loss is subtly encoded in the language of sea ice: still smaller fragments are known as 'growlers', after the bereft-bear sound made by released air as the growler drops off to make its own way in the world.

more here. The scientists tend to think of Antarctica as theirs – this last wilderness only they're allowed to f**k up.'

I drained my glass. A pause, and then Guy touched me tentatively on the sleeve.

'Why did you come, Graham?'

'I was led to believe that Sunita was here.'

'By who?'

'Daisy Rux-Burton.'

'Ah, Daise. Awesome girl. *Not* the brightest button.'

I left a pause. 'That picture on your blog. Of you and a girl on an ice floe. It's Paloma, isn't it? From the cruise ship?'

Guy shrugged. 'What can I say? It's lonely out here. And extremely male. Which is why it was probably just as well Sunita didn't come out in the end. I hope this doesn't sound sexist, but in many ways this *isn't* a very female-friendly place.'

I looked around me, at the drab walls, the brown carpet, the wall pinned with postcards and torn-out photographs of breasts, bottoms, fingers on glossy, pouting red lips, and thought of the in-ship magazine produced by Georges Lecointe, second-in-command on the Belgian Antarctic Expedition, semi-literately entitled *The Ladysless South*; of Roald Amundsen's stern injunction against all talk of the opposite sex; of Rear Admiral Jim Reedy, commander in the mid-1960s of the US Deep Freeze Task Force 43, talking wistfully of 'the womanless white continent of peace'. Gosling was right. For a hundred years men had been coming to Antarctica to get away from women, and I, fond fool that I was, had come here to find one.

'Do you know where she is?'

'Haven't the faintest,' said Guy. 'I was going to ask you the same question.'

'When was the last time you saw her?'

'I don't know. Late September?'

'So you're no longer together.'

'I suppose not. We were meant to meet down by the Gullet one Saturday morning. She said she had something really important to tell me. And then she never turned up. David Redfern was there so I assumed it was one of Sunita's little melodramas.'

'By which you mean?'

Guy winced into the distance. 'Oh, you know. The whole David thing, for instance. From the way she talked about him when we first met I assumed she and David were an item. Turned out they weren't. But then all the time Sunita and I were seeing each other she wouldn't stop going on about him.'

'So you were seeing each other.'

'Well, sort of. We were – actually, wait a second. Why am I feeling guilty about this? I had a fling with your wife, all right? She told me the marriage had been over before it started. And besides, it was only a bit of fun. Nothing remotely serious.'

'And how long did it last?'

'A couple of months? On and off after that night at the Walnut Tree when Peter Agnew lost the plot. Then for a few days in mid-September she came to stay with us at Alder Hall. That's when it all began to break down, really. My father rather took to her but I'm afraid she didn't really hit it off with Mum.'

'No?'

'*Really* no. We'd be having lunch and she'd start banging on about what a wonderful photographer David was, and how I'd be mad not to take him to Antarctica blahdeblah. Didn't go down well at *all*. And then she started getting all mysterious about whether she was on the pill or not.'

'At lunch? With your parents?'

'Well, you wouldn't put it past her, would you? No, in private. Everything was a game with her. "Chase me, chase me." Which I'm sorry, but I really don't find that charming. It just p*sses me off.'

'I can imagine.'

Guy peered at me over the table. 'You haven't murdered her, have you?'

'You're not the first person to ask me that.'

'Well, have you or haven't you?'

'Of course not.'

'No offence,' said Guy, with a sly smile. 'It's just I'd assumed by not turning up that morning Sunita was trying to make me jealous. But then it occurred to me you might have had enough, tonked her on the head and dumped her in the lake. *I'd* certainly have been tempted. Either way I wouldn't sweat it too much, mate. All due respect, but in my opinion you're well shot of her.'

I looked down at my whisky glass, and was surprised to find myself wondering what effect it would have if I smashed it on the side of the table, and drove it into Guy's handsome, practised face. Frowning, as if in deep thought, he turned to look through the window.

'Not that any of it matters very much. Not compared to the big stuff, anyway.'

Here Guy gestured at the meteorological balloon, a partially inflated silver sac, about the size of a male elephant seal, tethered to a weight by a cord the climate scientist was gently twanging with his index finger. Arranged in a semicircle around him, my shipmates from the *Oksana Antonova* listened, fingers to chin, legs crossed at the ankle, as he explained, so Janet was later to tell me, that due to the decrease in external pressure the balloon would inflate as it entered the upper atmospheres. The scientist knelt to untether the balloon, and as it rose into the cloudless blue sky I saw Janet grab hold of Phil's kagoule, pulling him, evidently against his wishes, closer and closer, until, with an easy readjustment, they were standing enfolded in each other's arms, staring up together, and the balloon was a colourless speck.

Guy shook his head. 'I'm just sorry you came all this way for nothing.'

'That's all right,' I said, to the balloon. 'I would have gone to Mars.'

Walk 15: Ledbury Circular

A ghost walk. At the time of writing a good part of this route still passed through the ancient broadleaf woodlands east of Ledbury. Even now, however, ramblers may feel this immaculate landscape, and others like it, slipping into the past. Only time will tell what scraps will remain once man, in his wisdom, has unmuzzled his chainsaw, and entombed the springy earth in obdurate concrete. The rest of the walk, which follows the route of several main roads, serves in its sooty verges and litter-strewn roundabouts as a stern reminder of what happens when the promiscuous spirit of nature is suppressed, although ramblers may gain some comfort from the nettles, brambles and dandelions that continue to defy the weed contractor's strimmer. Failing that, the walk begins and ends at a perfectly serviceable pub, and in the author's experience, even the end of life as we know it can seem of little consequence through the shifting amber prism of a pint glass!

Turn left outside the Full Pitcher pub on New Street in Ledbury. In the cold months that followed my return from Antarctica I saw

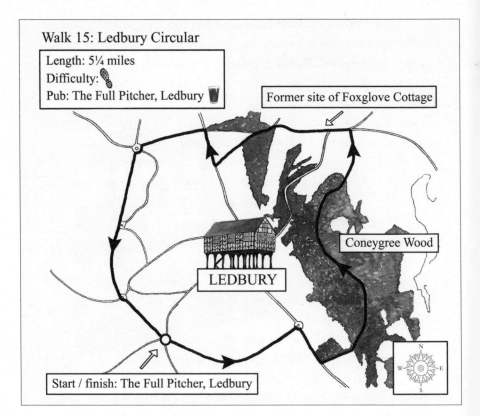

a succession of Sunitas, blurred in passing cars, doubled in shop windows, and once, heart-stoppingly, in the murkily firelit front room of a cottage in Ledbury, two doors down from my new rental property, through a small mullioned pane whose imperfections made her shudder as she glided out of sight. Indeed, on the fateful day I took the train to London, I saw a Sunita standing on the platform at Moreton-in-Marsh, shielding her face with one hand as she wept into her mobile phone. Less than a week previously I had been discussing Sunita with PCs Cox and Onions of the West Mercia Constabulary, and had it not run the risk of sounding highly suspicious, I might, in response to their understandable curiosity as to where she was, have in all truthfulness answered, 'Everywhere.'

'Excellent sound quality on the Olympus, isn't there? Very clear.'

PC Cox had brought round my missing voice recorder and laid it on the kitchen table between us. 'Shall we have a listen?'

I said nothing. PC Cox pressed play.

'Help!' said Sunita. '*Heeeelp!* I'm being *grabbed!* SOMEBODY CALL THE POLICE!'

'It was an argument,' I said, after PC Cox had paused the recording. 'Nothing more. And I wasn't "grabbing" her.'

'Yeah,' said PC Cox. 'You say that on the recording. You're just trying to stop Ms Bhattacharya starting the car. You're estranged now, aren't you?'

'Separated. That's correct.'

'And you have no idea where she is?'

'No.'

'No idea,' repeated PC Cox, consulting his notes. 'And you've recently returned from the South Pole, I believe?'

'From Antarctica, yes.'

'Holiday, was it? Get away from it all?'

'No. I went because I'd heard Sunita might be there.'

'You went to Antarctica because you heard Sunita "might be there".'

A patient smile. 'I had nothing else to go on.'

PC Cox nodded, and jotted something in his notebook.

'To the best of your knowledge,' said PC Onions, after a pause, 'does Ms Bhattacharya have friends or relations in the west London area?'

'I'm not sure. Why do you ask?'

'Because it seems a number of withdrawals have been made on her bank account. From a cashpoint on Ladbroke Grove.'

'Ladbroke Grove?'

'You seem surprised.'

A rumble of wind on the kitchen window. 'Yes. I suppose I am.'

'Why? Because you think she's dead?'

'What an absurd question. She's quite evidently *not* dead, if she's been withdrawing money from her bank account.'

'Unless somebody else had access to her bank card and PIN number.'

Unruffled as I may have appeared I had inwardly to admit to some irritation at PC Onions' line of questioning. Granted, I *did* have Sunita's PIN number, and had been in London on at least one of the dates in question,[1] but however inconveniently violent the quarrel on the voice recorder may have sounded, to imply that I had anything to do with Sunita's disappearance was as I'm sure ramblers would agree to take the professional duty of free speculation to extremes. Still, I agreed to 'give them a bell' if I heard anything, and with no small excitement committed the coming Saturday to an expedition to the capital. Having been offered a 'newly created' clerical position in my own department I had taken the hint, resigned from the council and joined the Gloucestershire and West Midlands Tidy Britain Partnership as a volunteer team organiser. This kept me busy three days a week, which would leave me a full three and a half to look for Sunita if I skipped the wake and left immediately after Alan's funeral – at which, as it turned out, a chance encounter yielded vital further clues as to where Sunita might be.

'Daisy,' I exclaimed, in grave tones, as we gathered in the churchyard after the service. 'I didn't realise you knew Alan.'

'Met him at the Walnut Tree,' she said. 'He had *such* a love of nature writing.'

Alan had succumbed to a gastrointestinal haemorrhage after drinking eighteen pints of Tribute and had died in hospital three weeks later, his three beloved daughters by his bedside. Michael, his elder brother, and no stranger to the bottle himself, had read Sonnet 60, 'Like as the waves make towards the pebbled shore', and if, in the circumstances, his inability very audibly to form a consonant had gained the audience's sympathy, he promptly squandered it by following his reading with a long, semi-comprehensible ramble on the

1. For an ambitious 'Hidden Rivers Ramble', supposedly taking in the variously culverted and asphalted-over courses of Stamford Brook, the Westbourne, the Tyburn and the Fleet, but ending (for me at least) somewhere near Notting Hill Gate, after an argument with Linda resulted in a bent walking pole and my quite possibly permanent estrangement both from her and the Gloucestershire and West Midlands Saturday Walkers' Club.

textual evidence for Shakespeare's chronic alcoholism. Alan's widow Heather had been too upset to respond to my condolences, but I was granted an insight into the distance that seemed to have developed between us during a brief exchange by a broken gravestone with her eldest daughter, Olivia.

'Is your wife well?'

'I couldn't say. We're separated.'

'What a coincidence,' said Olivia, with a brilliant smile. 'Just like Mum and Dad when he died. I wonder, Mr Underhill. Have you ever had your pr*ck teased?'

'Not to my knowledge.'

'I don't recommend it. It can drive you to drink.'

After this Daisy came as some relief. I had found her in the shelter of the lych-gate, lighting a cigarette, and as she leant forward to kiss me on the cheek she stopped and recoiled with a look of pantomime revulsion.

'Eww. What's that on your *face*?'

'Touch of frostbite. Nothing that won't clear up in another six months.'

'Oh, God.' Daisy grimaced. 'I suppose that's *my* fault.'

'No more than it was mine.'

'It can't have been an *entirely* wasted journey.'

'No, no. Extraordinary wildlife. Very informative. I think Sunita might be in London.'

That Daisy seemed unfazed by the abrupt change in subject may, it occurred to me, have had something to do with her appearing momentarily to pass out at the mention of 'wildlife', and coming round thinking it was several seconds later than it actually was. I filled her in on what PC Onions had told me.

'Hm,' she said, with a ruminative nod.

'Why "hm"? You know about this? Have you heard something?'

'No.' The shadow of an amusing thought flitted across Daisy's face. 'It's just . . .'

I resisted the temptation to stamp my foot. 'Just what?'

'I really can't say. She *swore* me to secrecy.'

'My dear Daisy,' I said, pointing at the thick black scab on my left cheek. 'I think you owe me this one, don't you?'

Alighting at Paddington, I made my way to the nearest internet café. During one of their many 'girly chats' – a phrase I'm proud to report Sunita never used – Sunita had told Daisy that if she were ever to find herself 'in a corner' she had met a writer at one of the Walnut Tree seminars whose friend owned a pub in London and might be in the position to give her a job. The name of the pub was, regrettably, outside the reach of Daisy's memory – she had a vague idea it was animally, or planty, 'something to do with nature, anyway' – but she definitely remembered it was somewhere near the river. Two hours spent cross-referencing pubs with nature-related names against pubs in easy reach of the Thames yielded eighty-eight results.[2] To make the project manageable I had restricted myself to a twenty-mile stretch of river between Richmond to the west and Greenwich to the east. Laterally speaking I thought it reasonable to stray no further than two-thirds of a mile from the river's edge. Rather than walking the entire twenty miles along the south bank of the river, and twenty miles back along the north, I broke up the route into sections divided by bridges, so that I might, for instance, walk the six and three-quarter miles along the south bank from Hammersmith to Richmond, taking in the Red Lion, the Coach and Horses, the Bull's Head, the Brown Dog, the Orange Tree, White Swan, White Horse and Red Cow, then six and three-quarter miles back along the north, ending at the Dove in Hammersmith, ready to hop on the tube to Pimlico for the twelve-mile Vauxhall Bridge–Hammersmith Bridge–Vauxhall Bridge loop. Allowing for the restrictions imposed by opening hours, need for sleep, etc., etc., completing the entire forty-mile circuit in three and a half days would demand a daily walking quota it would be callow to compare to Scott and Wilson's in their attempt on the Pole, but

---

2. The monotony of this process was broken, temporarily, by the sight of Sunita's actor/barman acquaintance Seb, trapped in a building-society advertisement on the sidebar of a pub-review website. The poor chap was waving frantically in an attempt to lure potential customers into activating the sound. I demurred.

which would nonetheless demand reserves of stamina, single-mindedness and at least partial resistance to the variously nutty, hoppy, biscuity temptations on offer!

I kicked off with the central Tower Bridge–Vauxhall Bridge–Tower Bridge loop. At just under seven miles in total this was considerably shorter than average, but naturally took in a considerably greater than average number of pubs, compared, say, to the sections of river-bank between Putney and Barnes, or, in particular, Hammersmith and Isleworth, revealed by my analysis as intriguingly short on floral and/or faunal pub names.[3] Between 4 and 8.30 p.m., when I rewarded myself with four pints of Flowers IPA (3.6%) at the Lavender in Vaux-hall, I visited the Bunch of Grapes, the Mudlark, the Wheatsheaf, the Slug and Lettuce, two Roses and Crowns, two White Harts, the Mulberry Bush, the Sloe Bar, the Walrus Social, the Camel, the Horse, the Three Stags, the Pineapple, and the Royal Oak, pausing for a moment to consider whether the Jolly Gardeners counted, deciding on the grounds of its proximity to the river, and Daisy's taxonomical ill-discipline, that it probably did, and knocking back a cheeky half of Erdinger *Weißbräu* before moving on to the Dog House, the White Bear, yet another White Hart, and the Rose.

As I left the Lavender, ramblers will understand if I had begun to feel the hour. It was a bleak, drizzly evening in February, and crossing Vauxhall Bridge on my way to the White Swan, the Royal Oak, and the White Horse and Bower, I stopped for a moment to watch as the river slid beneath me. Under the ambient light the water showed a sallow, sluggish orange, pockmarked by rain, and I wondered what it might be like to drown in it, whether that first foul gulp and misty intimation of solute would be any worse a death than a slow descent through clearer waters. Suddenly the enormity of my task, its enormous

---

3. Perhaps because the yearning for natural phenomena encoded in central-London pub names like the Wheatsheaf, the Bunch of Grapes, etc. has in these historically 'greener' outlying parts of London been satisfied by the real thing. The theory is lent weight by the corresponding fashion in Britain's dreariest semi-rural back-waters for bars with wistfully 'urban' names like 'Scene', 'Zoombar', 'Hub', 'Fusion' and 'Qube'.

pointlessness, weighed so heavily on me that I started to imagine that I had been deceiving myself from the moment Sunita left me on that windswept bench the previous September. Had I perhaps murdered her after all? The police evidently thought so, and I had noted a new revulsion, suppressed but unmistakable, in the faces and voices even of people outside my immediate circle of acquaintance,[4] as if my guilt, like a mark on the face, was obvious to everyone but its bearer. Even Daisy, even *Linda*, might simply have been waiting, withholding judgement until the matter was proved beyond reasonable doubt, and as the rain picked up it began to seem perfectly credible that I had done something so horrific that I would go to the ends of the earth to forget it. These and other harrowing thoughts dogged my steps as I called in at the Barley Mow, the Red Lion, the Theodore Bull Frog, the Lemon Tree, Hops!, the Coach and Horses, the Elephant, and another Bunch of Grapes, stopping for a pint – often of indifferently hopped, mass-produced lager – at each, until, stumbling into the gloomy environs of Tower Hill I received a text from Daisy informing me, with effusively capitalised acknowledgements of her idiocy, that she'd just remembered that the pub wasn't by the river, but the Regent's Canal, and might not have had an animal- or plant-related name after all.

I was in no state to continue my pub walk that evening – let alone cross-reference canalside pubs with pubs whose names Daisy might temporarily have misremembered as animal- or plant-related – and so retired to my hotel just north of Paddington, on a street of dingily blowsy Regency townhouses not far from Delamere Terrace, where Edward Wilson lived during his brief stint as a doctor in London. Sunday dawned dry, under a generality of white so seamless it might not have been cloud, but a perfect blue sky drained of colour. After a late and unabashedly greasy breakfast I set off under the concrete thunder of the Westway to Little Venice, where the Grand Union Canal, dawdling in eastwards from Birmingham, meets the Regent's Canal, built between 1812 and

4. For example the woman at the ticket desk at Ledbury Station.

1820 as the last link in a chain of navigable waterways that stretched from the industrial heartlands of the Black Country to the Thames at Limehouse Basin, and thence to India, China and the rest of the world. Eight and a half miles in length, it could, according to my researches, claim reasonable proximity to twenty-seven pubs, and it was with a combined sense of muted excitement, fear and resignation to Daisy's by now firmly established unreliability as a source that I looked in at the Bridge House, the (tragically boarded-up) Crocker's Folly on Aberdeen Place, and, the other side of Regent's Park, the Engineer in Primrose Hill, through whose large plate-glass window I saw my wife knifing smooth the cambers of a dozen butter dishes.

My wife. Sunita. I doubled back to check if my eyes had deceived me. They hadn't, but caught in a squall of conflicting feelings I had planted my hands, gecko-fashion, on the wall beside the window, and very slowly introduced my head beyond the jamb, without, I admit, much thought as to how it might look from the perspective of anyone inside. Sunita, praise be, was too absorbed in her task to notice, but for a bowel-loosening moment I caught the eye of a swarthily handsome barman standing polishing a wine glass, and pushing off the ground floor's attractively Italianate stucco dressings I set off up Gloucester Avenue at as expeditious a hobble as my coccyx would allow. Arriving, breathless, at the Lansdowne, the next pub up the road, I was at first treated as some form of vagrant, and it was only after a show of some considerable eloquence that I retired to a table by the gents' with a frothing pint of Thornbridge Hall's potent, pine-scented, playfully citrus-peely Jaipur IPA (a hefty 5.9%). It was, by now, a quarter past twelve, and groups of artfully dishevelled young punters had begun to assemble for a Sunday lunch that might feature braised lamb shank with cinnamon, green beans and pearl barley, or chanterelle and thyme tart with a chicory and pinenut salad. For at least the next couple of hours Sunita would, I inferred, be run off her feet serving a clientèle I dimly hoped might be a notch or two less attractive and conspicuously affluent than this one, and despite my complete lack of appetite, I forced myself to order a borlotti-bean and turnip-top risotto, the better to absorb the multiple pints I would need to regain my composure.

By half past two I had left the Lansdowne soundly, but not, I think, dismayingly drunk. Nevertheless, leaning against a wall in good if strategically indirect view of the Engineer, I soon became tired, and judged if I sat on the pavement wearing an alert expression, with my hands placed like marble lion's paws on my knees, I would maintain a level of dignity that, notwithstanding the unsightly scabs on my cheeks, might dissuade passers-by from thinking me the sort of alcoholic down-and-out for which I had at first been mistaken at the Lansdowne. I must, however, have nodded off, as when I came to I found not only that I was surrounded by loose change, but that Sunita was walking down the road towards me, arm in arm with the good-looking barman who had earlier caught me peeping through the Engineer's front window.

Desperate to attain full wakefulness I dealt myself a vigorous slap on the cheek. Regrettably, this succeeded only in reopening the wound frostbite had left there, and as I stood to greet the handsome couple I felt my broad smile wettened by a trickle of blood.

'My darling. You're alive!'

'F**k!' screamed Sunita, throwing up her hands, and in the confusion that followed I found myself almost nose to nose with the barman, whose white shirtsleeves had been rolled, as if in readiness for just such a combat situation, almost to his shoulders, revealing smooth brown biceps of exemplary bulbousness.

'Back off, tramp.'

'It's okay, Bruno,' said Sunita. 'I know him.'

From its starting point of pitiless belligerence Bruno's expression softened, as his blood pressure dropped, into a leer of vaguely thwarted contempt. Looking me up and down, he gave a snort, and absolved from further involvement by a nod from Sunita, strutted off into the hurting afternoon.

'F***ing h*ll, Graham,' said Sunita. 'You scared the sh*t out of me.'

'I'm sorry.'

'You look f***ing terrible.'

'And you,' I said, feeling a weight of tenderness that nearly sent me to my knees, 'look f***ing beautiful.'

Sunita cancelled me with the flat of her hand. 'I'm sorry. I can't deal with this.'

And she was gone. Twenty yards further down the avenue, at the brink of a bridge, metal steps led down to the canal, but with my coccyx the way it was I had only just reached the gap in the wall when Sunita clanked off the bottom step and out of sight. By the time I gained the towpath there was no sign of her, save for a distant ring of footsteps that might have been coming from either direction. Looking left, towards Camden, and right, towards Regent's Park, I chose right, and within less than half a mile was rewarded for the trust I'd put in fate by the sight of my poor, confused darling, catching her breath on a buckled bench by a mass of mottled ivy.

'Can't run any more,' she said, looking up. 'How did you find me?'

We sat side by side on the bench. Over the twelve locks between Little Venice and Limehouse the Regent's Canal drops a full 86 feet (26m), and its current was just discernible in the dreamy drift of debris on the surface. If, in the days before Sunita left on a more permanent basis, I returned from work to find her not at home, I would feel an ache so raw it was as if a part of me had been removed, and after an absence of nearly five months ramblers will understand if the urge came upon me to throw my arms around her and squeeze until I'd partially absorbed her. Naturally, I suppressed it, and not only because Sunita could be uneasy with overt displays of affection. The few pounds she appeared to have gained had, if anything, intensified her beauty, but she seemed by the same token reduced, somehow, slightly less there – and pale, inasmuch as someone of her skin colour could be pale, as if she had a bloom on her, like a fallow field after a light frost.

'Where are you living?' I asked, after a silence.

'Near Ladbroke Grove.'

'Alone?'

'No.'

'Right.'

'With a friend.'

I brightened. 'We could walk there along the canal.'

'Oh, please. Give me a break. It's *miles*.'

'Three and three-quarters. Come on. It's a miserable, cold, overcast afternoon. What could be more spiritually uplifting?'

And so we walked, not quite touching, at a pace somewhere between Sunita's and mine. Indeed, as we entered the cutting between the zoo and Primrose Hill it struck me that this was the first time I could recall us walking more than a few yards together without Sunita either taking a lead or falling behind. To our right, there soon loomed into view the immense broken umbrella of the Snowdon Aviary, home to night herons, green peafowl and, most spectacularly of all, the sacred ibis, like the fearsome honey badger a native of southern Iraq, its long black bill downcurved like a plaintive cadence. And to the call of a green peahen – ah-*eyy*-eh-ah – I ran Sunita through what had happened in her absence: my trips to France and Antarctica, the publication of *Holes*, its shortlisting for the Leipziger Bundesbank Wild Photography Prize, Karen's pregnancy and, of course, the sad passing of Alan.

'Nothing happened, you know. Between me and Alan.'

I made no response.

'I mean, God rest his soul. But really! Ugh. Can you imagine it?'

'No, of course not. And neither can anyone else. In fact I spoke to his daughter at the funeral and she asked after your health.'

'I bet she did, that sanctimonious cow. You know she told her mother I'd given Alan a h**d-j*b round the back of the Walnut Tree Hotel?'

'Golly, no. Why would she think that?'

'Because he *asked* me for one. We had just popped out for a cigarette. And all of a sudden he put my hand on his thigh and said he could understand why a woman like me wouldn't be interested in a creep like Peter Agnew. The implication being I'd be interested in a creep like *him*. As if! He was so drunk I doubt I would even have been able to get *hold* of it. Anyway, I told him to f**k right off, but I suppose somebody must have heard us and started spreading it around. Next thing I know I've got Alan on the phone begging me to keep quiet about the whole sordid episode. I mean, the f***ing *irony* of it.'

'If you'd only talked to me about these things, Sunita. I would have understood.'

'I know, I know. I'm sorry. For everything. You must hate my guts.'

'Far from it.'

'For lying to you. Betraying you. For making you eat sh*t. Come *on*.'

'No.'

We had reached a gently curving stretch of canal so densely wooded on either side that were it not for the background rumble of traffic we might have been deep in a forest, following the course of a river to its source far from human habitation. A gust of wind ruffled the trees, and with a sequence of soft, buzzing honks, like someone blowing a comb through tracing paper, a swan swooped low over the wrinkled water, and on outstretched feet skied to a halt with a self-congratulatory shake of its tail feathers.

'I meant to call, you know.' Sunita had stopped to clean the dried blood off my cheek with a wettened thumb. 'To tell you I was all right.'

But she had been too ashamed. As Guy Gosling had suspected, by failing to turn up that Saturday morning in September – and inviting David along to boot – Sunita had hoped to make Guy jealous to the extent that he'd reverse his decision to end the relationship. Taking the train to London, she had moved in with her Ladbroke Grove friend and waited for Guy's call. Which never came.

'I'm so sorry,' she said. 'You must have been worried.'

'I was, rather. As were the police. They thought I'd done you in.'

Sunita laughed, then, after a moment's thought, fell silent. It was a moment before she spoke again.

'You really went all the way to Antarctica?'

'Well, only to the Peninsula. It's really not such a big deal these days.'

Sunita shook her head, and looking down at the towpath, toed a smile, or its opposite, in the dirt. 'What did I do to deserve you, Graham Underhill?'

The light had begun to fail by the time we reached the bridge where

Ladbroke Grove crosses the Grand Union Canal. For one reason or another, Sunita preferred to walk the last few hundred yards to her – or her friend's – flat alone, but over the ensuing weeks we saw each other with increasing regularity. The 'friend', it turned out, was the aspiring writer who had helped secure Sunita her job at the Engineer. Having met him briefly at the Walnut Tree during one of his occasional 'writing holidays' in Malvern, she had looked him up when she moved back to London in September. Now, however, although Sunita was too discreet to state it explicitly, he was clearly using his struggles to get published as a pretext to extricate himself from the relationship. Sunita would soon have to move out, and rent a one-bedroom flat on a waitress's income that would in any case shortly come to an end when it became hard to stay on her feet for long periods. Her writer friend, having money troubles of his own, was in no position to help. And in any case, as he had pointed out, why should he? Sunita had already been three weeks pregnant when she showed up at his door.

I, on the other hand, *could* be of some assistance, not only by making regular payments into her account, but by setting up a trust fund that in the event of my death would continue to contribute to her finances and the welfare of her and Guy Gosling's child. As, to give Linda her due, I had been repeatedly forewarned, my travels in search of Sunita had rather depleted the proceeds from the compulsory purchase of Foxglove Cottage. But I had enough to live on, and could think of nothing better to do with the rest than ensure my darling Sunita some measure of comfort. Moreover, I like to think my weekly visits to London, when we would sit, and drink, and talk, and take (moderately) long walks along the river, or through the city's oases of green, helped in some small way to restore in Sunita the vitality it seemed her estrangement from Guy had depleted. Sunita was understandably reluctant to dwell much on the baby's future until she'd had her 23-week scan, but her frequent talk of Guy's 'mad schedule' and 'right to a certain amount of head-space' had raised in me suspicions as to exactly how much the father himself was involved.

'You haven't told him, have you?'

It was a cold but sunny Tuesday afternoon in March. I had picked

Sunita up after her lunch shift, and, taking it slowly, we had climbed to the summit of Primrose Hill, at 206 feet (63m) giving views over a cityscape of such abrupt density and reach it seemed all at once a hostile country, separated from our little enclave of wildflower and grass by nothing but a flimsy border of trees. When Sunita spoke it was almost at a whisper.

'No.'

'You must.'

'I will. I will, I will. It's just so *weird*.' Here Sunita began to cry, quietly at first, and then in wild, hungry sobs. 'I'm not used to being out of my depth.'

I took Sunita in my arms. I had foreseen this moment, my utterly humiliating admission of defeat, and expected to find it unbearable. But holding her, finally, pressing her to my chest, I thought on the contrary how good it felt, how right, as if buried in the folds of my coat Sunita wasn't further from me than she'd ever been.

That Friday night Sunita failed to turn up for the late dinner I'd arranged. I found her soon enough, smoking an obstetrically ill-advised cigarette outside the Engineer the next morning. She had, she explained, taken on some extra shifts at short notice, but after a mildly unpleasant scene agreed to meet me at my hotel late that evening after work. Contrary to my gloomy expectations, she turned up, and stayed over, agreeing to sleep top to toe in the room's rather narrow double bed. Indeed, over the next couple of days she proved to be in such pliable if somewhat unforthcoming mood that for a brief, deluded moment I could pretend it a surprise when, having promised to meet for a drink at the King and Queen on Cleveland Street, she stood me up the following Monday. With will enough, and time, people aren't in my experience too hard to track down, and no doubt, dropping round at her writer friend's flat to find a newly erected FOR RENT sign outside it, and at the Engineer, where a charming young waitress claimed never to have heard of a Sunita, I might have persevered, and found her eventually. But I knew that night when I returned to my hotel that I would only lose her again, and, like as not, that I had lost her for ever the moment we met.

At a roundabout, take the first exit onto the bypass. After

three-quarters of a mile, turn right at a second roundabout, then left onto a signposted footpath into Coneygree Wood. Ignoring paths to the right, continue north, enjoying the wood's deep silence while you can, and cross a field to join a farm track. Turn left at a junction onto the busy A438.

At a fork, bear right along Cut Throat Lane, and keep ahead at three crossroads to enter Knapp Lane. To your right, a few hundred yards beyond the railway tracks, a cairn-like pile of rubble marks the spot where Foxglove Cottage once stood. Squint and a few dozen yards further north you might just make out the remains of Peter Agnew's barn conversion. Turn right onto the Homend and left opposite the train station to rejoin the A438. One rainy evening not so long ago I bumped into Robin Entwistle at the Prince of Wales, a fine pub on Church Lane towards the southern end of town. He was on his way out, and Smoky was straining at the leash, but for all our long history of mutual suspicion I was touched that he took a moment to ask after Sunita.

'You know it's funny,' he said. 'We all thought you'd done away with her. Ridiculous, when you look back on it. As if you'd harm a fly!'

And hoisting the deep hood of his parka he stepped out into the rain.

In the Tibetan Buddhist tradition the *kora* is a form of pilgrimage in which the supplicant, instead of walking *to* a site of sacred significance – a temple, a mountain, a lake – walks *around* it, intoning *mantra*, rotating his cylindrical prayer wheel, or, in some cases, prostrating himself every few steps. Nirvana is attained once the pilgrim has completed 108 full circles. And although I have a way to go yet, I have in recent days found myself treading and retreading these paths that my father walked, past the burial mound of the house he built, and slightly further afield, around Gullet Lake, whose mesmeric depths ramblers are, for one final time, reminded to approach with proper caution. At a roundabout, take the second exit back onto the A417, and continue straight over the following two roundabouts to reach your starting point.

The Gullet